Jason was born in Pittsburgh Pennsylvania in 1974. Since he was eight years old, he delved into science fiction and fantasy, following the works of J.R.R. Tolkien and Gary Gygax. His favourite book however, is *Great Expectations* by Charles Dickens. Jason began writing during his many deployments and travels as a member of the United States Air Force. After travelling all over Europe and the Middle East for nearly 24 years in the military, he is ready to put writing at the forefront of his life. Jason's true motivations are his daughters Eve and Ella who have read more books by the time they became teenagers than he had in his entire life!

For Zoe, Eve and Ella for putting up with…me!

Jason Kalinowski

VORCLAW

AUSTIN MACAULEY PUBLISHERS™

LONDON · CAMBRIDGE · NEW YORK · SHARJAH

A CIP catalogue record for this title is available from the British Library.

ISBN 9781398407398 (Paperback)
ISBN 9781398415546 (Hardback)
ISBN 9781398415553 (ePub e-book)

www.austinmacauley.com

First Published 2022
Austin Macauley Publishers Ltd®
1 Canada Square
Canary Wharf
London
E14 5AA

Thanks to Austin Macauley Publishers for giving me a chance.

Table of Contents

Part I: Sorrow to Revenge

Chapter 1

The Elf-Boy

"Well, Magnus, why have you brought me up here? What find is so important?" asked Major Baltus Blackpool from atop his horse. His White Eagles atop his shoulders gave away his officer's rank. He was thin but a solid human in his late thirties. He was blond, with tight curls hidden underneath golden helm.

"Right! It appears I found an elf-boy, sir," replied Sergeant Major Magnus Foehammer. His eight, striped, gold chevrons, running up the arm of his green sleeve, gave away his enlisted rank. He was a tall and broad, red-head soldier. "Quite a malnourished elf-boy, I must say," finished Magnus with a smile. The black-haired elf child wrapped himself tight around Magnus as the major approached on horseback.

"I see the elf has taken quite a liking to you, Magnus," observed the major.

"I would too, sir. Especially if I was starving and someone offered me some vittles," replied the sergeant major.

"What would an elf child be doing alone so close to the foothills of the Spine-of-Vana mountains?" wondered as much as asked the major.

"Not sure, sir. Elves are few and far between in Vorclaw," replied Magnus who motioned for the malnourished elf to continue eating.

"Private!" shouted Sergeant Major Foehammer to one of his fellow scouts. "Any sign of a struggle or tracks?"

The rest of the Vorclaw scouts were returning on horseback from patrol.

"Nay, sergeant major," responded the two-striped private. "Only the elf-lad's tracks coming from the creek, sir."

"Right, now that is odd," said Magnus looking at the half-starved elf-boy trying to fill his face with biscuits and jam.

"Why do you say that, Magnus?" asked Major Blackpool.

"He has bruises on his arms and face. But those around his face have healed."

"You believe he survived an attack?" asked the major guessing.

"Well, that or he took a few nasty falls, sir," replied Sergeant Major Foehammer.

"So, we have an orphaned elf, abused and no tracks to follow," stated Major Blackpool.

The sergeant major's entire scouting party and Major Blackpool stared at the elf-boy as he devoured the biscuits and jam. All pondered how the lone elf child, barely into his teens, ended up out here in the forested foothills, south of the Spine-of-Vana.

"Does he speak?" asked the major.

"If he does, sir, then he was either too scared or too hungry to reply when I asked him his name," said Magnus.

"*Lain lonora nac tah?*" Major Blackpool asked in an elvish tongue.

No reply came from the elvish boy.

"What did you say to him, sir?" inquired Magnus of his commanding officer.

"I asked him where his parents were," said the major. "Strange that he did not even turn from his feasting once I spoke an elvish dialect."

Magnus scratched his red goatee. He felt sad for the elf. It was obvious to him that the boy had been without real food for days. He also believed that the boy likely escaped from a near-death incident. That would certainly have repercussions at this young age.

"Yes, well, let us be off then and return to our column," said the major referring to his battalion.

A Vorclaw battalion was comprised of four companies, usually of foot soldiers. At least fifty warriors comprised a Vorclaw company. "Ah, major, we just can't leave him here, sir," started Magnus.

"Quite right, Magnus. I trust you to look after him then," said Major Blackpool. The major turned his horse around and headed down the foothills toward the road from Cairnhold where his battalion was en route back to Sedgedunum, the Vorclaw capitol.

"Me, sir?"

The major did not reply.

"Me and you then, little one?" Magnus asked the young elf-boy.

Two of the other scouts gave a chuckle at their sergeant major.

Magnus petted the boy on the head. "Come on then time to go little elf," he said out loud. With his massive arms, Magnus scooped up the young elf and put him on his horse.

The elf-boy, surprised at first by the quickness and ease he was thrown into the saddle, was too hungry to protest and continued his feast atop Magnus's horse. Magus carried on down the hill walking by the horse's side.

* * * * *

The scouting party re-joined the battalion. The elf had no idea who these soldiers were in their green and gold tinted armour, but he felt safe among the large number of marching and mounted soldiers.

Magnus looked up at the elf and then to the sky. "Looks like rain for sure," said Magnus out loud coming up next to Major Blackpool.

"You think tents are warranted?" asked Major Blackpool, still on horseback.

"I do, sir."

"Surely, Magnus, a little rain will not hurt us, will it?" sarcastically asked the major with a smile. "I think we can march until dusk."

"Long journey still ahead, sir. I don't want any of the boys getting on with the cold or worse yet, trench-foot, sir," replied Sergeant Major Foehammer referring to a condition soldiers can get from marching in the rain and not drying out their boots. Results are soldier's feet being saturated and their skin tears with each step.

The commanding officer could not disagree with Magnus's logic. "Very good then, sergeant major," conceded Major Blackpool. "Break out the tents then, Magnus."

"Right, sir. Battalion, halt!" shouted Sergeant Major Foehammer. "Break out the tents, lads! Looks like rain!"

"Aye, sergeant major!" came back from several soldiers.

"Come down now, little elf, time to set up camp."

The elf-boy did recognise a few words. The elf-boy believed the large soldier was speaking the common language of the humans. The elf-boy also knew he was speaking to him; the words sounded familiar, but he wasn't certain he understood them completely. Nor did he remember where he had been nor his name – his memory was gone!

* * * * *

That night, the rain came down hard as Magnus had predicted. Most of the soldiers were huddled in their tents except for the few guards posted throughout. The pelting of the rain was hypnotic if not soothing to the elf. The elf-boy was more content than he could remember, even though he could not remember much. He had been resting next to a creek for at least a day. In fact, that one day next to the creek was all the memory he had.

For the next few hours, the elf-boy tried to remember something. The bruises remaining on his body told him he was running from something. Something terrible, he was sure.

Bits and pieces of visions came to him. He saw a sword of gleaming light, a beautiful valley and some warming smiles. But that was all he could recall. He also wore a thin golden necklace, but it had no clasp to remove it. Nothing in his memory, nor his bruising, nor his necklace made much sense presently. Finally, the elf-boy, feeling safe, gave up on trying to piece back together his young elven mind as the pelting sound of rain against the tent got the better of him. It was not long before he was asleep.

Chapter 2
Baltus, Magnus and Leif

Magnus, smoking his favourite pipe, stared on in amusement as the elf-boy fought hard to keep his eyes open. Magnus took comfort once the elf-boy finally fell asleep under candlelight. Magnus new the boy was safe from whatever danger he escaped from. Few would dare attack an entire Vorclaw Battalion. An organised battalion of arch-goblins maybe, but they've not been seen in that size many a year nor this far south from the Spine-of-Vana.

This battalion's name was known as the White Eagles. Several battalions rotated throughout the land. The rotation of battalions went from city to city, stronghold to stronghold and road to road. This method kept the soldiers fresh and offered them opportunity to learn about their homeland. This concept was revolutionary; it was put forth by Major Blackpool himself and the ruling council adopted it. The Major's White Eagles have just finished their rotation and would soon be returning home for rest and recuperation in the area where they were based, which was the Vorclaw capitol of Sedgedunum.

"Magnus, are you ready for our match?" came a question from a stern voice entering the tent.

A smile grew across the sergeant major's face. "By all means, sir," replied Magnus softly not wanting to wake the elf.

In walked a drenched Major Blackpool carrying a stool and box. It was a meeting the two figureheads established to pass the time; the two leaders, officer and enlisted, collided in a chess meet.

"Sorry for not coming by this evening, sir, but I did not want to leave the young elf lad," said Sergeant Major Foehammer.

"Understandable, actually I assumed it was on account of the rain, not wanting to get your feet wet!" replied the major with a smiling grin referring back to the sergeant major's decision to bed down early for the night instead of marching in the rain.

The sergeant major smiled back as he was getting out his small fold-out table and stool.

"You realise time for our chess matches are at a near end," stated the Major. "We should be back in Sedgedunum in a fortnight and I will not remain commander of the White Eagles."

"You don't know that for sure, do you, sir?" stated Magnus, intending the question rhetorical.

"But I do know, Magnus, I do," replied the Major with a smile offering out a piece of paper.

Magnus looked at him curiously and reached for it. He read it silently to himself first while Major Blackpool took off his cloak and set up the chessboard.

"Says here you're to become Commandant of the Academy of Arms!" said Magnus looking up at the major who was smiling and pretending not to pay him any mind. "Says here, you are to be promoted to the rank of colonel upon your return!" Magnus said with a smile. "Congratulations, sir! I mean Colonel. This calls for a celebration wouldn't you say?" Magnus went through his pack and pulled out a bottle of honey mead and two small glasses.

Major Blackpool's eyes widened, and his smile grew as his sergeant major pulled out a bottle of potent alcohol.

"Sergeant Major, I am absolutely shocked, disappointed in you for bringing *Hair of the Dwarf* on the journey home!" Baltus said with sarcasm, referring to an old code for soldier's smuggling alcohol. Alcohol was frowned upon during manoeuvres.

The two shared a toast of *Hair of the Dwarf* and began their match. It was a fine crafted chess set the major owned. It was white marble with gold inlay for the board; one side was blue crystal and the other white. The board matched with white and blue marble pieces.

Well into the match Major Blackpool asked, "Magnus, can you grasp the potential of what is contained in that letter?" not taking his eyes from the board.

"Sir?" replied Magnus sounding distant.

Blackpool paused and looked up at his sergeant major staring at the chessboard. "What then, sergeant major? What is the potential?"

Magnus did not take his eyes from the game board. "You will mentor in some way, shape or form the future soldiers of Vorclaw," he responded.

"Exactly, Magnus! Exactly!" he said out loud.

Magnus put his fingers up to quiet the major not wanting to wake the elf sleeping just a few feet away.

"The Academy of Arms can teach more than just weapons and combat.

I want it to teach leadership and decision making for and during battle," said the major. "I want to make it an institution for learning survival skills, for blacksmithing and even for free thinking!" he said excitedly. "Have you any idea the number of educated officers I have commanded and, for that matter, been commanded by? Very few!" asked Major Blackpool as if having wanted to say it for some time. "Most of which were appointed only because of nobility," the major continued. "They didn't earn any position of leadership by my accounts. No, they were given commissions by the council to satisfy titles of nobility and favour."

"Yes, sir, I am aware that nobility, whatever that is, grants special positions regardless of deed."

"Exactly, Magnus! So you too can see how dangerous this could be to our country's security," said Blackpool leaning over the game board pointing at Magnus.

The sergeant major lifted his head up from the game. A pause grew between them. "Perhaps I should put away the mead?"

"There is something afoot in our land. We used to engage arch-goblins, lizard-goblins and orcs quite regularly. That's why I suggested we rotate battalions between the cities of Vorclaw, it keeps us on the move and unpredictable," said Colonel Blackpool.

"Then your advice to the ruling council to rotate battalions has paid off for the nation and for you, sir. It is probably one of the reasons why you were chosen to be commandant at the Academy of Arms," put in Magnus.

"Yet, is it enough, Magnus? See our foot soldiers are, for lack of a better word, mindless," he said quietly. "Keep in mind they are good warriors, but I worry they may be hard pressed to fight an organised threat without the aid of dragoons, wizards and clergy," said Major Blackpool to Sergeant Major Foehammer. Dragoons were the heavy cavalry branch of the Vorclaw army. Some battalions maintained several companies of these dragoons while others did not have any.

"Sir, was this was your speech you gave to the Commandant of Arms just before we left Sedgedunum?" asked Magnus.

"This is *our* opportunity to forge new leadership for our armies," a smiling Major Blackpool said confirming Magnus' question. Magnus Foehammer, however, noticed the major accented '*our*' to make it clear that Magnus was to join him at the academy. "I want you to join me, Magnus. I will give you a new title of master instructor and you will head up training immediately. I want the best soldier I have served with and none I have met have the complete combination of skills, of strength and intelligence that you possess, Magnus. Join me, Magnus, at the academy. I can have you transferred there as soon as we return," begged the major his eyes wide now with vision.

Magnus took a deep breath and rested his hand on his chin and went back to the chess game. He moved his queen into position to take his major's rook.

"You forget, sir, I have reached the highest rank an enlisted soldier can achieve, and I have served for nearly thirty years. I have plans to retire and become a blacksmith," said Magnus.

"Magnus, you love the military too much. Why would you want to get out now?" asked the major.

"I have a wife and boy that I see far too little," he replied.

"So do I, Magnus. But as instructors in Sedgedunum, we'll no longer deploy to faraway lands and strong holds!" he replied. "You would see Disa and Bjorn more often, though not as much if you retired," said Baltus referring to Magnus' wife and son. "And I will finally be able to see Merriam and Dru every day!" he said referring to his own family.

"Intriguing offer, sir, but it is time that I spent more time with my family now."

"Bah! You have lots of time for that still. They will understand as does my family. You are the best sergeant major I have ever encountered. You command the respect of the men under you and all my junior officers hold you in the highest regard. You are an experienced tracker and have spent much more time in the field than most. You discipline your troops so well that never does anyone fall out of line. You're a natural leader, Magnus. Your sheer size probably plays a large part in that and no disrespect, you look like a large brute, but you have a disciplined mentality, Magnus. You must know this?" asked the major raising an eyebrow. "Not to mention that our families know each other already. So your wife and boy will be amongst friends," put in Major Blackpool.

Magnus put his head back in the chess game making a move that left the Major's knight no escape. "And the fact that I have combat knowledge of every weapon in Vorclaw's arsenal makes no matter to you?" teased Magnus who was smiling with glee from the list of compliments the major spit at him. Not to mention that Magnus was about to capture the major's knight.

"Ah, yes, you do know your way around weaponry," said Major Blackpool. His tone turned sour seeing that he may have to sacrifice his knight. "You will be the master instructor. You will govern the drill sergeants already in place. Replace them if you like. It would probably be best to replace those with soldiers you trust or already know over time. I will approve it. You will educate your sergeants to instruct *our* recruits to be loyal to each other and Vorclaw," he replied.

"Sir, you make a fine offer but let me ask my wife. I had promised her that this was my last deployment, short of war, and I had planned to retire to blacksmithing soon," replied the sergeant major. "And we will have to discuss what to do with this one," he said pointing his thumb in the direction of the sleeping elf child. Magnus also wanted to end the academy talks till he talked it over with his wife, Disa.

"Orphanage?" asked the major.

"No, sir! I grew up in one and I'm not partial to those places," replied Magnus.

Magnus was orphaned as a boy having watched his family and others of his countrymen slaughtered by orcs while travelling through the Spine-of-Vana. He was found wandering aimlessly by a caravan pack headed for Vorclaw. The men of the caravan left Magnus off at the first orphanage they found in Sedgedunum; he endured a hard life at the orphanage and, therefore, did not want this elf-boy to go through the trials and tribulations of orphanage life. No, Magnus rather wanted to give this young elf a home with a family.

"What then?" asked Major Blackpool. They both now stared at the sleeping elf.

"I will bring my boy home a brother?"

The major let out a slight laugh but only for a moment when he realised that Magnus was not laughing.

"You're serious?"

"I am, sir."

"Well, Sedgedunum has the best schools and he will need to learn our language. What better place then Sedgedunum?" asked the major. When Magnus did not reply, Blackpool asked, "What will you name him?"

"I have always liked the name Leif. It means heir in my culture. It just seems fitting to me, almost like a lost prince?"

Baltus mustered a smile in Leif's direction. "Yes, it is fitting."

Chapter 3

Homecoming

The remaining journey to Sedgedunum was uneventful for the White Eagles. Most of the attention was on Leif. Magnus walked Leif around like it was his own son, partly to pass the time but mostly because Magnus wanted to rouse the boy's memory. He wanted to awaken the quite shy elf and see what there was to know.

The soldiers liked their sergeant major; a sentiment that Major Blackpool and his officers slightly envied but admired too. So it was easy for Magnus to move the elf about and gain the soldiers' acceptance. Leif became their mascot for their voyage home.

During the fortnight, Leif tried to speak some common. It was broken common actually, but the more Leif tried, the more he was able to put together sentences.

Magnus learned what he could, asking all-important details: where he was from, what happened to his family, what was his name? All of which Leif tried to explain but he could not, for he knew as much about himself as did the sergeant major. The elf-boy, not knowing his true name, accepted the name Leif.

* * * * *

Once within the outskirts of Sedgedunum, the White Eagles began to disband. Some returned home to small towns and villages along the way, but most soldiers did return to the Capitol City of Sedgedunum. To the east of Sedgedunum is where Magnus departed the White Eagles. For a short while anyway, he was going to enjoy some recuperation time with his family. This is also where Leif was to meet his new family, in the sleepy coastal village of Sedge Fen.

"Pa!" screamed Bjorn Foehammer running up to hug his father. The boy was a spitting image of his father, red hair, tall and strong.

They met in the village centre of Sedge Fen's muddy Main Street. Sedge Fen was a small rural community about a day's ride from Sedgedunum.

"Bjorn me boy, I hardly recognised ya!" replied Magnus to his son. "Let's have a look at ya. You have grown nearly three inches, haven't ye? And look how red your hair is, like your ma's," said Magnus hugging his boy one more time.

Bjorn's eyes dropped over to the short black-haired elf just behind his father.

"Where is your ma?"

"At the bakery buying bread," replied Bjorn pointing into the store they stood in front of. "Pa, is he an elf?" asked Bjorn not taking his eyes off Leif. He had never seen an elf child before.

"Yes, son," replied Magnus motioning for Leif to come forward. "Bjorn, I want you to meet a special lad. His name be Leif," said Magnus letting his proper rhetoric fall away as he always did when unaccompanied by his soldiers.

Bjorn could sense in his father's tone that Leif had bonded with his father in some fashion. He did not like it. "What makes him so special?" he asked with a bit of arrogance.

Magnus, surprised by his son's tone of voice, looked at him curiously. "He's an orphan like your pa was." Magnus hoped that explanation would suffice and put an end to any petty jealousy. Magnus instructed Bjorn to keep an eye on Leif as he went into the bakery in search of his wife.

"Hello, me love!" stated Magnus with outstretched arms for his wife, Disa.

"Magnus my sweet! Is that you, love?" came a cry from a lovely ginger-haired lady.

The two red heads embraced and kissed with such passion that Disa nearly dropped her rolls all over the bakery floor.

"Oh, Magnus, it is so good to have you home," she said gazing into her tall soldier's eyes.

"Who is this?" asked Dru Blackpool, son of Major Blackpool. Unbeknownst to Magnus, Dru was presently staying with Bjorn and Disa. In fact he had not even noticed his commanding officer's son until he spoke.

"An elf that my father found orphaned on his trip home," said Bjorn.

Leif stared back at the boys. They were taller than he was, especially Bjorn; Dru was only just a finger taller. Leif was not sure why, but he was sizing them up. He felt threatened by Bjorn but Dru's warm face and blond curly locks seemed anything but menacing. However, the size of Bjorn set Leif on edge. Leif flexed his muscles, anticipating a strike by Bjorn.

It never came but Dru did come forward. "Bjorn, look at eyes, they're amber!" he said getting up close to Leif's face.

Leif reared his head in response.

"So what? He's nothing special. I am sure there are elves just like him all over."

"Yes, but have you ever seen one before?"

Bjorn did not reply. Instead, he folded his arms and rolled his eyes in protest.

"My love, what is Dru doing here? His father marched to Sedgedunum this very moment," said Magnus staring at the three boys from inside the bakery window.

Disa looked at him in horror. "Please tell me you're joking. Did you not get the news?" she begged.

Magnus stared at her blankly.

"Magnus," she started with her eyes welling. "Merriam is dead," she stated referring to the wife of Major Blackpool. "It was a horrible accident. She was killed accidentally by a battle between mage students from Sedgedunum's Wizard's College," she said. "Since he has no relatives in Sedgedunum and we were only a day away, Dru asked the watchmen to contact us."

"I know nothing of this!" said Magnus.

"There is more, love, and I beg you not to mention it to the Major," she continued. "Dru blames his father since he was away at the time. Also, the war mages at Sedgedunum said they were going to send word and have him come," she finished the sad tale.

"We've received no word by message nor magic!" he said in disbelief. "Tragic, simply tragic!"

"So he's to be staying with us till his father arrives," she said.

"Well, there is only one thing to do. I must be off for Sedgedunum at once," said Magnus to his wife.

"At once, love? You just got home."

"At once, love."

* * * * *

Magnus was off soon after he introduced Leif and gave his regards to dear Dru on the loss of his mother, Merriam.

Dru was none too happy to learn that Magnus was bringing his father to Sedge Fen. Dru's anger stemmed from his father's constant deployment to the far reaches. Baltus knew his son for a little over half his fifteen years. The rest, Baltus was away. Dru also despised his father for the lack of influence in his and his mother's lives. Dru honestly believed that had his father been home, his mother would not have been killed. The whole situation frustrated Dru so he turned his attention to where Disa and Bjorn focused – on Leif.

Leif sipped his bowl of beef broth from the wooden spoon, a taste he never encountered before or so he believed. He looked up at the trio sitting across the wooden table. He noticed all eyes were on him. Leif quickly put down his head and stared into the wooden bowl of broth.

"Poor lamb, do you know where your family might be?" asked Disa in a gentle voice.

Leif looked up and shook his head. "No memory, Mum."

"How well do you know common?" she asked.

"I know some, Mum," replied Leif.

Disa smiled at that. Her smile quickly turned sour once she noticed Bjorn's twisted face of resentment.

"Do you know where you are?" barked Dru breaking into the conversation.

Leif shook his head again showing that he did not.

"You're in the grand country of Vorclaw," said Bjorn.

"In the village of Sedge Fen," added Dru.

"In the home of Foehammer," added Bjorn.

"Your name is Leif," added Dru.

"What is your family name?" asked Bjorn.

"I know not."

"Then yours is Foehammer too," said Dru.

"It is not," said Bjorn.

"Why not? It sounded obvious to me that Mr Foehammer plans to keep him," said Dru.

"Well, he cannot..." Bjorn began to protest but was cut short by his mother's smack on the back of the head.

"Leif will stay here with us, boys. For the time, till we find out where it is, little Leif, you belong. You like Magnus, don't you?" asked Disa of Leif.

"Yes, Mum, I do."

"Good, it is settled then. Now, Bjorn, Dru, you two boys take Leif out around and play while I put on supper for tonight. Show Leif around the village and Dru, stay out of mischief," ordered Disa.

"Mrs Foehammer, I never get into mischief, that's Bjorn," lied Dru.

"Go outside boys and Leif you too. Be back in two hours for supper!" she yelled as the trio ran outside the cottage door towards the fields with Leif in tow.

Leif turned to regard her, hoping he might stay until Magnus returned. It was too late for any protest though. Disa closed the bottom and then the top of the split door – a kind of door Leif knew he had never seen before. Leif suspected he was far from home but still he did not know where home was.

* * * * *

"He is cute!" said Sylvia. The platinum blonde-headed lass stated to her fellow young girlfriends. The three girls in total giggled and laughed at Leif.

"And look at his eyes, they're amber!" pointed out Dru. He was displaying Leif as one might show off new clothes to get the attention to attract the young ladies.

All three girls got up close to nervous Leif.

Bjorn stood off to the side, his arms were folded across his chest in protest at Dru's display of Leif.

"So what have you got here?" asked the twins simultaneously. The black-haired twin boys were friends of Bjorn.

"Me pa found a stray elf and Dru is parading him around the village," he replied without looking at the pair.

"Wow, a real elf!" said Vocke Garboldisham, the short-haired twin.

"Where did he come from?" asked Roc Garboldisham, the long-haired twin.

"Somewhere up north?" reasoned Bjorn. "And now he is to be living with us."

"You don't say," came a new voice and the twins parted immediately. Between them from out of the reeds came three large boys – bullies.

Bjorn was not scared of the trio and could stand off two of them but not all three; still they all kept a respectful distance from the large Bjorn. A new kid, however, seemed a tempting target to the bullies, especially one as fragile-looking as Leif.

"What's your name, elf?" asked the freckled-faced boy with brown hair, strolling right up to Leif. The other two boys pushed Dru and the girls away from the now forming confrontation.

"His name is Leif," answered Dru when Leif did not reply.

"I did not ask you, golden locks," said the freckled-faced kid, grabbing Dru by his blond curls and landing an opened palm punch on Dru's forehead.

Dru stumbled back a bit, dazed from the blow.

"Leave them alone, Ickthorn!" shouted Bjorn, revealing the name of the freckled-faced kid.

Ickthorn just ignored Bjorn and turned towards Leif smiling. "What's the matter, little elf, can't speak our tongue?" he asked giving Leif a shove on his small shoulder.

"I am warning you, Ick," shouted Bjorn but the other two boys turned towards Bjorn to prevent any rescue of Leif or Dru.

Bjorn wasn't sure he even wanted to rescue Leif but his parents' good upbringing got the better of him. Bjorn made a move forward to intervene as Ick kept shoving Leif. Then Bjorn stopped in his tracks. His jaw dropped as he watched what happened next.

As if Leif could stand no more of the shoving, on instinct Leif caught Ick's right wrist with his own right hand and turned it so that Ick's thumb pointed down. Once Ickthorn was snared, Leif used his left hand to add to the force on Ick's wrist to topple the bully over. Leif now held Ickthorn's right arm upturned pressing Ick's shoulder and face firmly flat with the ground. Leif further subdued the freckled boy by placing his boot on Ick's neck.

Ickthorn screamed a high-pitched whine. Almost too high for a boy! The girls began to scream and run. Dru put forth a few nasty comments at Ickthorn's expense. The two boys that arrived with Ickthorn were about to intervene but noticed Bjorn coming for them.

"I speak your common fine, my friend," said Leif with his melodious accent to Ickthorn.

Leif's amber eyes burned with fury at his would-be attacker. His anger was turning into rage. Leif felt an uncontrollable desire to break the human boy's arm. "Why not? I have no home no family," he spoke in his elvish tongue.

Ickthorn screamed louder as his pain intensified.

The crowd froze with horror now as the small elf increased Ickthorn's anguish, a boy twice his size.

Bjorn moved forward between Ickthorn's friends and went to Leif. "Let him go, Leif. Let him go," demanded Bjorn in a commanding tone.

Chapter 4

Boys Will Be Boys

Disa was a priestess, a follower of Matronae, the Mother-Goddess. Disa went to use her clerical abilities on Ickthorn at his home and to sort out the scuffle that occurred between the boys. Disa did not want the boys to get up to any more mischief so she left Bjorn, Leif and Dru at the home of the Garboldisham family. She ordered the boys to sit on the floor against the wall and not to move.

The Garboldishams lived in a large cottage bought and paid for by Mr Isaac Garboldisham. Isaac owned the only leather working shop for miles around. Both he and his wife, Elle, worked the shop during the morning and afternoon. The Garboldishams were well-off but the twins ruled the tired parents by night; the twins were used to getting their way. The three boys sat quietly, as per Disa's instruction, in the Garboldisham living room floor. Only ambers burned from the remaining evening fire. So the room was barely lit.

Leif sat quietly taking in the sight of the wooden cottage. He took notice of the white walls and wood floors. He inhaled then the warm sent of burnt pine from the heath. He admired the primitive and rustic craftsmanship of the large table and benches that made up the Garboldishams' dining room. Strange as it was to him, all the surroundings seemed to fit well together. All these sensations were new to him yet somehow familiar. Leif still had no idea who he really was.

It was not long before the twins pestered their parents enough to allow them to go into the living room and see the three boys.

"Leif, could you teach me how to do that trick you pulled on Ickthorn?" asked the long-haired Roc.

"No, show me first," demanded Vocke with a smack to his brother's arm.

"No, me," said Roc who hit him back.

"No, me," said Vocke who started to use both hands and smack his brother again.

And the two began their usual pushing, shouting and slapping.

Leif watched in awe as the twins began a wrestling match over practically nothing. Leif had no intention of showing anyone what he did to Ickthorn. He was not sure if he could. He acted on instinct upon a skill from which he knew not the source.

Leif took in a huge sigh as he rekindled the Ickthorn episode in his mind.

"I think you should show them your cunning manoeuvre, Leif. Break both their arms so they might be done with their fighting," said Dru staring at the twins fighting.

"No!" said Bjorn. "Then we will have to contend with *two* boys screaming like girls," said Bjorn laughing.

Dru laughed too. Even Leif caught the comment as funny. Leif managed a smile and looked up at Bjorn. Leif understood that Bjorn was not fond of him and hoped that shared laugh might break some of the jealousy Bjorn had. Leif eventually understood that Bjorn had not seen Magnus for some time and returning home with another son of sorts would bring out the worst in anyone.

Bjorn knew Leif eyed him but did not look at him. He only stared on at the arguing twins. Bjorn was unsure of Leif and jealous of the tale his father told of Leif before Magnus left again. Jealous of the fortnight of travel they spent together with the White Eagles. Bjorn was never on a journey with his father. He never had the chance to be mascot of an entire battalion as did Leif. His father was very affectionate of Leif and that bruised Bjorn. Yes, Bjorn was jealous of the time Leif shared with *his* father.

All thoughts were silenced as the Garboldisham father walked in to shut up his squabbling twins.

"Shut your blooming mouths before I give you two a crack of me belt," said the tired large leathersmith already exhausted from the long day.

"But, Pa, he started it!" they both said pointing at one another.

Elle Garboldisham entered the room in a fury. She gave both the twins slaps on the back of the boys' heads and sat them on the floor with the other three.

"Now sit there with the other troublemakers and don't ye make a sound!" she said forcing them to the floor by merely pointing to it. Her temper brought out the best of her small-town slang.

* * * * *

It was well into the evening when Disa returned to pick up her trio from the Garboldisham cottage. She was not alone, Magnus returned with Major Blackpool, Dru's father.

Once Baltus entered the cottage, he went to his son immediately. Dru stood up and stared at his father. As soon as Baltus began to speak of Merriam, his wife, Dru's mother, Dru only turned around to face the wall in defiance. The other parents and children went outside to give the father and son some privacy.

Baltus went on for many moments talking to the back of his son. Baltus went on explaining how duty and defending the lands was vital to the security of their nation.

Dru would not hear of it though. What he wanted was to hear his father take the blame for abandoning them, abandoning him for nearly half his life and his mother for nearly half their marriage. Yes, Dru wanted the wizard's guild punished too. Yet he wanted his father to take accountability for his mother's death.

Neither father nor son would budge on how they saw the matter.

* * * * *

"What did he do?"

"He broke the arm of Bjorn's friend Ickthorn!" whispered Disa not wanting the children to hear.

The Garboldisham parents listened in.

Bjorn, Leif and the twins were sent off to wait with the horses by the stable, while Disa explained what happened.

"You sure it was not Bjorn or even Dru?" asked Magnus of his wife. "Leif is very frail and Ick is at least twice his size," he added. "I don't even think Bjorn likes Ickthorn?" asked Magnus.

"Magnus!" shouted Disa. "All the children witnessed it, love. The twins, Bjorn, Dru and that sweet blonde lass Sylvia, her mother came over our house because of the tale her daughter told her mum," Disa replied.

"What tale?"

"The tale that Sylvia told her mum of an elf lad who put a wallop on young Ickthorn. Her mum was to crack her on the arse for spinning stories till poor Sylvia insisted that she come over to our place and see for herself the elf," said Disa.

"Me boys said the same things, Magnus," added Mr Garboldisham, his wife nodding in turn.

Magnus pondered the story. He had heard of elves training their young for combat, but he had never met an elf child before Leif. It would make sense. Not many could survive at such a young age alone on the hills as did Leif.

"Well, how is Ick then?" asked Magnus who did not sound too worried. For he knew Ickthorn had a reputation for trouble in Sedge Fen.

"I healed his arm, but it will be sore for a while to be sure," replied Disa.

Magnus did not react to the comment. He merely stared across the field at Leif wondering if it was best to hand him over to the state or some family, an elf family, to take care of him. Magnus shook those thoughts from his head. He knew the crown would only send him to an orphanage and strangers might abuse or sell the boy into slavery.

"We are not to keep him, Magnus?" asked Disa as if reading his mind.

"Why not?"

"Magnus, I am sympathetic to orphans as much as you are. But he is an elf and our ways are foreign to him," she said. "What if that was Bjorn's arm? What then?" asked Disa getting a bit flustered.

"Well then, Bjorn would have provoked him?" stated Magnus.

That comment infuriated Disa.

"I think he is an adorable little lamb, but we may not be what's best for him. He should be with his own kind."

"No! He will be fine with us," said Magnus out loud. Now his voice carried. Magnus did not want to continue with the argument. Not there in front of the Garboldisham house. Not with the Blackpools mourning their loss. And not after the long journey he had just made to come home.

He had hoped the sound of his voice was enough to settle this conversation, at least for the time being. And it was – for now.

* * * * *

"You can hear them, can't you, Leif, can't you?" asked Bjorn.

The twins' faces brightened up in smiles as if they found a new secret weapon against their parents.

"What they saying, Leif?" asked Vocke.

"Are they going to give you a whooping for snapping Ickthorn's arm off?" asked Roc teasing and exaggerating the story.

The twins shared a giggle at Leif's expense.

Bjorn noticed that Leif was listening to something more serious. "What's the matter, Leif?"

"Mum does not want me to stay," he replied in the saddest voice.

Bjorn grew sad at the mere sight of Leif's disappointment.

* * * * *

"I thought I told you boys to wait over by da stable?" scolded Disa.

"Mum, Leif has something to say to you," said Bjorn leading Leif by the hand.

With a hung gulp of courage, Leif fought back the tears and apologised for the incident. "I am sorry, Mum, for fighting today," said Leif. "I promise not to hurt anyone ever again. Please don't send me away!" he begged. Tears welled in his eyes after his plea. "I don't want to go with other elves," said Leif tearing.

Bjorn looked at his parents with sympathetic eyes. He now felt something for Leif in the way of a friend or even a brother feels when the other is in trouble. Bjorn did not know why. Maybe it was for standing up to Ickthorn, which he admired, or maybe it was because he felt pity for his tragic loss of memory. Whatever it was, Bjorn knew in his heart that Leif was a good soul. He knew Leif never meant to hurt Ickthorn. In all reality, Ick got what he deserved. And Bjorn could not let Leif be abandoned for sticking up for himself.

"He heard all that you said," added Bjorn.

"With dem elven ears of his he did," piped in Roc.

"Mum, Pa, Leif is a good kid and I don't think he would hurt me. Even if he did attack me, I think I can beat him down," said Bjorn jokingly to put them all at ease. Bjorn even put his arm around Leif giving him a brotherly hug.

"Leif, you heard what we discussed?" asked Magnus stunned.

"Yes, sir."

"Leif, can you promise me that you will never hurt another boy like that again?" asked Disa with a stern look on her face equally stunned.

"Yes, Mum, I'm sorry," replied Leif.

"It was not his fault. Ickthorn…" started Bjorn.

"Quiet, Bjorn, your mother is talking."

"Also, Leif, if you want to live with us, you will have to pull your own weight around here and help out around the cottage and the forge. You have to take responsibility for your own actions. I hold Bjorn to the same standards too. Is this going to be a problem for ya?" asked Disa challenging the elf lad.

"No, Mum," said Leif sniffling.

"It is settled then," finalised Disa but her looks changed when she saw Magnus's face. "What's the matter, love?"

"Well, um, helping out around the cottage may not be necessary," said Magnus shifting in his boots.

"Why?"

"See um well, I have decided to take up a new position in the army on account of Major Blackpool's generosity," said Magnus.

"You—what?"

* * * * *

After Magnus explained at length the opportunity before him at the Academy of Arms and how it might be good for Dru, Leif and Bjorn to bond, Disa came around accepting Magnus' idea to move to the city.

She knew it was for the best when the Blackpools emerged from the Garboldishams' residents. Neither Major Baltus Blackpool nor his son Dru were crying despite their loss. However, both looked sapped from the sad reunion.

Disa looked at the pair with a sympathetic heart and as a close friend to Merriam Blackpool, she knew in her heart that both Baltus and Dru would need *her* family to pull them through their loss. She agreed to her husband's request to remain in the service of Major Blackpool, not for her own family, nor for her husband's opportunity but for Merriam Blackpool's sake.

Chapter 5

Transitions

Major Blackpool led his White Eagles in a march through the city streets of Sedgedunum. A return parade from their mountain deployment was typical and well received by Vorclaw citizens. It was a bitter homecoming for many of the White Eagles, next time they deploy to keep safe the minors in the Spine-of-Vana Mountains, they would do so without their commanding officer and sergeant major.

Back at the Spine-of-Vana, rotational battalions were sent out of Sedgedunum. The White Eagles were replaced by the Biting Dragons, another battalion of Vorclaw from Sedgedunum. The Dyer Wolves will replace the Bighting Dragons later in the year. The cycle comes full circle with the White Eagles replacing the Dyer Wolves after that. Three battalions, armed with foot soldiers and some boasting dragoons, rotate out of Sedgedunum to patrol the Spine-of-Vana protecting minors, travellers and traders Other Vorclaw cities patrolled other regions of the kingdom and they too rotated battalions to guard their regions.

Sergeant Major Foehammer called out cadence loud and crisp to keep his soldiers marching in unison. The soldiers filled the main street marching five abreast. Their boots reverberated as they hit the cobblestone streets. The sergeant major's cadence calls had his soldiers echo back with a response in unison. The cadence instilled a sense of pride and uniformity, symbolising they were one fighting unit.

The sergeant major not only wanted to make an impression on Sedgedunum but was concerned for his commanding officer. Magnus felt Baltus deserved a top send-off; the major returned home a widower, an unwanted father, all while assuming a new command. Magnus hoped the parade into the city might bring up his morale.

The sergeant major incorporated drums, emphasising the procession and letting Sedgedunum know the White Eagles had returned.

The officers mostly rode black steeds and brought the rear of the procession down the streets. Major Blackpool preferred the black mounts and demanded uniformity in his soldier and officer ranks; this was one of many reasons Foehammer and Blackpool got along so well.

The major made them ride four abreast. The horses were adorned in light battle armour but highly polished. The major was meticulous like that. He led this portion from atop his black mount.

The parade welcoming home the White Eagles snaked through streets of Sedgedunum. Onlookers cheered and threw flowers but the balcony where the ruling council would rest was empty. The White Eagles marched past the palace and seat of power of The Council of Twelve.

The absence of any ruling council present saddened Major Blackpool. Normally not an openly emotional man but since the news of his dead wife, he had been dismayed. Lack of representation by the council did not help. The Major's troops all received news of his loss and banded back together outside the city for this parade, why couldn't any member of The Council of Twelve show? Major Blackpool was to assume command of the Academy of Arms. Nearly all the White Eagles went out of their way to participate in the parade. The major hoped then the council might be at the Academy of Arms for the change of command ceremony.

One of the reasons he inquired about the commandant position at the Academy of Arms was that he knew he spent a great deal of time away from his family. Now, here he was taking a position that was to reunite him with his family only now his wife was dead. He went over and over in his head on who to blame: should he blame himself for not being there? Should he blame The Council of Twelve for deploying him so much? Should he blame the Wizard's College whose students struck her down accidently? Who should he blame?

* * * * *

The parade ended at Academy of Arms just on the western outskirts of the city. The White Eagles marched underneath the Warriors Archway which was the gateway to the stadium grounds. There in the stands sat the families and friends of the returning White Eagles, the outgoing commandant of the Academy of Arms and staff members of the academy.

For the White Eagles, this parade was more than a welcome home celebration march through the capitol, it was a bittersweet moment. It was a farewell and a promotion for the soon to be 'Colonel' Blackpool as he accepted the position of Commandant of the Academy of Arms and relinquished command of the White Eagles.

Leif sat with his new family watching the White Eagles march into the complex and surveyed the parade grounds. The Academy of Arms had their young soldier-recruits waiting in the stadium grounds. They were formed up in three one-hundred-man formations, five abreast. Leif watched as the White Eagles marched in from beneath the archway. The stands erupted into cheers. Leif noticed his new adoptive father leading the procession of foot soldiers into the stadium.

Leif admired how the White Eagles marched in perfect unison.

Magnus gave the command of counter march and the Eagles marched into action. The fifth column of soldiers went around the entire entourage of Eagles. The first went between the fifth and the fourth. The second went between the third and fourth. The fourth went between the first and second while the third column marched in place. Once the columns were finally facing the other way, the third column did an about face. Now all five were facing the way they came in. Magnus shouted the command of halt and the soldiers stopped marching. It was then that Major Blackpool and his officers entered.

The officers on horseback waited outside as Magnus gave the order for their next manoeuvre.

Dru, who was sitting with Disa's family, didn't even flinch when the crowd erupted. Nor did he even turn to view his father's entrance.

The officers on horseback went around the columns of soldiers. They went in pairs on either side. As soon as the major passed, Magnus gave the order to do an about-face and begin marching in unison inside the flanking horses. Drums were beating as every right foot hit the ground.

Guided by Major Blackpool, Magnus had the soldiers stop directly in front of the grandstand where the change of command was to take place.

Then Major Blackpool gave a call to Magnus. "Sergeant Major!"

Sergeant Major Magnus left the ranks and rigidly marched to the front of his major's steed. Major Blackpool dismounted and rigidly marched, only slowly, up to the ceremonial platform created for the major's promotion and his taking of command of the Academy of Arms.

Major Blackpool again noticed the lack of attendance by The Council of Twelve. Now anger began to fester in the man.

After defending interest of the people, the country, and the 'council' of Vorclaw, why does the council not have the decency to show? thought the Major. *My wife was murdered as I defended Vorclaw and no member of the council can show up for me – the new leadership responsible for training the future protectors of this country?*

The only one who was waiting for Baltus was the outgoing and decadent commandant General Larling Flinthouse. Major Blackpool noted the man's crooked posture. The general himself wore so many ribbons over his left breast that Major Blackpool wondered if he might fall over. Baltus was trying to think of something to take his mind off his rage and wondering of the old coot tipping over was doing the trick.

The old general smiled at Baltus, welcoming his replacement. Baltus knew for some time old General Flinthouse wanted to retire and now the light at the end of the tunnel was at hand for the old man. The major saluted the general as soon has he had come face to face. The general returned his salute and eagerly extended his hand.

"It is good to see you again, Baltus, this old man is ready to retire," stated the old general with a smile.

"You honour me, sir, with this appointment. I will be continuing your legacy of moulding our future warriors," responded Major Blackpool.

The old general gave a half-hearted smile and lifted a limp shoulder as if to say sure!

The half-hearted smile by the old general infuriated the already upset Baltus. However, Major Baltus Blackpool would not show it. His training was to remain calm and professional.

Up walked a young lieutenant carrying a blue velvet pillow. On this pillow were two shoulder lapels in the form of silver dragons with their wings spread wide apart. These were to signify the rank of colonel. The old general removed the major's gold griffins from his shoulders and replaced them with silver dragons.

"I promote you good soldier to the rank of colonel!" said the old general. The now Colonel Blackpool returned with a salute.

The White Eagles let loose a roar of admiration for their commander. "Hazah! Hazah!"

The old general turned to face the formation of soldiers and smiled back at them. "They admire you good sir, do they not?" asked the old general.

"Indeed, general."

"Are you ready to assume your new duty for your ruling council and country?"

"For country," he said under his breath, "I am."

Now up walked another lieutenant, this one carrying a black flag embroidered with a green castle, a shield and a sword; the flag hanging from a pole. It was the commandant's ceremonial flag symbolising ownership of the Academy of Arms.

The young lieutenant handed the flag to the outgoing commandant. "Are you ready to do your duty for Vorclaw?" asked the general holding the flag staff against his chest.

"Yes."

"Then I pass this flag and all that it represents; I pass to you the responsibility of training a nation's soldiers, to protect its people, its land and its rulers," responded General Flinthouse. With that said, the general forcefully held out the flagstaff. "Take it 'Colonel' Blackpool! Take over as Commandant of the Academy of Arms of Vorclaw from me!"

Colonel Blackpool reached out with both his hands and took the flag staff from the general. He forcefully pulled tight against his chest. He turned to face the soldiers of the White Eagles and new soldier-recruits on the parade grounds before him. Then he held the flag up high in the air and waved it!

The audience in the stands behind the colonel and his troops in front of him erupted in cheers.

All Colonel Blackpool could do was think about avenging his dead wife.

All Dru Blackpool could think of was blaming his father for his dead mother.

Chapter 6

City of Sedgedunum

For over a week now Leif marvelled at the sights, sounds and smells of Sedgedunum, Capitol of Vorclaw. Even though his memory had not been regained, he knew in his heart that Sedgedunum was alien to him.

Bjorn was no stranger to Sedgedunum, however, and neither was it to Dru. The duo had kept Leif close to them under Disa's orders. Bjorn knew his mother really wanted an eye kept on Dru too. Bjorn knew that Dru should not be left alone in light of his mother's passing. Also, Dru's father was busy at his new assignment at the academy. So it was up to Bjorn to watch the pair. Bjorn also knew that Sedgedunum was no place for a wayward elf-boy.

Leif was instructed to do whatever Bjorn said, which made it easy for Bjorn. Dru on the other hand was acting like a youth gone wild. To make matters worse, Dru pulled Bjorn and Leif into his mischief.

Unwittingly, Dru had Leif and Bjorn talk to the merchants about the price of apples, oranges and pears all the while Dru was stuffing them in his pockets. In the past three days, Dru had burgled fruit from the market and a lady's bracelet from a peddler in the street while Leif and Dru stopped to watch the shopkeeper juggling apples. Dru was starting to like his new trade.

Later that week, Dru set his eyes on a bigger purse. He wanted to see if he could steal a weapon.

"Common, lads, let's go down 'Cutters Corner' today!" begged Dru.

"Nay, Dru, you were not to be headed down that area of the market, Mum wanted us to be getting vegetables for the stew tonight," scolded Bjorn.

"Just for a minute, come on, it'll be fun. Anyway, Leif has never been down there and he should see a bit of everything," begged Dru.

"Come on, Leif," said Bjorn. "Just for a minute, Dru."

"Come on!" exclaimed Dru.

The young teens walked into the heart of Cutters Corner, a weapons' market in Sedgedunum. Many armoured figures walked these streets here. Many young would-be warriors made their rounds admiring while older experienced soldiers walked straight and unerringly to which ever tent held what they sought. Merchants bartered and swindled what they could out of any would be customer.

Dru walked up to one tent and ran his fingertips down the edge of a fine dagger's edge.

"Don't hurt yourself, Dru, these are not toys," said Bjorn.

"Yes Dad!" Dru replied sarcastically with a smile.

Dru and Bjorn were about the same age of fourteen, but Bjorn maintained a mature approach to weapons while Dru seemed like a kid in a candy store.

This was how it had been since Dru's mother died. Bjorn believed Dru's disobedience was a phase that Dru himself would need to work out. Bjorn's mother, Disa, thought the same and Bjorn new it; it became expected of Bjorn to try and keep Dru out of trouble. No small task for the Bjorn who was to also keep watch over his new adopted brother, Leif.

* * * * *

Magnus was not pleased with his new assignment thus far. He was honoured Colonel Blackpool chose him to train Vorclaw's future soldiers; however, he soon realised he had a lot of work before him.

His main problem was the lack of discipline instilled in the drill sergeants at his disposal. He appraised their abilities to train Vorclaw's soldiers and he found them wanting. Decadent these men were, not the same rough and tough breed he remembered. These trainers were spent and past their prime.

He made an appointment to speak with the colonel on this matter. He had replacements he knew of in the field that would greatly assist him. They were a lot tougher than his current lot of drill sergeants. However, Magnus would have to wait at the bottom of the stairs to his colonel's office until the current business was concluded.

A member of the council family and a member of the wizard's guild were visiting Colonel Blackpool. They were to attempt to express their organisation's sympathies to Baltus on the accidental death of his wife, Merriam.

* * * * *

"My aunt the Lady Sanne sends her condolences," stated the young Lord Handel Nightingale, Lady Sanne's nephew. The Nightingales, a family of wealth bricklaying and construction family; Sanne held a seat on the Vorclaw's Council of Twelve.

"My understanding is you two grew up together?" asked Lord Nightingale.

"I know your aunt well, we did indeed grow up together," said Colonel Blackpool, seated from behind his large oak desk, in his dark stone office. Baltus Blackpool appraised the council envoy. Although Handel was sincere in his intentions as was Lady Sanne, who was known to have no real love for the Wizard's College and their damaging buffoonery, Colonel Baltus Blackpool suspected Handel was sent only to gain experience in the art of savoir-faire instead of Lady Sanne coming herself. Yet Baltus was appreciative by the gesture by replying with a nod.

"Lady Sanne also offers her sympathy on behalf of the entire council," he added. "She says had she been in town, she would have come to your assumption of command. She also realises that no treasure she can offer can equate to your loss so in addition she has permitted me to offer you, on behalf of our own family, a sizable sum for you and your son," continued Handel. "Also, I am told commandants normally receive a sizable estate on the academy grounds therefore the council itself is offering three servants to care for your estate during your tenure as commandant."

"We too at the Wizard's College feel absolutely terrible," stated Horatio Mercutio suddenly as if missing his cue to speak. Horatio was another messenger.

Baltus had heard the name before. Horatio was an aspiring sorcerer out of the Wizard's College. He had made a name for himself in Sedgedunum. Yet he did not look as if he wanted to be at this meeting nor sounded sincere.

Baltus began to wonder if Horatio believed that this task was beneath such an up-and-coming wizard. That thought infuriated Baltus. Baltus stared over his desk at the wizard undaunted.

Horatio Mercutio tried to match stares but looked to Handel instead. "The Wizard's College will donate a substantial sum to make up for your loss as well," Horatio added staring back and forth at Handel and the stern colonel.

Baltus could sense the young Handle Nightingale was sincere. He was after all the nephew of his childhood friend, but it did not ease his anger with the council as a whole, especially Wizard's College and their envoy, he decided. The Colonel Blackpool's emotions began to stir, and he suddenly felt insulted by the young wizard's presence. To further fuel his anger, he was now commandant of the Academy of Arms second perhaps to Lord Ethan Brisbane, General of the Armies of Vorclaw, not some lab rat for the young envoys to hone their diplomacy skills. Baltus now believed someone with more importance should be addressing him. Not these boys! Baltus' mind, still frustrated by the sudden loss of his wife, wondered if the council was buying his silence in the matter in order to keep the peace with the Wizard's College since the college has done damage to city before and put people in harm's way in the past.

Baltus stood up from his desk, clearly agitated. He walked over to open his balcony door. He let the remaining light of the setting afternoon into his polished stone office. He put his hand to his lips and pondered their offer.

The two messengers sat waiting uncomfortably while the colonel pondered their offer. Colonel Blackpool had been scheming revenge of sorts since his arrival at the Academy of Arms. He never actually thought to go through with any of them but, thanks to his anger, he would try; this bribe, as the colonel saw it, cemented his desire for vengeance.

Money and loyal servants are what I require; however, if I am to have my revenge, then I will need more! Servants, yes! But I cannot take their servants, no. The offer from Lady Sanne will have to do, to demand more would arouse suspicion. But I will not take on council servants, spies for the council, certainly. However, I will try and take more from the Wizard's College, much more, Baltus thought to himself. The means to revenge were being placed right in front of him, so he believed.

The two envoys nervously waited in the uncomfortable silence. The caused nervousness was another natural ability Colonel Blackpool mastered – an ability he acquired long ago. Just as he could inspire soldiers through their leadership and charisma, he could also instil fear and doubt in the hearts of others.

Baltus did not turn to regard the pair when he responded. "My Lord Handel, please convey to Lady Sanne that her family's offer is more than I could have dreamed from such a family who owes me nothing. I am truly blessed to serve a caring family who would be so gracious during my tragic loss. I thank you," he said.

"By all means, commandant colonel," responded Handel now rising believing the business at hand was concluded.

"I will not need the servants though. I will procure my own military servants to care for my estate but my thanks to you and the council," stated Blackpool.

"As you wish, colonel, my aunt is only looking after her most favoured and dependable leadership. She is especially fond of you, sir," said Handel with a bow.

"Is she?" said Colonel Blackpool now turning to face the two men. His sarcasm was evident in the words he spoke. "We haven't conversed in half a decade, good sir. Are you sure she knows me or cares? And do you have any concept of my loss?" asked Baltus rhetorically. "And what about you, wizard?"

Neither man spoke. The colonel seemed larger than life to them and he was beaming with contempt in every word, this they knew. The colonel let them stand in uncomfortable silence for many moments. The charisma of Baltus Blackpool's scornful gaze had the pair of envoys motionless.

"Your pitiful bribe is not acceptable, wizard," Baltus said dryly turning to match gaze with Horatio Mercutio once again. Lord Handle motioned for Horatio to sit down as did he.

Horatio shifted uneasily in his chair. The young wizard spoke, "What else could I um, I mean what can we do to ease your suffering?"

"One, I want the young mages hung dead!" he said. "Two, I want some damn respect from you little slug when you talk to me. I despise your sarcastic tongues. While your precious self is sitting here in the safety of Vorclaw's borders, my soldiers and I are off killing arch-goblins and lizard-goblins to keep Vorclaw's interests safe. And for what? So pitiful fools can squabble in the streets and kill my innocent wife before my son's very eyes!" Colonel Blackpool said standing over his desk before the pair.

Handel and Mercutio were beginning to perspire.

"Three!" Baltus said angrily. "I want my wife back," he said looking back and forth at the pair. "Can either of you give me what I want? No, I think not. A bag of gold for my wife?" asked Baltus with contempt.

Neither Handel nor Horatio dared speak. They were sure that the colonel had more to say.

Baltus continued after an uncomfortable silence. "You say Lady Sanne favours me, did you not? Or was that a simple gesture, young man, to ease my suffering?"

The young Handel was now unnerved. His palms were sweaty. That was partly due to the fact of having never been talked to in such a manner and secondly, Colonel Blackpool was now handling the pommels of his sword and dagger.

"Of course she does, colonel. I…we do not wish to give offense to you, my lord. We have been permitted to grant some special concessions if the offerings were not suitable. What else might Lady Sanne and the Wizard's College provide?"

Horatio Mercutio's face made a subtle wince at Handel's statement and Colonel Blackpool did not miss it.

Baltus took a large gamble on faking his dissatisfaction with their offers, but it paid off. He now knew the initial offering was just that, an initial offering. Now he had to see what else he could get for himself, for his soldiers, for his son and for his revenge!

"Let us be fair and start with the good of the soldiers that protect this country and council who oversee it," said Baltus pulling out some parchment, ink and quills. "Then let us talk about what this rundown academy needs and we shall move on from there to what I need."

* * * * *

"Hey, Leif, ever seen one of these before?" asked Dru as he underhand-tossed a small dagger, handle leading the way, towards Leif. Then he tossed another in Bjorn's direction in the same manner, hilt first. Dru expected either of his friends to drop the daggers and cause a distraction.

Leif caught the dagger tossed in his direction with his right hand just before it hit him square in the chest. Bjorn on the other hand was not looking and would have received a nice bruise across the chin were it not for Leif's quick reflexes.

Leif stretched out fast with his left and caught it just before it touched Bjorn's face.

Dru did not get the commotion he expected but he did get a distraction nonetheless. The vendor and the patrons in the tent saw the incident play out. Everyone including Bjorn was staring at the quick reflexes of the little black-haired elf-boy. Dru's face was covered in shock of the near injury he almost created but he quickly shook that off and pocketed three daggers under his jerkin.

The vendor stood up and began to shout at the three disruptive youths, ordering them off. Dru got away with his first big prize!

* * * * *

"How did it go, sir?" asked Sergeant Major Magnus Foehammer.

Baltus stared at the contract he finagled out of the young upstarts. He did not even stare back at Magnus when he responded with, "Oh, it went well."

Magnus was not sure what the colonel was thinking or meant by that statement so he went right to the subject that brought him to his colonel's office.

"I have some disappointing news on the calibre of instruction here. I do not mind telling you, sir, that we have a lot of work ahead of us," said the sergeant major.

Baltus now looked up at Magnus staring down at him from across his dark oak desk.

"Go on," said the colonel.

I would like to replace three of the five drill sergeants immediately. One in particular is absolutely awful! I know some young staff sergeants in the field that would be better suited for these positions than these old master sergeants," said Magnus.

"You know your replacements personally?" asked the colonel.

"I do, sir."

"Very well then, I will approve it and the remaining misfit instructors will be reassigned," stated the Colonel Blackpool.

Colonel Blackpool smiled at the pact he worked out of his previous visitors. And he had to share the information, who better than Magnus. "Magnus, let me tell you about my recent meeting and what wonderful new weapons we are going to receive. But how about a game of chess while we talk?" he asked with a smirk.

Major Blackpool was hesitant at first to explain what he garnered from the meeting. However, he wanted to make it clear that he now thought it prudent the military leaders and soldiers train to do what was best for Vorclaw; in other words, to know when to depose poor leadership. If Colonel Blackpool came out and said this then Magnus might have him arrested for treason.

Baltus leaned over the chessboard and softly stated, "I have garnered a lot from Merriam's death, but I take it not for me or Dru, but to right the wrongs taking place in Vorclaw," he said.

Magnus merely looked on at him. Then looked back at the chess board.

"Now that I am more affluent," began Baltus, "I have the hope that once we trained *our* soldiers properly, then *our* men will know how to correct the actions of the appointed commanders. Perhaps even the ruling council itself."

Magnus sat up straight and looked hard at his commander. Baltus matched his gaze as best he could. Many moments passed before Magnus spoke. Baltus did not look nervous in front of the larger sergeant major, though nothing could have been further from the truth. Colonel Blackpool was worried Magnus did not share his point of view. That could cost the colonel dearly.

Magnus, however, was not sure what to say – his commanding officer spoke on the boarder of treason. Was he serious about disposing of poor leadership when it came to the ruling class or was he just merely speaking of working around appointed leaders when necessary due to their inadequacies?

Finally, Magnus spoke, well actually chuckled. "I cannot believe I almost fell for that one, sir. You really had me on starting a coup."

Colonel Blackpool let out a chuckle too, realising where his sergeant major stood – loyal to The Council of Twelve. Still he wanted Magnus to join him at the Academy of Arms.

"We will solve our leadership woes by training our soldiers to deal with foolhardy leaders and by teaching them how to correct their defects – to make them better leaders of course," stated as much as asked Magnus.

"Exactly," said the Colonel Blackpool.

"Not to cite a coup?" asked the sergeant major with a concerned stair.

Colonel Blackpool let out one more chuckle and reared back in laughter, a very rare sight indeed for the serious commander. "Magnus, you think too highly of me, sir. I have no desire to take over, I love Vorclaw too much to do that," he said smiling. Then the colonel's expressions changed and he leaned back in over the chess board. "Yet on the other side of that coin, Magnus, I love Vorclaw too much to watch fools run *our* military into the ground and kill a lot of good men when our country is surrounded by threatening agencies and hostile nations. That is why I need you. But enough talk, let me tell you about my fruitions meeting with the infernal wizard envoy."

Chapter 7

The Shape-Changer

The shape-changer Mimdrid was not at all pleased with the soldier he chose to replace. Mimdrid murdered, assumed the form of and mimicked the characteristics of one Master Sergeant Ian Coventry. Mimdrid chose Ian because he was a lonely sort with no family, few friends outside the army barracks and had expensive taste. While Mimdrid soon realised the master sergeant had a lot of debt and creditors after him, he still thought it might be fun to boss around some young human soldiers as a drill sergeant at the Academy of Arms.

Mimdrid came to Sedgedunum by way of the arch-goblins living deep in the Mistful Forest. The unfortunate incident occurred while he was travelling with a trade caravan along the Spine-of-Vana Mountains. He was posing as wealthy human-merchant when the arch-goblins raided his camp at night. Being at night, it was easy for him to assume the form of an arch-goblin he killed. When the arch-goblins returned to their city in the mountains, he uncovered terrible secrets there and did not wish to stay for risk of being discovered. So he made his escape and came to enjoy Sedgedunum. However, the recent arrival of the new Sergeant Major Magnus Foehammer made Mimdrid's delightful scheming and murder more trouble than it was worth.

Not only did the drill sergeants drill the new soldiers, as Mimdrid observed, Sergeant Major Magnus drilled the drill sergeants too. This training, as Magnus put it, Mimdrid had not counted on and it was obvious that Magnus was most displeased with his lacklustre performance.

Mimdrid could kill most humans with his supernatural strength. However, Magnus Foehammer's size, strength and abilities gave Mimdrid some cause for concern and decided against retaliating, keeping his true identity a secret.

Mimdrid was actually planning to merely leave the city for good when Magnus gave him new instructions. He, as well as two other drill sergeants, were given a choice to be reassigned to new posts or to report to the commandant's estate for duties there.

The commandant's estate sounded interesting to the shape-changer; he considered murdering and mimicking the commandant for a time. It would be a fun time indeed ordering about a bunch of pathetic humans, especially if he got the chance to order around Magnus Foehammer for a change. Mimdrid reported as ordered. The other master sergeants chose a new assignment to get them away from Magnus Foehammer.

The commandant, Colonel Baltus Blackpool, met him. The colonel explained Mimdrid's task. Mimdrid drew yard work for being late to his new assignment.

This was not what the shape-changer had in mind. It was still daylight so he could not just snap Baltus's neck, which was Mimdrid's preferred method of killing. No, he would study the colonel for a few days. Then, one night, he would then snap his neck – then Magnus' neck after that. Suddenly, it may be more fun to replace the colonel and torture Magnus!

* * * * *

The trio of friends settled down on the banks of a small creek near the outskirts of Sedgedunum. There Dru revealed his prize to an intrigued Leif but an upset Bjorn.

"You took these from the Cutters Corner, didn't you?" asked Bjorn of Dru accusingly.

"No, I paid for them!" responded Dru.

"When?"

"When you weren't looking," Dru responded again. He passed one of the rather plain-looking daggers to Leif.

"You're lying, Dru! We need to return these, right away," stated Bjorn.

"Bjorn, calm yourself," Dru said with smile. "No one will miss these old things anyway," he continued passing another old dagger to Leif.

"No, Dru! The last thing we need is to be labelled as thieves. Let's just return them and say we made a mistake," said Bjorn.

"Are you crazy; they will send for the City Watch!" exclaimed Dru referring to the guardsmen that kept the peace in Vorclaw's capitol. Dru passed a dagger to Leif but the elf instinctively took the whole set.

"Not if we tell them it was an honest mistake, Dru," said Bjorn defiantly.

Bjorn went on and on about honesty and integrity but Dru was no longer listening. Dru was watching Leif. Leif was juggling the daggers! Bjorn finally got the hint when he noticed Dru staring over his shoulder. So he turned around to regard Leif.

Leif was juggling the three old but nonetheless sharp daggers. Then he walked slowly into a position facing a tree. When his feet were firmly planted, Leif juggled the daggers higher and higher. When high enough for a dagger to take a few moments to drop, Leif caught them one at a time and stuck them into the tree one at a time with a forceful throw. Leif turned to smile at the duo.

The two boys wore different expressions. Bjorn had a look of shock, almost terror at the skill Leif possessed. Dru, on the other hand, wore a huge smile.

"That's outstanding, Leif; where did you learn that?" begged Dru. "Do something else."

"No, don't encourage him and we are taking them back!" scolded Bjorn.

"I don't know where I learned it. It just felt like something I could do, or have done before, or something familiar about it all," explained Leif.

"Well, let us see what else the great Leif Foehammer can do, shall we?" asked Dru.

Bjorn was about to protest but saw that Leif was smiling and even eager to try something else. Dru made targets by scratching a circle on the bark of trees. Then he asked Leif to make the mark. Bjorn too was intrigued. Leif brushed his black locks from his face and took the three daggers. He took aim and made the mark each time he threw them.

Next Dru challenged Leif again by setting him further from the targets.

It was clear Leif possessed an uncanny knowledge of weapons and he enjoyed exploring those skills. Before Bjorn confiscated the daggers, Dru blindfolded Leif and he still made the targets.

Bjorn eventually took the daggers back to the tents at Cutters Corner. He suspected Born would have little trouble returning the weapons; Bjorn had righteousness about him, like his mother. Dru expected Bjorn would make everything all right.

* * * * *

Bjorn and Leif made their way back to their family's new apartment outside the academy. Dru made his way to his father's new estate and observed his new estate from the grounds outside. Dru never expected to see soldiers filling the role as labourers. He was only a young lad, but he thought his father had gone a bit too far with reaping the rewards of his mother's death. That was how Dru saw his father anyway, an opportunist capitalising on his mother's death.

Dru did, however, fit into his new home nicely. It was big enough for him to hide and get away from his father when he was not out with Leif and Bjorn. Dru enjoyed having them here in the city. In the past when his father and Magnus would go off to some distant land, Disa would take Bjorn away to the Foehammer-cottage in Sedge Fen. Now that they were going to stay in Sedgedunum, Dru let himself feel happiness for a change.

Besides, Bjorn and Leif were great distractions to his targets while Dru perfected his future career. Dru daydreamed of being a great cutpurse, bandit even! And if he was caught, it could serve as a great way to get back at his father for leaving his mother to raise Dru alone over the years.

Dru's heart began to sink just then. The thoughts of his mother seemed to do that to him.

* * * * *

Over the few days, Mimdrid observed Dru from a distance. He could see that he was a troubled youth by the way he disrespected his father. He heard rumours from the other sergeants that the colonel lost his wife in a freak accident. If Mimdrid was to assume the role of the colonel, then he figured he best get to know the troubled youth and find out as much as he could.

44

Mimdrid approached Dru as the lad was sitting on a brick wall staring out over the dilapidated gardens. "She's be needing a lot a work," said Mimdrid in the form of Master Sergeant Ian Coventry.

"Yes, sir," replied Dru turning to regard the stranger.

Mimdrid began to rake some of the grounds so he might not arouse suspicion. "Are you looking forward, young master, to living in such a grand estate?" the false sergeant asked Dru Blackpool.

"Um, no not really."

"No? Why not? This home will be a grand residence indeed I reckon once we are all finished with her."

Dru did not respond.

"What be the matter, lad? You, your father and your *mother* are very lucky, don't you know? To have such a grand estate is rare thing," stated Mimdrid. He mentioned the boy's dead mum to see what the boy would reveal.

"My mum is no longer with us," said Dru.

"No longer with the lad you say. Dear lad, where is she?"

"She is dead," he said flatly masking his sorrow.

After a short pause and acting surprised, the shape-changer said, "I am terribly sorry, lad. My condolences to you, young master."

After that statement, the shape-changer had Dru talking. Mimdrid learned a lot from young Dru Blackpool. Mimdrid also had a secret weapon of sorts. He had a magical earring that could garner the surface thoughts of others.

Over the next few days, he learned Dru was deeply troubled and blamed his father. He also believed Dru was on a path of 'no-good' and the young lad had been a scheming cutpurse for some time. Mimdrid even learned that Dru used his friends as distraction during his thieving. It seemed that Dru would burgle a bit while his father was away on deployments.

Mimdrid learned, although he suspected as much, the Wizard's College and The Council of Twelve paid for the colonel's silence in the matter of his wife's death. Also, the colonel had much more coming from them in the name of condolences. Mimdrid learned that Colonel Blackpool was as much upset about the bribe as was Dru but accepted it anyway.

This puzzled young Dru but not Mimdrid. For what else could the colonel do but take what he could in this cruel world.

For days, Mimdrid weighed what he learned as he did his meaningless chores of raking the over-weeded garden. *With the colonel in such a position of power, receiving favours, money and whatever from The Council of Twelve and Wizard's College, the colonel may be the ally I sought after for so long,* he thought to himself. *Or was it better to kill the colonel and assume his identity?*

Chapter 8

Another Blackpool

"Halt, sir!" shouted the young lieutenant standing guard at the bottom of the steps to Colonel Blackpool's office. The shouting was procedural. It was used to alert the other lieutenant standing guard at the top of the stairs to listen in. It also informed the colonel himself that someone wished to see the Commandant of the Academy of Arms. "State your name and business, sir!" added the lieutenant at the bottom of the stairs to the dark-robed man.

His blond curls were barely visible from underneath his dark robes. The lieutenant took note to how this man resembled the colonel. Only the robed man was a bit younger.

"Tell the colonel his old friend Anthon wishes an audience."

"And what business, sir?"

"Oh? Family business."

"Rrrright," said the lieutenant slowly and with a bit of sarcasm. "A mister Anthon to see the commandant on family business!" shouted that young officer not taking his eyes off the robed stranger.

The other lieutenant at the top of the stairs turned and knocked on Colonel Blackpool's oak door and entered.

While waiting below the other lieutenant queried the stranger, "Who let you into the Academy of Arms, sir?"

The robbed man smiled and said not a word.

"How long have you known the colonel, sir?"

The two eyed each other neither backing down. Anthon only smiled while the lieutenant stared intently.

"The commandant says to let the man up!" came a call from above, breaking the tension.

Anthon gave the lieutenant a wink and moved past to glide up the narrow stone steps. The other young lieutenant at the top of the stairs told Anthon to stop as he got to the top step. Without turning away, the lieutenant opened the door and then he motioned for Anthon to continue. Anthon walked through the doorway and the lieutenant closed the large oak door behind him.

Anthon regarded the room. It was mostly large grey stones. Many crests, weapons and banners hung from the walls. This was definitely a warrior's room. A large oak desk sat in front of a balcony that overlooked the stadium grounds to the Academy of Arm. A small table sat on the wall across from the great oak desk; upon it sat what appeared to be an unfinished chess match. Two lavish chairs of purple and gold sat just to the sides of the great fireplace opposite the doorway.

"Why have you come back, Anthon?" asked Baltus sitting in one of those lavish chairs before the fireplace.

"To see you!" said Anthon with a smile. "How is Dru?"

"He is fine. Answer the question!"

Anthon walked over to fix himself and Baltus a drink. "I have told you. I have come to see you and see how the two of you are doing after Merriam's tragedy."

"And what do you care of it? It was your craft that caused her death!" said Colonel Blackpool staring into the fire.

"Yes. I know all of it. I still have contacts at my former school," said Anthon giving Baltus a glass. He sat down in the chair opposite and stared into the fire.

"I want them dead."

"I figured as much."

"My wife was a good woman."

"Yes, she was the best."

"She never hurt anyone! She raised our son practically on her own while I defended this country, these absent rulers and that thoughtless Wizard's College," Baltus said with venom on his breath.

"I know. These are some of the reasons as to why I refused to defend his land," stated Anthon.

"Don't you turn this into about you! I will never forgive you for joining that organisation. It is a betrayal to your country," exclaimed Baltus.

Anthon turned his back on Vorclaw after he graduated but was outcast from Vorclaw's Wizard's College, arguing for a change in leadership. Anthon felt he was headed for a life of servitude and wanted to rise above it. Anthon, like Baltus had ambition; Anthon left complaining of an absentee leadership and a close-minded Wizard's College. Although Baltus sympathised with Anthon's reasoning, Baltus believed Anthon truly left to seek power and riches rather than to serve his country. This actually embarrassed the proud colonel which set the two 'brothers' at odds. Anthon instead joined an underground network called The Shadow Company.

The Shadow Company was an organisation whose main purpose was to line its pockets with wealth and land. The Shadow Company was comprised of wizards, warriors, clergy and thieves; a mysterious leader or leaders sat and ruled at the top of the hierarchy. The members were mostly distrusted with societies' leadership and bureaucracy so many like-minded folks found homes in The Shadow Company.

There was a silence between the two brothers for many moments. Neither man really wanted to argue. Finally, Anthon gave in realising that he owed Baltus an apology.

"I am sorry, brother. I am sorry about comparing your wife's tragedy to my own issues with this land. I did not mean to downplay Merriam's death. It was wrong."

Baltus said nothing.

"Though I have not come for my brother's forgiveness for leaving Vorclaw," added Anthon, trying to break his brother's silence.

"Naturally, why have you come?"

"I have come for my brother's needs in his time of tragedy as a family should."

"I have everything I need so you may go," said Baltus.

"Really? Then why have you been requesting for enchanted weapons and an extortionate sum of money from the Wizard's College?"

"It is not for me personally. It is for my soldiers."

"Your soldiers?"

"Yes, mine!"

"You mean the Council's soldiers," he stated wickedly.

"Whatever, brother, how do you know of such things anyhow?" asked Baltus.

Anthon had to carefully answer this question. He had heard of his sister-in-law's death and his brother's return from his few remaining contacts in the wizard's college. Several of them were disgruntled like Anthon himself and therefore maintained connections with the organisation that Anthon belonged to – The Shadow Company.

This also meant that Baltus was correct in Anthon's ambitions but Baltus knew nothing of his brother or how many other graduates of the Wizard's College belonged to the company. Given this, it was a matter of time before news of Baltus Blackpool's requests for enchantments and favours from the Wizard's College reached Anthon Blackpool.

Anthon did more than just return though. He used scrying magic to see what plans his brother was scheming. What Anthon uncovered about his brother's personality was that he was an angry man bent on revenge. What form his revenge might take, Anthon was unsure. Anthon did like the tools at his brother's disposal though. Anthon also knew he could help his brother get some of the enchantments and weapons he desired thanks to his own contacts still within the college. Anthon intended to use Baltus' desire for revenge on the Wizard's College and to gain favour in The Shadow Company for himself.

Anthon also discovered other information about Academy of Arms' staff members that Baltus needed to know about.

Anthon also worried someone might try to scry on his meeting as he did with Baltus. Therefore, Anthon took precautions. He took out a hand-sized blue candle encased in golden inlay. The inlay was not only beautiful but also acted as a stand with three legs protruding at its base. Anthon set it on the small table between the two brothers and whispered the activation words. The lit candle let off a blue hue.

"There, now magic from within this candle will prevent anyone from scrying on us so we can talk safely brother. Here is what I know and why I have come home to see you!" said Anthon confidently.

* * * * *

Mimdrid, in the form of Sergeant Ian Coventry, made his way down the dark dirt road to the manor of Colonel Baltus Blackpool. He had decided that this was the night he would murder the colonel and replace Baltus with himself. Mimdrid had studied the colonel for several weeks while working as his groundskeeper. He also gathered what information he could about Baltus Blackpool from other soldier-workers, most of whom were substandard soldiers and sergeants themselves. That in itself made them candidates for menial tasks like grooming the grounds of their new commandant.

Mimdrid also continued to learn what he could from Dru Blackpool. If Mimdrid hoped to impersonate the colonel, then he would definitely need to convince the colonel's son, Dru. Certainly, he could kill Dru if he suspected anything but Mimdrid did not enjoy killing children and besides he grew fond of Dru. It was clear to Mimdrid that Dru would grow up to be a character to his liking.

Mimdrid understood on the outside that Colonel Blackpool was a warrior's warrior. The colonel believed in drilling and training soldiers hard, expecting exemplary results. In return, he treated his soldiers with fairness rewarding those that shined and relying upon Sergeant Major Foehammer to discipline those that did not. He led by example and trusted his senior sergeants and junior officers.

Mimdrid also understood that the colonel commanded a daunting presence. His uniform was always kept in the cleanest and highest regards. The shape-changer was aware that the colonel was a knight. Although Mimdrid did not know the colonel's entire skill set, he did know that it held a revered stature. He also knew that Baltus Blackpool had a dark side, one that was coming to life in the form of revenge of his dead wife.

Mimdrid knew that he could not completely mimic the colonel, but he only wanted to for a time. And what better way to explain any noticeable odd behaviour than using the man's dead wife as a source for it.

Mimdrid still held resentment for Magnus Foehammer too. He thought about killing him but instead he would make his life a living hell with some menial tasks before redeploying him to some far-off land.

* * * * *

The shape-changer, using his magical item, an earring, that allowed him to read the surface thoughts of a nearby person to survey the grounds of Colonel Blackpool's estate. It was the same device that allowed him to garner information from unsuspecting individuals that he replaced.

First, Mimdrid used the earring's powers to seek out individuals to avoid while approaching the estate. This got him to the southern wall where the balcony to the colonel's bedroom was. Next, the shape-changer used his greater than human strength and ability to elongate his body to scale the wall. The shape-changer again called upon the earring's ability to detect who was about but sensed only soldiers at their posts at ground level. Curious this was to

Mimdrid, since Colonel Blackpool was usually home this late in the evening; this could turn out to be a stroke of luck for the creature.

Mimdrid fashioned his finger into a key and inserted it into the lock of the balcony door. He was able to manipulate his skin to push down on all the bars inside the mechanism door. Once inside, the shape-changer surveyed the bed chamber; seeing the bed was still made Mimdrid deduced that the colonel had yet to return home. This suited the shape-changer fine. Now Mimdrid would simply lie in wait. He picked a spot where he could easily keep out of sight in the bedroom closet.

Over an hour passed before Baltus Blackpool returned to his manor. Mimdrid heard the footfalls of the horses and carriage wheels signalling the colonel's return. He also heard Colonel Blackpool talking outside and inside the house ordering to "not to be disturbed this evening". This was music to the shape-changer's ears!

The colonel announced where he was heading to the guards below, straight to his bed chamber! Mimdrid, waiting in the closet, heard the colonel's heavy footfalls coming up the steps and barking out orders as he went up the staircase. The shape-changer still engaged the colonel using his earring to read surface thoughts. Baltus was reflecting on his last moments with his wife and seemed unaware of the shape-changer's presence. Colonel Blackpool entered the room, shut the door behind him and produced a small crossbow.

"Come out, shape-changer, I will not harm you if you surrender peacefully," stated Colonel Blackpool who knew full well that Mimdrid lay in wait.

The colonel owed his brother dearly for his magical capability to scry and foresee this danger, or as the colonel saw it, this opportunity.

Mimdrid could scarcely believe it. He wasted no time; he burst forth from the closet to attack the colonel. Mimdrid, still in the form of Ian Coventry, lunged at the colonel. He only engulfed air; the illusion of the colonel did its work. On instinct, the annoyed and confused shape-changer made a dash for the balcony window only to be scared nearly to death by bursts of flames billowing from the hands of the invisible wizard. Mimdrid fell back onto the floor. When he regained his footing, there stood Colonel Blackpool and two wizards holding wands.

"Help me, colonel, I am possessed," beckoned Mimdrid trying to buy some time.

"Calm yourself, shape-changer," stated Colonel Blackpool who entered the room from the hallway. "There is no need for tricks among friends. Had I wanted you dead, you would already be so."

After several moments, Mimdrid changed back to his true form and stood up.

Mimdrid looked like an albino human with no hair and blue eyes. He was thin almost, frail looking.

"I don't care what happened to the man you assumed, nor do I care what your intentions were although I could very well guess," stated Colonel Blackpool. "I forgive you for the attempt on my life."

Mimdrid just stared at Baltus not saying a word.

"A thank you would be in order," said the colonel with a smile.

Still no response from Mimdrid.

"At least give me the pleasure of your name," asked Baltus.

"My name is Mimdrid, colonel," he said with an otherworldly voice and a polite bow. "Why have you spared my life, great colonel?" continued Mimdrid playing to Colonel Blackpool's ego a bit.

"Well, isn't it obvious? You're more useful to me alive," stated Colonel Blackpool. "Your ability to mimic and see into one's mind using your magical earring, and yes I know you can read mine right now, is quite useful to me. My associates have been aware of you for some time, Mimdrid."

Mimdrid knew much of the Colonel Blackpool's desire to take revenge for the death of his wife and knew that is why he had spared him. Mimdrid garnered that from the surface thought and from weeks of observing the colonel. Mimdrid tried to read the thoughts of the two wizards in the room but could not. They had spells or devices in place to keep him out. Mimdrid quickly deduced that he was studied and the colonel likely left his mind open to show his sincerity.

"I have a proposal, one that will include wealth, intrigue and power, Mimdrid," said Baltus now pouring glasses of brandy and handing Mimdrid one. "All you have to do is give me your input on certain matters and do what I ask."

* * * * *

That night Anthon returned to his apartment. He lifted up the rug he placed upon the floor where he had a pentagram drawn on the floor. He stepped in it, knelt down and said the incantation to open communications.

"My Lord of Shadow, I have done as you asked. I have manipulated my brother, laid the foundation for a war that will benefit The Shadow Company."

Chapter 9

Unholy Union

The next evening, a meeting between Mimdrid, Colonel Blackpool and Anthon Blackpool concluded with Mimdrid walking out of the colonel's house under a new guise. The colonel's new advisor, Mimdrid, was to become an officer, a captain, one tailored to Colonel Blackpool's design. Mimdrid took the guise of a slender man once known to him as Nigel Newman, a former merchant from Karthia he killed.

Anthon dismissed his apprentice, Erik, who aided in the capture of Mimdrid.

"A shape-changer was not to be taken lightly and assurances need to be taken to keep you safe from harm," stated Anthon.

"You're not worried about me, Anthon, are you?"

"Yes actually, shape-changers are not pets. They can be devious and have uncanny abilities. This is especially so with this one who has an earring that can read into the minds of those around him. A rare magical device, indeed; we should kill him and take his magical device for our own."

"I know but he is an asset worth keeping," replied Colonel Blackpool sipping his brandy with his brother. "Think about it! We have an ally who can be anyone and read into the minds of others. What an asset. And shape-changers are mostly interested in self-gain, not unlike yourself, brother. I think I will be able to hold his attention and keep him entertained."

"I am not convinced, brother. Therefore, I took the liberty to procure this for you," said Anthon handing his brother a ring. "This ring will keep your mind safe from him. What about you physically, the shape-changers have a deceiving frail structure as you have seen and…"

"Come, come now, brother," interrupted Baltus with amusement, "I have strength, skill and magical devices at my disposal to aid me in my entire fighting prowess, but thank you for the ring."

"Very well then, what of Magnus?: asked Anthon who had concerns that a man of Magnus' integrity would be a problem for them eventually. "Surely he will not indulge in your retribution."

"No, Anthon, he will not, you're right," said Baltus solemnly, "But I need him. I will keep him through the next year or so."

"Why? Why keep someone around who could uncover our plotting?"

"Because he is a magnificent soldier, and the soldiers respect him. And he has an uncanny ability to bring out the best in soldiers. Did you know he is known throughout the army? I need him to find me the best of each class that come through my academy. I need him to find me diamonds in the rough."

"For what reason?"

"Once he uncovers the 'diamonds' among the soldiers, I will mould these men into an elite cult of officers loyal to me. And from this cult, I will enact my revenge."

"Sounds charming, brother, I had no idea you thought this coup through so far!" Anthon answered but suspected as much from scrying on his brother.

Anthon also possessed a similar magical item to Mimdrid's – a small ring worn on his left pinky finger, one that could garner the surface thoughts of another's mind. However, Anthon was not sure his brother had the stomach to see coup attempt through and garner justice for his wife's death! The wizard was also given a ring that could influence others into agreement.

"Soldiers loyal to you are not enough. You need a cause to garner their support in a coup. You need a war!" said Anthon.

"A war, with who?" chuckled Baltus.

"With the arch-goblins of Mistful Forest, of course, and I am going to help start it," stated Anthon in all seriousness. "As you said, there is something amiss with them. I am also curious to see what they're about. However, first how do you intend to pay for my services, or should I say pay for the services of those I enlist to aid you in quest," beckoned Anthon Blackpool.

"I am sure the filth that employ you will gladly aid 'you' in 'our' quest. Especially if they get a piece of Vorclaw for their own," responded Colonel Blackpool coldly.

The reference to Anthon's dealings with The Shadow Company reminded Baltus of why he was displeased with his brother. Baltus was irritated that his brother abandoned Vorclaw even still.

Baltus, however, just realised that he was doing the same, betraying his country. Or was he? Or is this just a necessary evil?

"Wrecking and rebuilding a nation is not enough for them, they want assurances and something to prove you can back your cause," stated Anthon not bothered by his brother's comment about the order.

"For instance?"

"Well, what do you intend to do with all the money the Council and Wizard's College is granting you?"

"Why?" asked Baltus.

"I think we can sway them if we invest in their interests, locally, of course, and they may invest in ours in return. Well, make a tiny profit to be sure," explained Anthon.

"What local interests does The Shadow Company have in Vorclaw?"

"Piracy on the high seas, dear brother," said Anthon Blackpool. "Yes, that could fund your coup quite nicely," he said with a smile. "You are not the only one in a position of power that has ties to The Shadow Company," Anthon teased.

"Due till then?" asked Baltus.

"There is one member and one only on the council that has a tie to my company. Although he is indeed altruistic, his true loyalty is to his sons," said Anthon.

"Who?" asked Baltus, eager to know.

"A friend of yours of course. His son is also my pupil although I am not certain how much his father, Captain Drake Kahee, knows of it."

Baltus took it all in. He knew it would take years to get all the right pieces in place and by then, would he lose his nerve. An unseen alliance with The Shadow Company could prove to speed up things and be profitable? However, Drake Kahee having a son involved in The Shadow Company was truly unexpected!

"What of your son?" asked Anthon suddenly remembering his nephew.

"Dru is inquisitive and will likely uncover some of the plot; however, he must never know of the great sins I am about to commit," said Baltus refusing to look at his brother as he mouthed the words, for Baltus Blackpool wore guilt upon his face.

"We do this to avenge Merriam," said Anthon sensing the guilt in his brother's mind.

"For my wife," whispered Baltus.

* * * * *

The next day, Colonel Blackpool provided an officer's uniform complete with two shoulder epilates containing a silver X signifying a captain in Vorclaw's army.

"Mimdrid, I have to say I am pleased with the new appearance. Don't you agree, Anthon?" Mimdrid in his new form performed a bow to Colonel Blackpool while Anthon did not respond to his brother. Mimdrid in the guise of a slender man once known to him as Nigel Newman took notice and knew he would have to win Anthon's trust over.

There was another person in Colonel Blackpool's office. Erik Kahee, the wizard who aided in the capture of Mimdrid the night before. He kept his bad complexion and greasy hair concealed under his black hooded robes. Anthon dismissed his apprentice once he was certain the room was secure and Mimdrid did not pose a threat.

The three-remaining sat around a large oak table with Anthon's blue candle encased in golden inlay stood as the centrepiece, aflame.

Colonel Blackpool opened their meeting with questions of how Mimdrid came to Sedgedunum and what aspirations he held. Once all were in agreement on what this unholy union was to be, Colonel Blackpool laid out his plans for the future.

Baltus expressed his desire for revenge and plans for a coup. He wanted to topple The Council of Twelve and the Wizard's College. He planned to do so by building an elite class of soldiers, a cult, loyal to him – similar to the Knights of Uden, but with more power over the land. He also told Mimdrid he

54

hoped to guise his coup by inciting war with the arch-goblins in the Mistful Forest and get them to raze Sedgedunum.

"Let the arch-goblins sack the city, then I will take control of the army and retake the capitol thanks to my well-placed followers," Baltus went on to say.

Mimdrid believed the colonel could manipulate most soldiers. He was very charismatic and intelligent. He already had Magnus Foehammer to his side and although Mimdrid despised Magnus, he knew he was an influential asset in army.

"But for these plans to work, simple raids on the arch-goblins to draw them out of the Mistful Forest may not work," continued Baltus

"I do not believe the arch-goblins are interested in Sedgedunum? Their interests lay elsewhere," stated Mimdrid.

"What makes you say that?" asked Anthon.

"I have been to their cities. I have seen their queen." The blank stares back told Mimdrid these two human brothers did not know much about the arch-goblin hoards within the Mistful Forest. "They have at least three small cites, one in the forest, another in the Spine-of-Vana and another underground within the Spine-of-Vana mountains."

"My instincts tell me there is more to them than just a rabble," stated Baltus. "How large are these cities?"

"The largest city underground holds about five thousand. The other two hold about half that at best."

"You said they had a queen?" asked Anthon.

"Yes, and not just any queen, a vampire. She is rumored toto be an arch-goblin half breed but I don't know for sure. I do know she does keep the three chieftains in check. She is the reason why I could not stay there. I feared she would uncover my identity."

"Raiding them to pull them out and attack Sedgedunum may not work then. A creature like a vampire is usually very intelligent," said Baltus.

"As are arch-goblins," put in Mimdrid.

Several moments passed before anyone had a suggestion.

"We will need to form a union with this vampire queen," stated Anthon. Both Mimdrid and Baltus's jaws dropped open in protest! "We need to pull her into our union."

"What?" asked a shocked Mimdrid.

"Yes what?" asked Baltus equally shocked. "How are we going to convince her to join us?"

"And how are you going to get her to leave Sedgedunum? I presume you still intend to claim Sedgedunum as your own, do you not?" asked Mimdrid of the brothers.

"Mimdrid, you said that the arch-goblins' interest laid elsewhere. What is it they want?" asked Baltus not answering Mimdrid's question.

"They want the lands north of Panther-Paw-Pass."

"Why would they want that awful place?" asked Baltus. "There is nothing there except mines, farms and cattle."

"That's preciously what they want!" stated Mimdrid. "They want the mines and the lands there, to feed their people and livestock."

"It makes sense, mining towns are growing up all the time along the Spine-of-Vana. Riches and old artefacts are coming out of them. Plus, we just erected a small fort in the area that routes forces through there They know we are there to stay," stated Baltus.

"This is also why they have been quiet lately, they are plotting and scheming on how to deal with your recent encroachment," continued Mimdrid.

Baltus turned to all of them and smiled. "Then that area is what we will offer their queen," said Colonel Blackpool.

Anthon smiled.

* * * * *

Later that morning, the three members of the unholy union walked onto the balcony of the commandant's quarters, Colonel Blackpool's office. The view oversaw the parade grounds where Sergeant Major Magnus Foehammer was drilling the new recruits in the morning light. Some of his drill sergeants were marching recruits while others were teaching fighting styles with mock swords. At the far end, archery training was taking place.

Sergeant Major Foehammer was instructing a class of new recruits on the different weapon types. A variety of weapons on a large rack stood behind him. Some were wood for mock while others were for real combat, but all were optional weapons to be used by Vorclaw soldiers. Most of the young soldiers were already familiar with swords but some were familiar with other weapons and Magnus encourage the soldiers to stick with what they knew, for now. Magnus and his other drill sergeants matched mace and shields against sword and shield. One soldier even chose to fight with a glaive only. Another chose to fight with a war hammer.

Magnus clearly understood the need for a uniform fighting force, and most were equipped with the standard sword and shield, but with approval of Colonel Blackpool, Magnus did incorporate a diverse few into the army ranks. Simple yet different thinking like this by Magnus, is why Colonel Blackpool kept the large red-haired soldier at hand.

"You see..." said Colonel Blackpool pointing at Magnus, directing Mimdrid and Anthon to look. "I need Magnus in order to create my elite class of soldiers. I also ordered Magnus to find the most talented top five soldiers of each class for officer school."

"Do you intend to corrupt all the officers?" asked Anthon.

"No, brother, several other officers housed here at the Academy will be taught leadership and decision-making skills during battle. But I will instruct the top officers. It would be from these top officers that I would build my cult. And Magnus would find them for me."

"I have to ask, how you are going to keep this cult a secret from the rest of the academy?" questioned Mimdrid.

"Follow me," responded Colonel Blackpool.

The trio went back into the colonel's chamber. The colonel opened what was presumed to be a closet. It led to another hallway. It was a short hallway. The hallway's end, opened to a private bedroom and office but off to the side was another door.

The colonel took them through this side door and went down spiralling stairs reaching far below ground level. The temperature change was apparent at the bottom.

The colonel mouthed a word silently, clapped his hand, and the wall torches grew to life illuminating the chamber. "Here is where I will train, teach, and hold my council," said Colonel Baltus Blackpool out loud so it echoed.

Anthon and Mimdrid's jaws hung open as they marvelled at the underground chamber. Ancient statues of when long dead elven kings reigned were all around. Glyphs of elves conquering orcs and decorated the reliefs along the walls. Marble bleachers ran down the sides. An arched stone roof capped the top of this ancient monument.

"I am told this once belonged to the elven kind, a gift from the General Flinthouse. He claimed he never used it when he was running the academy but here is where an elven court once resided and it is here my cult shall meet, away from prying eyes."

"What if he was lying?" asked Anthon. "We don't want to risk anyone else knowing of this treasure."

A moment passed before Colonel Blackpool responded. "Good point. Mimdrid, seems I have a tasking for you already. Please take care of the good General Flinthouse, and make it look like an accident," stated Colonel Blackpool.

"That should not be too difficult, he looks so old, he must be near death as it is," said Mimdrid. "And what will you call *your* cult?" asked Mimdrid with a smile, starting to actually like this jaded colonel.

"*Our* cult will be called The Black-Masks," responded Colonel Blackpool.

Chapter 10
The Arch-Goblins

Dearest Queen Ooktha, ruler of the arch-goblins within the Spine-of-Vana, I beseech an audience under a flag of truce. I wish to speak of a merger where we both might profit greatly in land and title through downfall of certain parties in Vorclaw.

I know you maintain impressive weapons cache for the ten thousand mighty arch-goblin warriors and lizard-goblin fodder within your two cities above and underground. I know of your kind desire to conquer rich mining lands in the Spine-of-Vana. Finally, I know your quest is doomed to failure and will never come to fruition without my aid.

Please forgive my bold statements but I hold great knowledge of Vorclaw's strengths and weaknesses in matters of war – and of yours. The fact that I know of your existence lends credibility to my knowledge base. However, I wish to aid you in your endeavours.

Without revealing my identity, know this, I command great importance in Vorclaw. I have travelled throughout this country, defeating all manner of goblinkin and orckin to keep its people safe from harm. I have the ear of the several members of the wizard's guild, the army, navy, and the council of this land.

However, I have come to an impasse and desires toward revenge. Along this path, I have uncovered new allies and established new alliances in order to aid me in my cause. I grow more powerful and influential by the month.

Dearest Queen Ooktha, meet with me to hear my plan. Aid me in my cause and I will in turn provide you with additional admiration of your people.

Sincerely, B.

* * * * *

"For the last five years I have received letters such as these," said the Queen Ooktha to her undead council members. Queen Ooktha, ruler of the arch-goblins, belonged to a secret society known as the Union of Undead. It was a confederacy of powerful undead forces. Their members were vampires and revenants.

The vampires were the undead creatures who drained the blood of the living to survive. The turning to undead granted them everlasting undead life, strength and unique powers but only if they had a sustenance of fresh blood daily.

The revenants, however, passed from the living to undead through the magical manipulation of soul-separation. While their bodies decayed slowly, their consciousness and powers remained often enhanced. The majority of the soul, however, was separated and stored in a vessel called a soul-sepulchre. For if the soul could not depart Vana in death, one's consciousness could remain in their decaying body. Many reasons exist for becoming a revenant, most personal but some of the traditional examples are simply fear of death, the desire to achieve powers beyond what they could in true life and some even take on this form to guard lands or treasures they hold dear.

Rarely did any of the Union of Undead meet in person but all could view one another through mirrors that projected one's image through another mirror over vast distances around Vana. The mirrors came in all shapes and sizes with décor to the taste of the owning undead.

"Before the letters were simple pleas and invites but now they reveal much more about my hoards. They mention of my numbers, weapons, cities and fodder. This tells me I have a spy or spies and I can no longer afford to ignore this if I am to proceed with my plan," continued Ooktha, several of the twelve undead members nodded in agreement, of those that could still nod.

"Some lord wishes to make a name for himself is all," said Revenant Rom-Seti. This skeletal visage was always adorned in some snake-like head dress, like that of a cobra. "Ignore these letters and proceed with your plan to remove those people from your territory."

"I disagree!" exclaimed Revenant Niss, a recluse mage who kept her whereabouts hidden to the undead league; she is thought to reside in a tower that changes location monthly or at least at her mere will. While others believe she lives within an undisclosed ruined city. "First you must seek out the spy or spies and interrogate them, they will reveal much to you." Revenant Niss had particular hatred toward Rom-Seti for reasons she kept to herself. It was not surprising she disagreed with Rom-Seti.

"Agree, reluctantly, to terms and then discover a weakness and press your will upon whoever this creature is."

"Do not listen!" exclaimed Rom-Seti. "You waste your efforts! Even if this 'B' is genuine, he will not likely be so trustworthy if he's willing to betray his own kind!" stated Revenant Rom-Seti.

Queen Ooktha admired the Revenant Niss for her ability to stand firm in a male-dominant union. Revenant Niss and herself were the only female members of the Union of Undead.

The rest of the mirrors kept silent beyond the two comments for many moments. All knew of the distaste Niss and Rom-Seti had for each other and no one wished to incite another argument as had happened in past meetings. Ooktha herself disliked Rom-Seti as well; however, she liked Rom-Seti's suggestion.

"Meet with 'B'!" announced Lord Drim, breaking the tension. He was another revenant who also kept both his identity and location secret. His dark his kept his visage hidden. "Uncover his true intentions by whatever means you have available and report back to us. You must understand his motives. Meet with 'B' and embrace this as a chance to gain knowledge about your enemies," he said from beneath his black robes. Lord Drim was a most evil creature that all the Union of Undead revered and feared, all except the cavalier Revenant Rom-Seti.

Queen Ooktha heard his advice loud and clear. "I thank you all my friends for your council. Especially yours, Lord Drim, I will meet with this person and uncover his intentions. I will keep you all informed. I ask you all to please support me in my decisions. I know I can count on you all to aid me in my endeavours and conquests." She closed her mirrored portal and others followed suit.

With a wave of her hand the candle-lit room door of this antechamber opened. Down the hall she walked to her throne room. There her council of three, her chieftains, were waiting.

* * * * *

These were the three great arch-goblin warriors, the chieftains, who ruled her three cities.

Chieftain Gutter, a rotund arch-goblin who governed the western city on the northern outskirts of the Mistful Forest. Ironhold, as it was known to the arch-goblins, was part in the forest and part in the mountains.

Next was Chieftain Merka, the tall and slender but crafty leader of the eastern city Blood-helm. His city was small and built more like a fortress and atop older ruins. It was near the area known in Vorclaw as Panther-Paw-Pass.

Finally, there was Chieftain Blist who claimed to be Queen Ooktha's distant cousin. He was a giant arch-goblin who ruled the large underground city of Skulls-thorpe; a magnificent city cared out of rock nestled atop an underground lake.

Queen Ooktha had elven ears with short black hair. She told everyone she was one quarter arch-goblin. The rest of her past she kept quiet to all. She did make it clear that she found the bigotry of elves, humans and dwarves intolerable and demoralising. She then left her elven past behind to seek out her arch-goblin family. This led to an unfortunate or fortunate brush with a vampire. This vampire, whom she never speaks of, aided her in locating Chieftain Blist, her cousin. Soon after, she became ruler of all three-warring arch-goblin clans, with her cousin Chieftain Blist at her side. Queen Ooktha had it all, a sanctuary underground, the protection of the arch-goblins and a haven from daylight. This great feat made her petition into the Union of Undead too hard to ignore – so they welcomed her in.

To the three chieftains, their queen was not ugly to them but not beautiful either, more unique in appearance. She was slender and muscular but lacked the broadness of arch-goblin women. Queen Ooktha's face was mostly elven to them. The closest resemblance she held to an arch-goblin was her skin tone. While an arch-goblin's was light blue, hers was nearly bone-white.

Before her, each chieftain held a captive in front of them. They were always humanoid and still living but the sacrifices were kneeling, gagged and bound, and covered by red blankets. The victims knew not a vampire was before them. Queen Ooktha enjoyed this game immensely as did her chieftains, all relished at the creature's expression once the blanket was removed.

Queen Ooktha herself was not picky but only took one of the sacrifices which sometimes lasted her over several days to several weeks, depending on how active she was. She never knew what manner of humanoid lay beneath the covers. It was up to the chieftains to locate her victims and convince their queen to select their sacrifice. It was a deadly game they all enjoyed.

"Powerful mistress of the arch-goblins," shouted the mighty Chieftain Gutter. All the victims began shifting nervously from under their blankets. "I bring to you a delightful treat whose blood is fresh and sweet! I have for you a young female halfling captured passing in the Spine-of-Vana."

"Great Queen Ooktha," began Chieftain Merka whose voice sounded more like a wicked buzzard than that of a hearty arch-goblin. "I have here a fresh offering from which you may drink. Mine is most unique and never before seen in your throne room. My offering is male, slender and evil as night. Yet to make this game more fun, dare I say, I dare not tell you, my queen, but please choose mine and see," stated Merka smiling the whole time.

Queen Ooktha delighted at the tale and laughed aloud at the crafty chieftain's offer.

"Take mine, dear queen and cousin," said Chieftain Blist. "My offering of flesh and blood is powerful and hearty. It was not easy not an easy booty, this one, for this mighty dwarf we captured in the caverns below killed many an arch-goblin and deserves your wrath!"

Queen Ooktha was already sold on Chieftain Merka's offering. "I choose yours, Merka, reveal your sacrifice to your queen."

Merka, beaming with pride, lifted his blanket to reveal a bound male dark-elf; Dark-elves live within Vana and not on the surface. This particular breed of elf had an ashy-coloured skin, red eyes and golden hair like the rest of his kin. This dark elf immediately began screaming through his gag.

All the arch-goblins laughed at the dark-elf and applauded such a capture. Dark-elves were known for their cunning and evil ways; to capture one was no easy task. Queen Ooktha simply said one word, "Delicious."

* * * * *

Satisfied after she partially drained her dark-elf victim to nearly the point of no return, she had him shackled and removed. The other victims were removed as well, given back to the arch-goblins who found them.

"Let us now discuss what we intend to do about this 'B'," stated Ooktha rubbing the dark-elf blood from the corner of her mouth.

"Ignore this scum, mistress," stated Chieftain Gutter, governor of the western city. "Our defences are now prepared for any attack they might bring through the forest."

"I agree, no one could possibly breach our positions," smiled Chieftain Merka of the eastern city. "So, they have spies, we have spies. We know we can conquer the whole land around and they are not poised to stop us."

"Let us attack now!" announced Chieftain Blist. "Even if the some Vorclaw citizens know of our plans, our spies do not show any new defences. They must think us incapable of an assault on their small mining town and timber fort around that elven ruin they call the Tor. Their spies must not be that skilled."

Queen Ooktha smiled and was delighted at her arch-goblins' eagerness and confidence but needed to be sure her chieftains thought things through.

"We are ready to strike, my friends. We are powerful enough to repel any invader to our lands," she said coyly. The three arch-goblin leaders howled in agreement.

"But are we ready for a war on two fronts? Can we defend our lands and hold onto what we have taken from the Vorclaw nation?" she asked with some authority. "How long can we secure our own lands if attacked while we're out taking someone else's?"

Chieftain Merka's smile diminished considerably, and Chieftain Gutter growled at the questions but backed away waiting for a strike from the vampire queen.

Chieftain Blist played this game before with Queen Ooktha and knew she was fishing for answer from them and knew she already had a plan. Arch-goblin always have a plan, but unfortunately some arch-goblin plans are overzealous. Therefore, Chieftain Blist presumed his vampire cousin was against their plan of ignoring 'B'. He assumed she wanted to meet with him after five years of messages. "Then it may be wise to see what he wants and see, um, what we can learn?" announced Chieftain Blist to all.

"Delicious," said Queen Ooktha responded with a smile.

* * * * *

Mimdrid, in human form, painstakingly set up the meeting between Queen Ooktha and Colonel Baltus Blackpool. It took him years to cultivate any connections with the arch-goblins near Pather-Paw-Pass; it often ended in an exchange of insults and even weapons would clash. The Arch-goblins he found were not the easiest to negotiate with. Eventually, both Mimdrid and Chieftain Merka agreed on a neutral location, a high outcrop in the Spine-of-Vana Mountains. It was a moonless night with heavy overcast and a cold wind. It was agreed only Baltus and Ooktha would meet on the outcrop, even though reinforcements and support were well in hand for both sides.

Baltus came prepared with holy water saturating in his gloves and clothing. He already had his enchanted sword unsheathed and rested both his hands on the pommel as the tip pointed into the ground. He maintained a few other enchantments and weapons just in case. He knew he had to use the best of charismatic abilities to persuade this vampire into alliance.

He had seen Queen Ooktha many times through his brother's scrying, but even he was enchanted by her presence as she floated into sight. She did not arrive as a flying bat or a dire wolf as many vampires do. Ooktha arrived as a form of black smoke that took shape of a beautiful creature dressed in red and black scandalous garb. Her features were elven he noted. Her black lips smiled to reveal her deadly vampire fangs.

"You are quite the beauty, Queen Ooktha, and your dress, all the same," started Baltus.

"Who are you?" she asked.

"I am the one who has been trying to get your attention for the last five years."

"To what end?"

"To aid me?"

"I warn you do not toy with me, be more specific. I will ask you one more time and if you do not answer, you forfeit your life for one of solitude as source of nourishment," stated Queen Ooktha, her fangs growing and face contorting slightly to accommodate her enlarging maw.

"Well, let's get right to the point, shall we, my dear?" Baltus responded unafraid. "I want you to destroy Sedgedunum."

Baltus just stared at her intently, beaming with confidence at the request. By the look on the face of Queen Ooktha, more a look of confusion, it was an offer she was not prepared to answer but was intrigued. Her fangs and maw retracted and the vampire's face returned to beauty.

Confident he had her interested, Baltus continued, "And in return I will broker you a deal and hand you over what you desire most. All wrapped up in the form of a treaty."

"The land in the Tor?" she asked.

"Yes."

She let loose a chuckle at the proposal. "Delicious indeed but why should I attack a city I do not desire when I can simply take the land from you?"

"Because I know of your plan and know it will not succeed, not for long anyway. You cannot sustain a war on two fronts. If you attack our mining town near the Tor, I will be forced to attack you from Sedgedunum in the Mistful Forest while the rest of Vorclaw wipes you from mountains. And they will not stop. We will bury you into the Spine-of-Vana for the next one hundred years," announced Baltus, his confidence turned to antagonism.

The vampire, angered by his arrogance, leaped at Colonel Blackpool. He sent a wet hand up to the face of the attacking maw while he let his sword drop and pulled forth an enchanted wooden dagger he had hidden up his right sleeve. It went into her flesh too easily.

Queen Ooktha backed off and let out a hiss at the Colonel Blackpool. She hid well the pain from the holy water on the colonel's glove. Her burned undead flesh already started to heal but the point of his enchanted dagger went through her like a knife through butter.

"It doesn't have to be his way, my lady, we can join forces to get what we want," he shouted in return, his enchanted sword now in his hand.

"Why would you want your capitol destroyed?" she hissed with her fangs out. The wind started to pick up. Both their capes started to flutter in the breeze.

"Because!" shouted back Colonel Blackpool, his breathing intensified, and his muscles tightened for the strike or to strike. "My wife, my wife," he said angrily yelling over the wind. "They killed my wife and I want revenge!" he shouted. "I want that city and the people to pay for their crime." His anger gave way to irritation as he recounted the last moment, he saw his wife. Then his mind flashed to the grave where Merriam rested.

Over the last five years, bitterness had grown in the man. He used this negativity to channel his strength and resolve. It made his skills in combat sharper, deadlier but also at the cost of the trust of his true friends. He was not about to make the last five years all for naught. This vampire would either join him or he would all end here tonight.

"The choice is yours, queen, join me in my request for revenge, be sure to choose the correct one," he said with deadly sarcasm.

"Calm yourself, my dear," soothed Ooktha, her form now converted into a more heavenly beauty. "I too have felt pain like yours. I can feel the hate in you, can see it. I am in the same place as you."

"How so?" he inquired, the wind dying down.

"Clearly, I am not fully arch-goblin, I am mostly elf. Shunned and scorned by my own elven kind but fully accepted by my arch-goblin kin," said the vampire. "Even when I moved to Vorclaw many years ago, I was eschewed again by the humans and dwarves in the region."

Both Colonel Blackpool and Queen Ooktha stared at each other for several moments.

"So we are akin, you and I, we both want the same thing, revenge," said Baltus.

"Delicious!" she said nodding in agreement.

Chapter 11

Boys Become Men

"I still say you look nothing like an elf," said the drill master.

"Yes, drill master!" responded Leif standing perfectly still and at attention.

His drill master, a tall lanky sergeant, stood eye to eye with Leif. Leif did not move a muscle. His father, Magnus Foehammer, now retired from the Academy of Arms taught Leif what to expect at the academy. Leif knew not to move a muscle, follow orders and agree with whatever comments were made – learn to obey, only then will you be allowed to think for yourself.

Bjorn, Leif's older brother, looked on smiling at his 'little' adopted brother, who was not so little any longer. The drill master spoke the truth though about Leif. Leif did not look like an elf. Like Bjorn, Leif was taller than an elf. He grew to be larger in height and size than any elf. The family all presumed it due to the diet Disa Foehammer served over the last five years.

Bjorn Foehammer, having gone through basic combat training over a year before with his childhood friend Dru Blackpool, reminisced of the days he was being yelled at by the same skinny drill master, one of many that his own father trained for the position of drill master. The training was similar, lots of yelling and antagonising at first, followed by serious discipline, combat and followership training. The yelling and provoking never let up though, even today at the graduation.

"I could not be more pound of him," said Bjorn to Dru Blackpool as he came to join him on the bleachers of the Academy of Arms training ground. "The drill master that replaced my father told me he is going to graduate as the top student, just like you."

"Outstanding! Surely, he is a better student than we were," said Dru. Dru had to fake his enthusiasm for Leif. For Dru, the top graduate of the class last year just above Bjorn, knew well the cult his father created--The Black-Masks. This fraternity was an underground network of soldier loyal to his father. Often, the top few graduates were recruited to join. He knew his father would attempt to assimilate Leif into The Black-Masks as he did Bjorn and Dru.

Both Dru and Bjorn had become young captains after a year of assignment to the White Eagles and specialised training thereafter. They both got their starts in the army with the same battalion their fathers once belonged to, coincidence, surely.

Bjorn, in taking after his mother, Disa, who was a priestess of Matronae, handled the spiritual needs of soldiers, but his specialised training was much more. Colonel Blackpool sent Bjorn off to *school* for months so he might fine tune his priestly professions. The cost would be for young Bjorn to specialise in one of the fields the colonel prescribed.

Dru's training was just the opposite, not only was he trained as a soldier, but his father ensured Dru's talents for thievery were embraced. Originally, Dru's father explained to the young man that he should embrace his talent as an experiment to see if it might be useful. However, Dru suspected his father and his uncle Anthon to have more sinister plans for his talents.

Still, Dru obliged his father as did Bjorn at his school. Everyone obliged Colonel Blackpool. Bjorn especially as the large man admired Colonel Blackpool, just like his own father did. And when he was assimilated in the Black-Masks, the young Bjorn so it more of prestige than sinister.

"Should I ask my father to put him in the White Eagles?" asked Dru.

"If he can make it so, that would be ideal. And we can order him around as often as we like when we return to the White Eagles!" said Bjorn with a chuckle.

"If we return," stated Dru.

* * * * *

Today was graduation day and bleachers were filled with spectators. Magnus Foehammer, now retired in Sedge-fen, thriving as a black smith, joined Bjorn and Dru to watch the commencement. Disa joined them as well forcing a seat between Dru and Bjorn, taking in both their arms. Disa had been like a mother to Dru since his own mother, Merriam, had passed.

Dru smiled at the adoptive family he joined but was still troubled about Leif potentially joining The Black-Masks. As far as Dru knew, Leif knew nothing about The Black-Masks. Dru's father had ominous plans but he was not entirely sure how far they would reach. All he did know was his father had contacts with sinister sources and had officers commanding all over Vorclaw that were loyal to him. Dru suspected Magnus knew about the cult but assumed he no longer worried about such things being retired from the military and his blacksmithing being so lucrative. Oddly Magnus never spoke much of Dru's father and never asked after him.

After the graduation ceremony finished, Magnus, Bjorn, Disa and Dru all went down to the parade grounds to congratulate Leif on being top of his class.

"I owe much of my training to you, father," said Leif to Magnus after all the hugs and praises from his adoptive family. "But my patience and discipline come from my mother," he said smiling at his adoptive mother, Disa.

Magnus was about to protest in jest but Disa pushed forward for a big hug from Leif; tears of happiness and pride watered their eyes, just like she did at Bjorn and Dru's graduation. She saw all three of these boys as her sons. "I am so proud of you, Leif my boy," she said looking up at him, her hands holding his angled cheeks.

Magnus too could not be prouder. He spent countless hours training all 'three' boys as soldiers even before they went to academy.

"Congratulations Lieutenant Foehammer," came an all too familiar voice. All turned to regard Colonel Blackpool, all except his own son, Dru. Leif and Bjorn snapped to attention. There was an uncomfortable silence for a moment. Dru eventually turned but folded his arms in protest at his father's presence. Baltus did not even acknowledge Dru in response.

"It is good to see you, Baltus!" exclaimed Disa, breaking the silence and reaching out to collect a hug from the colonel who returned it with a smile.

"You're crying, tears of joy I hope?" asked Baltus.

"Of course!" she said wiping tears.

"These young officers are about to embark on great adventures. Stand at ease, gentlemen." The Foehammer boys stood down from being at attention.

"Bjorn tells me you assigned Dru and him to the White Eagles, where might ye be sending Leif?" asked Magnus.

"Not sure just yet, but don't worry, I am sure he will have an assignment where he will excel," responded Colonel Blackpool. "But surely, now is not the time for such things, now is the time for celebration. Let us all move to the banquet hall."

As the family departed to the hall, Baltus stopped Dru with a firm grasp. "When I signal you this evening, bring Leif to my office to discuss his future."

"Father, I beg you do not include him in your scheming."

"All I ask is you bring him, we'll let him decide. Do as I command," stated Baltus and he walked off, leaving Dru standing alone on the parade grounds.

* * * * *

Leif had not interacted with much of his own kind. Not surprisingly he marvelled at the underground elven court in ruins beneath Vorclaw's Academy of Arms. It is true, he was more robust than the elves depicted in the statues and glyphs decorating this underground chamber. These elves were slender in the shoulders and legs. Leif's body was that of a smaller version of his brother, Bjorn.

Dru brought Leif but left him in the middle of the chamber floor. Then a door to his right opened and in walked soldiers of Vorclaw, wearing Vorclaw's colours but all the soldiers wore black masks and cloaks which not only hid their identity but also their rank.

Leif took note of thirty soldiers staring back at him from the marble bleachers to his right. The door behind him locked and another door, opposite the one he came in, opened; from that door, entered the only members not wearing masks, Colonel Blackpool and Dru Blackpool.

"Leif, welcome, and well done, my son," said Colonel Blackpool smiling, his arms out praising. "Your father had prepared you well for the academy. As I expected, you graduated the top of your class. In fact, many of these soldiers are also top graduates of the academy," he said pointing to the masked soldiers.

Leif quickly tried to discern what he could from the lot. Like a detective, he did his best to profile at least one of them. He discerned one to be a female and knew a female graduated top of her class, several classes before Bjorn's and Dru's.

By now Baltus had joined Leif and put his arm around him. Leif was not offended in fact welcomed the endearment. Never had his family spoken ill of the colonel and for all Leif knew, all the family held Baltus Blackpool in high regards. "Sir, what is all this?" he asked.

"Why it is your future if you choose to accept it. We are the protectors of Vorclaw. We are the guiding body that shapes the military might of our homeland and keeps Vorclaw safe from harm and the corrupt. We are a secret society, Leif, comprised of military members of the highest calibre of warrior. Each of us also possesses special skill sets other than fighting prowess. Known only to a few of us, each person before you holds unique expertise, some are warlords with specialised fighting skills, some are practised in magic use, others are devoted to religion and still others are skilled at infiltrating while others are simple assassins," explained the colonel.

Leif stared at the Colonel now standing with the masked warriors.

"We are the Brotherhood of the Black-Masks," stated the masked female he located earlier.

"Make no mistake we are a secret society, young Foehammer," said a large soldier on the front row next to her.

"We are loyal to the protection of Vorclaw and to Colonel Blackpool," the female dragoon explained.

"Why?" asked Leif.

"Why what?" replied Colonel Blackpool.

"Why, everything? Why me, why have I never heard of you all, why a secret society?"

"Leif my son," began the colonel smiling, "Why not you? You are star among your peers; your fighting prowess proves it."

"Perhaps young Foehammer is not the soldier you said he was, colonel," announced a large man stepping forward. Other Black-Masks rumbled in discussion.

"This soldier is the son of Magnus Foehammer, one of the most talented warriors I ever served with and responsible for much of your own training," proclaimed Colonel Blackpool stepping forward from the crowd. "He has his father's metal!"

"I don't think your skills with the blades as a good as mine," stated the large man now out on the floor with Leif. "He questions our motives, colonel, and yours. Foehammer or not, he has not yet earned the right to speak to you in this manner. I invoke the right of challenge set down in the guidance of our brotherhood."

"This is inappropriate; you will stand down," stated the colonel coming before Leif and the large soldier.

Dru in the background had two knives pulled ready to throw or stab with if he felt Leif was to be attacked. The room erupted into shouting as the colonel tried to contain it all but when Leif put his hand on Colonel Blackpool's shoulder and asked for his sword, the room went silent.

"I accept your challenge," stated Leif, holding Colonel Blackpool's sword.

The large man, who stood a foot taller than Leif, pulled forth a large sword that glowed. "Let's see if your father has taught you anything new."

Leif exploded into attack. His slashing put the large man back on his heels immediately. He could only defend with his larger sword; Leif was too quick to allow the man time to generate any kind of formidable counter assault. The large soldier did only what he could and took a chance, accepted a strike by Leif but instead of reeling back the man pushed forward.

Leif's blade cut him in the left arm, but Leif took a hit from the large man's right shoulder, square to the chest. Leif, presumed by most to be a normal elf, was assumed to be unable to take a shoulder block from someone much larger than himself. Leif was no normal elf – he was a Foehammer.

Leif accepted the hit and did not rear back as much as the large soldier had hoped. Instead, Leif used the close quarters to land a left punch across the man's face. The men went spinning around and back into the corner were Dru lay in wait.

The man regained his composure. He never noticed Dru standing behind him, but he did see Leif standing there staring back at him with the colonel's sword outstretched pointing his way. The man wiped the blood from his face and regained his composure. "Magnus has taught you well, young Foehammer, seems you are ready to join us."

"You've done well, my son," said Colonel Blackpool coming up next to Leif and taking back his sword. "You will make a fine addition to us and to the salvation of Vorclaw."

The large man shouted out, "Leif, Leif, Leif!" and the room erupted the same.

Nor Leif, nor Dru knew if the fight was staged, nor did they know that Anthon Blackpool was attempting to charm Leif into their cult at the same time. With the excitement, adrenalin and the charm, Leif accepted the entry into the Brotherhood of the Black-Masks.

* * * * *

The two met alone on the academy parade grounds that evening to discuss the Black-Masks.

"Magnus doesn't even know about it I think, nor does your mother," stated Dru to Leif.

"Why not?" asked Leif.

"Think about it, Leif, your father the righteous, your mother and brother both clergy of Matronae, they would never agree to a secret society."

"So, Bjorn doesn't know?"

"Bjorn does but sees the cult more as prestige than anything else. I am not sure what Bjorn suspects about my father but I am certain he knows little of the Black-Masks," said Dru.

"And am I not righteous enough then?" demanded Leif wondering if he was just insulted.

"Of course 'you' are, Leif, you are no doubt a Foehammer, and that is what I do not understand why my father recruited you. I do know this, Leif, you cannot reveal yourself to anyone other than members of the Black-Mask cult without prior approval form my father. To do otherwise would lead to death, of this I am certain."

"Would your father have you or I killed?" asked Leif with a smile.

"Yes, because I believe he has done it before," Dru said callously. Leif's smile quickly disappeared.

After many moments under the star-filled night, Leif asked, "Why me?" not fully believing Dru's concerns.

"I don't know, but watch yourself? If there is member of the Black-Masks in your battalion, they will make themselves known if ordered. Eventually, after some time in a battalion, my father will send you for more specialised training."

"What do you mean?"

"He assigns each of us a special skill to be determined by him and his agents, developed by his agents. Hidden talents, Leif, the Black-Masks all have hidden talents."

"What agents? What hidden talents? What is our real purpose?" asked Leif.

"Leif, I cannot tell you much more as I don't know," lied Dru who already knew of his father's plan to make contact with the arch-goblin queen but not certain why.

"Wait, what is your hidden talent?" asked Leif.

"He sent me to be trained by a former thieves guild member."

"Well, you did have the talent," said Leif with a chuckle.

"No, Leif, my father sent me there to learn how to become more than just a common thief. But I will tell you more once I finish my training. Now I am certain Bjorn is missing us and we have a graduation to celebrate!"

"Wait, what's Bjorn's talent?"

"For some reason he has been training to fight the undead but I don't know why," replied Dru. "And neither does he."

Part II: Soldier to Leader

Chapter 12

A New Foehammer in the White Eagles

"My name is Master Sergeant Dunkin Saltclaw and I will not tolerate disobedience in this company," shouted the company sergeant through his long and upturned moustache.

He had six striped chevrons upon his sleeves and save for the officers, this rugged master sergeant was the ranking soldier in Gold Company, one of the four companies of soldiers in the White Eagles Battalion. For these thirty new soldiers, this was their first assignment away from the academy. It was custom to greet the new recruits fresh from the Academy of Arms in such a stern manner.

"The White Eagles have four companies, gold, silver, blue and green," he continued. "So you thirty know, you are assigned to Gold Company. In addition to all you new lads, Lieutenant Foehammer is our new company commander," he said pointing out Leif. "He is our liaison to our battalion commander Major Bartholomew Titus and therefore an extension of the battalion commander, so if I see or hear of any disrespect in his presence, you are disrespecting our battalion commander and I will have your arse for it. Is that clear?" shouted Saltclaw.

"Yes, Master Sergeant!" all the new recruits echoed in return.

"I suggest you get some rest and say your farewells tonight. We march in the morn for the White Eagles' new assignment."

"Where is our new assignment?" asked a private.

"We heard rumours we're to be going into mountains of Spine-of-Vana," said another private.

"Did I give you permission to speak, soldiers?" shouted Master Sergeant Saltclaw running up to stand nose to nose with the first soldier that spoke. All thirty soldiers snapped back to attention. "You will go where your officers tell you and when they tell you," he shouted.

Moments passed before Master Sergeant Saltclaw spoke again. Leif watched as Saltclaw eyeballed the new soldiers. He took note of Saltclaw's ability to control the formation of new soldiers by tone of voice and presence.

When Master Sergeant Saltclaw was sure he was in control and would not tolerate speaking unless given permission, he turned the formation over to Leif. "Lieutenant Foehammer, did the commander release any information regarding our assignment?"

This was the first opportunity for Leif to address a group of soldiers, soldiers not unlike himself only with more training. His father, Magnus Foehammer, warned him long ago first impressions were paramount to garnering respect.

"Thank you, Master Sergeant Saltclaw, men, the White Eagles will start manning Fort Adamant. It is our country's new fortress built to protect the growing mining town northeast of Sedgedunum," stated Leif. "That is all we need to know for now. As more information becomes available from Major Titus, I will make it available to you, if the Master Sergeant Saltclaw and I deem necessary. Is that clear?" shouted Leif.

"Yes, sir!" the soldiers shouted back.

Shortly after Saltclaw dismissed the new soldiers, veterans of the White Eagles came to pair up with a new recruit to further train and acclimate them into Gold Company. Master Sergeant Saltclaw went straight for the new Lieutenant.

"I wanted to thank you, sir, for the speech. Sharing decision making with your enlisted leadership, such as myself, honours me, sir, and will gain loyalty to the men," said Master Sergeant Saltclaw.

"I know, Master Sergeant, my father…"

"But don't give away such power too quickly, mind me saying, sir," interrupted the master sergeant, purposefully but not rudely. "I don't want them thinking you are not willing to accept command and responsibility."

"Well then, don't interrupt me, Master Sergeant, and you will not have that problem," stated Leif dryly.

About ten seconds passed between Leif Foehammer and Dunkin Saltclaw before anyone spoke. It was a battle of wills Leif knew. His father, Magnus, warned him he would be tested quickly. Leif matched gazes with the experienced enlisted man refusing to give into the mounting tension.

Eventually, Master Sergeant Saltclaw cut a small smile and said, "I have seen many fine soldiers come from Sergeant Major Foehammer's teachings. I am sure you'll do him proud, lieutenant."

Both had a small laugh at the end and a friendship was formed.

* * * * *

It was a misty morning on the march out from Sedgedunum. The sky remained overcast for the two days it took to march the White Eagles to the low mountains. It would be another overcast day into the low mountains where Fort Adamant sat. It did not take long for a sprinkle of rain to come down.

"I knew we would get some rain on this leg of the march," said Master Sergeant Saltclaw. "You ever been up these ways, sir?"

"No, master sergeant."

"Wait till we see Fort Adamant, sir. I am told it be a damnable sight. It is a loosely constructed timber and stone fort built around a tall hill, so I am told. The only proper stone standing fixture there is the Tor."

"What is the Tor?"

"An ancient tower, sir, believed to be built by elves centuries ago. And a well-built, well-thought place to have a tower too. It overlooks for miles around."

"Where does the name Tor come from?" asked Lieutenant Leif Foehammer.

Master Sergeant Saltclaw did not answer, Leif turned to regard his silence.

"Tor," said Master Sergeant Saltclaw.

"Yes, what does it mean?"

"It's elvish, sir, it means tower," said Master Sergeant Saltclaw puzzled.

"Oh," responded Leif.

"You are an elf, sir?" asked Saltclaw with a chuckle.

"Yes, but I don't speak it!" said Leif sharply.

"Sorry, sir."

An uncomfortable moment passed between the two until Leif spoke up. "I am sorry for snapping, master sergeant."

"It's all right, sir."

"No, it is not, and I owe you an explanation. I did speak elven but barely do anymore. I have lived with humans as long as I can remember and I can't remember anything before the day I met my father that day in the mountains. I know nothing before that."

"I had no idea, sir, my apologies."

"No, I am the one who apologises, you could not have known."

"Have you nothing to tell you of who you are?" asked Master Sergeant Saltclaw.

"Only this," said Leif pulling out his necklace. "It has no clasp, and it grew in length as I grew. My mother says it radiates magic, powerful magic, likely of protection. She warned against me in trying to remove it. It is what may have kept me alive before I was found?"

"Fascinating, sir, fascinating."

Leif went on to cite tales of his uncanny knowledge of weapons and how his father, Magus, cultivated that talent. He spoke of his brother, Bjorn, a priest of Matronae, like their mother, serving in the army. He thought to mention the Order of the Black-Masks but remembered what Dru told him that a member of the order would make himself or herself known to him when instructed to do so.

"Any idea why Captain Blackpool was reassigned?" asked Leif wondering why Dru and Bjorn were pulled from the White Eagles.

"No, sir, and I did not know the good captain well; I came from Blue Company after I was promoted."

"Seems we're both new to Gold Company then," stated Leif.

"Yes, sir."

"Did you know my brother, Bjorn?"

"Captain Foehammer if you please, sir. How could I miss him, sir? He stood nearly seven foot with boots and a helmet on. But I hardly spoke with the good priestly captain, I have not many battle wounds."

"So you boast, master sergeant, or have you not seen much combat," said Leif with a smile.

"Yes, sir, I do boast, I am a good fighter."

"Tell me, what skirmishes are we to encounter here in the Spine-of-Vana then?" asked Leif.

"Not sure, sir, this is the first time the White Eagles have rotated into the Spine-of-Vana. Hopefully we'll see just bandits and bar brawlers if we're lucky."

"And if we are not lucky?"

"Well, sir, my sources tell me it will be arch-goblins."

"What you know of them?" asked Leif.

"They're smarter than any orc, lizard-goblin or troll, that's for sure. Arch-goblins always move with purpose and have a plan. Good fighters too but they're no match for my old faithful," said the master sergeant referring to his glaive he secured alongside his horse. His glaive was modified a bit with a shortened stock to be better used in close combat and in conjunction with a shield.

"I can't say I have seen anyone fight with a glaive before. Most our soldiers battle with a sword and shield. How did you come to fight with that?" inquired Leif.

"It was your father actually, sir," replied Master Sergeant Saltclaw. "When I was in training, he gave some of us students the chance to fight with other weapons, and I wreak havoc with my glaive and I haven't looked back, sir. She hasn't let me down yet."

* * * * *

The two continued to get to know each other and the men of Gold Company over the next two days. When they came to their last day of travel, still some miles off on the distance, the Tor came into view. Within hours, a large weather worn hill rose before the White Eagles. Half the hill was rocky outcrops and the rest was short grassland. The semblance of a stonewall was going up around the hill. Atop stood a solid six-sided stone tower; larger at the bottom, it narrowed at the top.

"It was clear why the site was chosen by whoever made the tower and why Vorclaw wanted to build around it, the tower overlooked approach from all angles up to mountains," said Leif.

The approach to the fort was through Panther-Paw-Pass. Once the pass was merely a means for water to flow out of the pass from the hills, now it served as the main approach.

Panther-Paw-Pass itself was a frontier town. Its hills were honeycombed with minors seeking fortunes and all those looking to capitalise from mining. The entrances to these mines connected to the main road with muddy footpaths.

As the White Eagles passed, smithy's peddling equipment, farmers and bakers selling goods and pubs for all to spend their pay! Still others were minors and trade folk. To Leif and most of the White Eagles, it appeared a haven for ruffians.

Panther-Paw-Pass gave way to open space, which was now covered by makeshift huts, tents and log cabins. This makeshift town gave way to what was called Fort Adamant which surrounded the Tor. Many of the workers quarried rocks and cut timbers to build the fort.

After the White Eagles made their way into garrison at the fort, the garrison commander greeted the White Eagles battalion commander Major Titus. He was followed by a warrior not wearing a Vorclaw uniform and a distinguished looking individual with fine clothes and appeared out of place for a frontier town.

"Welcome, friends, to Fort Adamant," said the garrison commander Major Isaac Goldwater who seemed too eager to see them.

Major Goldwater had the officers of the White Eagles brought to his private quarters inside the middle level of the Tor for drinks.

"May I introduce Lord Ethan Brisbane, mighty warrior-priest of Matronae and member of The Council of Twelve." The White Eagle's commander Major Titus, Leif and the other three company commanders nodded in respect.

"No need to explore my titles, dear Isaac," stated Lord Brisbane with a disarming smile. "Gentleman, please be seated and at ease."

"His lordship is observing our progress and to report on the arch-goblin issue in the area," stated Major Goldwater.

"And speaking of arch-goblins," interrupted Lord Brisbane. "May I present Mr Night, our resident expert in these parts and on those devils."

Mr Night, who wore no uniform or rank, nodded to Major Titus and Leif but never took his eyes off Leif.

"May I present my company commanders," announced Major Titus. "I present Captains Ty, Ickingham and Norwich of Blue, Green and Silver Companies. As well as my newest commander, Lieutenant Leif Foehammer who is commanding Gold Company," said Major Titus.

"Not kin to the same Foehammer who taught at the academy?" asked Lord Brisbane.

"Yes, sir," Leif responded proudly.

"I met your father several years ago at the Academy of Arms. Magnus is a good man and a credit to our forces," stated Lord Brisbane.

"Thank you, sir," said Leif while being handed a glass of Vorclaw's finest brandy by Major Goldwater.

"And your mother and brother, they too are clergy of Matronae, are they not?"

"Yes, your lordship."

"Oh, I like your new lieutenant already," stated Lord Brisbane to Major Titus with that disarming smile.

"We're all familiar with your father's work at the academy, young Leif," stated Mr Night.

Leif nodded in return and noted the comment from Mr Night. It revealed to Leif that Mr Night at least did serve in the Vorclaw army.

"Let us get down to business, Isaac; we've had a hard march up here," stated Major Titus of Major Goldwater, calling him by his first name. Irritation was heavy on Major Titus's tone. "What brings us here this late hour after marching all day in the rain?" He even put his hand up to pass on a drink from the man.

Leif noted the annoyance on his battalion commander's words in addressing the garrison commander. Leif deuced the pair met previously since Major Titus called Major Goldwater by his first name. "Quite right, Bartholomew, let us get down to business then," responded Major Goldwater as if expecting the comment.

"The Mining Guild believes they discovered something in the mountains, about five miles northeast of here. What, they are not saying," stated Lord Brisbane grabbing everyone's attention.

"They're not saying?" asked Major Titus.

"Likely it is a vein of some material," Mr Night intervened. "We presume they don't say because they don't want rivals nor the Thieves Guild getting their hands on the territory."

"And so, they request military protection Bartholomew," said Major Goldwater. "And that is what you are going to provide them."

"Blue Company, led by you Major Titus, will set up a perimeter at the base of the entrance until Lord Brisbane have assessed the find and negotiated terms," said Major Goldwater.

"So I will be travelling with you," said Lord Brisbane smiling.

Major Titus, infuriated, wanted to interject; how dare a major of equal rank and no authority in his battalion dictate what he does with the White Eagles. Major Titus looked at all with suspicious eyes. Normally he would admonish Major Goldwater for being so bold but Lord Brisbane, a member of the Council of Twelve of Vorclaw, already stated his lordship would be joining 'him' on this journey. "Very well then, we have our orders, we shall turn in for the evening," said Major Titus ending the meeting abruptly.

* * * * *

"Clearly Major Goldwater and yourself have a history," said Leif to Major Titus walking to their tents that same evening.

"You could cut the tension in the room with a knife," said Captain Ty jokingly.

Anger in Major Titus's eyes confirmed such. He disliked Major Goldwater since the days they were at the Academy of Arms together. "I don't trust him," said Major Titus in reply to Leif and the other three company commanders. "And I don't trust his mentor either."

"Who is that, sir?" asked Captain Ty.

"Colonel Blackpool, of course," said Major Titus.

The company commanders remained silent at the notion, all knew Colonel Blackpool and received training under the man, including Major Titus but he suspected something of the Colonel Blackpool and did not trust the man and his teaching.

"Something is false about Colonel Blackpool and something was false about the meeting tonight."

"I agree, sir, on both accounts," said Captain Ty. "How dare Major Goldwater dictate which company goes out on this mission, he is the bloody garrison commander."

Captain's Ickingham and Norwich nodded in agreement.

"What have you to say about Colonel Blackpool?" asked Major Titus of Captain Ty.

"Only that the colonel pushes rhetoric of loyalty to the country but never mentions the council. I mentioned loyalty to the council once and the face of disgust was unforgettable. I too thought something was afoot in the conversation, but I don't see a connection to our orders and Colonel Blackpool," said Captain Ty.

"Agreed," said Major Titus.

"But I don't see a need for Major Goldwater to dictate how you run the White Eagles and send you out with me."

"Agreed! That is why we are going to send Gold Company," said Major Titus.

The men all stopped in their tracks.

"If he wants me out of the Tor, then I want you here in the Tor Captain Ty as my eyes," said the major. "Especially since you Captain's Ickingham and Norwich have been silent about the matter. They were about to protest but the major winked at the pair disarmed them with a quick smile. "Leif, I know this is your first command, but I will be with you and I gave you Saltclaw, the best Master Sergeant I have."

"Sir," announced Leif in feeble protest to defend Colonel Blackpool. "Surely Colonel Blackpool thinks highly of you enough, why else would you hold command his former battalion? If he disliked you, then I am certain he could have worked it out so you did not lead his former command."

"Lieutenant, don't be fooled, there is something foul about us being here I can assure you. The White Eagles have never posted in the mountains before; we have always rotated further east. And don't let your allegiance to the colonel overshadow your obligation to me. I know your background and your family's connection to Colonel Blackpool. Furthermore, I had his son, Dru, under my command if you recall, briefly, too brief for him to gain any real command experience. There is some scheming going on with the colonel, I'm sure of it," said Major Titus warning Leif.

Chapter 13

What About the Trees?

On foot it took them all morning to get to the meeting point of where the minors requested security, the steep side of a mountain with a cave at the bottom. The journey eventually snaked through a thick grove of trees to get there.

"A strange mixture of trees wouldn't you say, master sergeant?" asked Leif noting newer and slender trees spread throughout the older pines and oaks that seemed to have been growing there for centuries.

Master Sergeant Saltclaw merely shrugged not noticing the different trees, nor actually caring what his new lieutenant was talking about. "With respect, sir, we should start scouting for defensible positions, escape routes and signs of an ambush," replied the master sergeant.

"Lieutenant, master sergeant," called Major Titus riding on horseback to join them. Only Lord Brisbane and the major were on horseback that morning. "Set up the perimeter while Lord Brisbane and I meet with the minor's guild."

"Right, sir," replied Leif.

"Teach my lieutenant well, master sergeant," ordered Major Titus.

"Right, sir," replied Saltclaw as the major road off to meet the three guild members waiting up ahead.

"Take in the scene, lieutenant. We have a cliff face, a sloped hill at its base leading to our three Minors Guild party – looks like two dwarves and a scrawny man. Opposite we have a dense forest with a bunch of trees and your new trees," said Master Sergeant Saltclaw with a chuckle.

"Not the most ideal situations but we do have the high ground with the slope leading up to the cliff face," replied Leif. "It is defensible though nowhere to retreat to. Any attackers would be fighting an uphill battle against Gold Company. And no humanoid could well hide behind those new trees," replied Leif, sharing in the teasing of his own observation and drawing a smile from Master Sergeant Saltclaw.

"Right! But they can hide behind the old ones still," he responded smiling.

* * * * *

"Greetings ye lordship! Just put on a pot of water for some tea," exclaimed a red-bearded dwarf at the top of a stone and dirt worked staircase.

"Nothing wrong with making the guests feel welcome, wouldn't you say?" asked Lord Brisbane quietly to Major Titus.

Lord Brisbane waved his hand to the trio as a gesture of thanks as Major Titus and himself made their way up pre-cut steps, freshly dug out of the dirt and rock. Some fifty steps winded their way up to the waiting dwarves and an old man. The dwarf gave a wave to the approaching warriors and walked off into a cave at the top while the dwarf and the old man continued to sit by the small campfire stoking the ashes.

"Do they seem a rather odd pair to you, major?" asked Lord Brisbane near the top of the steps.

"I see a dwarf and an old man prodding the campfire, my lord. But where did that red-haired dwarf go?" asked Major Titus as they continued their climb.

"Major, I did not have a worry out here with nearly one hundred of the White Eagles, but these two seemed a bit sickly and are causing concern for me? Look at their appearance," whispered Lord Brisbane as they were within earshot of the dwarves at the campfire.

"They look dirty and likely from the cave, your lordship," said Major Titus.

"No, look closer, their skin looks grey underneath that dirt. You can see it clearly at the neck and ears," said Lord Brisbane.

"Well met you two," shouted Major Titus with his hand on his sword hilt as they continued their ascent.

The two neither turned to regard the approaching warriors nor responded to the major's call.

"They're not alive, they're not undead, they're animated," said Lord Brisbane not understanding.

A series of explosions detonated at the position of Major Titus and Lord Brisbane. Clouds of dirt rock, debris and body parts from the dwarf, old man and the two warriors went flying.

* * * * *

Chieftain Merka, the tall slender chieftain of the arch-goblin city of Blood-helm, had over two hundred warriors disguised as small trees and stumps. A *mass illusion* spell performed by their new mage ally, Anthon Blackpool. With the sound of the explosions, Merka's arch-goblins emerged from their illusions, took aim with their bows and fired into the scattering Vorclaw company.

"Fire a second volley and a third then form up as planned!" shouted the Chieftain Merka.

Chieftain Merka struggled to see through the debris cloud to ensure the warrior-priest was dead or at least maimed. Lord Brisbane, the great Warrior-Priest of Matronae was the prize on this assault as set by Anthon Blackpool.

Anthon told Merka a spy would also infiltrate and finish off the warrior-priest if need be during the fight. The spy would have red hair was all Merka knew and believed it would be a Vorclaw soldier but now wondered if it were the dwarf that ducked into the cave before the blast. Merka thought the wizard must have magically transported the dwarves and the old man into the cave; they definitely did not pass his hidden soldiers.

Merka made his way up to his formation of nearly two hundred warriors. His quick assessment of the situation was there were barely seventy healthy soldiers defending the warrior-priest. "Three to one, I like these odds!" he shouted from his toothy grin. "Warriors of Blood-helm!" he shouted as he drew his favourite weapons, his trusty axes. "Kill the humans and take their ears as trophies!"

* * * * *

"Get behind your shields, lads, and form up or we're all dead men!" shouted Saltclaw as he lifted Leif from the ground.

Leif was covered in small rocks and dirt. He spit to get the grit out of his mouth and rubbed his eyes to clear them. His ears were ringing but he could make out screams from his soldiers. And they were his soldiers as he saw Major Titus' mangled remains not far from where the man once stood. The blast sent debris fragments throughout the area and many of his men were dead or dying. As for Lord Brisbane, Leif could not see him.

"Come on, lieutenant, get your shield off your back and form the lines!" shouted and pulled Master Sergeant Saltclaw. The two quickly got behind their shields at the centre of the makeshift formation. Eventually, the remains of Gold Company crouched into two rows deep forming a small crescent. The soldiers were now neatly tucked behind their gold shields.

"You were right, lieutenant, about the high ground, they have to come up the hill at us!" shouted Saltclaw peeking out from his shield.

Strangely, Leif noted Master Sergeant Saltclaw's excitement about the pending battle.

"Who is attacking at us?" asked Leif.

"Arch-goblins, sir. Nasty buggers, looks like a three to one fight in their favour, sir," shouted a soldier in the middle.

"Where's our priest?" asked Leif trying to assess the situation. No response came even after Leif shouted for the clergyman.

"Where's our mage?"

"Dead, sir, he is lying over there!" pointed out by one of the soldiers.

"How many archers have we left? Archers, sound off!" screamed Leif. About ten archers responded. "When the arrows stop, make your way towards the rear and centre of the formation and make ready your bows, for they're going to charge us when they stop shooting!" stated Leif.

"Come and get me arch-goblin scum!" shouted Master Sergeant Saltclaw, trying to instil confidence into to the soldiers.

Three more volleys of arch-goblin arrows slammed into Gold Company before an all-out arch-goblin charge made its way up the hill.

Lieutenant Foehammer took a smile from his master sergeant's taunting of the arch-goblins as he rallied the archers in the rear of the formation. Leif directed a return fire as the arch-goblins charged up the hill. Their concentrated effort by the ten archers in Gold Company's rear ranks surprised and downed several arch-goblins. A few sporadic arrows from the arch-goblins still flew by but single shots from the distance were easy to avoid and Leif himself was deflecting incoming arrows with his shield as he directed the return volley of arrows. In all, the archers downed about twenty arch-goblins and injured at least that many as well before the arch-goblins were upon them.

"Keep them arrows a-flying, lieutenant and don't let them flank us!" shouted Master Sergeant Saltclaw as the arch-goblins engaged. Saltclaw was the first to strike a kill in mere seconds actually. No novice in battle, the master sergeant cut open the throat of an approaching arch-goblin with his mighty glaive. He then forced another on to the left so the soldier next to him could make an easy kill. Gold Company, from the battalion of the White Eagles, engaged in combat!

A trio of arch-goblins, two with shields, worked their way around to the left of the battle. Leif ordered a volley their way, dropping all three with a five-arrow volley. The attention to the left allowed another five arch-goblins to come up the slope and try to flank to the right.

The remaining five archers were ordered to move forward to take out arch-goblins in the centre at point-blank range.

Leif shouted warnings and the crescent formation of soldiers attempted to compensate by curving the crescent a bit more but were hard pressed as nearly everyone was engaged. Master Sergeant Saltclaw gave orders to the two soldiers supporting him from behind to leave the centre and assault the flanking arch-goblins.

Soon the formation began to break up as combat became one-on-one, two-on-one or three-on-two but always in favour of the arch-goblins. As the formation dissolved, so too did the volley of arrows but not before Gold Company could send a combat-burst into the sky. It was an enchanted arrow that could reach a mile in altitude with the slightest pull of the bowstring; when it reached height, it burst into a shower of red sparks. It would alert the remaining White Eagles Battalion in Fort Adamant to ride out and reinforce.

* * * * *

The sounds of the battle were music to Chieftain Merka's ears. He didn't much care for this ambush or allegiance set in motion by Queen Ooktha or Queen Ooktha for that matter, but he hated the humans for invading what he perceived as his domain and was glad to see them begin to fall.

As he slowly made his way up the hill to the battle, he was focused on the warrior-priest. Merka knew what a powerful foe one could be. Now that the debris cloud was slowly clearing, he could navigate his way through the battle. Merka kept near the sides of the battle so he could make his way up the hill quickly, while his arch-goblin hoard pushed the Vorclaw soldiers backwards.

Merka, towering over a human, easily blocked a sword attack with his enchanted axes that enhanced his speed! He slammed down his other axe upon the golden shield of his human attacker. Two more arch-goblins came to their chieftain's aid, but the crafty arch-goblin chieftain was so tall that he sent the Vorclaw soldier tumbling down the hillside after two quick chops of his axes followed by a boot to the chest. The two arch-goblin soldiers followed the soldier down the hill to finish the job.

Now at the top, Merka saw what the trap set by Anthon had done. It maimed many humans and severed limbs of their commanding officer, but the warrior-priest was alive! Merka noticed him rise from underneath a rubble pile. Anthon warned the magic properties of the warrior-priest's armour might save him. Merka waded in toward his warrior-priest target. He looked around for the red-haired spy Anthon promised but did not see anyone fit the description. Merka smacked aside another assault and then downed a Vorclaw soldier with an overhead chop by one of his enchanted hand axes – it went right through the helmet. As he pulled free, his axe from the skull of the dead human, before Merka stood a mountain of a human. This soldier with his six striped chevrons on his sleeves with a long and upturned moustache held no shield, only a large glaive. Merka knew he would have to go through this soldier to get to the warrior-priest.

* * * * *

Leif had never killed anyone or anything before. At least nothing he knew of prior to his childhood memory loss. The sound of a shattered arch-goblin nose against his own shield-edge made him nauseous. The feel of his sword sliding into an arch-goblin was a sickening sensation. Yet it all passed as the heat of battle increased. He went back to the training Magnus, his father, had taught him. He focused on the nearest threat until it was no longer a threat because he killed it. Then he widened his gaze to identify his next target. He did not enjoy killing, even if he was killing arch-goblins, but his father assured him he would be good at killing.

Leif engaged two in combat now. Both arch-goblins carried two weapons, one with a sword and mace and the other with a spiked club and an axe. Their barrage put Leif on the defensive, using his shield to absorb the blows, Leif back peddled. Then Leif began a dart to his left only to quickly jump right and do a full spin to the side of his right attacker. Spinning, Leif swung around his round shield into the neck of the right arch-goblin and a roundhouse swing of his sword for head of the other; Leif cut open the face of that arch-goblin with his sword. Both arch-goblins reeled back. The one with his face cut open stumbled into the back of another arch-goblin fighting some other Vorclaw soldier causing both arch-goblins to collapse. Leif's other opponent recovered his footing, but Leif didn't waste time and went after the creature. The hit from Leif's shield prevented the arch-goblin from raising his left arm Leif realised and finished the creature off with a thrust to the gut. It was the first time Leif made a kill and would not be the last.

* * * * *

Screams of human soldiers and painful screeches of arch-goblin warriors filled the air. The only sound to overshadow was the noise of metal swords and other weapons ringing against shields, armour and bones. Master Sergeant Saltclaw had been in situations like this before, outnumbered, fighting arch-goblins and surrounded. The arch-goblins had no effective answer for Master Sergeant Saltclaw. With his shortened glaive, he was able to use it like a bastard sword; he could use it as a one-handed weapon or two hands, but the large blade played to his great strength, making him a difficult opponent to defend.

Saltclaw worked the centre of the battle. He first repelled attackers coming up the hill. Then he started to use his strength and skills to push arch-goblins off balance and place them to the left and the right of him so his fellow soldiers could pick them off. As arch-goblins began to spill around the sides, he moved from the centre of the battle to the rear. He went to opposite side from where his lieutenant was. Once he saw Leif Foehammer's fighting prowess, he went to the other flank. With great strides, Saltclaw cleaved and hacked any approaching arch-goblin with his mighty glaive. He took the head off one arch-goblin and sliced open two more who were engaged in combat with his soldiers.

Saltclaw then saw Lord Ethan Brisbane lying on the ground. He also saw a tall but slender arch-goblin holding two axes, heading towards Lord Brisbane. Without hesitation, Master Sergeant Saltclaw made his way to intercept, smashing, belting and hacking any arch-goblin in his way.

The arch-goblin leader Chieftain Merka halted with surprise when Master Sergeant Saltclaw stood poised before him.

Merka struck first with a series of blows with his enchanted axes.

Saltclaw felt the unusual weight of those blows by Merka's axes and quickly understood they were producing a greater effect than they should. The magic imbedded in those weapons was strong but so was Saltclaw.

Saltclaw refused to give ground and brought his glaive in tighter to his body to deflect the blows. Saltclaw knew if he gave too much ground, he would put Lord Brisbane in jeopardy, but he also knew if tried to make a stalemate eventually one of the magical axes would make for the kill.

The constant deflection of his assaults began to irritate the arch-goblin. The deflections also kept Merka somewhat off balance. No novice to battle though the arch-goblin chieftain changed tactics and attacked with both axes together, surely the magic within his weapons would overwhelm this human's defence. Merka was correct in his assessment and the overhead assaults from both axes together were too much for this large human soldier and his strange weapon.

Saltclaw found himself back peddling now. However, he quickly saw a way to use this attack to his advantage! Remembering how Lieutenant Foehammer dispatched three arch-goblins moments earlier, Saltclaw decided to attempt the same. The man forcefully deflected both attacking axes to his left and spun himself around to his right. The move forced Merka forward and to the side of Saltclaw. Much like Leif's spin-attack moments before, this move provided

Saltclaw the opportunity to spin all the way around and with two hands on his glaive, Saltclaw brought a roundhouse swipe at Merka's head.

The glaive was slowed by the magical axe in Merka's left hand, but the glaive made it through the meagre defence. The arch-goblin's helmet took most of the hit, but the glaive's blade dug into the side of the arch-goblin's helmet removing flesh and the left eye of Merka. Blood sprayed forth along with that flying eyeball.

Merka let out a yell of terror and pain and landed on the ground, losing both his weapons. He began a meagre retreat on all fours, away from Lord Brisbane. The retreat was cut short by the heavy boot of Master Sergeant Saltclaw. Chieftain Merka, forced under the boot of his mighty opponent, figured this was his end and closed his remaining eye.

Master Sergeant Saltclaw surveyed the scene with his foot planted firmly atop Merka's back. The image was enough to make some of the arch-goblins weary of the man, but it also infuriated them seeing their leader under his boot. In response, several arch-goblins disengaged from their outnumbered opponent and went for Master Sergeant Saltclaw.

Chapter 14
The Red-Hair

The red-haired dwarf viewed the scene from a cave opening. Now that the dust cloud cleared from the explosion that created it, he could see the arch-goblins were slowly defeating the Vorclawean soldiers and he could see the downed warrior-priest, but alive! Lord Brisbane's armour did indeed save him and could see the man stirring. It seemed to him the arch-goblins weren't able to finish the job. He could see the warrior-priest moving and knew if the man regained his footing, this battle could take a turn for the worst.

The red-haired dwarf's body began to elongate, and the bones began to break and snap as the red-haired dwarf's body began to grow in size. His skin began to take on the colour and composition of an arch-goblin. The red beard recessed, and the skin turned pale blue. The semblance of an arch-goblin's face began to take shape. With the transformation taking mere seconds, the red-beard dwarf now stood over a foot taller and took on the guise of an arch-goblin. Down the red-haired arch-goblin crept, past the rubble remains of the pre-cut stairs.

As he crept, the red-haired arch-goblin observed the battle. He noticed how the Vorclaw soldiers kept their backs to one another to protect their rear from arch-goblin assault. He watched in awe as Leif escaped death several times and instead of falling to the sword or axe, Leif dropped several arch-goblins using his shield as a weapon and several slashes of his sword. Then the red-hair watched in horror as Merka fell in a bloody heap, yet still alive at the hands of Saltclaw and his mighty glaive.

The red-hair then took cover quickly to avoid detection from Saltclaw. It would be a disastrous, he reasoned, to come across that man unarmed with any metal weapon. All the red-hair had was his fists that he could morph into solid fist-like hammers, no match he reasoned against Saltclaw and his glaive.

Saltclaw eventually engaged with several more arch-goblins, soon the red-hair could make his way to the downed warrior-priest. In seconds, the red-hair quickly morphed his fist into a solid appendage and slammed down hard onto the face of Lord Brisbane, pushing bone fragments into the brain of the helpless man and killing him.

"It is a sad end to a mighty warrior indeed," said the red-hair.

With his fists still solid like hammers, he made a mad-dash and a leap to Master Sergeant Saltclaw who had downed several more arch-goblins in his wake. The red-hair brought those mighty fists down upon the back of the neck and head of the unsuspecting man, rendering him unconscious and near death.

The sight took some of the wind out of the soldiers and although at first stunned the arch-goblins, the fall of Saltclaw rallied the monsters onward!

The turn of events was so sudden that within minutes, only one soldier remained.

* * * * *

From the corner of his eye, Leif watched helplessly as Saltclaw dropped by the surprise attack from the odd arch-goblin. Saltclaw's fall was a blow to morale and eventually led to the demise of Gold Company.

Within minutes, Leif was the only one standing, surrounded by the remaining arch-goblins. Leif, who was extremely winded but with only minor cuts, couldn't help but laugh at the sight.

"I think it was four to one at the onset you filthy beasts and there are about twenty of you, one of me!" said Leif breathing heavy and constantly spinning around whacking at probing blades and looking for a means to escape.

Leif smacked down another blade with his shield and went for a return stab but was pushed back as the two arch-goblins next to the assailant went after Leif in retaliation. Leif knew he could not get out of this situation, not even if he ran through a pair of arch-goblins at full speed. But he had to try something and so he did just that Leif stormed forward with his shield, taking hits and assaults while trying to dash down the hill, hoping to disappear into the forest. Luck was not on his side. The brunt of the assault forced him to trip down the small slope instead. He found himself rolling down the rocky hill. Within seconds, the arch-goblins were atop him, holding him down and disarming him.

Leif struggled helplessly against the barrage. He settled down as soon as he saw that huge blade tower above him about to be thrust into his neck but then that odd arch-goblin with the larger than normal fists shouted orders in the arch-goblin tongue. The remaining hoard seemed a bit standoffish from this brut. The arch-goblin with the blade hovering over Leif moved away and the red-haired arch-goblin leaned over at Leif. One of his hands turned to normal and pulled off Leif's helmet, revealing his elven heritage.

The hoard let out some grunts and chats at the sight of his ears, his elven ears. The red-hair looked more satisfied than anything with that wicked smile. The red-hair let out some more grunts and barks then followed up with a quick punch to Leif's face. Leif quickly fell into darkness.

* * * * *

None of the arch-goblins of Blood-helm had ever seen this arch-goblin before. The red-hair could sense the uneasiness around him.

"I am not of your clan but know I am your ally in this endeavour. I have knowledge of the humans and this elf as well. He will make a great sacrifice to your Queen Ooktha."

"She is your queen too!" announced one of the remaining arch-goblins, pointing with his mighty sword.

The red-hair did not want to argue knowing he had no weapons to save himself from an argument and knew soon reinforcements from Fort Adamant will be arriving, so he nodded in agreement.

"Soon the enemy will be arriving with reinforcements. Take your captive and your wounded. Return to Blood-helm, you haven't much time."

"You will not be returning with us?" asked another arch-goblin.

"No. And you must hurry if you wish to avoid a pursuit," said the red-hair.

And the shape-changer darted down the rocky hill and into the forest.

The remaining twenty or so arch-goblins picked up their living wounded that might be salvaged, to include Chieftain Merka who was minus his left eye. They killed the rest of their kin who would not survive the journey and made off into the mountains with their prize – Leif.

* * * * *

The arriving soldiers were able to withhold two other injured arch-goblins they found in the mass of dead but they refused to talk or were too wounded to do so. There was a third who eventually died from his wounds.

The White Eagle's company commanders, Captain Ty of Blue and Captain Ickingham of Green, met at the sight of the battle where Gold Company was decimated. The two stood over the beleaguered Master Sergeant Saltclaw, apparently the only survivor.

"There was an ambush," he said in between taking in gulps of water. They appeared from nowhere after the explosion. "The commander?" he shouted referring to Major Titus. "Where is he?" But it started to come back to him that Major Titus died in the initial explosion. "Lord Brisbane?" he said looking in the direction where his lordship fell unconscious. Saltclaw tried to stand but fell over from the concussion he sustained from his earlier assault to his head. "Where is Lieutenant Foehammer?"

"They're dead," said Captain Ty. "It appears everyone is dead except for you, master sergeant. You're lucky to be alive." Master Sergeant Saltclaw covered his face in despair. "Rest easy, master sergeant."

"We have one missing," said Captain Ickingham to them both. "We cannot locate the remains of Lieutenant Foehammer. Not yet at least," he said.

"My lieutenant is missing," said Saltclaw to himself but now standing tall.

"We crossed paths with Mr Night and a few soldiers from Fort Adamant and they joined us. He identified a few tracks heading off into the mountains and led his team in that direction," stated Captain Ickingham.

"How was this an ambush, Master Sergeant, the field before us is quite bare? Surely you saw their arrival?" asked Captain Ty.

"What, sir?" queried Saltclaw. "That forest is…" started Saltclaw but he stopped mid-sentence. He paused a moment and walk towards the forested area before the battlefield confused.

"Master Sergeant, what's wrong?" asked Captain Ickingham.

"The forest, sir, it is not as I remember it. It is missing trees?" he said as much as asked himself.

Then it dawned on him suddenly, the trees, Leif, missing trees.

"The lieutenant knew! He knew it wasn't right," rambled the Master Sergeant. "Where is he, where is Lieutenant Foehammer?"

"Knew what? What are you talking about?" asked Captain Ty. "You have just been through quite an ordeal, good sergeant. You must calm yourself."

"He is talking nonsense," stated Captain Ickingham. "We'll find Leif. Let us get you back to the fort," stated Captain Ickingham.

It was then that Mr Night rode up with his soldiers permanently stationed at Fort Adamant.

"I found tracks going into the crags and higher mountains but couldn't follow on horse, nor see how far up into the mountains they've gone," he stated to Captain Ty and Captain Ickingham as he dismounted his horse.

"And what of my lieutenant?" demanded Master Sergeant Saltclaw.

"What about him?" responded Mr Night.

Saltclaw responded with fist to the face of Mr Night sending him tumbling down the hill. "He is missing, you pompous arse!" shouted Master Sergeant Saltclaw following him down the hill.

Protests went up from both Captain Ty and Captain Ickingham but the soldiers that arrived with Mr Night drew their swords and moved on the Master Sergeant.

"You're supposed to be the expert here concerning the arch-goblins and they ambushed us! They killed my entire company, you fool!" shouted Saltclaw.

Captain Ty and Captain Ickingham ran down after the master sergeant trying to restrain the angry soldier. They motioned their own soldiers from Blue and Green companies to help retrain the Gold Company Master Sergeant.

"They also killed my commander and Lord Brisbane, you fool!" he shouted kicking Mr Night further down the rocky hill.

It was then the Fort Adamant regulars travelling with Mr Night were able to intervene with swords pointing. Captain Ty of Blue and Captain Ickingham of Green drew their swords in defence of Master Sergeant Saltclaw, as did the rest of the soldiers of blue and green, though pointing at the regulars, not Saltclaw.

Several moments passed before Captain Ty broke the tension. "Let us all back off here, there's been enough bloodshed for one day," he said. "Everyone stand down. Master Sergeant Saltclaw, you're to collect your things and your self-control and return to Fort Adamant with a handful of soldiers from my company. Is that clear?" demanded Captain Ty.

"I request permission to search for Lieutenant Foehammer, sir."

"No, you're to return to the fort at once, you endured enough today."

"But, sir!"

"You're under my command now, Master Sergeant. Follow my orders and return to the Tor and report to Major Goldwater," said Captain Ty sternly.

Captain Ty then put his hand on Master Sergeant's shoulder and said, "You have endured enough for one day, leave finding your Foehammer to us. I will discuss everything with you upon my return," he said with all concern.

Mr Night stood up then and recomposed himself. He dusted himself off and looked surprisingly unharmed for having taken a punch from the largest man within miles to include a thirty-foot tumble.

* * * * *

Leif was rudely woken by an offensive smell. His left eye hurt and he knew it was swollen as was his nose. He could feel the dried blood that had dripped from his nose when he was knocked out. He could not see due to the sack over his head, but the offensive smell gave way to his other senses. He realised he was indoors based on the feel of the air around him. The air was moist and warm, he could feel and hear the fires burning around him. He was disrobed, save for a loin cloth. His wrists were bound as were his ankles but he couldn't resist the urge to try and free himself. Then he heard the grunts, barks and growls of arch-goblins and the presence of someone or something moving nearby.

The sack over his head was removed suddenly and a large overweight arch-goblin woman, an old woman, stood over him. She was holding a wet cloth and began cleaning his face. Leif pulled his face away in protest, but the old woman grabbed him by the chin, looked at him and grunted.

"Moving around will make cleaning your face painful," she stated.

"You speak common?" asked Leif.

"Of course! I speak many languages."

"Where am I? Where are my soldiers? Why am I here? Where are my clothes?"

"Too many questions, large elf, be still so I can prepare you," she responded.

"For what?" asked Leif. It was then that he realised he had been washed from chest to toe, by her presumably.

"For Queen Ooktha," she said. "You are to meet with her and be judged worthy. And we do not send gifts to the queen filthy," responded the old arch-goblin woman. "Your clothing is being washed and will be returned. I normally remove pretty gold necklaces from captives, but I cannot find a clasp to remove such a pretty necklace. If she takes off your head, I'll remove it then – ehh!" she said with a raspy giggle.

Leif was not surprised by the necklace comment. That necklace had been around his neck for as long as he could remember. It seemed to grow with him. Even he tried pulling on it to no avail. His mother, Disa, sensed it held great power but didn't know its source nor what it did.

Next in came a priestess of some description or a shaman at least to some heathen god – presumably Crom-Cruach, the crooked god of the underworld. An odd character dressed in beads and bones of various animals. It was another female and she seemed to pray over him. The energy directed from her hands alleviated the pain and swelling in his face. Next in came an assortment of young and old arch-goblin males carrying his armour and clothing. They stood Leif up and with hands bound still they dressed him in his clothing and armour. Lastly, they tied his wrists to a bar, parallel to the ground and around his lower back. Leif realised he was their trophy!

Chapter 15
Revelations

Chieftain Merka, the tall and slender leader of the eastern arch-goblin city of Blood-helm seated on his throne of bones, cushioned by animal furs, sat irritated and stared, in defiance of his pain. He sat viewing his prisoner with his remaining good eye. Most of the bleeding had subsided from stitching and salves placed of the wound. His head was wrapped in a bloody cloth and he had several shamans around him praying to Crom-Cruach. Before him stood the commander of the opposing force he just ambushed, relatively unscathed.

Merka was angry at the whole situation. He had planned his assault with the assistance of the human wizard ally and cornered the Vorclaw soldiers perfectly but still his own warriors were decimated, only twenty survived. The only reason Merka didn't kill this Vorclawean officer was because he needed to appease his queen for losing so many warriors in what should have been an easy victory; Leif was to be the offering of appeasement to Queen Ooktha.

"We should kill him and make a feast of him. I haven't had elf-flesh in so long," stated one of the soldiers in the room who battled alongside Merka.

That thought appealed to Merka. He didn't care much for Queen Ooktha, but his clan was the smallest of the three tribes, and he didn't want to be visited by the vampire in the middle of the night. So he thought best to appease her, for the sake of his clan.

"No, we should offer him as a sacrifice to Queen Ooktha as a spoil of war!" said Lorez, Merka's trusted advisor, one of his best warriors and what an arch-goblin would consider a friend if they had a word for it.

"Agreed," said Merka in a dry tone.

Merka then rose from his throne of bones and stepped down towards Leif. The two soldiers escorting Leif smacked him in the back of the knees to make Leif knee before their chieftain. Merka stepped before the elf and grabbed him by the chin so Leif would look up at Merka.

"Why does an elf fight with these humans, ehh?" asked Merka in the common tongue and slightly shoving Leif by the chin.

"Answer him, elf," stated Lorez also in common.

"I can answer that. But first tell me why you would risk open war with Vorclaw over a cave?"

Lorez let out a chuckle as did a few other arch-goblins who spoke common but Merka's glare from his one good eye quieted them.

"The cave!" stated Merka returning to his throne. "The cave matters not, elf. What matters is the Vorclaw advance on our territory and fortress around your ancestry ruins, elf," he said pointing. "For what reason, elf?"

Merka asked. Merka knew he was just a pawn in Queen Ooktha's game with some Vorclaw army commander and this battle had been staged. It served as a means to evaluate the Vorclawean troops but also to keep the Fort Adamant soldiers from venturing unabated into his domain. It also showed good faith on this human military leader and human wizard that they were willing to sacrifice their own to gain Queen Ooktha's favour. The whole idea disgusted the chieftain but had no choice in the matter. All he could do now was to try and save face. Merka also hoped this capture might also uncover some important intelligence.

"If it is a matter of territory, I am certain a treaty can be established. Conflict doesn't need to continue," replied Leif, although Leif wanted to jump up and cut down the arch-goblin chieftain.

The arch-goblins in the room laughed but not Merka. That statement gave the chieftain pause. He wondered, could he strike a bargain and have his own kingdom while keeping the humans out of his region?

Lorez did not laugh either for he knew his master wanted a sanctuary for his arch-goblins. Even though they were a warlike race, there were plenty of enemies to be had underground, above it, in the mountains or in the forests. The incursion by Vorclaw was the last thing this clan needed.

Merka dismissed that notion suddenly realising he still needed to appease his queen.

"Lorez, take him to Queen Ooktha, unspoiled," Merka stated in the arch-goblin tongue and the room quieted down once again. "Our battle with the enemy has given us much to think about, including both in allies and tactics. Our defeat will likely go over easier if we bring her an elf to feed upon."

"You want me to take him?" asked Lorez who had met Queen Ooktha once before and found her revolting. He thought she looked too much like an elf and the fact she was a vampire unnerved the arch-goblin.

"I am not well enough to go just yet and I am certain she will want a report if her wizard ally hasn't provided one already. Go immediately!" he commanded.

* * * * *

Having survived that encounter, Leif started to regain his senses and take note of what he saw. If he ever got out of his arch-goblin captures, his information may be of importance.

Once outside, it became clear to Leif that he was in some form of mountain castle or fortress. To Leif, it looked more like a less impressive fortress built upon an older one; the older ruins at the base and lower walls seemed the more solid construction. Definitely two distinct architectural forms were at work here from two different eras and races. The base construction must be elven he deduced since elven ruins were abundant throughout Vorclaw, but one this big had never been mentioned to him before and the arch-goblins clearly built upon it to their liking.

In the courtyard was a small thriving village, complete with smithy and a butcher. From his vantage point, he saw something that struck him, arch-goblin long houses and barns dotted the land outside the fort. Then he saw arch-goblins tending sheep, goats and bison. He also saw smaller creatures, lizard-goblins!

Arch-goblins, Leif knew, kept the small bipedal lizard-like creatures of various colours as servants and fodder. Their scales were often seen as either green, red or orange. They had no real relation other than arch-goblins always seemed to keep them for those purposes – so that's what the humans tend to call them. Seems they also acted as shepherds for the livestock as well. All around the castle walls were winding paths leading down into the forests or up even higher into mountains.

"No children," Leif said aloud. It was then he was shoved by the head down a flight of stairs and inside a lower part of the keep.

The castle complex inside was definitely elven in the lower levels at least. A set of stone stairs wound down, meant more to impress than for defence, gave way to lower levels and eventually a great hole into the wall. All around that cave opening in the wall laid dozens of defaced, cracked and broken elven statues.

Leif was shoved through the busted opening that led to a set of cut stairs in the rock. Those steps led into a steep cut tunnel. The underground tunnel ended at the bank of an underground river. Leif was shoved up onto the dock where some other arch-goblins were waiting.

Leif then noticed the unusual boat on the dock. It had spikes protruding down towards the water, outward on a horizontal plain and upward at an angle. The front of the boat was fashioned into an angry dragon's head. It wasn't overly large, forty feet at most. It had six oars on each side and soldiers with spears, crossbows and tridents at every corner. This was a war ship, Leif deduced, equipped with a ballista above the maw of the dragon.

As the arch-goblins chatted in their grunts and growls, Leif thought to quickly jump into the water and swim, but to where and could he swim and with his arms bound behind him? What about those spikes protruding downward to the water; are they trying to prevent something from climbing out of the water? His decision was made for him shortly though, as he was pushed up the boarding plank and onto the boat.

"I am Lorez, your master henceforth," stated the large arch-goblin chaining Leif to a seated position along the starboard side wall. "Obey me and you may get to Queen Ooktha in one piece. Defy me and you will have a slow watery and undignified death," he finished.

Leif nodded in agreement as the boat began to row from shore. All firelights were extinguished then. Everyone, including Leif, went to their *night-vision*.

"Am I permitted to speak?"

"You are but I am likely the only one to understand and you must speak in moderate tones, so not to alert any creatures looking for a meal."

"Why must I go to your queen? Is it to negotiate my suggested peace treaty?"

Lorez let out a half-hearted laugh, but it seemed to Leif, a peace accord was not the plan as Lorez walked away.

Leif closed his eyes and prayed. Leif prayed to Matronae, the great mother, the Mother-Goddess, the goddess of his adoptive mother, Disa, and brother, Bjorn, who were clergy of the deity. Leif had often attended their ceremonies, along the woods, glens and fields. They were beautiful ceremonies, breathing life into flowers, fruit and vegetables, securing harvests and nature. However, he never felt that he truly belonged to that deity, Matronae. Try as he could to pray to Matronae, he often found it difficult. Moreover, this day, he couldn't take his mind off the events that just unfolded. He wasn't sure how long ago the battle took place due to his injury, but he remembered the ambush, countering, winning and then his Vorclawean soldiers being overrun. His men it dawned on him then. He lost them all likely. So many dead. Why did it happen?

Leif was saddened then by the loss of soldiers. He wished he died with them on the battlefield. But then he changed his mind as he refused to die in vain. He would avenge his soldiers.

He tried to change his thinking and consider why he was sent to the cave in the first place. What was the significance of that cave or was it just a spot to pin the soldiers down and slaughter? Or was it more...

"Why do you mention treaty?" asked Lorez, breaking Leif's thoughts.

Leif almost didn't believe his pointed ears and almost raised an eyebrow in confusion. He didn't expect this conversation to continue but when he looked at Lorez, who stared into the water as if deep in thought, Leif sensed this arch-goblin was interested in the concept at least.

"I...mentioned it because we both have nothing to gain in warring," stated Leif, although unconvincingly.

"I do," he responded. "My people do," said the arch-goblin looking out to the water as the boat slowly oared down the dark cavern.

"What then and at what cost?" asked Leif chained to the floor looking up at the arch-goblin.

"What cost you ask? Everything!" stated the Lorez. "Enemies to fight, worthy enemies, lands of our own unchallenged and trade with other nations!"

"So you wish to be a nation or a city-state?"

"Yes! And more but your people encroach upon our lands and that challenge must be met," said Lorez looking down upon Leif with a venomous smile, fist in hand.

The arch-goblin walked away but Leif wouldn't let him go that easy, stubbornness he learned from his adoptive parents.

"Propose a treaty with Vorclaw and your queen could have all of that."

"She is not my..." Lorez turned in anger. That sudden outburst put Leif into confusion, and he wore the surprised look on his face. Lorez knew it and regretted his outburst. Lorez reverted back to his arch-goblin language and stammered off through a door into the hull below.

"You can have it all!" announced Leif at the shut door. It was then Leif received a slap from a nearby arch-goblin who then motioned for him to be silent or his neck would be cut.

Leif obliged and again closed his eyes, trying to pray again to Matronae. He thought of prayers his mother taught him, songs to the harvest and forgiveness of his sins. His mind then wandered to when his father taught him the study of arms, weaponry and chivalry. He could see Magnus on the parade grounds of the Academy of Arms. A smile grew across Leif's face remembering Magnus teaching how to parry with sword and shield to Leif, Bjorn and Dru. Magnus served as his father, mentor and instructor. Leif remembered how Magnus was adamant they learn to use several different weapons. This served not only to find their strengths, but their own weaknesses using the array of different arms. It also served as means to counter the threats of different weapons. Leif's eyes remained closed as his smile grew wider reminiscing of the first time his brother, Bjorn, sent him toppling over backwards from a crushing blow of Bjorn's mace to Leif's shield. He saw Dru looking over him with his shield laughing intently. The slenderly built Dru Blackpool fared no better against Bjorn.

His mind then drifted to his two best friends, his adoptive brother, Bjorn, who always seemed so chivalrous and his friend Dru Blackpool who always seemed to be mischievous. Polar opposites in fact but somehow the two seemed to get along like two peas in a pod. When the three were out in the city of Vorclaw, Dru seemed to always find the shadiest of characters that would end in either a fight or a deal in his favour. Leif wondered how he fit in and how the pair saw him?

Leif then delved back into his training. Magnus' teachings continued to ring true in his head. He remembered that if captured, escape by any means possible. The Academy of Arms instructors elaborated on this teaching, stating that establishing camaraderie with capturers and gaining trust was one way to achieve freedom, as long as it was not at the expense of fellow prisoners. Leif believed this doctrine would likely be his best chance at returning home.

Over an hour into the voyage, Leif's thoughts faded suddenly when a commotion on board forced his eyes open.

"Kelpiefolk!" shouted one arch-goblin. His yelling was cut short when a trident pierced his back. A tether attached to that trident pulled the arch-goblin overboard, bouncing off the spikes protruding from the hull. More tridents and spears came forth but the now alerted arch-goblins seemed well capable of defending against the assault.

"Alarm!" shouted Leif.

Lorenz and other arch-goblins burst from the door onto the deck with spears and shields. From his seated position, Leif watched as arch-goblin shields held against the barrage. Then the arch-goblins returned fire with crossbow bolts and spears of their own.

Leif peered over the side to see what was assaulting them. It was humanoid, short and aquatic but had the two arms and two legs but all webbed. Its skin was dark and smooth, like an amphibian's. These creatures had great dark orbs for eyes, small fins protruding from their frog-like head. Their attacks were scattered and unorganised, submerging quickly and resurfacing only for a moment. He surmised they were water breathers; the creatures appeared to remain submerged for long periods and no bubbles surfaced to signal they breathed air.. The melee was over as quickly as it began, and the boat rowed on.

"What were they?" Leif dared to ask Lorez.

"Stupid kelpiefolk! A water breathing nuisance. They like to attack unsuspecting ships."

"I hope you speared a few, for the sake of your comrade," said Leif. Lorez's face looked puzzled and it was then he noticed one of the crew was missing!

Lorez started speaking in the arch-goblin tongue to the others on board to confirm their loss.

"You saw what happened to Zeth, the warrior on the bow?" asked Lorez of Leif.

"It was he who alerted of the attack. But they speared him and pulled him over."

Lorez climbed up the stairs to the steering and looked back from where they came, hoping to see a glimpse of his fallen comrade. Leif, knowing full well there was no hope of that arch-goblin called Zeth surviving.

Leif made a point to address Lorez when the arch-goblin was back in his presence. "If it is any consolation, he died saving us. He shouted the warning, alerting us all."

Lorez gave a slight nod. "But it was your voice I heard," he said but did not make eye contact with Leif. However, another arch-goblin made his way to Leif with a whip for speaking to Lorez. Lorez stopped him though and turned the arch-goblin back to his post. Leif couldn't be sure if it was because of the compliment or the cause they entered a great underground cavern they now entered.

As Leif tried to stand and get a better view, Lorez actually unlocked some of the chains so Leif could rise on two feet and see the spectacular setting. Leif gazed upon an underground lake within an enormous cavern, easily two miles across at places and seemed to stretch for additional miles. Pillars of rock reaching to the ceiling and small islands dotted the lake. There were other ships on the lake too.

"Orcs!" exclaimed Lorez and spat in the direction of a ship similar in size to their own. The orc ship was heading off away from the centre of the cavern towards another tunnel.

Up ahead Leif noticed lights of green and gold. It was a large island where many boats of all sizes moored, leaving and heading to it. It was a walled island where much noise came from. In the centre was a great natural pillar that reached from the ceiling of the overhead cave to the bottom of the lake in which it sat. A waterfall ran down the centre of the pillar feeding the lake.

Lorez gave some command to the ship's pilot and they veered far out to the left of the island.

"Is that where your queen lives?" asked Leif.

"No!" announced Lorez with an arch-goblin chuckle, which was more like a bad cough. "That's Skagsnest, a market town where the races of the underground trade goods, services and meet to discuss all sorts of things, like terms during war."

"Do you not fear the kelpiefolk attacking there as well?"

"The kelpiefolk don't venture this far away from the smaller tunnels like the one we came through for fear of other creatures in the water that would feed upon them. The differences being those beasties don't come out of the water like the stupid kelpiefolk."

"So it's a neutral territory for arch-goblins and orcs?" asked Leif.

"For any race," he said. "Arch-goblins, orcs, merfolk, dwarves," stated Lorez.

"Neutrality and trade among those who would otherwise harm one another, but you still war with one another, do you not?" probed Leif.

"We do when it suits us or provoked. However, since Queen Ooktha established her reign over the three city states, war has not come to our people much, just small skirmishes underground," said Lorez. "But my tribe at least still has battles above ground to contend with."

"So a treaty is something not unheard of among the tribes of your race?"

Lorez let out another chuckle that again sounds like an old man coughing. "I know you're bargaining for your life, large elf, and I don't blame you, but it won't work with me as it is not up to me. You're just a young elf in the army you serve. You couldn't possibly produce a truce between Vorclaw and my chieftain."

"You underestimate me and the influence my family and friends have," sated Leif dryly.

Leif watched Skagsnest's lights fade in the distance of the great cavern and many moments passed between Leif and Lorez before either uttered a word.

"If you survive this, large elf, I might take you up on your offer of a treaty," said Lorez.

Leif smiled as his father was right – it is important to establish some trust and connection with your captors if one is to survive.

Chapter 16
What of Leif Foehammer?

Major Goldwater, Captain Ickingham and Mr Night all met in the evening at the top of the Tor.

"I promote you to the rank of major, assuming the role as commander of the White Eagles," stated Major Goldwater of Captain Ickingham smiling and handing him a glass of honey wine.

"Thank you, sir," stated Major Ickingham.

"Don't celebrate too soon, Colonel Blackpool will not be pleased?" stated Mr Night.

"It didn't all go to plan, but it went well enough," stated the new Major, Ickingham.

"You lost one of his favourite students, captured and likely tortured to death," stated Mr Night. "And Captain Ty still lives."

"Surely the good colonel won't mind? We delivered Brisbane and got Titus out of the way," stated Major Goldwater. "That should be enough to sate him."

"If you say so, you can ask his brother when he arrives tonight!" replied Mr Night. Concern grew on the two officers' faces. As members of the Black-Masks, Colonel Blackpool made clear to all members that his brother Anthon Blackpool held a high place within their cult. The highest-ranking mage in the Black-Masks was never a soldier and considered somewhat of a rogue amongst their order which made him unpredictable.

Mr Night now knowing he had their attention scribbled something onto a parchment, only to roll up the paper and place it into a scroll tube. Mr Night then stood up and locked the door to the room. Seconds later Anthon Blackpool appeared before the three of them, having come through a *mage's gate* into the room wearing his black mask and black robes.

"Well met mage of the Black-Masks," stated Major Goldwater.

"What news have you for me to bring to the colonel?" asked Anthon Blackpool, getting right to business.

"Great news!" exclaimed Major Goldwater pouring Anthon a glass of wine. "All went as planned, Lord Brisbane is out of the way and Major Titus is no more," stated a smiling Major Goldwater handing Anthon the beverage.

"That is great news indeed," said Anthon. "They were both getting too close to our cause."

"How faired the arch-goblins?" he asked.

Both men chuckled a bit at that. "Although the White Eagles' gold company was wiped out, save for one survivor, nearly four arch-goblins were killed for every Vorclaw soldier," replied a jovial Major Goldwater.

"You mean reen company?" asked Anthon.

"Um well, Major Titus was so furious at being instructed which company to send, that in defiance he sent the gold company."

"Without our knowledge mind you," piped up the new major, Major Ickingham.

"Was Captain Ty with him? You know he was also under suspicion?" asked Anthon.

"No," said Major Ickingham. "He still lives but I don't see him as a problem now that I am in charge of the White Eagles."

"What officer commanded gold company?"

"Leif Foehammer," replied Major Ickingham.

"What?" asked Anthon in anger. "Please tell me he was the one survivor?" demanded Anthon in the most serious tone of voice.

"Uh, no," said Major Goldwater. "It was the master sergeant, who is remanded into custody I might add, for striking Mr Night," said Major Goldwater.

All waited for a response from Anthon, but he gave none. However, the mage's breathing increased, and his face began to show signs of agitation. Finally, Anthon rubbed his hands over his face in a symbolic attempt to wipe away his frustration, knowing full well there could be a backlash to the death of Leif Foehammer by both Baltus Blackpool and Magnus Foehammer. Neither were as close as they used to be, as Magnus began to suspect Baltus was up to something sinister. However, the death of Leif could potentially complicate matters and could get Magnus to start meddling into their affairs again.

Anthon finally broke the silence. "Where is Leif's body?" he asked.

"It was taken by the arch-goblins," stated Mr Night.

"What!" responded Anthon sharply. The three shifted uncomfortably.

"Seems the reports of one survivor were premature as Leif was taken into their custody. Alive or dead, who can say but they took his body with them," said Mr Night.

"Why? To what end?"

"Perhaps they recognised him as the remaining commanding officer, for negotiations later," said Major Ickingham.

"Don't be so dim-witted," said Anthon with agitation, who was now standing and began to pace the room.

"Likely he is dead or eaten or sacrificed to their queen," said Mr Night. "But there may be time as I just met Queen Ooktha yesterday and she made no mention of an elf sacrifice to her.

That gave Anthon a pause. With working with these arch-goblin tribes on projects for both his brother's designs and The Shadow Company, he was aware that Queen Ooktha liked sacrifices to her by the three tribes.

"How do we know he is not out wandering the wilderness wounded? How do we know they took him?" asked Anthon.

"The master sergeant saw Leif still standing before he was knocked unconscious," said Major Ickingham.

"Wait! Did you say he struck you?" asked Anthon of Mr Night.

"He did," replied Mr Night.

"Why would he strike you?"

"Because I am the resident expert on arch-goblins and therefore, he blamed me for the ambush."

"I see," responded Anthon. "How did Leif get captured?" Mr Night merely shrugged as if he didn't know.

"Well, it has been more than a day since the battle, so he is likely a prisoner of the Chieftain Merka and I am certain Baltus would want Leif returned alive. He was after all supposed to come here and learn from you all. Perhaps even take over the White Eagles, in due time," he said looking at Major Ickingham with anger. "But he was not supposed to be part of this!" shouted Anthon standing over them.

The three men sat back in their seats uncomfortably at Anthon's outbreak of emotion.

"I must return to the arch-goblins and barter with the chieftain or even Queen Ooktha for his life if it's not too late," stated Anthon. "Pray he lives, otherwise there may be repercussions."

"And what of the report to the colonel? Are you not going to inform him first?" asked Mr Night.

"No, that will be your job now, Mr Night," Anthon replied.

* * * * *

The nearly all-day journey aboard the Bloodknuckle, as Leif came to know the name of the arch-goblin ship ferrying him, was coming to an end. With the great cavern far behind, the Bloodknuckle travelled down another tunnel to open into another cave. Not nearly as big as the last cavern where Skagsnest lay, but large nonetheless, and bright!

The cavern glimmered of orange and gold from magical lighting, open flames and the red granite that comprised this massive cavern. A marvellous red and black stone city dominated the cavern lake at the centre and it reached back up against the wall to the right of the caves entrance. The city stood high off the water, about fifty feet. It was further protected by a great wall that ringed the city reaching up another twenty feet at places. A great bridge reached from the city to the opposite wall. At the base of that bridge opposite the city were docks and what appeared to be a small town made of wood and stone. It was the Bloodknuckle's destination and once moored, Leif would be moved off the boat, up a great staircase to the entrance to the bridge.

"Behold the grandeur that is Skulls-thorpe, Queen Ooktha's citadel," said Lorez once up on the bridge. "For it will likely be the last splendour you will lay your eyes upon," said Lorez.

Leif barely registered the comment, for he was taking in this massive city of rock before him. Leif quickly regained his wits, looking for an escape opportunity before they started the long walk across the bridge expanse. Of course, there was not. He thought to jump off the bridge if he could get away, but on the other side of the bridge, opposite the tunnel from where they travelled from, was a large waterfall. Leif could not see the bottom. It was the end of the river so to speak.

"A splendour the city is," stated Leif. "But why do you think this will be the last splendour of my life? I thought we were still thinking of negotiating a truce?" stated Leif with as much conviction as he could. Leif began to feel the nervousness from within as he spoke about his final moments soon coming. Lorez looked doubtfully if arch-goblins had such a look. Lorez and his small arch-goblin horde prodded Leif along the bridge.

"I admire your courage, large elf, but we are a warrior race and a treaty with the humans you serve will not likely come to pass."

"So you will not assist me in my endeavour then?" Leif asked.

Lorez didn't respond. For Lorez knew Queen Ooktha conspired with the humans to start a war for many months now and confrontation was inevitable. The problem as Lorez saw it, his arch-goblins at Blood-helm were the most vulnerable. Additionally, arch-goblins admired good warriors and leaders and by all accounts, in Lorez's mind, this large elf was both. Therefore, this was not an easy task for Lorez, to deliver this elf to the jaws of Queen Ooktha. It somehow seemed inappropriate.

Intoxicating aromas hit Leif as soon as he neared the city portcullis. Stone statues that looked like apes with large maws, gargoyles he presumed, stared down at him. The air was thick and humid inside the city. The place was teeming with activity, noise and even music. Arch-goblin craftsmen of all sorts, slaves and animals chained to either their arch-goblins master's hands or to each other or even to the walls of buildings. Leif even thought he spotted a pub! He could easily slip out into the crowds given half a chance, but it was then he realised Lorez and his soldiers held tightly his chains and surrounded him. Where would Leif break away to anyway?

Then Leif noticed some young arch-goblin children being shepherded by what looked like priests. The youth threw small rocks and chanted taunts at him. Leif began to wonder if his surrounding arch-goblins were actually for his protection. Lizard-goblins were abundant too. The little creatures were all over the places. They seemed to do the cleaning of the streets, and run errands, probably for arch-goblins masters. A few other races were noticeable.

Several more neighbourhoods, a few more walled gates and the party arrived and at a large black-domed building, the walls were a mixture of black with red and two large double recessed doors of crimson red. One had an arch-goblin face on it for décor. Two arch-goblin guards armed with halberds halted the party and exchanged arch-goblin-speak before they were allowed to advance up the stairs to the large building. One of the guards spoke to a face, an angry looking arch-goblin face onto the wall of the door which came to life as he spoke to it. It seemed to repeat the comments back to the guard and they waited. Nothing happened as the remarkable face turned back to stone.

"The face on the door announced our arrival," offered Lorez who seemed to take a delight in Leif's puzzled look.

Just then the face reanimated saying something in the arch-goblin tongue and the door opened. Out came an enormous arch-goblin adorned in fine armour, apparently for arch-goblin elite. A small entourage followed.

"It is good to see you again, Blist," stated Lorez in his native tongue.

"It is Chieftain Blist to you, Blood-helm dogs," responded one of the arch-goblins surrounding Chieftain Blist, the arch-goblin chieftain of Skulls-thorpe.

"My apologies great chieftain," said Lorez with a slight bow.

"Enough!" said Blist. "Where is Merka, your fearless leader and architect of the battle with the Vorclaweans?"

"He is alive and well, oh great one. Just recovering from battle," replied Lorez.

"I think not," said Blist. "Our Queen is a mage as you know and she has informed me on the loss of Merka's eye and many of our warriors from all three of our cities. Queen Ooktha is not pleased," Blist responded looking down the stairs at Lorez then to Leif in chains. "Is this her prize then, a Vorclaw officer?" motioning for them to come up the stairs. Blist grabbed Leif by the chin as soon as he was at the top step and lifted Leif's face forcefully up to meet his gaze. "A lot of guards for this large human," said Blist aloud but more to himself.

"There is something you should know about him," said Lorez to Blist, who seemed more interested in looking at Leif's features, armour and helmet. "He is not human, but elf." That grabbed Blist's attention and motioned for everyone inside the citadel.

Inside, Blist immediately removed the helmet from Leif's head to reveal he was indeed an elf. Leif instinctively surveyed the scene for an escape plan but could not see one. It was in a large room held up with ten pillars, five on either side. He could make out a throne covered in fine furs at the far end of the dimly lit chamber. Lit by dozens of large white candles and a few braziers, Leif also saw plush rugs and hides along the side walls, lizard-goblin servants and a few female arch-goblins. Leif thought them be arch-goblin concubines as this seemed to be the throne room of this large new arch-goblin that seemed to be in charge.

Blist then grunted something else in his arch-goblin language and a black hood was placed over Leif's head. Leif was taken up some stairs left of the throne and through a door where he was forcefully made to kneel. He heard a few more arch-goblins grunting and laughing and then there was silence.

Chapter 17
Queen Ooktha

After much talk and some rant by Lorez that Leif didn't understand, Lorez lifted the black veil that covered Leif's face. He was kneeling before a small set of steps that led up to a black throne. The throne room was lit by numerous red and white candles. There, at the top of the throne sat a beautiful elven woman. She was dressed in red and black scandalous apparel that revealed the tops of her thighs. Her lips were painted black and black eye make-up that covered her eyes like a black mask. Her black lips were parted, revealing her pointed teeth. Her face was majestic, but her skin colour was a bone white, similar in colour to the arch-goblins who were pale blue, but she had no other distinctive arch-goblin features of an arch-goblin, just the skin tones.

"You are an officer among the human filth infesting my lands," stated Queen Ooktha. "You appear elven, but I never seen one as large as you. Tell me are you a half breed then?" asked Ooktha.

Leif was struggling to answer at first, he was mesmerised by her beauty. "I don't know really," replied Leif. "I was orphaned long ago, and I believe that I am elf as my parents told me so. But I have no memory of my life beyond eight years ago."

"Curious," she responded getting up from her throne and now walking down the steps to the kneeling Leif. "No memory and you don't even know if you're truly an elf. Raised in an orphanage I presume?"

"No, I was raised by two loving human parents," he responded.

"Oh, how delicious, an elf or half elf pretending to be a human," she said with a chuckle and some of the arch-goblins joined in the laugh. "A lot of good it did you, human-elf. Now let me take a closer look at you."

Her shapely legs protruded from her dress with every step down the steps. She stood over Leif, her hands touching the tops of her legs, slightly showing them off to Leif. Suddenly she kneeled down in front of him face to face. Her gaze never matched his, she seemed to look him over from his black hair down to his face, like a child scans over a new toy. Her fingertips danced over his face, feeling his strong cheekbones then, curiously, over his lips.

"And what of you?" Leif asked suddenly breaking the uncomfortable moment. "How did you end up here?" he asked as Queen Ooktha stood up suddenly but still sliding her fingertips seductively, now over the breast plate of Leif's armour.

Queen Ooktha found this elf quite intriguing, most cower or scream in fear but never had anyone asked questions before. Not to mention, this black-haired elf was handsome, and it had been so very long since she had conversed with anyone elven, aside from the despicable dark-elf whose blood she happily drained. She now moved behind Leif, placing her hands upon his shoulders, her great vampiric strength holding him firmly in place.

"My arch-goblin brethren took me in when I was seeking refuge from the daylight after my elven clansmen abandoned me. It was my other blood ties, my cousin, in fact, that took me in," stated Ooktha as she leaned in closer behind Leif.

That didn't sound plausible to Leif. Arch-goblins did not have monogamous relationships that would produce cousins as one would know it—so Leif had been taught. Their young were raised in communal orphanages, reared by the elderly or the infirmed who are too battle damaged to be of use. At least that's what he was taught at the Academy of Arms. Another piece that did not make sense to Leif was he was not frightened. He felt warm in fact as if some great energy protected him. Not even when Queen Ooktha firmly planted her hands them upon his shoulders. She leaned closer so her face touched his right cheek.

"Do you not fear me, warrior from Vorclaw?" she asked with her lips whispering into his ear. She even dared let the tip of her tongue touch his earlobe. She was attracted to the elf she realised and contemplated how she might make him her concubine. "How will you pay for your crimes against my kingdom?" she asked seductively.

Leif slowly turned his face to meet hers. Again, he was surprised that he was not frightened. "You make me sad, my lady," he said to her after matching her gaze. "Being a vampire matters not to me. I too am different from those I call my people. However, what saddens me is that I see such beauty hidden behind your teasing play and pointed teeth. I would have loved to have met you before you became so scorned by those of our kind." Leif then turned his head the left exposing his neck, upper shoulder and necklace. He began to pray to Matronae.

A puzzled look came over Queen Ooktha. Her teasing and vampire powers of persuasion seemed wasted on this handsome elf. Several moments passed as she digested his message. Was he being sincere about her beauty or merely trying to weasel his way out of this? Was he really an outcast like her? Furthermore, she was taken aback by this elven soldier even mentioning her beauty. It had been so long since she had seen or felt the tenderness of one of her own. But she was queen here in this domain and with nearly a dozen arch-goblins staring at the two of them, she could not afford to lose face. At last, she decided Leif's words were nothing more than pity, and that irritated her. She was a survivor and didn't need anyone's pity.

"Do not pity me," she said in an angered voice grabbing him by the neck. Her strength squeezing hard, making Leif very uncomfortable. "I have turned from our kind long ago and found a new and more powerful home," she said.

And to think she thought to take this elf to her bed. Then she dug down deep onto the skin and necklace of Leif.

To Leif, the next event happened in slow motion. First the warm sensation upon his neck, followed by the powerful force of her grip securing him as she struck. Next, her bottom lip touched his neck and then felt two pin pricks of teeth push onto his skin. What should have been a sensation of warm blood spurting from his neck and searing pain of fangs ripping into his flesh, another sensation was present instead. It was a warm sensation but more like love, like a mother's love he reasoned.

A brilliant rainbow of colour burst forth from his thin necklace. It was followed by a blinding white-light that radiated from that necklace of his. It repelled that vampire's mouth and sent Queen Ooktha rearing back in horror and in pain. She stumbled back into Chieftain Blist screaming, sending him reeling back as well. Her face was burned badly; her lips were burnt off! She quickly covered her face as she felt the brilliance that came from Leif's necklace; it was divine light for sure as her undead skin began to turn to ash!

The blinding light had the arch-goblins on their heels too. Some had arms raised up to shield their eyes, others ducked down into a ball and turned away.

Fearing for her undead life, Queen Ooktha quickly transformed into a great bat and flew away behind her throne and into her private chambers. Smoke trailed behind her as she was still smouldering, even in bat form. Once there, she changed back into her humanoid form and grabbed a crystal decanter filled with blood from a previous victim. She poured it into what remained of her mouth and swallowed, rejuvenating her strength and life force, healing her wounds.

* * * * *

The event was over as soon as Queen Ooktha fled the throne room. The brilliance was gone, and the throne room returned to the candlelight.

"What just happened?" Leif dared to turn and ask Lorez. Leif was now eye level with Lorez. The arch-goblin was seated in rearing position on his behind, not far from he once stood, his mouth agape.

"Kill him!" shouted Blist in the arch-goblin tongue.

None of the arch-goblins actually moved, either fear or shock held them in check. Not Chieftain Blist though, he pulled forth his mighty katana and moved in quickly on Leif. So too did Lorez who got up, pulled forth his scimitar and moved in. Leif, sensed the danger coming, quickly jumped to his feet and backed up, retreating up the throne room steps. His arms were still chained to the bar behind his waist but with the vampire gone, maybe he could take down some of the arch-goblins surrounding him.

"Hold all of you!" shouted Lorez. "Do not touch him, he is my prisoner!"

"Kill that filth, he may have killed your queen!" screamed Blist back at Lorez and all others present.

"No, he is my prisoner and I'm taking this elf to be interrogated!" he announced.

"No, he is to die here and now! And your queen will drink his blood!" argued Blist in a roar.

"We can't kill him, not, not here, we don't know what else could happen," said Lorez. "Let me take him back to Blood-helm and I will bring Queen Ooktha another gift. And I will kill him a safe distance from Skulls-thorpe. You need to worry about the Queen and make sure she survives. I will kill him on the surface," explained Lorez.

Leif stood there, realising Lorez was defending him although he had no clue what they were saying to each other. Chieftain Blist gritted his yellow teeth and his face began to contort. Leif could see Blist was torn between about what just happened and what Lorez was saying.

Blist finally made a decision about the fate of Leif. "No!" he said calmly, pointing with his large katana. "To the coliseum with this one."

* * * * *

Located behind her throne room, Queen Ooktha was safe and secure. There were her private chambers. She lay in large red-velvet bed, recovering for hours now. She kept the door locked and would not come out until her face fully recovered. She was healing, the blood of her previous kill that she had bottled, was doing its work.

She lay there troubled, confused, excited! She wasn't sure if it was her near-death experience or just having conversed with another elf. But why would the encounter excite her?

It had been so long since she had a conversation with another elf, she wondered if it just stirred long lost feelings of a time before she was a vampire. Or was it more of a homesickness that would pass? But she felt, attracted to the one who nearly killed her. "Did he really try to kill me?" she asked aloud to herself sitting up suddenly. "Or was that a defence of that powerful magic necklace? It didn't activate when our faces touched. Only when I tried to bite," she reasoned aloud.

Perhaps she might keep Leif alive as her concubine. "Was it because he did not judge me being a vampire? Maybe I'm fascinated because he said he saw beauty in me? Did he really see me as beautiful?"

"No, it was pity I saw pity in his eyes!" she said aloud, remembering the moment before her bite. She grew upset with herself for being captivated by this black-haired elf called Leif. She stood up angry, feeling her face and confirming it has nearly healed.

"I will watch his blood spill in the coliseum."

* * * * *

"I wish I could help Lord Anthon," said Chieftain Merka seated from his bone thrown. A female arch-goblin priestess was tending to his bandaged eye. "The one you seek is likely dead at the fangs of our queen. Every victory must have a sacrifice to my queen. You know this."

Anthon did not respond immediately. He was trying to surmise the repercussions of it all. Anthon knew how fondly his brother cared for the Foehammers and to lose Leif in a battle they all helped stage perpetrate might jeopardise his work in the eastern arch-goblin city of Ironhold. While his elder brother Baltus wanted revenge, Anthon wanted respect and power and to lose Leif may drive his brother mad with anger and endanger his own Shadow Company plans and schemes.

"What value of this elf is to the great Anthon?" inquired Merka.

Anthon responded with a spell which put the room on alert drawing weapons by the arch-goblins present. A quick chant, release of some components and a twist of his fingers and he was gone in a flash.

"Scribe!" shouted Merka. "Take down a message and have it sent to Lorez immediately. I want that elf back!"

* * * * *

Anthon teleported to his prearranged spot, outside Queen Ooktha's black-domed citadel. He quickly made his way to the large double recessed doors of crimson red, on one door hung the arch-goblin face. Two arch-goblin guards armed with halberds shouted but quickly backed off once the recognised Anthon. The wizard touched his pinky ring on his left hand. The magical properties allowed the wizard to converse in arch-goblin.

"I must see Queen Ooktha or Chieftain Blist at once," announced the wizard.

Cheers erupted off in the distance.

"Human wizard, her majesty and Chieftain are at the games," responded one of the guards.

"Take me to them at once!"

Chapter 18

The Coliseum

"Name is Ko-ko, Ko-ko the troll. Pleased to meet you," said the old smelly troll who outstretched a pointy green and brown hand through the iron bars of a cell. Ko-ko smiled a yellow sharp-toothed grin.

"Don't you be trying to eat my elf, Ko-ko!" shouted the arch-goblin jailer, aptly named Grim. Grim brought a lit torch to the troll's outstretched claws. Ko-ko the troll repelled instantly. " Me hates the fire," he remarked to Leif.

"Grim not nice today," shouted the troll who picked up some straw bedding and threw it at Grim to no real avail.

"I will feed ya soon enough just wait until I'm done with this one!"

It amazed Leif how so many creatures spoke the human language.

"What am I doing here? Where am I?" asked Leif to Grimm.

The noise from above the prison which is where Leif presumed to be was odd. It sounded like cheering.

"You're in the coliseum, Leif," came a voice from behind. In the door way made of iron bars stood Lorenz.

"You are to fight for your life, my friend," said Lorez.

Grim paid them no mind as Leif was secured in chains to the floor. Instead, Grim fed Ko-ko the forearm of some creature.

"We're friends now, are we?" asked Leif.

Lorez did not know how to answer but after his discussions with Leif aboard the Bloodknuckle, he did feel this soldier was genuine and willing to try for a truce. Additionally, Lorez also saw potential in Leif, or at least his necklace, if his power could damage his Queen, what other devices or means might the elf have to counter Queen Ooktha's hold on the arch-goblins of Blood-helm.

"Am I to fight you then, Lorez?" asked Leif.

"Hardly," responded Grim. "You have to fight the pussy-cat first!" he said with a chuckle and motioned for Leif to stand to unbind him.

Lorez heard that statement and now the notions of peace and separation from Queen Ooktha seemed moot.

"I come to wish to say I believe you," said Lorez as Grim brought Leif thru another set of prison bars in the form of a door. In this area was a weapons rack of swords and bucklers. "I believe you would try to champion a treaty for my kind."

"Put your hands back through the bars and I will remove your locks. Then pick a weapon and a buckler off the rack and wait by the door," said Grim.

"And if I refuse?" Leif asked.

"Then the pussy cat will come in here for you."

"Don't refuse old Grim, pick your weapons and fight like you did against my kin," said Lorez.

Leif selected a buckler and sword, followed by a leather helmet.

"It is a shame you send me to my death if you believe me," stated Leif in a serious tone eyeing Lorez.

"Farewell, elf, and thank you for alerting my soldiers to the kelpiefolk assault," was all Lorez could muster. He turned and walked off upset for missing an opportunity for his clan.

Leif now stood before a wooden door with cheers and screams of the dying on the other side.

* * * * *

"What do you mean Leif Foehammer is dead?" shouted Colonel Blackpool.

Mimdrid, using the guise of Captain Nigel Newman, stood calmly enough but was hiding his true nervousness. Mimdrid and the Blackpool brothers all put a lot of work into their plans over the last few years and didn't want it all to come crashing down. Their simple plan to give the arch-goblins an easy victory, show how genuine Colonel Blackpool was in this war and to provide a taste of Vorclaw tactics, did not go according to his designs.

"Seems he was captured and killed, we cannot be sure, but your brother is trying to uncover his whereabouts," stated Mimdrid dryly. "The plan was not executed properly because Major Titus switched companies. The entire Gold Company was slaughtered. He at least is dead as is Lord Brisbane. However, your soldier's tactics are far superior than you may realise. The cost of arch-goblin victory decimated their ranks." That did not brighten his expression as the loss of Leif was extremely unexpected and unfortunate.

In the wake of his wife's untimely death, Colonel Blackpool's need for revenge increasingly caused him to value soldiers by what they could do for him both personally and professionally. However, Leif was a Foehammer and beloved by the colonel. He was not sure how to inform Magnus let alone Disa.

"All is not lost for your beloved Foehammer-elf. Anthon might yet retrieve him before arch-goblins foul him," stated Mimdrid. Secretly Mimdrid hoped just the opposite. He hated Magnus Foehammer from when he first met him, which in Mimdrid's mind, Magnus' kin were to be equally hated. Mimdrid even wondered if the elf might return as an undead creature to haunt his family. It was sheer luck that Leif Foehammer was the last remaining soldier standing when Mimdrid arrived on the scene an arch-goblin during the battle. "I will have you know there is no way I could have prevented the loss of Magnus' son. I didn't even know he was there," explained Mimdrid.

"Well, I will have to put my faith in my brother that he lives but if not, then this justifies the training I sent Dru and Bjorn on."

111

"I am not following?"

"Leif's death will motivate them in their training."

"How so?" asked Mimdrid not catching on.

"They will want to avenge the loss of Leif."

* * * * *

Leif came through the doors and into the coliseum. The air was thick and warm due to it being surrounded by the thousands of arch-goblins jeering at him from the stands! It was an open ceiling and the pace was lit by torch light and by orange and yellow magical lights. Leif saw Queen Ooktha seated high above in a special boxed balcony draped with sheer black curtains and pillars to match, clearly seating for the elite. Her face healed and black eye makeup smeared across her face like a mask from ear to ear. Leif rationalised it was to make her more menacing. Next to her was that large arch-goblin who tried to kill him earlier.

Leif turned his attention to arena area itself. Stone floor lightly covered in sand to draw up the blood on the floor. And there was evidence of fresh kills marked by blood in the sand. The top of the red walls was ringed with metal fence barbed with spikes pointing downward towards the coliseum floor, to prevent climbing out and into the crowd.

Leif dressed in small shorts, a buckler, and leather helmet closed his eyes and began to pray as his mother taught him. To Matronae, for strength, to take care of his family, who took him in as an orphan and for the soldiers he had lost in ambush. Leif did not ask for revenge; it was not yet in his nature.

Then the door opposite opened and his training from the Academy of Arms took over. The tutelage of his father, Magnus Foehammer, surfaced in his consciousness.

A large feline roar came forth from that dark opening and the crowd of arch-goblins, lizard-goblins and a few other races privy to be in attendance had gone wild with anticipation. It was a bizarre creature to Leif but deadly looking nonetheless. It had the body of an orange tiger without stripes but a long whip-like tail that was constantly twirling in the air; the tail had spikes at the end. The tail was not the oddest thing about the creature. It had the oversized head of a man whose face was covered in orange fur and whose maw was filled with sharp teeth.

The strange feline did not attack Leif but instead used its great claws to try and scamper up the walls to look for a way out but several arch-goblins with pikes forced the creature back to the coliseum floor.

Leif took notice that this strange beast seemed to change positions along the wall once an arch-goblin tried to prod it off the wall. One arch-goblin unknowingly poked the illusion of the tiger-like beast but once the trick was sprung, another arch-goblin was better able to locate the true location of the beast, a few feet away. Leif now had a sense of what he was up against, it must be a mantikhoras.

It was just a few moments before the beast started to fixate on Leif. Leif waved his sword at the beast to keep it at bay and shouted at the thing. The mantikhoras circled around Leif, judging how best to make the kill. The spiked tail went out and nipped Leif in the buckler.

The arch-goblins cheered the beast on.

Leif backed up to the wall but kept moving to his right. The mantikhoras followed suit but kept probing Leif for weaknesses with its wicked tail but Leif's buckler was up to take the hit. Suddenly the mantikhoras appeared in a spot a few feet away but launched assaults with its tail from its actual position. The crowd again cheered as Leif was hit in the ribs. Leif instinctively shifted back to his left when he felt the spikes hit his torso. He pushed his sword and buckler in downward sweeps to break the connection.

The connection was broken and not a moment too soon as the mantikhoras lunged with four clawed paws open for the kill. The orange beast plunged into the wall but was unharmed from the impact, more surprised. Leif was lucky he realised.

The mantikhoras quickly pursued along the edge of the wall now. Arch-goblin's in the stands leaned over the wall in effort to see the battle. Leif shouted and waved his sword to keep it at bay, but the beast seemed unafraid and Leif knew it.

Leif tried not to panic and remember his training. He remembered teachings from Magnus, in the wilderness, when he explained the importance to keep wild beasts in front of you, don't run away and if escape is impossible, try and intimidate such a foe any way you can.

Leif kicked some of the sand in the air to try and blind the creature which had no effect because the mantikhoras was not where Leif thought it was, again! He instinctively side stepped to his left quickly as a large spiked tail went for his face. Leif's quick sidestep and sword thwarted the attempt as a whipping spiked tail met Leif's blade.

The noise grew louder in the coliseum at the near miss.

Leif kept his back to the wall so the beast might not appear from behind and surprise him. The attacks from a spiked tail continued. The strange feline seemed to be displaced at times but did not attack with its paws again; Leif began to suspect that it would not, unless it landed another spiked hit.

Leif continued to kick up sand at the creature hoping to get on the offensive, but the beast was never where he really appeared. However, Leif noticed a pattern, the strange cat was always to his left after each kick of the sand. Might it always be to the left and the cat before him always the illusion? Leif had to hold onto that thought for a later moment as another spiked tail bludgeoned his right torso. The crack of the tentacle like tail definitely caused serious pain to his ribs, perhaps even cracked them. Leif continued his sidestep but sliced at spiked tail. Then Leif spun around and back to the right going the opposite way he was a second ago. Leif waved his buckler arm in the air during the spin as four claws again pounced for him. The beast raked at Leif's arm, tearing into the elf's flesh but let go when Leif's sword jabbed at its face.

Queen Ooktha shifted uncomfortably in her throne watching the display. She hoped her prisoner would survive the assault but now feared he might not. She did her best to hide her emotions from her face as several thousand spectators were in attendance, but she doubted anyone would notice. Even Chieftain Blist, who was seated nearest to her, was intently engaged in the battle between Leif and the mantikhoras. That odd feeling concerning this elf was back again. When she sat down for *The Games* as it was known in Skulls-thorpe, she was angry with Leif, not only for nearly killing her, but for looking at her with pity as she prepared to drink him. However, after seeing him nearly naked and in fighting prowess, her desire for this elf returned. No longer did she care that she almost died, nor cared that she interpreted his look as pity, all of which could be construed as self-defence. Now she just wanted him to survive – so she might get to know him better.

Lorez too, who looked on with eagerness from the bleachers, wanted Leif to survive. He was impressed by this elf who helped save his clansmen aboard Bloodknuckle. And although Lorez's kin were a warrior race, he believed a truce between his clan and that of Vorclaw, which Leif promised to broker, could aid Blood-helm in breaking away from Queen Ooktha and the Chieftain Blist's Skulls-thorpe clan. Lorez also hoped to understand the power behind Leif's necklace and perhaps it could help vanquish Queen Ooktha.

Anthon, covered in black robes and a hood, just arrived at *The Games* but was unsure if the gladiator was indeed Leif. He made his way through the crowds with escorts but not sure he could stop what was already in motion. By Anthon's guess, that warrior would not survive for long. Anthon never actually met Leif Foehammer and that poor person fighting the mantikhoras did not look the build of an elf, more of a well-fit human, but he really couldn't discern due to the leather helmet over the fighter's head. Over the last decade, Anthon learned that his brother Baltus is very sentimental regarding the Foehammers and Leif's death could prove an end to this alliance; never seeing his work come to fruition could also have dire consequences for him in the Shadow Company.

* * * * *

Leif was not certain how much longer he could last against this beast. Leif's left arm was badly bleeding from the clawed assault. He also realised one of the spikes from the tail was embedded in his torso. A small chuck of flesh or muscle protruded from the bloody wound. The elf now backpedalled pressing his arm left against his torso to stop the bleeding. Leif took heart as the evil cat pursued cautiously as its own spiked tail was visible cut from the encounter with Leif's sword.

Remembering the mantikhoras' nasty trick of seemingly to be to the side of where it actually was, Leif kicked out some sand to the side and struck home, seeing the cat reappear to exactly where he sent the sand flying. The beast wiped its eyes with its paws to clear the sand and shook its head. Leif seized his chance to do a running pass and take a swipe with the blade.

The stunned crowd *ow-ed* and *aw-ed* as Leif's running swipe to the cats left side sliced an opening in the beast's orange hide. The beast stunned, hissed at the retreating Leif and then roared a spike-toothed grin.

The great cat pursued angrily now. The elf ended up backed against the door he entered from and then the crowd's excitement increased sensing a kill to come. The great cat pounced like before, all four clawed paws outstretched to encompass the seemingly helpless warrior. Leif did what he thought best; he quickly ducked down into a ball pinned against the door and braced his sword against his body pointing up towards the lunging cat.

The great cat came down in a heap upon poor Leif. All four claws made contact with Leif, all doing serious damage to his legs, arms and torso. Luckily, the cat's spiked teeth could not get to Leif's neck as its head banged against the wooden door. The crowd, overjoyed with the fray, shouted and cheered.

Normally, the cheers lasted longer as the mantikhoras usually rakes and tears its opponents to pieces but instead remained motionless. The cheers went quieted to mumbling and discussions. Eventually several arch-goblins and lizard-goblins exited from the door opposite where the two combatants lay in a ball. After much prodding from the spears of the lizard-goblins, the arch-goblins moved in to reveal a dead mantikhoras. Leif's sword submerged in its stomach to the hilt!

Leif lay beneath the beast seemingly dead too, covered in blood of both beast and elf.

The crowd went wild with excitement at the kills!

* * * * *

"What news have you of Leif then?" asked Colonel Blackpool of his brother upon his return.

Anthon simply shook his head from side to side signally Leif's death.

"We will go through with the war but add a new target to the fold, Queen Ooktha herself."

"How so?"

"Read this letter I have prepared to send to our training facility in the Pirate Isles," stated Baltus, handing his brother some parchment. "When our pirate captain returns to our port, I want this brought to your Shadow Company agents and delivered to the Island."

It is with my deepest sympathies that I must inform you of the untimely death of their brother and dear friend, Leif Foehammer. He was killed during a surprise attack by arch-goblin forces. His entire company was slaughtered by these wretches. I hope I do not sound insensitive when I ask you to please continue your training in earnest! As I will have need of your new talents in order to avenge our dearly departed brother in arms as I recently became aware of the source of this assault. I will need your trained talents to exact revenge upon the one who took dear Leif from us.

Chapter 19

The Island

Bjorn ran his large hands through his thick red mane. His eyes closed and he dreamt back to the day he last saw Leif. Just after Bjorn's return from his first posting with the White Eagles, just after Leif's graduation from the Academy of Arms. Magnus and Disa were unusually giddy. And for good reason, their father Magnus, had been crafting the wonderful item under the prayers and guidance of their mother, Disa.

It was Leif who met Bjorn at the gate of their house at Sedge Fen, smiling at Bjorn. Leif guided the large red-headed man around the back of the house.

"Mother and Father had been working on this over the last year. So you better like it," said Leif with a wink and smacked Bjorn on the back of the shoulder.

Bjorn hardly registered the hit as he was mesmerised by the large flower garden that had never been in the backyard earlier that day. Disa was kneeling and hands raised praying to Matronae, the Mother-Goddess, he presumed, being a priest himself of Matronae. Magnus, his father, dressed in brilliant silver chain armour stood opposite her, mouthing a quiet prayer. Between the parents was a finely tilled small patch of dirt. A pink haze radiated just above the patch. Bjorn remembered feeling frozen in place watching the spectacle, until recalling Leif prodding him forward with another shove from behind. A playful brotherly shove.

"The Mother-Goddess Matronae has blessed you, my son, has blessed this family. Your father and I have worked together on this for you," stated Disa getting up from her kneeling prayers.

"On what, Mother? What is all this?"

"Reach down into the Cradle of Matronae and receive her blessing, my son," she replied.

Magnus motioned him forward, but Leif of course did another brotherly push.

"Reach down, my son, into the soil," said Magnus.

Bjorn did as instructed. His hand breached the pink glow and drove into the dirt. The soil was soft and warm, but not wet. Buried within, Bjorn gripped something metal. He pulled forth from the soil and haze, a wondrous mace. Its stem was long but not unusual for someone of his stature. Atop was a sliver round ball adorned with four rose-coloured crystals. The crystals themselves were fashioned in the shapes of roses, four evenly spaced around the equator of the ball. The stem was patterned in faint golden noughts and crosses its whole length. There was a handguard, not unlike those found on sabres. Etched into that handguard was the holy symbol of Matronae: an X that displayed the sun within the top of the X; a circle represented the planet Vana in the bottom of the X; to the left within the X was a wavy line that represented water; finally to the right in the X was a cloud formation that represented the wind. As Bjorn breached the pink haze, the light infused with the mace.

"A blessing from Matronae," stated Leif from behind.

"Your brother is correct," stated Disa. "The loving energy the Mother-Goddess gave to this weapon will radiate and protect you from the undead. It will help heal your wounds should you encounter any from such creatures. Your holy symbol of power is etched and infused upon the handguard."

"It was your father's idea, to be sure, to make the whole mace your holy symbol to guard against the undead, heal the sick and provide benedictions to the people."

"This...this is a blessing indeed, thank you!" exclaimed Bjorn. "But this is an expensive item. How could you afford such a wondrous gift for me to wield?" responded Bjorn in disbelief.

"It was commissioned by Baltus," responded Disa referring to Colonel Blackpool.

"He paid for the materials, your mother blessed it and I well, I constructed it," said Magnus proudly.

"I helped as well, before I went to the academy of course," piped in Leif.

Bjorn's eyes swelled with tears at the memory of Leif proud that he smithed with Father. The large man wiped his wet eyes and let the memory fade there. Back to his present reality, Bjorn lifted what he called the Rose-Mace.

* * * * *

"I swear vengeance," stated Bjorn aloud suddenly.

The sounds of the undead nearby amplified Bjorn's anger.

"Open the door!" Bjorn shouted. With the Rose-Mace and shield in hand, mighty Bjorn, full of anger and the power of a cleric of Matronae, the man charged through the portal.

It was a maze; it was always a maze and always different. He darted left, straight and then right. Stumbling upon a pair of armed skeletons, Bjorn went to work immediately with his mace, obliterating one with his spiritually amplified weapon – the Rose-Mace.

Bjorn then sent the other crashing against the wall with his shield. Bjorn could have used his clerical powers to vanquish these two undead into dust, as was the power of a warrior priest, but Bjorn was angry and wanted to satisfy his rage. The man again smacked his shield into the skeleton and crushed bones and skull between his shield and the wall. The bones fell away in a heap against the wall.

Around another corner, another turn and another, Bjorn went until he reached a rectangular chamber. Stooped in the corner gnawing on bones of some recently killed animal were two ghouls, horrible undead humanoids who were equally evil in real life unlike skeletons who were either animated to follow orders, ghouls hungered for flesh and bone of the living. They could even sense Bjorn's as he entered the chamber.

Bjorn's cleric didn't wait and went after them without fear. The two growled loudly at the approach and they charged one after the other. Bjorn swung the mace fully at the one on his left, who was nearest. Using the momentum from the swing, Bjorn spun his whole body around, shield leading the way, to crash into the face of the next assailant. It was a technique he learned from his father.

The creature was upended by the powerful blow. Bjorn finished the ghoul with a crushing attack with his mace. Certain both creatures posed no threat, he called upon his divine powers to smite the two creatures. With his mace outstretched, the Rose-Mace which dubbed as a holy symbol beamed a rose-coloured hue, a divine hue and ended the undead lives of these two creatures completely. Satisfied the ghouls were now dead husks and sapped of all undead life, Bjorn moved onward through the maze.

A rush of armed skeletons awaited Bjorn a corridor away. His senses tuning with the divinity of Matronae, he could sense the undead lurking in the dark. He called forth the power of his mace to enhance the light in the passage and now could see the twelve skeletons waiting. They charged him as soon as he saw his pinkish light. On instinct, Bjorn again called forth the divine powers to counter the undead and with a silent prayer, the divine radiance beamed from the Rose-Mace. The skeletons burned away to ashes as they approached. All twelve were quickly dissolved to dust before they could even reach the priest.

* * * * *

The warrior, the priestess and the mage watched Bjorn's challenges unfold.

"He was supposed to merely subdue and make the ghouls cower away with his divine magic. Damage them yes so they can no longer harm him but not destroy them," stated a priestess only known as Shanna. She was a priestess of Lir, the water god, hired to manage undead shipments to the island – to train Bjorn.

Erik the mage, hired to oversee the creation of the mazes, merely shrugged at her and continued to watch Bjorn through the scrying globe before them.

The black-haired warrior and Pirate Captain who laid claim to the island where this training was being held merely smiled. He was the estranged brother of Erik. The two had very different career paths.

While Shanna and Erik were Shadow Company agents, Captain Ruko Kahee saw himself more a privateer than a Shadow Company pirate. Yet, even he knew those lines were easily skewed. He garrisoned over a hundred pirates and controlled three vessels. A lot of it had to do with his brother Erik the mage controlling the scrying.

Aligning with The Shadow Company and Colonel Blackpool over the years had been pure profit. Captain Kahee did legitimate trading of goods but also transported people, stolen items and undead for darker purposes. He asked no questions other than what's the risk.

Ruko Kahee practically owned this island, for now. As long as he was in good favour with The Shadow Company, thanks to his brother Erik, Colonel Blackpool allowed the transport of goods through the country and lastly the one who safeguarded the island through ties to the Vorclawean Navy, his father, Admiral Drake Kahee.

As for the other pirates in the Pirate Isles, he had ties with them as well. But certainly, his alliances allowed him to reign supreme on the sea and in the Pirate Isles.

"It seems the message I delivered, had the effect his master wished," stated the Captain Kahee.

"It is amazing how loss can drive a person's abilities," replied Erik.

"Too much a matter of fact!" announced the irritated Shanna throwing open her black and purple robes to exaggerate her agitation. The brothers both managed a chuckle but did not argue with the always irritated priestess of Lir.

* * * * *

Both on the island, Dru and Bjorn were told together the night before. After much sadness and a few shared drinks lamenting Leif's supposed demise, the two went back to their training. On the island, Dru Blackpool found concentrating on his training seemed to soften the blow of the loss of Leif.

Dru was an accomplished fighter thanks to both his father and Magnus Foehammer. It was further fine-tuned at the Academy of Arms. However, here on the island, Dru Blackpool practised his new craft, a craft he always enjoyed, thievery!

Sitting at his workbench, Dru was going beyond pick pocketing which he learned on his own. Dru was learning the art of stealth, opening and disarming locks, setting traps and discovering an array of tools he never knew existed. He could hardly believe his father sanctioned such training; however, he presumed his father had ulterior motives for such a course.

The locks and cutpurse tools were only a temporary distraction. Dru's mind wondered and began to reminisce. He pondered if Leif would approve of this training. "Likely not," he reasoned out loud with a chuckle.

Dru knew Bjorn always turned a blind eye, though he knew not why exactly. Maybe because Bjorn knew the relationship between Dru and his own father to be jaded after his mother's death and just figured Dru was just rebelling.

If Bjorn turned a blind eye, then surely Leif would too? "Likely not," he reasoned out loud with a chuckle. Leif would follow both Bjorn and Dru to a bitter end for sure, loyalty to his brothers, even though no blood tied the three together. Leif was caring, wicked with the blades but also pure of heart. Dru then closed his eyes and smiled, reminiscing of Leif. Remembering that one day on how he played on Leif's goodwill, innocently enough.

It was three years ago on the streets of Sedgedunum. The three of them, Bjorn, Dru and Leif, had been together as boys for years living in the capitol while their fathers worked at the Academy of Arms. Dru was planning to pick pocket, selecting a target, he got good at it. Dru smiled remembering who it was he stole from. It was another pickpocket and member of a local thieves' guild and he used Leif unwittingly to help.

Bjorn and Leif hadn't caught on to what he had been doing that day at the market or at least Leif had not, but it was common for them to be out during market day. It was a typical market like any other, sun was shining, the fishmongers were peddling their catch and goods had come in from across the sea. There were fruit and vegetable venders, blacksmiths, and potion peddlers. The cobble stone square was alive and bustling with activity.

Dru had been scoping out this young man for weeks. The three took their usual seats outside a pub and inn called Dead Cat, watching the world go by and enjoying some local brew. At least Dru and Bjorn were, Leif preferred wine, something the two never understood about Leif. Bjorn went back into the Dead Cat to get more drinks and some food, so Dru decided to move on his target.

"I say, Leif, do you see that man over there, the man dressed like a sailor?" asked Dru. "I been seeing him here on market day about every week, but he never buys anything."

"Some folks are picky, my friend," replied Leif but did make an effort to overlook the sailor in question.

"Watch him, Leif," asked Dru. "See! He wears a large overcoat on a nice day like today, plenty good for storing stolen items. See! He examines different venders, talks to them but never buys. I could have sworn I saw him lift from that same jewellery peddler once."

Leif was indeed watching the sailor in the overcoat now. Wearing the heavy coat just did not make sense.

Truthfully, Dru watched this thief steal before and expected the man to pick again at any moment. He knew he already picked several items. Now Dru wanted Leif to catch him in the act.

After several moments, Dru announced, "He did it! Just now, he burgled another patron in front of that linen vender."

"Come on!" demanded Leif.

"Shouldn't we wait for Bjorn?" asked Dru hesitantly, not expecting this to happen so fast and not without some proper muscle behind them.

"There is no time to lose," said Leif staring at the culprit from across the market. "Circle around and prevent his escape, I will confront him," said Leif, eyes transfixed on the thief.

"Careful, Leif, he could be skilled with a blade or armed with magic."

"I am skilled with the blade too you know, and I know what I saw."

"Hey, Bjorn, some assistance please!" announced Dru who was moving to circle around the tents and stands to cut off any escape.

Leif went to the person pick pocketed who turned out to be a local vender named Shamus and confirmed the man was missing a small pouch of coins. Leif pointed out the pickpocket dressed as a sailor who was creeping away slowly. That was until Dru rounded the corner.

"I think a friend of mine wants to have a word with you," stated Dru to the pickpocket who was about ten years senior to Dru. Dru was also pointing over the man's shoulder. The thief turned to see both Leif and the merchant closing in from behind. Dru winked and with a held-out hand said with a smile, "Just hand it over and we'll avoid any mess."

The thief immediately grabbed what he could to throw at Dru. Unfortunately, the nearest vender was a vegetable merchant and the sailor-thief threw a sack of potatoes at Dru and took off. Leif sped past Dru who appeared to be stunned. Leif caught up to the man in short order tackling the man into a bunch of barrels of herring and drawing protests from the fish mongers.

"He is a thief!" stated Leif. "I saw him!"

Dru and Shamus caught up with the pair as did three of the City Watch. Dru immediately went for the thief pulling off his over coat. Dru pulled from the coat the money pouch and handed it to the Shamus. The three watchmen took charge of the thief.

Shamus rewarded the pair with some coin which Leif quickly refused, as did Dru reluctantly. But it was a great victory for Dru as he removed a villain from the streets and lifted several valuables from the thief's sailor-coat before handing it over to the city guards. The two returned to their table outside the Dead Cat, Bjorn already eating. His chewing slowed seeing Dru rubbing his forehead where the apple sack clobbered him. Then he turned his attention to Leif who was all wet.

"You two look a sorry state. What happened to you two?" asked the red-haired young man, laughing over a half-eaten plate of seafood, smiling and beginning to laugh.

A click of the lock Dru had been slowly opening brought Dru back to his present state, on the island.

* * * * *

For Dru Blackpool, it was becoming second nature, opening these locks. This latest one was normally used to secure closets, chests or other items used to keep valuables. He unlocked three this morning and one even set with a poison needle, and although no poison was actually used, Dru was becoming good at unlocking devices. Yet this was not all his master taught him. Dru was becoming skilled at finding hidden passages, moving with stealth and developing his senses.

Dru mused about how he came to be here in the first place. With his father knowing and endorsing such training, Dru reasoned it was to give his angry father some reason to be proud of his son perhaps, but why learn on the island in the pirate isles with pirates, thieves, angry clerics and wizards? What was his father's original purpose for him and this training? All that did not matter now he knew. Dru was given a new mission or at least the objective. He and Bjorn were being trained to avenge Leif. But was odd was the training did not seem to change, but instead it intensified.

Dru then turned sensing a presence in the room. The door, locked before was now slightly ajar and so he quickly scanned the room. His master was in the far dark corner.

"Your capabilities seem to be progressing well, but your situational awareness still needs perfecting," said the assassin known as Damon Crag. Damon, an expelled from the Knights of Uden, or so rumoured, was a well-kept man of black hair and a goatee to match. "You were so deep in thought a stumbling drunk could have got in here and killed you before you even picked that lock."

"I knew you were there...master," lied Leif who said it thick with sarcasm and a dismissive hand.

Dru had an air of arrogance due to his father's station in the military. Normally Damon would not let any pupil talk to him with such disrespect; however, Dru Blackpool was the nephew of Anthon Blackpool, Damon's handler regarding the Shadow Company and Dru knew it. Otherwise, Damon would have smacked Dru across the back of the head with his blackjack.

"It is time for young Blackpool, for the next part of your training," stated the assassin throwing Dru a small bag of metallic items, more locks for sure, upon Dru's workbench. "I also expected you to be finished with the locks by now," continued Crag but his voice trailed off seeing that Dru was finished and with more locks than expected.

Dru didn't miss the trailing voice and turned to his master with a smile.

Chapter 20

Playthings

Darkness slowly became light. There was not much light, it was candle light in fact. Immediately, Leif tried to sit up but found he was racked with pain. He fell back into the bed, yes it was a bed, and he lay on a soft pillow, warm blankets coloured red and silk black sheets covering his body. It was the bed for wealthy to be sure as four black posts with a covering of fine garments hung all around the bed. Candles and oil lamps adorned the walls and furniture. Beautiful tapestries draped the walls. The room smelled of some exotic perfume.

Leif looked, closed his eyes and shook his head to make sure he was not dreaming. The last time he awoke from a battle, he was being cleaned by an elderly female arch-goblin. This time, no old arch-goblin woman was in sight, not a person and best of all no chains. Leif was not bound and therefore forced himself up. He quietly thanked Matronae that he was not naked as he was clothed in a tan shirt and black shorts.

Leif felt a warmth emanate from his necklace suddenly. The thin chain seemed to be full of wonders as the warmth sent waves of healing energy to his many wounds...all nearly healed! Scars remained where claws dug into his torso. He had full movement of his body as he sat up from the right of the bed. He stood up and felt sluggish and thirsty. Across from him he saw a glass pitcher and tumbler and headed for it. It was water he determined after careful inspection and testing with his senses.

"Help yourself, soldier. Drink, it is safe," came a familiar female voice.

Startled, Leif stared hard at Queen Ooktha in a dark corner opposite him. Wondering what his next move should be, he surmised it was she who saved him but why. She was dressed in sheer clothing and no longer wearing her black eye makeup that covered her face like a mask. She was beautiful in the physical sense, to Leif's eyes anyway. She walked slowly towards him, Leif eyeing him up and down.

"How long have I been here?"

"Here, just a day but unconscious for three. I instructed my people to heal you immediately while your necklace seemed to do the rest."

Leif instinctively went to ensure it was still around his neck even though he had felt its healing energy moments before. It seemed to have been the very thing that saved him, twice. "I am sorry about my necklace, I didn't know it could do that," stated Leif, trying to establish rapport as to why he was alive.

"It is an interesting device. But I healed nicely from your assault. Do you mean to harm me again then?" asked Ooktha.

"I didn't mean to harm you in the first place, you assaulted me, and 'it' merely reacted it seems."

"So if I am nice to you…it won't harm me?" she asked coming closer.

"I do not believe so," he replied taking another gulp of water and turning to fill his glass once again.

Leif suddenly felt the touch of her hands on his back. She ran her fingertips up over his shoulders, careful not to touch his necklace and then gently touched his biceps.

"Why did you save me?" asked Leif forcing his glass down to the table and turning to face her. His amber eyes had a penetrating gaze.

"I don't know honestly," she responded but was she now certain after looking into his beautiful eyes that she desired him.

"I am looking at you and all I see is beauty."

"You flatter me," she said looking into his eyes.

"And I think we both know why you saved me. It is your secret, isn't it?"

"My secret?"

"Yes, there is not an ounce of arch-goblin blood in you, arch-goblins don't keep blood ties or so I been taught. You are of no real relation to that chieftain, are you?"

Queen Ooktha did not answer but merely stared at the Leif.

"You are an elf like me, lost from your elven lands like me, making the best of the situation before you, like me. We have more in common than we both initially realised," he said taking another gulp of water.

When Queen Ooktha failed to reply and merely stared blankly at Leif as if she had been unmasked.

"Thank you for saving me," he said. Then Leif put down his tumbler of water, turned to face Queen Ooktha, leaned forward and kissed her passionately.

And the queen gladly accepted!

* * * * *

"Is he to be your toy for the time being, my queen, or are you actually fond of this elf?" asked Chieftain Blist.

Her mind was not presently there at the dinner table with her chieftain. The two of them often shared meals together, actually Ooktha's was a goblet of blood from a fresh kill. No, her mind was on her new lover.

"My queen?" stated Chieftain in order to gain her attention.

She really didn't know the answer. She sated her desires, for now; however, she was conflicted by her anger with the surface world but her lack of companionship, elf companionship, tugged on her desire to keep Leif from death. She thought of turning Leif into a vampire, save that cursed necklace of his but that was not her way anyway. She vowed not to turn others into vampires unless absolutely necessary. In fact, one of the reasons why she took on this union with Chieftain Blist was to prevent the need to kill mortals for her bloodlust. Her mere presence kept the other two cities in check while they, in turn, provided her with fresh victims who came across their paths. After she drank their blood, they were killed, and the remains were given to her minions.

"A toy for now," she replied drinking from a golden goblet filled with red liquid.

The chieftain was sceptical to be sure but did not show it. Chieftain Blist drank with her but ate as well. He enjoyed raw meat and blood, though arch-goblins could not be sustained on blood alone. It was an unlikely union, but it served both of them really well.

"The war is coming soon but our forces were well decimated in the mountains by your toys' soldiers. If we continue as planned," he began but stopped to swallow some meat.

"Does this trouble you, my friend?" Ooktha interrupted during the pause of the chieftains swallowing. "You yourself said that Merka was a fool of a leader. Did you really expect to have better results?"

"I did indeed expect to have more warriors return alive from that endeavour! That concerns me greatly. For I now worry of our other plans, to war with the vile orcs of the north. Those plans may be in jeopardy if we also engage in our hidden agenda in the south."

"How so?" she asked, not being a military strategist.

"If the battle is not won swiftly with the orcs in the north, we may not be able to carry out the assault on Vorclaw as effectively as we promised the Vorclaw traitors. We cannot afford a war on two fronts, one with the humans and the other with the orcs, I am not certain we will still be able to accomplish our hidden plans for that area they call Panther-Paw Pass. However, perhaps we can get the good wizard or the Vorclaw colonel to aid us with the orcs. After all we are doing them a favour?" the chieftain put in.

Queen Ooktha shook her head in disagreement as she had discussed assistance before with other tribal woes, but Colonel Blackpool always deferred until after the Vorclaw assault happens.

"Perhaps send your toy with Merka's forces then? Maybe they could learn from him?" stated the Chieftain.

"Why would he help our forces fight the orcs?" she asked. "And do not presume because I have seduced him that he is completely loyal to me."

"I presume nothing, my queen, but you could ask him to join our cause against the orcs, which every race despises. Perhaps in exchange for his freedom and show good faith?" he asked slyly.

"Ah, you have heard his willingness to barter for a peace treaty with us, especially at Blood-helm?" she queried.

"I have indeed, my queen. Although he clearly does not know any of our plans, we could use him to our advantage. Let's not forget my lady, you will be preoccupied with the war soon, will you not? Let us send him to the north to kill orcs on our behalf and let him prove his intentions. Challenge him to return to you and only then would you consider his offer at a treaty. Although we both know you never will," schemed the chieftain.

* * * * *

Queen Ooktha sat in her chamber of mirrors. It was her usual meeting with the Union of Undead. Topics of discussion ranged from acquisitions, plotting coups, offering advice and sharing stories. However, Queen Ooktha's mind kept her thoughts on the night she spent with Leif. She was definitely smitten for the large elf, but she was still uncertain if she was truly interested in him as a lover or a play thing. So she was not paying attention when her least favourite revenant, Rom-Seti, inquired about her dealings with Vorclaw.

"Dear Ooktha," asked Rom-Seti, again. "Are we to hear from you this month? How fares your upcoming war? We have been waiting for it to happen for months now," he said laughing.

"It is near, my friends," said Queen Ooktha addressing everyone and ignoring Revenant Rom-Seti's mocking laugh. "We are ready to strike the city and moreover, unbeknownst to the Vorclawean traitor's, our plans extend beyond merely sacking their capitol city."

"Do tell, my dear," inquired Revenant Niss. Revenant Niss actually knew the particulars being Ooktha's most trusted advisor.

"It is a delicious tale. Allow me to weave it for you all?" she begged. "Now that the traitor wizard has completed his construction in my city of Ironhold. The traitor colonel has decided on a date which puts the majority of the city residents at the harbour and docks; we will begin our assault at the end of the month."

"What is so significant about the end of the month?" asked Rom-Seti dryly.

"It is a holiday to the Vorclaweans, where they give thanks to the sea's bounty or something like that. It will be in the evening where the town's folk celebrate next to their seaside, far from the gates we intend to smash through!" she said delighted.

"Do you hope to push them all into the sea?" asked Rom-Seti with what sounds like a snicker, but no one could be sure if he was excited or being sarcastic as he no longer had lips or muscles upon his face to see such a telling sign.

"I intend to sack the city and plunder it for as much wealth as I can take," she responded. "However, what Vorclaw does not know is that when we also sack their capitol, we also intend to…"

"You should push them into the sea and create a legion of undead and wage an even larger war upon the land!" stated an excited Rom-Seti, his finger pointing at her through the mirror. "Let me run your war young 'pup' and I will bring your hordes to glory!"

"Enough!" shouted Queen Ooktha who was visibly upset by the insult of being called a 'pup' in front of her peers. "How dare you!" Queen Ooktha stammered and stood up from her black throne. "I had enough of your disrespect over the years, you decrepit thing. I wouldn't ask for help from the likes of you even if you held the key to my salvation, let alone allow you the honour to lead my minions," she said with outrage. "Go and find a new war to wage and stop living in the glory of when you decimated that city you constantly boast about."

The mirrors were silent by her outburst. None had seen Queen Ooktha be so aggressive. She wished she could take back calling the revenant decrepit, in light of other revenants present, but she quickly changed her mind when she saw smiles, of those that could smile, for putting Rom-Seti back into his place.

"Let the woman speak!" stated Revenant Niss who also disliked Rom-Seti. She could still smile. Other members nodded in agreement, for those that could still nod.

"You insolent whelp!" shouted Rom-Seti, now standing pointing back at her through the mirror. "I offer you a chance for glory beyond your pitiful plans and you disrespect my offer and insult me."

"Rom-Seti," came a booming voice out of Lord Drim. "Be silent and let the vampiress lay her plans to us!" Rom-Seti complied and sat back in his throne. "Continue vampiress, queen of the arch-goblin hoards," stated Lord Drim, showing all, respect to Ooktha.

"Many thanks, Lord Drim," she responded with a bow.

* * * * *

After the Union of Undead adjourned, Queen Ooktha reconnected with Revenant Niss via the mirrors. "I presume you contacted me to discuss Rom-Seti my dear?" asked Revenant Niss.

"Hardly my mentor, I have no time for that sap!" she replied gleefully. Revenant Niss, had enough skin tissue remaining to provide an approving smile.

"I do have news though I wish to share with you my mentor," stated Ooktha gleefully.

"Do tell, my dear."

"I am, infatuated," she said, not certain how she felt about her news. Her news was about Leif but was not sure how to explain it to an undead human wizard who no longer felt such emotions, or so she believed. "It is with a male elf captured by my arch-goblins and he perplexes me."

"How so, my dear?" she asked through the mirror.

"His name is Leif, clearly not an elvish name but I don't understand why I'm infatuated so. In fact, he almost killed me, on accident it seemed. His gold necklace protects him somehow, but it did not stop our love making. He even killed my mantikhoras in my arena. But see, I am rambling about him like a smitten young kitten," she said finally and shrugged her slender shoulders.

"Well, enjoy him while you can, my dear. However, be cautious, as once he learns of your war against his people, you run the risk of his wrath do you not?" replied Revenant Niss. "Best to use him and be done with him as soon as your war begins," warned the revenant, waving a bony finger while shaking her head back and forth.

"I know, my mistress," Ooktha said in frustration, her hands over her face. "And I have no intention of telling him about my war," she said suddenly, looking up from her hands. "But I just cannot bring myself to kill him, drink him or turn him," she said with futility.

"And how does he feel about you?"

"He made love to me without hesitation, without my influence, many times," she said aloud, almost without having to think on an answer. "Before then I had him in my arena as food for my mantikhoras, which he cunningly dispatched," Queen Ooktha said, laughing aloud at the irony of making love to a male elf she had intended to feed to her pet.

"So he has interest in you too. That's good, my dear, use that against him. Perhaps you can convince him to fight for you or even reveal secrets that your Vorclaw associates have not?"

"You sound like Chieftain Blist," she said with a slight laugh. "He suggested as much but also recommend I send him north to fight along arch-goblins of Blood-helm against the orcs there."

"Perhaps he too sees the danger this elf is to you and fears for you," reasoned Revenant Niss referring to Chieftain Blist's suggestion.

"I think it's more that he has concerns Leif will change my mind about the war and rob Chieftain Blist of his power over the other two arch-goblin tribes. But I reassured him he had nothing to worry about."

It was that moment a humming noise began to resonate in Queen Ooktha's private chamber. It came from another mirror from the Union of Undead, Rom-Seti's mirror. Revenant Niss heard the call as well but not from within her own chamber of mirrors but through Queen Ooktha mirror meaning whoever wished to converse with Queen Ooktha, they meant for it to be with Ooktha alone.

"It's Rom-Seti, my mistress," stated Queen Ooktha. "Do you think he wishes to apologise?" she asked with a chuckle of Revenant Niss.

"Answer him, my dear, but make no mention that we are conversing. And with your permission, my dear, I wish to eavesdrop on what the wretch has to say," requested Revenant Niss.

"Of course, Revenant Niss," agreed Ooktha.

Queen Ooktha made for Rom-Seti's mirror, touched it to activate the portal and stood before it with her arms crossed in defiance.

"I presume you are contacting me in order to apologise," stated Ooktha. Just then Ooktha felt a pull inside her, like a sickly feeling, demanding she go somewhere. It intensified and Ooktha fell to her knees in pain.

"Apologise, my lovely, hardly," stated Rom-Seti.

Ooktha crawled for her chair. It held magical properties to protect her from more powerful assaults through the mirrors. It was a gift from Revenant Niss but it seemed so far. A few feet mind as well had been miles away.

"I am going to teach you a lesson in pain!" Rom-Seti shouted, happily viewing Queen Ooktha wincing in pain. "Never again will you disrespect me in front of the Union. I am going to teach you respect by pulling on your soul." The revenant's power to call upon other undead creatures extended itself to inflict pain upon those called. That pull on the soul, upon the life force, if unheeded, transcended beyond the soul onto the undead's corporal form;

however, in some cases a revenant could inflict that pain upon other undead at will. Just then Ooktha let out an aching scream in pain!

"I can feel your life force, I am pulling on it, pulling it from your body. I can feed upon it if I choose to, add it to my own. And you would become a worthless zombie!" shouted Rom-Seti.

He begun another pull upon her lifeforce. A wave of pain rolled over Ooktha, dragging her backwards towards Rom-Seti's mirror. She could not speak as every muscle in her body ached. She felt fear, a dread like no other as if Rom-Seti was indeed beginning to pull her life from her body. It stopped suddenly as she heard what sounded like curses and sensed a frustration from Rom-Seti. She could not understand him, he spoke in some ancient tongue at first but gave away to common. She could not make out any sentences but clearly, he conversed with someone or something. She tried to gain her strength and get up from the pull on her life force. Slowly she crawled up the steps where her magical seat awaited her. She glanced up at the mirror of Revenant Niss, but it was dark. Did she abandon her? Ooktha did hear her voice, coming from Rom-Seti's mirror. Ooktha quietly thanked her for she interrupted Rom-Seti's assault by contacting him through her own mirror into Rom-Seti's lair.

Rom-Seti noticed Ooktha's slow climb up the throne and would have said something but did not want to let Revenant Niss know he was 'mentoring' Queen Ooktha. The mentoring will have to wait," he said allowed and dismissed the connection between his viewing mirror and Queen Ooktha's.

Chapter 21

Strike a Deal

The mental plea to "bring my decanter of blood immediately" did not go unheeded by Chieftain Blist. Had he not, he knew Ooktha would drink the first living creature she came into contact with, which might have been himself. He poured the blood into her mouth immediately and picked her up off the floor once the decanter was emptied. Then he took her back to her private chambers for her to recuperate. She did not speak a word, merely rested. Hours turned into days as he helped pour the decanters of blood into her daily.

He took great care of her for she was the glue that forged the three arch-goblin tribes into a union. Fear of her alone scared Chieftain Gutter and Chieftain Merka to fall in line behind him. Without her, his desire for uniting the tribes and laying waste to the capitol of Vorclaw would never come to fruition. That was the arch-goblin mindset, achieve a great military victory, garner great spoils of war and become a legend to behold. Chieftain Blist, Queen Ooktha's pretend cousin, the giant arch-goblin who ruled the underground city of Skulls-thorpe wanted a legacy.

As his mind grappled with this predicament, he wondered if she was poisoned or assaulted and by whom. She would not respond to his query as to what happened either. He began to worry if she would ever return fully. Her colour was returning which was a good sign, although she was soft white to almost pale blue already, but she would not communicate. Chieftain Blist knew of the Union of Undead and although it is possible, she was attacked by another member, surely the remaining would prevent such. Therefore, he now wondered if her new lover had something to do with this. After three days of silence by Queen Ooktha, Leif was back to the jails of the arena, but not before some interrogation.

* * * * *

Lorez took pity upon the elf although he knew not why. Leif sat chained to the wall, his face a bloody swollen mess from the interrogation by Chieftain Blist and his warriors. The Blood-helm clan wanted nothing to do with the impending attack upon Vorclaw and perhaps Lorez's infatuation with Leif was the key to Blood-helm's autonomy again? That seemed like a farfetched idea and Lorez wasn't even sure why he came to see Leif although it was nearly impossible to get in as he was not originally granted access until he came across the original jailer Grim, from when he left Leif in the arena prison. Lorez's mind began to sway towards this battered elf putting a spell of friendship upon him. That notion left his mind believing spells like that wouldn't last for days, compounded by the site of the elf before him. Bloodied and bruised in face and body. Lorez in fact was just about to leave the city of Skulls-thorpe when he heard the queen was taken ill and possibly an attacked. Another rumoured surfaced about a small band of dark-elves found nearby. The dark-elves turned out to be rogues and were quickly dispatched; however, one was captured. Now a special event was to take place in the arena so Lorez remained in the city to uncover what he could.

"Why are you here? Come to see me battle in the arena again?" asked a groggy Leif.

"I think I come to see why you are still alive. I thought you died in the arena. Seems you defeated our queen's great cat."

"You are a paranoid race, Lorez of Blood-helm. Do you know they questioned me about conspiring with Blood-helm to kill the queen? They questioned me whether I was an assassin come to kill your queen...on your chieftains' behalf."

"What? Why would they ask such?"

"Probably because I almost killed her once already, did I not?"

"Did you try and kill her again?"

"No, but someone did. The chieftain found her lying on the floor near death and thought I had something to do with it."

"Did you?"

"No! Of course not," replied Leif.

"I find you hard to believe, my large elven friend. What surprises me though is why you are alive in the first place. I thought you dead after the battle with the mantikhoras."

"I think it did kill me or nearly had. It seems your people saved me, however, at the request of Queen Ooktha."

"To what end?"

Leif snickered with a quick laugh but then shook his head in confusion. Lorez caught on and let out a great laugh. "You're her mate!" he shouted pointing, still laughing. "Or at least you were. Not up to performance, my friend?" asked Lorez, giggling.

"Actually, I thought all was well, but I hadn't seen her in days and then the chieftain came, questioned me, tortured me and sent me here."

"So you didn't try to kill her again?"

"No! And I never tried to kill her in the first place," replied Leif.

"Well, who did then?"

"I do not know, and I am not sure she is even alive. If she is, she is either recovering or she has abandoned me altogether," said Leif.

"Why didn't the chieftain kill you?" asked Lorez.

"I know not," stated Leif shaking his head.

"He is to fight the captured dark-elf, he will die soon," stated Grim the jailer in the arch-goblin tongue.

Lorez turned to regard the jailer, more to the point that the old arch-goblin spoke the common tongue but Lorez recounted and realised he had not said anything incriminating to his clan. Nor did he say anything revealing that he wanted this elf to return with him to Blood-helm to at least try and establish a treaty with the Vorclaw.

"By comparison, how fares this elf compared to the dark-elf? Is the dark-elf equally damaged?" asked Lorez.

"The dark-elf is barely hurt. Whispers say the dark-elves sacrificed his own brethren to save himself from certain death," responded Grim.

"Does he know what he fights?"

The jailer shook his head not knowing, nor caring. Lorez then took out his purse and handed over a few coins to the jailer arch-goblin.

"For your information and your silence!" said Lorez in the common. Grim looked puzzled but accepted and realised what he meant when he pulled forth another vile to give to Leif.

"Drink this, elf, it will heal your wounds and make the fight fair today," said Lorez and Leif had no reason to doubt him. It tasted bad but soon felt its energy throughout his body, but it was different from the energy of his necklace. This feeling was more a strengthening of his muscles than a healing of wounds.

"Do not disappoint, I am betting on you to win," Lorez said with a toothy grin. "Remember, dark-elves are devious. They have powers to cast simple spells at will."

A shudder went through Leif's body when he heard the word 'dark-elves'. He only read about them but knew they were evil, most of them anyway. Yet something deeper within made him angry at the thought of a dark-elf.

"Did you know you were going to fight a dark-elf?" asked Lorez and Leif shook his head in response.

"They are tasty sweet meat!" shouted Ko-ko the troll from across the jail who had been listening in. "Save me some, large-elf," shouted the old troll.

"I will feed you soon enough, my happy old troll!" shouted Grim back at Ko-ko.

* * * * *

Somehow the roar of the crowd outside seemed less frightening this time. Even the smelly old troll Ko-ko seemed comforting.

"Don't get yourself killed, large elf. And bring me back a treat, please!" said Ko-ko.

Grim the jailer didn't say much but he did fit Leif with a leather jerkin, small shield and a sword.

The gate opened suddenly, and Leif stepped through. The crowd roared and Leif immediately looked for the seating where Queen Ooktha sat during his last fight. She was not present, Lorez was there seated alongside Chieftain Blist. They were conversing and occasionally pointing at Leif. Across from Leif stood a grey-skinned elf with blond hair.

"Wow, you are a large elf," shouted the dark-elf in the elven tongue.

Leif gave no reply because he could not understand him.

"If we work together, we can get out of here!" he said while looking up to the ceiling of the massive cavern. "These arch-goblins are such idiots. I have some magic yet to play, my brother. I can levitate us both to the ceiling and we can escape through the cracks to the surface. Do you understand?"

The dark-elf wasn't certain that this was a true elf, perhaps a half breed and asked the same but in the human language.

Leif did not know whether to take this dark-elf at his word or not. Lorez told him they were devious and a fire inside him told him that dark-elves are inherently evil.

"Do you understand me?" asked the dark-elf. "However, we have to make it look good to throw the beasts off their guard. Just fight me for a bit first!"

On came the dark-elf, brandishing two short swords. The dark-elf's movements were fluid and had Leif retreating immediately. The hits to Leif's shield and sword were more forceful than Leif expected but it mattered little as Leif was much larger than the dark-elf in height and mass What did matter was that Leif was nearing the wall sooner than he could have expected as the dark-elf's assaults were relentless. Leif did not even hear the cheers of the crowds of arch-goblins, lizard-goblins and whatever other wretches were in the coliseum. Instead, he focused. Leif counted the hits and movements looking for a pattern and then it stopped. The dark-elf backed down and backed up shouting at the arch-goblins in their language. He was taunting the crowd bringing their cheers louder!

"Come on, large elf, you will have to do better than that, for the crowd at least." On came the dark-elf again, pushing Leif back once more around the arena.

"How do I know you won't kill me when we rise up?" asked Leif.

"I cannot survive on the surface on my own and will need a companion. And besides, if I wanted you dead, I would have killed you already," laughed the dark-elf.

Insulted by the statement, Leif began his assault. It was clear to Leif that this dark-elf was much older and likely wiser but Leif found a pattern in his movements. A quick assault and slash from Leif and then a simple retreat confirmed the dark-elf fought right-left-right-left-right-left-left-left-right and repeat.

"You cannot defeat me large elf, dark-elves' tactics are far superior to any others and I am exceptional with the blades. And even if you did kill me, that large arch-goblin up there in the stands wants you dead. He even offered me riches and freedom if I kill you."

Standard tactic, deception or not? Leif took advantage of this dark-elf's fighting pattern. When the last right in the pattern came forth, Leif countered with his shield thrusting up at that right-side sword, forcing that arm of the dark-elf up high. Leif quickly followed by a chop from his own sword and then a swing back to the dark-elf's left to counter his other sword. Leif scored a direct hit on the right forearm exposing bone, flesh and streaming blood. The dark-elf reeled in pain and jumped back out of the way from Leif, part of his right forearm hanging limp. The dark-elf shouted curse at Leif in what he believed to be the dark-elf language.

After several moments, Leif's opponent backed down some distance away. It was then Leif realised he had not been unscathed in his assault. The dark-elf's blade sliced open Leif's right shoulder.

The two engaged again but Leif still held some advantage as both his arms could still function. The dark-elf then threw his sword from his left hand at Leif. It happened so quickly that Leif barely had time to react. Had Leif not jumped, that sword would have sunk into his chest but instead cut into his arm. Leif no longer had use of his right arm, just as the dark-elf did not.

The dark-elf was now tearing a piece of his clothing off to stem his own blood flow and Leif on cue did the same. However, the dark-elf finished first and came on running at him with his left hand wielding a sword. Leif was out of time to dress his wound, instead shoved some his clothing into the wound to stem the blood flow and oh how it pained him to do so but knew if he did not stop the blood loss, he would die.

The dark-elf hacked and sliced but Leif was marvellously good with a shield and battled back with that shield. Now the gladiators circled each other in the centre, neither gaining ground.

Suddenly, the dark-elf kicked sand up and into Leif's face. Leif was now backpedalling, appeared blinded and instinctively tried to shake the sand from his face. On came the dark-elf hoping for such confusion. The dark-elf had his opening to finish Leif; however, thanks to Lorez, Leif was expecting some kind of dirty trick. Leif's back peddling and blindness was a ruse.

The dark-elf's stabbing thrust missed completely as Leif jumped and spun to the side. Although the dark-elf's miss was easily corrected with a backhanded return swipe, it was overpowered by Leif's shield edge and sheer strength. The shield caught the dark-elf across his right temple first and then the sword. The dark-elf fell limp to the floor, his body shook once, and the life of the dark-elf was over.

Leif went over to make sure the dark-elf was dead by stabbing him in the chest. The crowd went wild at the spectacle. Then Leif did something unexpected. He used the dark elf's own sword to cut the rest of dark-elf's damaged forearm. The crowd went crazy with blood lust and cheered wildly; Leif even waved at the crowd of creatures but also looked up to the Chieftain Blist as well and locked stares. Leif then walked back to the jailer's door which opened for him.

"Ko-ko!" shouted Leif.

"Large elf, you alive!" replied Ko-ko seeming happy to see him.

"I have a treat for you." Leif tossed the dark-elf's hand to the old troll, who marvelled and then began to devour the dark-elf arm!

* * * * *

135

"I was certain the dark-elf would have killed him," stated Chieftain Blist. "I was told he was a good fighter, killing four of our own kin, himself."

"How did you capture him then?" ask Lorez counting the purse the two arch-goblins wagered.

"We had the numbers is how. In fact, he even killed one of his own to save his skin and proved he was worth more as a prisoner than dead."

"A lot of good it did him," stated Lorez. "But it did me plenty of good, my lord," he teased shaking the purse of coins he had just won from the chieftain off a bet of the outcome.

"I was actually surprised he fought so well after I, I mean my interrogators treated him so badly."

"It seems he is a resilient elf," responded Lorez. "He was the last standing in Chieftain Merka's battle."

Chieftain Blist did not reply.

After a moment of silence, and while waiting for the next battle in the arena to commence, Lorez probed a little further. "So the rumour is our queen was attacked in her own citadel and was not present because she is recovering. Is this true? Is that why she does not watch her lover fight?"

The Chieftain looked at Lorez with open hate but Lorez, the clever arch-goblin, never looked at the large chieftain but merely stared at the arch-goblins removing the dead dark-elf from the arena. A large streak of blood seeped out of the severed arm.

"Lorez, had you asked those questions anywhere outside the coliseum, I would have cut you down for asking," responded Chieftain Blist. "However, here in the coliseum, members of the other two tribes are present and I want to maintain my alliances among our tribes."

Lorez did look at the large chieftain who was staring at him intently but Lorez decided not to back down.

Blist let out a belly laugh and slapped Lorez hard on the back and shoulder but did not let go. "Rumours are just that...rumours," he said but now wondered how he could have known that information.

"You should let me take him back to Blood-helm," said Lorez talking about Leif. "He would do well on our front lines when we battle the orcs. Surely, he would kill them in exchange for his freedom, don't you think?"

"No, I will kill him myself," Blist responded.

"But you can't," said Lorez.

"And why not?"

"Would the queen truly ever forgive you for killing her lover?" replied Lorez. "All it would take is her and you to be at odds over something, anything and she might remember that you also killed this elf and decide it was time to kill you, or worse," teased Lorez.

Lorez saw he got Blist to think differently about killing Leif outright. A death in *The Games* would at least be honourable and easily explained while she did recover. So too would a death fighting for the arch-goblin causes.

"It would also be prudent to have him removed from our queen's presence when the war comes with Vorclaw," pressed Lorez. "He would be a distraction to her, would he not?" Lorez stated as much as asked.

"Ha! You must have been reading my mind. For once you and I agree," said the large arch-goblin chieftain.

"It is settled then, I leave on the morrow," said Lorez.

"But he is not mine to give you," stated Blist staring at the cleaning of the arena awaiting the next match.

"A pity," Lorez stated and did not know how to counter that.

"He belongs to our queen and I do not wish to incur her wrath without some form of compensation," said Chieftain Blist. "I could give him to you but perhaps a payment for the risk in handing him over to you," said Blist now playing a game.

After a few moments, Lorez realised a price had to be paid in order to take this elf from the chieftain. Lorez then threw the winnings from their wager onto the table between them hoping that would be enough.

The chieftain picked up the purse smiling a toothy grin and said, "Make sure you get your money's worth, but he is not to survive for long."

Part III: Love and Hate

Chapter 22
Council Rules and Treaties

The Council of Twelve ruling Vorclaw was based on who had the most influence and wealth but must be voted on by eight of the twelve members.

Although Lord Handel Nightingale's family has been on the council for decades, he was a relatively new member to the council; his aunt Lady Sanne Nightingale stepped down to oversee the family businesses. However, the young lord's influence has grown increasingly, thanks in many ways to Colonel Blackpool's insistence of the Nightingale family's familiarities with the mason's and supplies needed in the construction of Fort Adamant.

"The losses of an entire company, not to mention the loss of the late Lord Brisbane, are exactly why Colonel Blackpool has been petitioning for a battalion to be posted in the mountains," announced Lord Handel Nightingale at The Council of Twelve meeting. "The gods only know what would have happened if the White Eagles where not training there," he continued. "Therefore, until Fort Adamant is finished, I motion for the White Eagles to remain at Fort Adamant until it is complete and properly garrisoned," stated Lord Nightingale.

The remaining members of the council agreed with motion cast by Lord Nightingale. Thinking himself clever, he now lobbied for his next motion.

"And may I dare say to the business of replacing our departed Lord Brisbane as commander of our military," stated Lord Nightingale, surprising the council.

"Quite right, young lord," stated Boyd Draconian, Headmaster of Sedgedunum's Wizard's College. He was also known as the hairless one. He was one of the few wizards who refused to grow a beard and boasted a bald head, by choice. "I have prepared a comprehensive list of candidates based upon wealth, experience in commerce, skills in diplomacy and years spent in the military."

"We three have developed a list, similar to yours," announced Archbishop Zelana Spool, a high priestess of Matronae. She was also speaking for the two other pious council members, Archbishop Storm Evander a priest of Dagda and Archbishop Elman Wisemind, a priest of Ogma. "Lord Ethan Brisbane was a Warrior-priest of Matronae after all. It stands to reason a warrior-priest of one of the three council faiths should replace the man."

The other council members included wealthy members of Vorclaw society, similar in wealth to Lord Nightingale's family and were representatives from the cities within Vorclaw. There was Lord Igor Frothbeard, a dwarven arms dealer from Irons-by-the-Sea. Lord Evan Ester, a human and the leader of the miner's guild in Cairnhold. Lord Taywin Ray, a wealthy ship builder and maritime entrepreneur, represented Cairnloch. Lord Syngen Anglewood, a wealthy retired warrior was from the frontier town of Exbury. There was Lord Dremil Dissmee, a retired half elf rogue who settled in Wrexbury, also extremely wealthy. Lastly, there was the head of the admiralty, the white moustached and elder, Admiral Drake Kahee commander of the Navy, who kept his headquarters in the seaside town of Seaforth.

All had to have the consent of the mayors or district leaders of those they represented. This ensured interests of all of Vorclaw was brought to the table. Of course, each had their own nominee, except for Admiral Kahee, who seemed uninterested. As the table erupted into debates and arguments, it was Admiral Kahee that calmed everyone down and asked that each put forth their name and speak for their nominee's qualifications. Each council member explained their nominee in great detail and the whole process took roughly two hours to come to conclusion. Only Lord Nightingale remained.

"Ladies and gentlemen of the council, I know that I am new to this governing body, but I have the full trust of my family. They have full confidence in my abilities to make sound decisions for the good of Vorclaw. Therefore, I have chosen my nominee very carefully. I have spent much time with this person over the last few years. A man whom I met after his dear wife was callously murdered in the streets. I have come to understand him as a master in the art of leadership. As a combat veteran, a commander and with practical experience in the science of war, he has established credibility in the eyes of this council already. Not only has he been charged with the training of our soldiers over the last half dozen years but also is a wealthy entrepreneur in the shipping industry. He understands the delicate art of leading people and is savvy enough to govern a small business. Therefore, I nominate Colonel Baltus Blackpool next to sit on The Council of Twelve."

The room remained silent as Blackpool was never considered by any of them before. Slowly Baltus Blackpool had been building his own wealthy empire in warehousing in addition to his role as the commandant of Vorclaw's military training. Those facts influenced the council to take Lord Nightingale's nominee under consideration. However, when the votes were cast, everyone voted for their own nominee of course. Therefore, it was up to Admiral Drake Kahee, Commander of the Vorclaw's Navy, to decide.

* * * * *

"Well done, lad, well done! And thank you, councilman," stated Colonel Blackpool shaking the hand of Lord Handel Nightingale.

"I wanted to come to your office and tell you the news personally," he said.

"Captain Nigel Newman!" shouted Colonel Blackpool. "Bring us some brandy at once!"

"I have learned much from you over the years and you deserve to be a part of this council as much as anyone. Councilman!" replied Lord Nightingale.

Mimdrid the shape-changer, in the guise of Master Sergeant Coventry, poured the brandy for the two councilmen.

"Now that you're on The Council of Twelve, I got them to assign you the duties of the departed Lord Brisbane," stated Lord Nightingale.

Both Colonel Blackpool and Mimdrid could not hide their surprise!

"I never suspected such!" stated Colonel Blackpool.

"You have taught me well in the art of negotiation, sir. Once I realised Admiral Kahee did not have a candidate, I appealed to his military background and he was the deciding vote my dear colonel, sorry, general!"

"What did you say?" asked the Blackpool.

"The title of general is only suited for commander of the Vorclaw's army and that is now you," General Blackpool. "It was Lord Brisbane's rank as you recall. There will be a ceremony of course. You will also have to find a suitable replacement for your position as commandant, as you will be expected to tour. I made sure you may keep your military estate since you are the new military leader," stated Lord Nightingale finishing he drink.

After another round of drinks and discussion, Lord Nightingale took his leave of the soon-to-be General Blackpool. Both Baltus Blackpool and Mimdrid in the form of Master Sergeant Coventry made their way down the secret stairs and into the hidden underground elven court in ruins beneath Vorclaw's Academy of Arms. There waiting in Black-Masks were Admiral Kahee and his son, the pirate Captain Ruko Kahee.

* * * * *

Leif had recounted the steps of his predicament. He was ambushed by a horde of arch-goblins that left his entire company dead as far as he knew. He should have been dead then and there. Instead, he was ferried underground as a sacrifice to the arch-goblin queen. He nearly killed her, unintentionally. As a result, he was thrown into an arena to fight a mantikhoras to the death. After barely surviving that, he was seduced by the vampire queen for days. Then suddenly thrown back into the arena to fight a dark-elf, where he discovered and unknown hatred for the kindred race; a hatred he wasn't certain came from. Finally, he was sold into the slavery to the arch-goblin Lorez.

Lorez's rules were simple, fight for him against the orcs and live, otherwise meet death. There was no promise of freedom in those rules. However, Leif was smart enough to know that his own hand at friendship did not go unnoticed by Lorez.

Warning the arch-goblins of the kelpiefolk attacks aboard the Bloodknuckle did well for saving his elven skin. Talk of brokering a treaty was something Lorez was interested in, or at least Leif believed. Save the loss of his own men, this entire journey might seem comical to an outsider. Leif managed a small crack of a smile beneath his helm and mask.

Now, however, was not the time to wonder the past or how he might organise a peace treaty. Instead, Leif now faced a horde of orcs while surrounded by ranks of arch-goblins and lizard-goblins.

Leif was kept chained by the neck and kept next to Lorez and two other arch-goblins. Leif was given a sword and shield, knowing full well an attempt to kill any arch-goblin would result in his own death. They painted Leif's face a light blue, similar to an arch-goblin's. His mask only covered the lower part of his face, no amount of make-up could disguise Leif's lack of pointed teeth. So, at a distance, he appeared arch-goblin. If Leif was lost to the fray of battle, a light blue circle painted across the back of his armour showed Lorez Leif's whereabouts.

Leif looked around the large cavern chosen for this battle. Several hundred orcs lined the walls with bows while foot soldiers formed less than impressive ranks across the way. The arch-goblin lines were just the opposite of orcs, they were well formed and straight as could be in uneven floors of the cavern. The arch-goblins too had archers lining the walls opposite the orcs. If this battle was to be a war of attrition, the numbers seemed even. Just then, dozens of short, bipedal creatures with a lizard-like appearance, began to filter through the arch-goblin ranks. Some of these scaly creatures were green, others were red or orange.

To Leif, the small and upright walking lizard creatures appeared as a cross between a small lizard and some small two-legged creature. The small creatures who were not up to Leif's waist filed in behind the first two rows of the arch-goblin company. Individually the little creatures seemed harmless but in mass, Leif thought they could be very deadly.

It was then he noticed a runty lizard-goblin, red in colour, being shoved and abused by his fellow lizard-goblins. It was definitely due to his small stature, small even for a lizard-goblin. Leif watched the two lizard-goblins prod the runt, even tease him, likely about his chances about the upcoming battle. The runt looked nervous indeed.

Leif then snapped his fingers and pointed at the trio and the teasing stopped. Leif motioned for the runty lizard-goblin to come over to him. Nervously, the runt complied as the other two scurried away.

Lorez let the scene play out and did not let the other arch-goblins interfere. Leif asked one of his keepers to ask the runt for his name. Lorez nodded with approval and the arch-goblin stated, "His name is Sker."

"Tell Sker to stand next to me where it is safe," stated Leif.

"I know the human tongue, master," replied the little lizard-goblin.

Lorez nodded approval with a laugh as did the other two arch-goblins holding Leif's chains. However, Lorez's attention was in the centre of the cavern. There Chieftain Merka met with the orc leader, Chieftain Longtusk. The two leaders were talking for nearly thirty minutes before the two returned to their respective sides.

"He has agreed to most of our terms," said Chieftain Merka to Lorez in the arch-goblin tongue.

"Except?" asked Lorez.

"Not one I care about, mining rights along the border is all," replied Merka. "But they will keep clear of us on the surface which allows us to go to war with the Vorclaweans without worry."

"Are we going to battle over mining rights then?" asked Lorez, excitingly and believing full well they would establish a victory here if they did.

"No! One champion per side battles for the mining rights. The losing side gets some concessions," stated Merka.

"I am up to the challenge!" stated Lorez.

"No!" said Merka. "Send your treaty-maker. Send the elf-slave to fight for us. He wants to make a treaty with us and the humans, let him start with orcs. You painted and dressed him to look like one of us, he should do nicely."

"What if it is discovered in melee that he is not an arch-goblin? Will not Chieftain Longtusk and his orcs be insulted?" asked Lorez.

Moments passed before Merka reacted and said, "I don't care." Then Merka growled forcefully at Lorez and pointed at Leif. It did not go unnoticed by other arch-goblins, lizard-goblins and Leif.

"What say you?" asked Leif of Lorez when he came over.

"Congratulations, you are to be our champion," stated Lorez in a less than an enthused manner. "The battle is over for us all but not for you. What is left is for single combat between two champions who will fight for the undecided terms of the treaty. You have been selected by Chieftain Merka to represent us."

"Oh well aren't I the lucky one," said Leif as Lorez and the two arch-goblins escorting Leif prepared him for battle. "Should I let them know I am elf?"

"I wouldn't," stated Lorez.

"What do I get if I win this battle for you?" asked Leif of Lorez.

"Come back to me alive and I will let you lay with some of our women?" stated Lorez.

Leif reserved comment.

"They're just orcs, you will be fine," stated Lorez but started to second guess himself once Merka started laughing. "You get to bring two weapons and a shield. What do you want?"

"I will take a sword, a shield and a mace. My squire Sker will carry my mace for me," stated Leif. An outburst came forth from Lorez and the other arch-goblins joined in the laughter, as did the lizard-goblins, except for Sker, who understood some common and was thinking he was better to take his chances with the bigger lizard-goblins. The laughter quieted down once the orc champion emerged and went to the centre of the cavern, it was an enormous orc!

"Probably bred with ogre to make that beastie," said Lorez.

"If your slave is as good as you believe, Lorez, I am certain that ogre-orc thing will be no match for your elf champion," said Merka. "Put some weapon black over his eyes to hide his elven face."

Lorez did as instructed blacking out Leif's face. "There under the helmet and the camouflage, no one would know you're an elf."

"Go secure my treaty, elf!" said Merka in the common tongue. "And who knows maybe I will reward you."

Leif did not like Merka, not in the least. If Leif could, he would have surely slain Merka right then and there. He was the opposing commander in the battle at the mines. Leif held Merka accountable for the death of his company and would not forget nor forgive the arch-goblin for ambushing his men. One thing Leif's father taught him was patience. And, of course, what choice did Leif have? So he did as he was told.

"Come along, Sker," stated Leif.

Leif let the desire to avenge his company give him incentive to succeed in this task. As Leif exited the ranks of the arch-goblin line with his squire Sker in tow, Leif prayed to himself a prayer his mother taught him. It was a prayer honouring the blessed Mother-Goddess. It comforted him when he was young and a prayer to the Mother-Goddess when facing adversity was the best way to keep calm.

He finished his prayer just before he got to the centre of the cavern and motioned Sker to stand a way off to his left. "Do you know their word for yield?" asked Leif of Sker.

"*Yenyea,*" replied Sker. "But I doubt master will need it, orc looks to kill you."

"Thank you for your confidence," Leif replied but was certain Sker did not hear him.

Leif's sword, which was known as a *dao* sword, a curved blade sharp on only one side, remained sheathed but had his metal shield ready. Leif was no small or slender elf, having grown up amongst the humans and ate as they did; he could pass for arch-goblin size. He had to hope his makeup and face mask would get him through this undetected.

His opponent was a giant of an orc and truly interbred with an ogre. Standing nearly a foot taller than Leif, the menace taunted Leif all the while with insults and with the one-handed swings of his large mace. Leif could not understand the beast but understood that a direct hit by the mace would break several bones. Even a direct hit to Leif's shield would reverberate throughout Leif's body. To make matters worse, the ogre-orc held the high ground from where the battle was to commence. It was a sloped floor that favoured the orcs, making Leif's opponent another foot taller. The ogre-orc was a well-armoured beast complete with a war-helm to cover his huge head. After many insults and taunts from the onlooking crowd of orcs, none of which Leif understood, the ogre-orc made the first move.

Instinctively Leif backed away when the ogre-orc made a leap towards him. That awful mace came to crash on the rocky surface, missing Leif's feet. Leif drew his *dao* sword quickly, slashing out in the same manoeuvre directly from the sheath to strike upon the forearm of the ogre-orc. Leif would have severely opened the right arm of the beast were it not for the armour along the forearm. The ogre-orc reared back his right arm holding the mace still and countered with a thrust of his shield from his left. Leif met the assault by propelling himself into the shield with his own shoulder leading the way. The two met each other and surprisingly stalemated. Although the ogre-orc was bigger and taller, Leif was no small adversary and used all his leg muscles to counter the bombardment.

Leif spun when he sensed the ogre-orc beginning an overhead swing of the mace. The nimbler Leif did his own quick overhead assault. The *dao* sword struck the large helm but did little damage as Leif had to back away to avoid the mace. The mace did connect with a scrape onto Leif's shield creating a spark, briefly lighting up the cave. The orcs howled with delight but after Leif landed two blows, so too were the arch-goblins rooting for Leif.

"Bloody arch-goblins, I'm not doing this for you lot. I'm doing this to stay alive!" said Leif dodging another blow of that wicked mace.

Leif sent a barrage of minor strikes to the ogre-orc's left and up high. The intent was not to do damage but to turn the beast so Leif might get a chance at taking some higher ground. The strikes also kept the ogre-orc at bay. The beast had to keep his shield up high to protect his head which allowed for few swings of the mace. After several nicks to the helmet the ogre-orc moved around and Leif gained the high ground, which actually made them about equal in height.

The monster sensed the error in giving away his advantage and pressed with a rage. The mace went flying in a series of fluid swings, not for Leif but more for his shield. The angry assault had Leif reeling and on the defensive. The hits were bending the outer edges of the shield and severely denting its front. The ogre-orc knew the pain would eventually take its toll on his opponent's arm, as did Leif. After five serious hits to Leif's shield, he finally began to back well out of the way. Once Leif put some distance between him and the ogre-orc, Leif countered.

Leif now worked the right side of the beast, the mace wielding arm. He started with a back-handed slash from his own left onto the beast's right. He had to turn his body to the left in order to produce any kind of hit, exposing his left. Leif did a series of thrusts upon high to keep the beast from taking a real swing with the mace. The beast attacked with his shield then, shoving it forward in hopes of knocking Leif back and regain momentum.

It worked as Leif went backwards from the blunt force of the shield. The ogre-orc now was able to get an overhead swing again. The beast thought of the kill to come, the thought of the bursting head of his opponent, like so many other opponents before.

Leif though, hoped for this assault. This opponent was not too different from when he battled his own brother Bjorn. Leif and Bjorn sparred often, Leif wielded a sword while Bjorn wielded a mace, both used shields.

Leif studied the beast's swings and arcs and knew what was to come. Leif could only hope his shield would hold up to the assault if it did not go as he planned. Leif saw the swing coming up over the head of his opponent. Leif saw the brief flicker in the monster's eyes, the flicker of absolute assurance; it was a similar look Bjorn had when he finally thought he caught Leif in error.

Leif though was prepared and attacked back, not with his *dao* sword but with his shield. Leif thrust the bottom edge of the shield forward and up high to meet that mace during an overhead assault. As he did, the ogre-orc was not able to get his full force of strength behind the mace and was stopped up high. The ogre-orc's armpit was now exposed. Moments before, Leif carefully brought his *dao* sword low to the side of his sheath just before he attacked with his shield. Leif was in perfect position and angle for a strike with the *dao* sword in a backhand swing. He did so with a diagonal swing upward into the armpit of the ogre-orc and cutting a gash through the unarmoured clothing, tearing into the muscle and flesh of the beast's armpit. Leif's blade cut deep into the flesh.

The beast howled in agony and backed away instinctively. The ogre-orc dropped his shield from his hand and tried to stem the blood flow from his armpit. Leif continued the assault with his *dao* sword pointing and poking the beast evermore in retreat, backing the creature away from its dropped shield.

Leif then charged in with his beat-up shield slamming into the creature. It stumbled on the uneven ground and went flying backwards to the rock floor in a tumble. Leif pounced and stepped onto the creature's mace, pinning it and the ogre-orc's hand to the cave floor. Leif's other boot pushed down onto the ogre-orc's chest, further flattening the ogre-orc. The beast stopped squirming once it felt Leif's *dao* sword next to his throat.

Oh, how the arch-goblins cheered!

Oh, how the orcs were silenced.

Leif motioned for Sker to come over.

"Yenyea?" asked Leif, remembering the word for yield.

"My master does not speak your dialect well and wishes to know if you yield?" asked Sker.

"I yield!" it said and relinquished hold on its mighty mace.

It was over almost as quickly as it started and the treaty was won for the arch-goblins, thanks to the work of an elf.

Leif removed his sword from the ogre-orc's neck and stepped away. After a few foot steps away, Leif told Sker, "Go tell him he fought well and hope they fight along the same side one day." Sker did as asked.

Lorez later asked Leif what he told Sker to tell the ogre-orc. After Leif informed him, Lorez had a perplexed look on his face and asked him why. Leif responded, "I wanted to ensure peace was maintained between you all for as long as possible."

Chapter 23
The Request for a Quest

The march in the caverns, caves and darkness was uneventful enough. Were it not for possessing *night-vision*, the ability to see in the dark, Leif would have been blinded while travelling with his captives. Arch-goblin, lizard-goblin, orcs and elf all possessed *night-vision*.

Many lizard-goblins though did not return with the march. It seems a handful of the creatures were used as compensation to the orcs for Leif winning the mining rights for the arch-goblins. As a reward for Leif, Chieftain Merka let Leif keep Sker.

Sker found himself happy for once. Most of the harassing lizard-goblins were now in the hands of orcs, likely being eaten or resold at Skagsnest. Furthermore, Sker was given a ride upon the shoulders of his new master, Leif.

Once the army returned to Blood-helm, Leif's victory earned him Sker as a translator and teacher of the arch-goblin language. Leif was always chained though but taken on walks, even had debates with Lorez, which both found gratifying. Leif was also forced to act as a labourer. Leif boasted that he could blacksmith, and he could thanks to his father. Leif sometimes was found repairing weapons, horse shoes and mending shields.

"You should have killed him," said Lorez laughing one evening while having Leif work with the old arch-goblin blacksmith repairing shields.

"I told you, I had no desire to do so and I was only asked to champion your cause, death was not mentioned as a condition and I refused to kill my opponent," said Leif chained once again and hammering a dented metal shield.

"Bah! I would have slit his throat and took his mace as a prize. That looked like it could fetch a nice price in the Skagsnest markets," said Lorez eating a partially cooked lamb shank and washed it down with some arch-goblin ale.

Leif looked at the arch-goblin brute, not certain what to make of him sometimes. One moment Lorez seemed civilised, a creature anyone would enjoy a good conversation with. The next, he spoke of taking life as if it was no minor thing.

"I do not enjoy killing, not arch-goblin, orc, human, lizard-goblin or elf..." said Leif but his words dropped off when he mentioned elf and his thoughts went to his encounter with the dark-elf. It was anger, rage, betrayal or something else. Leif could not quite put a finger on it. Lorez saw Leif was mulling over something.

"What say you, Leif? You clearly got some satisfaction out of the arena in Skulls-thorpe, did you not?" Lorez inquired wondering if that might be it. "You dispatched your ashen kin; did you not take any satisfaction in killing him?"

"He is no kin to me," Leif replied abruptly.

"He would have killed you, Leif," Lorez suspected he hit a nerve with Leif. "That dark-elf sacrificed his own people to save his own skin, so I was told. You did right by killing that one," said Lorez, eyeing Leif for a reaction. "And what of the queen's pet, surely you must be proud to have survived that battle?" asked Lorez who thought he might lighten the mood with playful banter about Queen Ooktha and Leif.

"Why am I here?" asked Leif.

"To mend shields," responded Lorez with a chuckle.

"I have been working for weeks in the forges and doing mason work. I thought I was going to help you lot secure your borders from Vorclaw?"

"That's what you wanted, elf, what Chieftain Merka wants is another matter. You're alive, are you not? What more do you want?" said Lorez with a belly laugh pointing a lamb shank in his direction while sitting back on a chair in the forge.

Leif could not argue with that. He thought he should be dead or a vampire. He was treated as fair as he could have hoped, honest work for decent treatment. The door opened suddenly letting in the winter breeze and in came Sker in a hurry. Leif had just then realised the few weeks in captivity had passed. It was late summer when he was captured and was definitely lucky to be alive.

Sker said something in arch-goblin or lizard-goblin to Lorez and the other arch-goblins that Leif did not understand but the dire look on their faces gave Leif concern for his safety.

"What say you, Sker?" asked Leif pretending not to notice the seriousness of all their faces but holding tight to the hammer and other tools nearby. Although Leif was still chained, he was certain he could take out one if not both arch-goblin jailers, and maybe the old blacksmith but Lorez on the other hand might present a large problem. Even if he did escape, the cold mountain air at night may prove fatal.

"Seems you are being summoned," said Lorez with a spine-chilling laugh.

* * * * *

Sker had a hot bath prepared in a separate room in the Blood-helm compound. Several candles were placed around the room. Fresh clothes, or what would pass for clothes as arch-goblins, were set out on a chair. Leif, who hadn't had a full bath in weeks, tested the water, looked around for a suspicious activity. He actually was worried the bath was to make him into soup! It was Sker who convinced him to get in by prodding Leif for his filthy clothes. Once in, Leif quickly relaxed and then scrubbed.

At first, he thought it was the warmth of the water but quickly realised his necklace grew warm as if alerting him.

"I have missed you," came a melodic voice.

"You sent me away," replied Leif. Leif calmed himself and laid back in the water. He recognised Queen Ooktha's sweet voice.

"No," she said walking around the bath to Leif's right, peering into the tub and letting her fingers touch the water. "I was attacked by someone and had to recover."

"What? Who attacked you?" shouted Leif standing up from the tub and reaching for her hand.

"I will tell you later," she replied. Ooktha let her black dress slip off her shapely body, stepped in the warm water and kissed Leif passionately.

"I hear you have done a great service for me and my clans," she teased. "Merka thinks highly of you."

"I care not for him. He killed my men," said Leif.

"Do not be so proud, my soldier. Warriors die all the time when they encounter one another. It is rare they find one as merciful as yourself."

She then kissed Leif and he pulled her into the bath with him.

After an hour of lovemaking, Queen Ooktha opened up about her absence.

"It was an enemy of mine, an evil and jealous revenant named Rom-Seti. 'It' covets my powers and my arch-goblins," said Queen Ooktha.

Both Leif and Queen Ooktha lay in a magical tent that Queen Ooktha brought. The room was five times the size on the inside than the actual size on the outside. "Rom-Seti wants to control my hordes so as to wage war, needlessly upon the world," said Queen Ooktha. She didn't actually lie to Leif, Rom-Seti would gladly take over control of her arch-goblin ranks.

"Is it over? Did you vanquish him? Or should we expect him to return?" asked Leif.

"I was not able to defeat him, but I might know a way to do so," she said bating Leif.

After several moments, Leif asked, "How can I help?"

"I want to send you somewhere with a party of warriors and priests to vanquish this revenant," she said openly. "I will supply all the essential supplies and some magical items to aid you in this quest."

"Does this party know where to find this creature?" asked Leif.

"Not yet, in fact you're the first of the party. One of my allies will provide the map to Rom-Seti's layer, and another ally will provide the rest of the party, although he doesn't know it yet."

"Well, I might know of several sources for your party if interested? But if I do this, will you leave Vorclaw be," replied Leif.

"What are your sources in Vorclaw, my brave military lieutenant?" she asked excitedly on the bed.

"My mentor, Colonel Baltus Blackpool, has the ability to find the finest warriors, I'm sure," said Leif. Queen Ooktha got up from the bed trying to hide her surprise that she knew the man Leif spoke of.

"Why would this man know of great warriors?" she asked trying to hide her smile.

"He is charged with the training of Vorclaw's forces at the Academy of Arms. My father worked alongside him for many years, so I have known the man all my life," Leif replied. "If you let me contact him to explain the terms, I am certain he could get the council to come to terms and establish boundaries for the Blood-helm and Vorclaw. Maybe even go as far as to trade?"

Queen Ooktha was now worried, her mind raced thinking Leif was some kind of informant for Baltus Blackpool. Was he manipulating her this whole time to some end she knew not? No, it couldn't be. Why would Leif reveal he has knowledge of the man if he was a spy?

"What troubles you? Have I not proven myself? My victory helped secure the treaty with the orcs, did I not? Have I not survived the many challenges your arena has bestowed? Have I not been a good lover to you?" he asked coming up behind the vampiress, kissing her neck.

Ooktha turned around and kissed Leif hard. "Tell me more about this man and how I might get a message to him so I can offer a treaty?"

* * * * *

"Anthon explained you wished to meet personally. What vexes you my dear?" asked General Blackpool of Queen Ooktha. The two stood across from one another at their appointed mountain top.

"I have an obstacle that I need you to remove," toyed Queen Ooktha.

"I give you your promised war and spoils, I get my revenge. That was the bargain and nothing more," replied the general.

"You haven't even heard my request yet."

"Your orcs in the north are of no concern of mine."

"It has nothing to do with orcs this time and my source tells me you have the resources to end my problem," she said slyly.

General Blackpool's interest piqued now. "Your source?" he asked.

"Do you recall the skirmish near Fort Adamant? One of your officers survived?"

General Blackpool's interest turned to anger as he presumed it must be Leif Foehammer. Did she make him into a vampire? All the other officers were killed and accounted for, save Leif. So too were the men, save for Master Sergeant Saltclaw who is held in the stockade for assaulting Mr Night. He also knew he had to tread carefully if he was to find out what she was referring. He was so close to his revenge for his wife's death and for Vorclaw's leadership that spurned him, the leadership who he blamed for his wife's death.

"I am listening," he replied if uninterested.

"The poor thing thinks you will broker a deal to create peace in Fort Adamant region in exchange for his return. Is there no honour among your young officers?" she teased the general. The two conspirators' relationship has grown strenuous over the several months now that the war the two have created is upon them. "However," she said before Baltus could get in a word, "I have a proposal. I will return him to you safe and sound, unspoiled even. Only if you allow him to lead a party of your choosing to do a great deed for me?"

Taken aback by this, a quest was not something Baltus figured. "What is this deed and who is the man of which you speak?" he asked.

"Don't insult my intelligence, human," Ooktha responded. "You know the elf of which I speak."

To Baltus that was proof that she was bargaining for Leif's life. If he did get Leif back, what information could Leif provide about the network of the arch-goblins and more importantly, what did Leif know of his scheme with Ooktha?

"He knows none of our plans if that's what you are worried about," she said as if reading his mind. "He does really believe he can broker a treaty between Vorclaw and the arch-goblins near Fort Adamant, poor lamb. Let us indulge him. Oh, and Leif is not a vampire, not unless you do as I ask. Besides, letting Leif lead a quest to faraway lands puts him out of harm's way from the coming war and any secrets you hold will stay with you."

"Tell me all you know about your problem and how I can help?" he said dryly.

* * * * *

"He is alive?" responded Mimdrid unceremoniously in the guise of Captain Nigel Newman. The three met in General Blackpool's estate. "You said he died in the arena?" asked Mimdrid of Anthon Blackpool.

"Seems he is more resilient than I gave him credit for," said Anthon who just returned from Chieftain Merka to confirm it all. "So I made a mistake? I confirmed it as you asked, and he is in good hands shall we say. But I honestly don't care, and I have to make the finishing touches before we begin this war. This should make you happy, brother, does it not?" asked Anthon of Baltus.

"It does but I am amazed how he survived for so long or why he isn't turned into a vampire," stated Baltus.

"No, I meant the finishing touches on the golem, not Magnus' elf-son. And who cares about Leif Foehammer? He likely cannot be trusted; my sources tell me Queen Ooktha and Leif are intimate."

"That partially explains how he could remain alive for so long with the arch-goblins," stated Mimdrid with a chuckle.

"My worry is he may know more than she lets on," said Baltus.

"Or he could know nothing," stated Anthon. "I do know Chieftain Merka doesn't want him around but keeps him alive from fear of his queen. He has even bonded with one of his best warriors."

"Resilient young lad," stated Baltus.

"Or you could send him on the mission she requests and deal with whatever he knows or doesn't know when he returns," said Mimdrid. "By then, the deed will be done. This adventure sounds like it will take several weeks at least and we are ready to commence in a fortnight. This would also give your would-be assassins a chance to practise what they were trained for. Revenants surround themselves with undead and Bjorn is proving to be quite good at destroying them."

153

"They weren't trained to end a revenant though, they were being trained to get into well-marked places secretly and kill a vampire," responded Baltus, not sure of the best course of action.

"Did she not say she had an ally to provide the location and the means to end this creature?" asked Anthon.

"She did say an ally knows where this *Rom-Seti* resides and will provide the means if they can get to the revenant," replied Baltus.

"What do you mean if they can get to him?" asked Mimdrid.

"They will have to face some obstacles along the way, Rom-Seti has minions of his own," replied Baltus.

"Perfect then, the means are provided and if your assassins are any bit as resilient as Leif, this should be within their abilities," stated Anthon, thinking he solved the puzzle for his brother and was preparing to leave.

"Who are the assassins you sent to be trained?" asked Mimdrid, knowing the answer and knowing Anthon did not. Mimdrid liked to see the reactions of these humans when surprised.

"Oh, Bjorn Foehammer and my son Dru to name two," said Baltus. That halted Anthon in his tracks.

"What!" asked Anthon. "You intend to send Dru and Bjorn against her?"

Mimdrid silently laughed to himself. He hated the Foehammers, especially Magnus Foehammer, Bjorn and Dru's father. Mimdrid thought it would be sweet irony if the Foehammer sons became vampires.

"But I don't see any other way if I am to maintain her trust in this endeavour," said Baltus.

"And it might draw suspicions away from our other dealings with the arch-goblins if we send the lot at her behest," piped in Mimdrid.

"I will see what other protection I can afford them," said Anthon dryly. "However, if battling a revenant, they will need powerful magic on their side. I may have to send Erik with them in fact and the assassin Damon who is training your son. Damon is dangerous mind you and costly. He will not take to this assignment without great payment."

"Will Bjorn, Leif, Dru, Erik and Damon be enough to defeat such a foe?" asked Baltus.

"With magical and divine items to aid them, perhaps," replied Anthon.

"Good! Then see to it they all survive. And there is one more thing, she will be sending an arch-goblin warrior to ensure we keep to the task," said Baltus.

"Where is the Rom-Seti's stronghold?" asked Mimdrid.

"Oh, in the mountains just south of the Land of the Great Glaciers," said General Blackpool stoically.

"Where exactly, that does not narrow anything down?" asked Mimdrid.

"Well up and over the Spine-of-Vana, to the north," said Anthon.

"And further north still," finished Baltus.

"Why is it that someone so far can affect her so?" asked Mimdrid.

"Magic," replied Anthon. "It reaches across stretches of land or even plains of existence."

"So you can transport the lot to this place?" asked Baltus.

"Potentially, but I will need to know precisely where to open a *mage's gate* else the spell will not work. Also, the revenant will likely have magical warnings to such a magical intrusion. Revenants are very weary of outsiders and although these types of undead are rare, they are always powerful. So best if I transport them some place close. I just need to know where on a map, scry that area and then cast the spell."

Chapter 24

Fort Adamant

Bjorn's new orders were unlike any he ever received, save for the orders that brought him to the island.". Bjorn wondered if orders like these were why he had such unique training and the new normal for Dru and himself.

The orders instructed, *"Captain Bjorn Foehammer and Captain Dru Blackpool, proceed directly to Fort Adamant this day! Damon Crag and the wizard Erik are to accompany you and they should check with their superiors if in doubt. Upon arrival at Fort Adamant, Major Goldwater will provide a new set of instructions. Wear no rank and carry no items that could affiliate you with Vorclaw. Regards, General B. Blackpool."*

Bjorn didn't care much for sea-going voyages and was the happiest of the party to make landfall just east of Vorclaw's capital city of Sedgedunum. Horses were waiting with a military escort at the pier. Within a day of hard riding, the party arrived late evening at Fort Adamant. The swiftness was in thanks to the prepositioning of fresh horses at the midway point for a change out. The party of four handed over their exhausted horses and made their way directly to the Tor, the Fort Adamant headquarters. The whole journey took about 5 days. Major Goldwater greeted the foursome and brought them into one of the conference rooms of the Tor where Mr Night and Anthon awaited them all.

"Major Goldwater, it's good to see you again, sir," stated Dru. "Uncle Anthon, I see you're still dabbling in the affairs of the nation. For my father no doubt?" badgered Dru of his uncle.

"Oh, so this is your uncle you spoke of?" asked Bjorn. "Your nephew says you have been a great asset to our military and nation."

A concerned look grew over Anthon's face that Bjorn quickly diffused the situation when he stated, "However, what you do for the good of our realm I know not, as Captain Blackpool has never divulged what you do," stated Bjorn with a smile and a wink. "So any state secrets are safe with you and him," said the large red-haired man, smiling.

"Is that the famous Rose-Mace I have heard about," asked Mr Night, the skinny man seated in the back-left corner behind Anthon.

"I am afraid I never had the pleasure, sir," asked Bjorn of the inquisitive man.

"I have heard that your mace was created by your family and is very powerful, especially against the undead."

"This is Mr Night," stated Major Goldwater. "He is a former military commander in Vorclaw who now acts as a consultant and expert in these parts of the frontier lands."

"At your service Captain Foehammer," nodded Mr Night.

"Let us continue on to the matter at hand. Time may be of the essence," said Major Goldwater.

"What brings us here?" asked Damon Crag dryly and honestly did not want to be on this mission.

"You must be the famous Damon Crag," said Mr Night. "I have heard your skills in getting into places thought impenetrable are legendary."

"You already know more about both the priest and me. And I do not like that so get to the point that brings me here," said Damon.

"Enough," said Anthon. "You are all assigned a mission to bring home Lieutenant Leif Foehammer from his captures."

"He is alive!" said Bjorn and Dru simultaneously.

"Yes, but it is complicated," said Anthon.

* * * * *

Bjorn made his way through Fort Adamant looking for his friends in the White Eagles. Dru and the rest of the party spent the night preparing themselves for tomorrows journey. Bjorn eventually met with Captain Ty who explained what happened to Leif's company and their mission. He also learned about Master Sergeant Saltclaw's imprisonment for striking Mr Night.

The pair made their way to the fort's reformatory and demanded to see the master sergeant. After much consternation with the jailor, the two were granted access.

"We were ambushed," stated Master Sergeant Saltclaw. "Your brother thought something wasn't right. He tried to tell us but none of us could put a finger on what he was referring to. He is very insightful, that one."

"What do you mean?" asked Bjorn.

"It was the trees! They weren't really trees, they were arch-goblins I tell ya, but no one believes me!" he responded. The two officers looked at the master sergeant sceptically. "I am not mad! There was an explosion killing the commander. Then the trees were suddenly arch-goblins! Don't you see they have a mage, a powerful one that can cast spells that explode and make arch-goblins appear as trees!" said the man in a fit state.

"Calm down, master sergeant," said Bjorn.

Bjorn cast a divine spell that allows a priest to discern the truthfulness in a conversation. As the master sergeant was recanting his story, Bjorn could sense the truth in the tale.

"I believe you," responded Bjorn. "Did you see what happened to Leif?"

"No, I was knocked out by then. What I did see was a great young warrior he became or was. He controlled the scene as best he could, ordering archers and laying out arch-goblins with both his sword and shield. He killed several for sure. He died a hero."

"He is not dead," said Bjorn.

"What!" questioned Master Sergeant Saltclaw.

"In fact, we're going to barter for his life it seems," said Bjorn.

"What?" interrupted Captain Ty.

"It's complicated but I can say no more about my mission. Rest assured I intend to bring my brother home. In the meantime, keep my words between us for now. Also, I will petition for your release, good sir," trying to end the conversation. Bjorn then said a prayer for Master Sergeant Saltclaw, blessing the warrior and giving him strength to his soul for surviving such an ordeal.

Afterwards the two officers spoke some more on the walk back to the Tor.

"We all thought he was mad and Major Goldwater was not willing to release the man after striking Mr Night," stated Captain Ty.

"And no one thought to bring the clergy to discern the truth? Who is that man anyway?" asked Bjorn.

"We don't really know honestly, only Major Goldwater trusts him," responded Captain Ty. "The man appears sporadically, occasionally accompanying a wizard known as Anthon or something."

Bjorn did not let Captain Ty know he recently learned that the wizard Anthon was in fact Dru Blackpool's mysterious uncle.

"It's rumours mostly but Mr Night seems to be some form of expert in the area with the arch-goblins in the north. Best guess he is a ranger in these parts, but he looks too scrawny a man to be one," speculated Captain Ty.

"Looks can be deceiving," responded Bjorn.

"I honestly don't know more than that and I have been occupied with ensuring the immediate area remains safe while Fort Adamant's construction continues," said Captain Ty.

"From one captain to another, keep my mission secret for now, my friend, or at least until I return with my brother," asked Bjorn.

"Of course, my friend," responded Captain Ty.

"I will see if Dru Blackpool has influence enough to persuade Major Goldwater to release Master Sergeant Saltclaw, even reassign him, perhaps to you," stated Bjorn. "He has been through a lot and doesn't deserve imprisonment, especially since he is telling the truth about the ambush."

"I agree and I have petitioned for his release before. Hopefully you will have better success, but I doubt he will be reassigned, more released from the army instead after striking Mr Night."

"Anything is better than rotting in prison," said Bjorn. "If the man is released, give him some coin please," asked Bjorn digging into his pockets for some silver. "Tell him I said to see my father and mother in Sedge Fen and to tell them Leif's story. My father served with Saltclaw and will help him," responded Bjorn.

"I will help Saltclaw as best I can and pass on your instructions to him Bjorn. Find your brother, my friend, and let me know if I can be of any other service to you while you are here or away. He is a hero and needs to come home."

"The general is agreeing to this to reassure our commitment to the plan with Queen Ooktha," stated Major Goldwater.

"More importantly, if we do not agree to this, Queen Ooktha will pull her support," stated Mr. Night to the rest of the new party that arrived with Bjorn. Anthon elaborated on the Major's point. "If Queen Ooktha was to have a change of heart, the general would still owe gold and positions of influence to those that have invested in the aftermath we are about to create. Not helping her with her request would be dangerous to us all," put in Anthon, referring to his counterparts in The Shadow Company.

"So we're all caught in our own web," responded Damon.

"His web, not mine," stated Dru Blackpool. "I never agreed to Father's plans but felt compelled to follow the man's direction, nothing more. But I truly do this to get back Leif."

The young wizard in the party Erik, who was the apprentice of Anthon, moved the conversation along since he did not care about any of the reasoning. "Master," he said addressing his mentor Anthon properly, "what tools have we to defeat this Revenant Rom-Seti?"

"To the point, Erik," responded Anthon who then moved to place a small decorative wooden box on the table. No one could see inside the small chest, but everyone understood the small box was magical as Anthon pulled several objects that could not possibly fit inside it.

On the table he placed four small wands or at least they appeared to be wands, five rings, three large bottles, three small vials and five copper bracelets.

"The wands are from the clerics of Matronae. They are called Lavender wands. They're blessed items. Shake them and the lavender inside will repel weaker forms of undead while confusing others. They will do little if noting against a Revenant The rings possess the power to instantly turn spells back against their casters. Against a Revenant, they would be good for two or three spells at best. The bottles are vials that would cure the most serious of wounds. The vials also cure diseases that may be associated with the undead. The bracelets will reduce the impact of spells upon your body."

"That's it?" asked Damon Crag. "A bunch of liquids, some flower-power to ward off the undead and some rings to redirect spells," he said.

"Relax, Damon," stated Erik. "You just keep the Revenant minions at bay while Bjorn and I dispatch this Rom-Seti."

"I will be stunned if we all survive this," Damon replied with an eye roll, arms folded over his chest.

"What about Leif?" inquired Dru. "How much does he know about our overarching plans and subplots we have in play?"

"He only knows that we must attempt this quest in order to secure his release," said Anthon. "He will also have one arch-goblin escorting him as well. As a witness likely to ensure we complete the mission."

"You mean us, Lord Anthon. You're not going," said Damon sarcastically.

Normally Anthon would dispatch someone speaking to him in such a manner; however, Damon Crag was an experienced assassin and an incredibly valuable asset to his superiors. If ever there was a non-magic-user able to speak to Anthon with impertinence, it was Damon Crag.

"True but I am placing you on the door step," said Anthon. "I have other tasks as you know, and I trust you will not let this mission fail. Now may we continue?"

Damon nodded in response.

"I will transport all of you to a location known only as Sanctuary. It's a camp of sorts in the mountains about three days' journey from Rom-Seti's layer. Or at least so I am told. There you will receive the map from the mistress of Sanctuary."

"Sanctuary?" asked Damon. "What is this place? Is it some resort town you are sending us? And who is this mistress?"

"The mistress is a mystery I must admit. Even Queen Ooktha isn't certain but she is rumoured to be a ranger or priestess or a mage or maybe all three but she befriends all and detests violence in her Sanctuary," stated Anthon.

"So we don't know what she is then," said Dru.

"This Sanctuary is just what the name implies. It is a patch of land in the mountains that welcomes all. The mistress of Sanctuary does not discriminate among the races and welcomes all into her reservation. Therefore, you may end up sleeping next to a group of orcs or outlaws. However, Queen Ooktha assures that you will all be accepted at the camp."

"I will gut the orc if I find one sleeping next to me," stated Damon.

"No, Damon, you will not," stated Anthon who was not afraid to be direct with the deadly assassin. "The mistress has one rule, do no spill blood at Sanctuary," finished Anthon. Damon was not amused by the directness of the wizard and eyed the mage dangerously. Damon was about to retort but Dru intervened with his own question.

"Is Leif there waiting?" asked Dru trying to end the standoff.

"No. We will all meet with him tomorrow in the mountains and I will transport you all to Sanctuary," replied Anthon. "I am told that Leif knows the mission and is to meet with the Mistress of Sanctuary for the directions. I also know he will be given a device to aid us in this endeavour but I know not what that is."

* * * * *

Walking around him like a prized trophy, Queen Ooktha marvelled at the handiwork her arch-goblin armorers produced. Leif stood in the centre of the Blood-helm throne room being dressed in that armour. It was black with brass trim that simulated the appearance of gold. Queen Ooktha placed magical enhancements upon Leif's armour to better the odds of success in the quest.

Neither Leif nor Queen Ooktha cared that any arch-goblin knew of their love affair. Lorez was present and donned similar armour but lacked Queen Ooktha's enchantments. Lorez presumed he was expendable anyway but also his orders were to ensure Leif was to enter Rom-Seti's layer and not to proceed in with Leif. Queen Ooktha did not want ties back to her for this assault but need to ensure that Leif's cohorts were actually going to go through with the plan.

It did not bother Lorez when his queen kissed Leif passionately in between spells. Lorez looked on with amusement as it was not the arch-goblin way to be passionate. Queen Ooktha's relationship did, however, cause concern for Lorez's chieftain, also present in the room.

Merka was restless of late. If Leif did not survive this dangerous mission, Merka could very well lose his head with her anger. He already intended to use his secret pact with the Vorclaw warlord, the one Queen Ooktha knew nothing about, to serve his own aspirations and to severe some direct ties to her capitol. Now that he was backed by those Vorclaw warlords Merka hoped that the information he provided General Blackpool by way of Mimdrid about Queen Ooktha's own plan to double cross them, would assure his own success and never lose his head. If his own betrayal wasn't enough stress, Merka now had to worry about Leif's success.

Sker the lizard-goblin entered the room. "The horses are ready, Master Leif." The lizard-goblin lowered his head in respect of the arch-goblin queen.

"Thank you, my friend," replied Leif. "Are you ready for this adventure?" asked Leif excitedly.

"I go where master Leif goes," replied Sker and the lizard-goblin headed off.

After Sker scurried away, Queen Ooktha asked in disgust, "Why do you keep company with that little thing?"

"I value his company," he responded. "He is quite helpful too. Sker has taught me some of the arch-goblin, orc and lizard-goblin tongue." Languages were not the only talents the runty lizard-goblin possessed. Sker had to learn other skills in order to remain alive.

"As you wish," she responded. "As long as he is useful to you."

"He is," replied Leif with a wink and a smile. Queen Ooktha then dismissed the remaining arch-goblins for a more private conversation.

"Are you excited to reunite with your brother?" asked Ooktha.

"That's an odd question? Of course I am," replied Leif. "Why do you ask?"

"No reason," she replied.

The observant Leif pressed her. "Are you concerned about something? I remind you I was the one who requested him and warned you about him being a priest. But his skills will be needed on this journey."

"It is difficult to let you go," said Queen Ooktha. "I worry you will not come back to me after this business is finished."

"What!" exclaimed Leif. "My queen," Leif began as he often did in addressing her, "I told you I will come back for you, did I not?" Leif then pulled her in tight against him with his arms. "When I come back, I want us to run away together from all of this. Let us journey the world together."

Ooktha looked up at Leif with sad but loving eyes. She wanted to go away with Leif in reality. But without the arch-goblins to support her need of fresh blood, she knew she would become a monster. A hungry beast she could not control and might even devour Leif. So she kissed him and whispered, "Just come back to me."

Leif winked back at her. "Of course I will," he whispered back.

"I have one more gift to give you to make your mission successful," said Queen Ooktha. "Your armour will defend against many of his magical attacks, but I also have for you a Soul Sucker." She produced a small green object. It was a small piece of jade cut into the form of a miniature tower. Similar to one might see on a chess board. It fit easily in Leif hand.

"What does it exactly?" he asked.

"Once you weaken Rom-Seti, he will likely turn and flee. When the revenant is in a weakened state, say the command word in his presence and it will pull his soul into this small Jade Tower. Then bring it to me. Remember you all must weaken him first else the Soul Sucker may not be strong enough to restrain him."

"Sounds easy enough," said Leif with a sarcastic grin. "How do I activate it?"

Several moments passed before she replied. "Lorez has the command word," she replied ominously. "Ask him for it after you leave the gates," she replied.

"As you wish," replied Leif seemingly unaware of her concern he might use it upon her. "Are you spending the evening with me before I leave in the morning?" asked Leif.

"How dare you even think you would have to ask!"

* * * * *

Bjorn made his way back to the base of the Tor after praying at a nearby shrine to the Mother-Goddess. Bjorn often prayed for guidance but was worried he was more motivated by revenge over what happened to his brother than for the grace of Matronae. However, now that Leif was alive and about to be returned, his prayers have been answered and felt owed the deity his gratitude. Bjorn made his way around the blocks of stone for the wall construction and the tents of sleeping soldiers. He was met by Mr Night.

"Well met young Foehammer," greeted Mr Night.

"Mr Night," acknowledged Bjorn with a nod. Bjorn tried to push past the slender man, but he was surprisingly strong for someone so small in comparison to Bjorn. "Is there something I can do for you, Mr Night?"

"I wanted to ask how your father was. I trained under him you know. A long time ago it was and so I doubt he would even recognise me or remember," lied Mr Night who never trained under Bjorn's father.

"He is well," replied Bjorn.

"That's good, he was a great warrior. So forgive my curiosity, why did you become a man of Matronae instead of a warrior like your father?"

"I am a warrior!" stated Bjorn. "Just like my father and a follower of the Mother-Goddess, like my mother. I emulate them both in my own way," he responded.

"Well put, young Foehammer," he said but still blocking the door.

"What do you want?" said Bjorn irritated by the man. Bjorn towered over Mr Night by at least a foot.

"I just wanted to know how your father was doing," said Mr Night. His real motivation was to find out what Master Sergeant Saltclaw revealed. "And while we are on the subject, Master Sergeant Saltclaw served under him as well, did he not? Did you see him over in the reformatory? He hit me good, that one."

"The master sergeant did serve under my father, yes. Why did he hit you?" asked Bjorn suddenly.

"The man blames me for the loss of Gold Company," said Mr Night. "It was no one's fault really. It was an ambush and superior numbers that did in the company. Nothing more," he said matter-of-factly.

"And what of the wizard?" asked Bjorn.

"Wizard? Ah! So you did talk to the master sergeant then. He is quite mad you know," said Mr Night.

"Perhaps but I doubt the arch-goblins could lull a company into an ambush so complete," responded Bjorn. "But once I talk with Leif tomorrow, I will know the truth," stated Bjorn.

"I hope so, young Foehammer. However, a word of caution, the young Lieutenant Foehammer may be compromised by the vampire. Those creatures have ways to manipulate the living. I hope for his sake he is still one of us and not one of her disciples." And with that, the man walked away. A seed of doubt about the mental health of Leif was planted.

* * * * *

"Do you think he will be there tomorrow?" asked Bjorn lying in the bunk next to Dru.

"I hope so," stated Dru who was thinking the same thing.

"Do you think he will be Leif or something else?" asked Bjorn.

"He won't be the same. After being one of the only two survivors of the ambush and been a prisoner all this time, I am not certain in what state to expect our Leif," replied Dru.

"If he is *vampeer*, I will wage a holy war against the arch-goblins. And Queen Ooktha will feel my wrath," stated Bjorn.

"Well, let's hope for everyone's sake she did not," said Dru.

"Mr Night stopped me this evening, asking after my father. Claims he knows him." Dru, slowly dozing off, didn't respond. "During the brief meeting, he told me to be concerned about Leif becoming a servant of Queen Ooktha."

"Come on, this is Leif!" said Dru. "He has more morals than both of us," said Dru trying to comfort Bjorn's concerns.

"Yes, but vampires have the power to manipulate the mind."

"If I could sum up Leif in one word, it is incorruptible. Sure, vampires have that ability but if anyone could withstand such a power, it is Leif. Now, let us get some sleep, my brother. We'll need our wits tomorrow to discern the particulars of this operation," said Dru.

* * * * *

It was an early autumn morning but the sun still felt warm in the early hours. Leif, Lorez and Sker stood in the open field up in the highlands. A small contingent of arch-goblins were just along the tree line watching the meeting that was about to unfold between the arch-goblins and the Vorclaweans. That small contingent of arch-goblins was there by design. Watching an agreement unfold between forces without incident would show trust between brokering parties but in case the agreement did not hold, the small contingent of arch-goblins would run in and kill anyone that was not an arch-goblin.

"Do you really think this plan of Queen Ooktha's is going to work?" asked Lorez. "What's to stop them from cutting my throat and having the little one for dinner once we're gone from here?" he snorted.

"I will prevent such an action, I give you my word," said Leif.

Lorez did not respond but merely stared at the approaching party from Vorclaw.

"Master Leif, not let them eat me?" asked Sker.

"Of course not, my friend," replied Leif who reached down to pat the creature on the head. Sker had revealed unknown talents to Leif and wanted the lizard-goblin by his side, especially for this mission. Leif had a plan for Sker in this endeavour. Sker himself was a scribe of sorts to his kin being runty. Therefore, Sker developed a basic understanding of several languages and was familiar with the gods of Vana. Leif sometimes wondered if Sker only stayed with him to remain safe. That was fine of course with Leif but hoped it was something more altruistic.

"Lorez...Sker, let me do the talking," stated Leif. "My brother can be, well, difficult."

"Fine by me," replied Lorez. "Something tells me this is not going to go well anyways, at least in the beginning."

"It will be fine, my friend," stated Leif. Leif had a momentary pause as he called Lorez his friend. He turned briefly to see Lorez staring back at him, smiling or what constituted as a smile for an arch-goblin.

"As you wish, large elf," said Lorez. "Look, here they are."

Chapter 25

Reunion

"You are a sight for sore eyes, my brothers!" shouted Leif smiling with open arms as the Vorclaw party approached up the hillock on foot.

"Aye, brother, as are you," replied Bjorn dryly.

Dru, however, smiled warmly back at Leif and tried to pass Bjorn but the ginger-haired clergyman would not let him. A confused look came of Leif's face when he saw the movement by Bjorn.

Bjorn held out his Rose-Mace instead which began to glow in a soft pink hue. Bjorn then held the mace upright and shouted, "Be gone unclean, by the graces of Matronae I command thee!"

Moments passed but nothing happened. Damon Crag let out a mocking laugh but cut it short noticing Bjorn's eyes locked. Everyone froze in place, even Anthon.

"Be at ease, my friend," began Dru. "Brother Bjorn is just making sure you're not a vampire or anything else," said Dru smiling. Still moments passed without a response from Leif nor a move by Bjorn. Dru thought the matter settled and again attempted to pass but Bjorn again stopped him.

"How do I know it is you?" demanded Bjorn.

"Ask me a question, any question that only you and I would know the answer to?" replied Leif who wore a serious face.

Bjorn approached with his mace ready to strike and removed his shield from his back, preparing for an attack. Leif did the same, pulling forth his *dao* sword and readying his shield.

"On the night I pulled this weapon from the ground, who was there?" asked Bjorn who then struck just as Leif was about to answer. The assault struck hard against Leif's shield, but the enchantments absorbed the blow of the Rose-Mace.

"It was Father, Mother, you and I," shouted Leif backing away. The elf then swiped back out with a back hand of his *dao* sword that clanged against Bjorn's shield.

"What happened when I pulled forth the mace from the rocks?" demanded Bjorn with an overhead assault, landing squarely on the shield. The blow actually got through the enchantments and into the bones of Leif knocking him backwards and off balance.

"You didn't pull it from the rocks, you pulled it from the ground, you large lump of coal," replied Leif. "And when you did, a pink enchantment rose with

165

the mace from the garden! Are you satisfied, you arse? It is me!" shouted Leif who threw down his sword and shield.

Bjorn threw down his weapons as well and took a swing at Leif, narrowly missing his jaw.

"I had to be sure, we were told you were dead," he said to Leif.

"Well, I am not," replied Leif with a quick jab to Bjorn's chin. "Although I should be," he went on. "I should have died with my men but was taken prisoner because I was the last man standing and was to be a sacrifice. But I survived that too."

"How?" asked Bjorn.

"By using my mind, my wits and common sense," replied Leif, a phrase that his father often said to use during times of stress.

"It is you," stated Bjorn.

"Of course it is him, you big oaf," said Dru. "Look at him, listen to him." Dru then came past Bjorn and put his hands on Leif's shoulder. He looked Leif squarely in the eyes and said, "We thought we lost you, brother." He then pulled him in close to hug Leif and let out a huge shout of happiness.

Bjorn then moved in to embrace the two friends. "It is you, isn't it?"

"How is your chin, you arse?" asked Leif and Bjorn bear-hugged the two of the brothers together. "I thought we lost you," he said with his eyes welling. Then Bjorn got a look at the arch-goblin on horseback.

"And you!" Bjorn began after breaking the hug pointing at Lorez with his large mace. "Don't think I owe you any gratitude or compassion on this mission."

"Bjorn, stop! He is with me," said Leif.

"I will kill you if you lead us astray. Do you even understand me, creature?" admonished Bjorn, now walking towards Lorez.

Leif moved to get between Bjorn and Lorez. "He saved me, Bjorn! You have him to thank for my life," said Leif.

Bjorn did not break eye contact with Lorez. The arch-goblin knew this might happen and resisted any retaliation.

Dru came again between mighty Bjorn but now next to Leif holding him at bay. "Let's just do this mission and get on with our lives my brother."

"I expect you to explain everything to me, Leif," said Bjorn, trying to calm down.

Damon Crag found this opportunity to interrupt. "Yes, let's just do this mission and get on with our lives. Anthon, if you please."

The wizard moved forward and took over the meeting. "We all know why we're here. General Blackpool has agreed to this unethical union in order to ensure Leif's release and keep the peace in the region. Therefore, I will transport you all to a place known only as Sanctuary. It is guarded by a witch of sorts with great allies at her disposal, so I am told. Her home is in the mountains far to the north from here. She will provide you the location to Rom-Seti's location. Her only rule, I'm told, is violence, strictly forbidden on her land. Is this understood?"

Leif nodded as did Lorez but no one else.

"The arch-goblin is going to ensure you all carry out your duties," said Anthon.

"Why don't you just transport us instead to Sedgedunum?" asked Bjorn.

"Otherwise we will have war," stated Lorez.

"Oh you do speak," said Bjorn with venom. "And what of this lizard-goblin, why is it, here?"

"You will have to ask your brother," responded Lorez.

"Sker has been my companion during my incarceration," stated Leif.

"Iza go where master Leif goes," stated the lizard-goblin.

Damon Crag leaned over to Dru and quietly conveyed, "The Foehammers are odd indeed."

"So the witch is expecting us then?" asked Dru getting away from his teacher.

"She is," replied Anthon. "Any questions?"

"How do we get back?"

Erik the junior wizard to Anthon had the answer. "Once the mission is complete and we are to return to Sanctuary, I will contact Lord Anthon to open a gate for us all to pass."

No more questions came forth.

"I will open a *mage's gate* just outside Sanctuary for you all to walk through. No horses, Mr Night and I will take them back, you will not need them," stated Anthon.

Anthon then put his thumbs and index fingers together to form a triangle. He whispered several words, stuck his hands forward, index finger tips pointing the way. A green dot developed at the point of his fingertips. He then split his index fingers and two green dots now existed at both fingers. He then traced the outline of a doorway with his green fingertips, green light trailed as he traced in the air. Once the outline completed the green light filled in and then spilt down the middle like a door opening to another place. A cold breeze poured through that door way.

Bjorn, Leif, Dru, Sker, Lorez, Erik and Damon walked through the doorway.

* * * * *

They came to a gentle slope surrounded by large pines and shrubs. A path existed just off to their left.

"It is colder here," said Lorez.

"Wow you can state the obvious?" said Bjorn.

"Follow the path up," said Lorez and led them up the trail.

"How do you know?" asked Erik.

"I can smell smoke?" Lorenz responded.

"From camp fire," said Sker.

They came to where the path split off into the mountains and the other to a large old quarry cut into the shape of a crescent. In the centre of the quarry was the source of the smoke, a long house constructed of pine and mud.

"A curious place?" said Bjorn. "Look around, there are shrines all around the quarry," noticed Bjorn. "There is a shrine to Ogma over there. And to Matronae up there," said Bjorn.

"And that one?" asked Damon. "The one etched in a rock?"

"I think that one is Terra, for the dwarves," said Dru referring to the one with the wave lines that formed a misshapen triangle.

"No it is Magmum, the fire deity for the orckin," corrected Lorez. "That is a symbol for fire, Magmum's symbol," explained Lorez.

"Here is one with a fish on it?" said Leif.

"It is for the merfolk," said Lorez.

"It is Sanctuary, all gods are welcomed it seems," said Lorez who walked onward to the long house.

It was not lost on the party that several small windows and a door also lay with in the rock wall of the quarry.

"No doubt the home to our host," said Leif.

Lorez went up to the longhouse and opened up the large double doors. The warmth of a central hearth washed over them. Lorez entered first, walking in slowly, cautiously but with no weapon in his hand. He felt eyes upon him. As his arch-goblin eyes adjusted to the light, he confirmed several races throughout the hall. In particular, a pack of lycaons, rare creatures indeed. They claimed a section halfway down the longhouse to his right. The lycoans were humanoid creatures with jackal-like heads whose tall pointy ears extended above their heads. Their skin was dark with short dark hair that covered their shoulders up to those tall ears.

A few black and green skinned creatures also eyeing him on the left side. They were orcs. He then realised they weren't just eyeing him but the party he led into longhouse.

There was also a small figure he could barely make out at the far end covered in what looked like a large pile of furs.

"We'll rest here until our liaison arrives," said Lorez pointing to his left. The orcs looked less threatening with only three of them, as opposed to six lycaons to the right. The orcs gave angry glares but when the large ginger haired priest walked over towards them and met their glares; the orcs went back to cooking their mutton in the hearth.

Inside, Dru prepared the meals, Damon sharpened his knives and Erik read though his spell book. Lorez and Sker, however, watched the orcs and lycaons.

"What manner of arch-goblin aligns with humans?" asked one of the lycaons in the arch-goblin tongue, or as best a lycaon could speak the language.

"You prisoner, eh?" asked another.

Lorez did not answer, just folded his arms and looked away. He again tried to make out the figure at the end in the furs. He thought maybe to ask Sker but remembered lizard-goblins' eyesight was not very good.

"Humans cut out your tongue?" asked the first lycaon. "I never liked arch-goblins anyways, it is probably for best, they keep you safe eh," he said with a hyena-like laugh that caught the attention of the entire room, especially when the other lycaons laughed too.

"Do we have a problem?" asked Damon of the arch-goblin.

* * * * *

Bjorn and Leif decided to have a walk around the compound while the party unpacked their gear and settled in.

The brothers, Bjorn and Leif, stopped before the small shrine to Matronae. "What happened to you?" asked Bjorn of Leif. "Where have you been all this time?"

Leif told him everything he thought was relevant. He told Bjorn about the odd meeting between Major Titus, Major Goldwater and Mr Night then he spoke of the ambush and the demise of Gold Company. Leif then explained how Lorez saved him from being repeatedly submitted to the arena and how he was the champion for the arch-goblins at the orc and arch-goblin standoff; that was how he his new companion, the lizard-goblin Sker came to meet.

Leif tried to explain his relationship with Queen Ooktha and what she was – an elven-vampire – and was merely trying to make the most of her unfortunate situation.

Leif, however, also suspected something sinister was afoot regarding the arch-goblins; Leif recalled hearing Anthon's name spoke by the arch-goblins before he had met the man.

Bjorn then inquired about the mysterious Mr Night but Leif did not know what to make of the man other than he was bad at being the expert in the parts around the Tor.

Lastly, Leif hoped that this mission would result in an end to arch-goblin hostilities in Vorclaw and that the loss of Gold Company would not be in vain.

It was a sad, almost unbelievable tale to Bjorn. The story seducing or being seduced by an elven vampire made Bjorn uneasy. Bjorn after all was a cleric of Matronae and the undead were not usually friends of goodly deities.

"But not a night goes by when I don't think about that ambush," finalised Leif. "If only I was more convincing when I suspected it as such. But they are dead."

"Not all, Master Sergeant Saltclaw survived," said Bjorn.

"He did!" asked Leif with surprise. "I thought he fell. How does he fare?"

"Not well actually," started Bjorn. "I found him in the Fort Adamant brig for punching Mr Night, in the face," said Bjorn with a smile.

Leif had a look of surprise. But that gave way to a slight laugh at the thought. "We have to get him out of the brig when we return."

"Seems he blames Mr Night for the ambush but he also shares your suspicions over that man, as do I. After I met with Saltclaw, Mr Night was waiting for me at the Tor to find out what Saltclaw said to me."

"The master sergeant is not to remain there, is he? He is not to be hung?" asked Leif with concern.

"No, Dru and I would not allow it. Dru convinced Major Goldwater to release him. Captain Ty is there still and will ensure he reaches Father to tell him you're alive and the story of what happened that day. Major Ickingham has command of the White Eagles."

It was a lot to take in between the two of them and Leif wanted to change the subject to Bjorn and where his travels had led him. Bjorn began to speak of the training General Blackpool was putting both him and Dru through on the island but halted as a commotion emanated from the long house. Then saw Sker running out the doorway to look for them. The creature waved for them both to come down to the longhouse and both started running towards it.

* * * * *

"Let's step outside dog-face so I can carve out your eyes and feed them to your friends," said Damon Crag to the lycaon who was teasing Lorez.

Lorez interjected, "No, ignore them."

"Oh I see now," said the lycaon, "the arch-goblin is your protector little human cub," said the lycaon in response.

"No blood spilling, no violence in Sanctuary," said Lorez to Damon. "These are the rules, ignore those filth!"

"Oh the human cub wants to fight," said the lycaon with a toothy grin. The lycaon picked up his spiked mace and his five lycaon companions picked up their weapons.

Both Damon Crag and Dru Blackpool drew their short swords they wore across their backs. Erik drew out a wand. Sker ran outside the long house. Lorez held out his hands unarmed to try and calm everyone but the place erupted into a verbal shouting match. It was then that Lorez noticed the three orcs remained in their corner, staring over at the dark figure he could not make out at the far end covered in a like a large pile of furs. The furs began to move.

The orcs kept their weapons sheathed and nervously looking back at the end of the longhouse at the pile of furs now moving.

The pile of furs began to take on a shape and Lorez could kick himself for not noticing the great grizzly at the end of the room earlier that emerged from those furs. In his own defence there were other furs and skins that could be mistaken for blankets, but the grizzly was the only fur moving. It let out a large long growl. In doing so, spittle sprayed from its mouth. The beast reared up on its hind quarters, taller than the lycaons it reached height of nearly double the height of Lorez.

Leif and Bjorn entered the room then and saw everyone was frozen, not certain what to do next.

"Oh, look a bear," said Leif.

"Everyone calm down and put away your weapons slowly," said Bjorn.

"You know the rules of Sanctuary," came a young woman's voice from behind the bear. "No violence!"

A small grey-skinned girl with black hair stepped out from behind the bear. The girl appeared to be in her mid-teens but held a silver bow in her hand and a quiver filled with arrows on her back. She was dressed in green camouflage of a sort with grey cloak.

The orcs to her right bowed and sat back down. The lycaons backed off as well save for the one who taunted Lorez. It took his companion lycaons to reel him back to the group for the young girl and her enormous grizzly.

Dru who already sheathed his swords motioned for Damon to do the same and did so but never took his eyes off the lycaon.

"Forgive me, forgive us all, mistress of the Sanctuary," said Lorez.

"I am not the mistress," she replied with a smile. "I am her daughter and we have been expecting your party. Who is the one called Leif?" she asked.

Bjorn pushed Leif forward with a brotherly nudge.

"I am, my lady," replied Leif.

"Mother is expecting you and you alone," she said.

Sker suddenly jumped onto Leif's leg. The lizard-goblin let Leif know another bear, much larger than the one before them, appeared behind Leif.

"Go," said the girl. "Follow Grommel, he will take you to her," she said pointing to the second large bear outside.

As Leif left to follow the bear, Bjorn turned to Dru and said, "What in the nine layers of hells did your father get us into Dru?"

"You know my father as well as I. No clue what goes on in that man's head."

A moment later, the bear in the room lay back down to sleep but the young girl walked past the orcs, lycaons and the party to join Leif. It was then everyone noticed the pointed ears on that black-haired and dark-skinned girl.

* * * * *

Leif followed the bear to the door that lay within the rock wall of the quarry. It was open and wide enough for the bear outside to fit through. Leif followed the bear through.

For being cut into the white stone, it surprised Leif to see plants of all kinds hung from baskets and vined throughout. Light peered in through the windows cut out of the stone and the small glass ceiling that allowed more light in from above. The large room smelled of fruits, flowers and vegetables were growing from the small potted plants and potted trees spread all over.

The bear Grommel laid down on the stone floor in a heap in front of the warm hearth. By the fire sat a raven-haired human woman in her forties, dressed in green camouflage and a grey cloak. An outfit not unlike the girl who escorted Leif.

"Mistress of Sanctuary I presume?" stated the large elf and bent his head forward in respect.

"You cannot be him?" she mustered.

"Ah, yes, Mistress, I am the one sent by Queen Ooktha to participate in the vanquishing of the evil Rom-Seti. I get a lot of confused looks given my size and strength as an elf. I was raised by humans in Vorclaw. I ate, played and grew as they did."

"Oh, I see. And how did you come to be raised by humans?"

"I have no memory of my past, my lady, beyond when my father found me along the hills of Vorclaw seven years ago."

"I see, I mistook you for someone else which was why I was staring, forgive me. A young elf lost to me some fifteen years ago. That young elf saved my life."

"I assure you it wasn't me."

"Quite right, you would be too young," she said. "You have met my daughter, Denisia," the mistress said. "She is elven too."

"She is elven?" asked Leif in a surprised manner.

"Half-elf," she replied. And Denisia revealed her pointed ears from under her black hair. "Do you know what kind?" asked the mistress.

"I do not?"

"She is half dark-elf."

Leif sensed it was some test. His only encounter was with the dark-elf in the arch-goblin arena where he felt that anger wash over him during battle; it was a feeling he did not understand. However, with this young girl, he felt no such hatred. Therefore, Leif replied, "Pleased to meet you, Denisia, I am Leif Foehammer."

"Have you ever faced a revenant before, Leif Foehammer?" demanded the mistress, drawing back Leif's attention. "Have you any idea the power they contain? Do you know what potential allies Rom-Seti has at his disposal?" she asked looking at her daughter.

Leif did not know the answers nor why she looked to her daughter then. Dark-elves have known to be evil and associate with other agents of evil. Now Leif wondered if Denisia was not conceived under unfortunate circumstances. He let that thought drop for now.

"Mistress, I have not faced one."

"Then why do it all? Why throw your life into harm's way so recklessly?"

"I do it because I am a soldier and I have been ordered to do so. And I will not do it alone. But more to the point, if I accomplish this mission, it will have a lasting effect in Vorclaw, for the betterment of its people. It will secure peace between the arch-goblin hoards and the inhabitants of Vorclaw. I will also be allowed to return to see my family," he said. "The risk is worth the reward," Leif said looking back at Denisia, smiling.

The mistress stared at Leif, measuring his words. Looking at his calming face and genuinely smiling at her daughter, she then thought him not a fool after all.

"So be it then, Leif Foehammer," she said after a brief moment of silence. "I was asked to aid you and I shall do so with the location to Rom-Seti's lair. It is three days from here, but he must not know of me or my assistance."

"Thank you," said Leif with a slight bow. "And I am sure Queen Ooktha thanks you as well."

"I know not who that is, nor do I care," she said rising up and going to a cupboard to pull forth parchment, a map.

"I presumed you knew of her? That she asked for your assistance?"

172

"You presumed wrong. I was asked by my guardian to help you. My guardian shall remain nameless of course," she said passing Leif the map. She stared again with intensity, as if trying to figure out if she knew him once.

"As you wish, my lady. What can you tell me about Rom-Seti?"

"He is a murderer, a thief, controlling, even charming, so I am told!" she said swiftly. "But he only cares about his own agenda! That abomination was once a powerful ruler of an ancient kingdom that is not of this world, but he unfortunately remains on Vana."

"Not of this world?" asked Leif thinking was it a metaphor or was she being literal?

"He has been known to align with dark-elves, amass an undead army and create powerful golems," she continued without answering Leif. "He does not know of me nor do I wish him to. That is all you should know. Now, leave me and get some rest. In the morning you leave with my guides into the mountain forest for the first day. After that you will be on your own."

Leif thanked her and departed back to the long house. Leif, although aware, never mentioned the other person hiding in the room. Her guardian Leif presumed. Leif's keen elven senses were not dulled by living among the humans and arch-goblins.

Leif returned to the longhouse with the story of the encounter and the map. The map shown that would take about three days to get to Rom-Seti's stronghold. And it was evident to all then that they had to travel through a subterranean path with in a mountain to get there.

Leif then noticed both the orcs and the lycaons all departed the longhouse.

* * * * *

"It is him!" stated the Mistress of Sanctuary.

"It cannot be the prince, he is too young," stated the elf in the room that was hiding during the meeting with Leif.

"It looks just like him."

"The prince was lost fifteen years ago," said Teodor, the elf who was hiding during the meeting with Leif and the Mistress of Sanctuary. Teodor was also the one who delivered the map of Rom-Seti's layer. "That elf would have to been taken in by the by humans about fifteen years ago, not seven years ago like he mentioned," explained Teodor. He was an older elf, but his face was narrow and hair was a dull blond.

"He only remembers seven years ago, you elves age differently than humans, it could be him."

"Felicia," said the elf referring to the proper name of the lady known as the Mistress of Sanctuary, few knew her real name. "They are from Vorclaw, leagues away from here!" he reminded. "You humans are an odd superstitious lot, you know that? That elf could be anyone, but he cannot be the lost prince of Archangel," argued Teodor referring to his home, the hidden elven city of Archangel. "He is too young and likely dead, like his brother."

Those words stung her profoundly and Denisia saw it upset her mother. "Then return to your master, elf," she said coldly.

"Very well," said Teodor.

"Wait," she said suddenly. "Indulge me one request. Ask your master to scry and to see for himself, to prove me wrong."

"I shall," he said after thinking about it. His master would surely be interested to see how this plays out regardless.

"Does your master intend to help them through this?"

"Ha! What do you think?"

* * * * *

"It is the best I can do for you, my friend," said Captain Ty to Master Sergeant Saltclaw. The captain handed the former prisoner some clean clothes, his glaive and some silver pieces.

"Bjorn Foehammer says to travel to the town of Sedge Fen, on the outskirts of Sedgedunum. His father is there. Bjorn asks you to tell him that Leif is alive and tell your story to the retired Sergeant Major, Magnus Foehammer. He says you know him?"

"Aye, I trained under the man, good man," replied the man.

"You keep your rank Master Sergeant but are forced to retire, per Major Goldwater," said the captain.

Chapter 26
Journey to the Lair

Dru and Bjorn spent the night reacquainting with Leif some more. Leif spun a sad tale of the loss of his troops but vowed not to let them have died in vain. He elaborated on his reasoning for taking on this mission – the hope to bring a truce to the land and end the fighting.

Quietly, Bjorn questioned Leif, "Why not blame the arch-goblins, the ones who actually obliterated your company?"

Those words stung Leif as it was his soldiers that were killed. Leif, however, countered with something he never spoke aloud before. Not Sker nor Lorez. "I believe something more sinister was at work, I am certain. I believe the arch-goblins were a mere tool to something else."

Bjorn and Leif disagreed on the matter but that was the case among siblings. Leif suspected more and did not want to reveal what he believed just yet. Although he now wondered if Anthon Blackpool may be involved somehow.

Dru remained calm but he did know more than Leif and Bjorn. So he believed and, therefore, did not enter the discussion. Dru knew the danger of this mission and came well prepared thanks to his uncle Anthon. But entering the discussion might reveal more than he cared to share. Dru was well aware that his father and uncle had dealings with the arch-goblins. Dru suspected he and Bjorn were sent to training in order to vanquish undead and to get into places that proved difficult. Dru suspected that he and Bjorn were to kill Queen Ooktha but that was just a theory he had.

Since the three friends decided to not completely divulge what they knew or thought they knew, Dru decided to change the subject to Leif's companions, the lizard-goblin Sker and the arch-goblin Lorez. Leif assured they could be trusted.

Bjorn then shared where Dru and himself have been assigned, to include there training. General Blackpool invested resources and time into them. Dru was concerned Bjorn may reveal too much as Leif was very inquisitive and he may discern why they were there. However, Bjorn stated that the true purpose for their training remains with the general but assured the pair that by working together, they were capable of this task.

After several hours into the night of talking, joking and recanting old times the three went off to sleep. Damon Crag though was awake, and the assassin listened intently until they all fell asleep.

"The Mistress of Sanctuary said she was going to have a guide for us on the first day," stated Leif walking out of the Long House.

There sat atop a great bear was the teenaged daughter, Denisia. She wore green and brown leather armour, had that silver bow over her shoulder and short sword at her hip.

"Hello," stated Denisia.

A startled Leif asked, "Ahh…do you know who we should expect as a guide for our journey?" he asked her.

Damon Crag, being the observant one, responded for her, "It's her, isn't it obvious?"

"Are your bellies full from your long breakfast? I been waiting since sunrise" she teased.

"Yes, young lady," replied Leif who was not much older than her. Denisia's face clearly showed she did not like being called *young lady*.

"Come along then," she replied and motioned for her mount the bear called Brommel who was smaller than Grommel, to lead the way. The team set about on foot falling the young elf riding the back of a large grizzly bear. The other bear, Grommel, who was waiting outside sanctuary sleeping and woke up to join them.

Grommel actually paired up with Bjorn for some reason. Bjorn seemed to be the only one not intimidated by the larger grizzly. Bjorn even dared to stroke the back of the beast without negative effects. "I could get used to having a pet-bear at my side," stated Bjorn.

"Grommel and Brommel are not pets!" said Denisia sharply. "They are our companions, our friends. And we treat them with respect," stated Denisia smiling.

"Says the girl riding on the back of her friend," interjected Damon Crag. That caused a chuckle to come from Dru, Erik and Lorez but not Bjorn who respected the bond the elf had with the creatures. Neither did Leif laugh at the insult and made a stern face to the others but was only received by Lorez and Dru who quieted and quit smiling. Leif also reassured Sker he was resting upon his shoulder.

"Tell me, young warrior, what manner of beasts might we encounter in these parts," asked Damon.

"Let's see," she said pondering. "In these mountain forests you might see lycaons, orcs, arch-goblins, no offense," she stated to the Lorez. "Lizard-goblins, no offense she said again," referring to Sker who took up a seat on Leif's shoulders. "Humans of course, no offense. In fact, many races make their way up north to this land. Not all of them live through the year though. Winters are unforgiving and so are the yetis, and giant kin. I have seen a dragon flying around on occasion."

"What is a chimera?" asked Dru.

"A cruel wizard joke," said Damon Crag looking at Erik.

"It is thought to be a magical creation by one of the gods," interrupted Erik. "It has three heads from three different beasts. My studies have revealed front quarters of a great cat but the body changes into that of a goat or some form of bovine. And it has great wings from a bat or dragon or bird. The three heads reflect which body-types the chimera has."

"Oh, there are rumours of a mantikhoras," interrupted Denisia.

"A mantikhoras!" exclaimed Lorez. "I would not worry about them with Lieutenant Leif Foehammer in our midst. I watched him defeat one in them in our arena. It was a glorious battle!"

"All on his own?" inquired Damon.

"He was alone in defeating the beast, yes," replied Lorez.

"What a load of shite," replied Damon.

"Believe it or not human. I know what I saw. Leif Foehammer earned much respect from my kin that day. He also defeated a great ogre in single combat."

"It was an orc," stated Leif.

"Half ogre, half orc," stated Sker.

"So you killed a half-ogre and a mantikhoras all on your own?" asked Damon Crag with a bit of humour on his tone.

"I did not kill the ogre," said Leif.

"Half-ogre," said Damon.

"I wounded him so he would submit," said Leif.

"It is true!" stated Sker.

"He saved the lives of hundreds of orcs, lizard-goblins and probably a few arch-goblins," said Lorez. "Much respect the lieutenant."

"Sounds like a bunch of lizard-goblin shite to me," said Damon.

"Are you calling me a liar, human?" asked Lorez who stopped and stared at Damon.

"Who cares what they say," stated Erik, trying to prevent a confrontation between Damon and Lorez. "Lets us just continue with this journey and more importantly, what else might we encounter beyond this mountain forest?" the wizard asked of Denisia.

"Let's see," began Denisia. "You might encounter some giant kin in the mountains with their dire wolf pets or if you are really lucky, some wandering zombies left from wars of over decades past."

"And what of inside the mountain?" asked Bjorn.

"Yes and within Rom-Seti's lair?" asked Dru.

"Who is Rom-Seti?" she asked. "You are going into the mountains?" she asked. "It was nice knowing you all," she said. "I do hope some of you will survive."

The journey took a silent turn after Denisia's comment. In fact, not much was said among the party after that until several hours later when they came to rest at a picturesque waterfall. There they took a rest, replenished their water and began to have a meal.

"Tell me, young warrior," began Damon Crag addressing Denisia, what manner of giant kin are in the mountains?

"Occasionally a dumb giant makes their way down in these parts but rumours of larger kin reside higher, ice giants, I think. Other visitors to Sanctuary claim to have seen..." she stopped suddenly at the growls of Grommel and Brommel.

"What is it?" asked Lorez, but no answer was given, and everyone drew their weapons.

The two bears were now standing on just their hind legs making them easily eight and ten feet tall. They stared at the path that was coming from down the mountain, the path they intended to take. From out of the forest came two of the three orcs that stayed at sanctuary when the party arrived.

They were bleeding, bandaged and moving quickly down the hill. It wasn't until the orcs were in the open that they saw the party before them with weapons drawn and two large bears staring back at them but that did not seem to stop them. In fact, they hurried closer to the waterfall. Once there the two orcs nearly collapsed of exhaustion and drank heavily from the pool before the waterfall.

"I presume they recognised us from Sanctuary?" asked as much as stated Leif.

"Are they the same orcs?" asked Erik. "They all look alike to me."

Lorenz began to ask them in orcish what had happened but was cut off by Denisia who also spoke to them in orcish with the same question, what happened?

One of them responded, presumably their leader, in the orc tongue. "We were ambushed by lycaons, the same ones from Sanctuary. They took our food, pelts and our brother. They said it be payment for staying silent in Sanctuary during your confrontation."

"Is he alive still?" she asked the orc.

"He was when we left him but was bleeding from the fight. We were told to leave, and he would remain alive as a slave. So we left to tell our chieftain."

"Or we would have all died," put in the other orc.

Denisia explained what had happened to the party using the human tongue and asked questions from Leif, Born and Lorez as to the whereabouts they were ambushed, how far and how lycaons. Denisia offered the orcs to return to Sanctuary where they might heal.

After the two orcs departed, Damon Crag said, "The orc is probably dead by now so let us just continue."

"We do not know that," put in Leif.

"Who cares?" responded Damon.

"You did provoke them after all," stated Lorenz.

"You ungrateful arch-goblin!" stated Damon Crag. "They were going to kill you. I am now going to kill you."

"You provoked them," stated Denisia. "I was there. It is both your fault and the lycaons, the orcs are the victims here."

"Who cares?" Erik responded. "They are orcs!"

"It is six lycaons and seven of us and two bears. Bartering for the orc's life is the right thing to do," stated Leif.

"Barter?" said Damon, Dru and Denisia in unison.

"Yes," said Leif. "We use threat of force."

"And if that does not succeed?" asked Dru.

"Then we fight," said Leif.

Damon Crag rolled his eyes and Bjorn let out a giggle.

"Tell me, Bjorn," began Erik the wizard aloud for all to hear, "has your brother always been such a saint?"

"He tries to be," replied Bjorn. "But I support him," stated Bjorn who reassured Leif's idea, even though the large cleric of Matronae didn't believe this would be a bloodless outcome.

* * * * *

The party saw the lycaons camp from afar and foreseeing the danger of a frontal advance from below, decided to take a winding path around the camp to put themselves up above it to the camps own right. From this point they could simply pass the lycaon camp without even being noticed but Leif insisted on trying to free the orc held captive. They could see the orc nearly naked orc tied to a tree, lycaons around him kicking and prodding him.

From above the camp, they watched six lycaons taking turns beating and berating their orc prisoner, tied to a tree. The lycaon encampment was up in the southern mountains just before the treeline began to give away to rock. The lycaons found a nice flat plateau with a few trees to protect them for the elements but with enough wood around for a fire. They also had a good view of anyone or thing approaching from below so they felt secure in their surroundings.

"I like these odds," said Dru with a smile overlooking the camp and Damon Crag cracked a smile but Bjorn and Leif looked at them both with incredulity.

"I could wipe them out with one fireball, you know," whispered Erik.

"I would like to consider that as a backup plan," stated Leif. "I think the best approach is we all go down there and demand release."

"There is no time, they are planning to brr...mm...ive," began Bjorn but the clarity and remainder of his words were spoken over by Damon.

"That's your plan, to walk in and say please?"

"No, walk in as a show of strength," replied Leif.

"It is a sound plan," said Dru. "And if they do not submit, we can get in some practical experience battling living creatures. Up until now all Bjorn and I have vanquished were the undead."

"Master Leif," stated Sker trying to get Leif attention.

"So you have not killed before?" asked Lorez.

"Just some wild animals like deer, goats, wild boar."

"Master Leif," stated Sker again but Leif motioned with his hand to wait, listening to the discussion between Lorenz and Dru.

"And have you killed before, large human?" asked Lorez of Bjorn who did not offer an answer, because he was no longer present.

"Master Leif," stated Sker. "Large brother is going to lycaon camp on his own!"

* * * * *

Bjorn felt overcome by a sense of purpose. They set out to save a life and although it was an orc, the task and purpose was cemented in his mind. Even though his faith was that of a lawful deity and orc traditionally were opposite in faith, Bjorn was also a soldier, and soldiers followed orders. Lastly, Bjorn recognised the danger the orc was in. So Bjorn charged off knowing his friends would follow. However, when he turned to ensure just that, his companions were not with him. Had they not heard him state there wasn't time? The lycaons are planning to burn him alive! No matter, Bjorn pushed forward with the Rose-Mace and shield to lead him. Within moments Bjorn burst into the clearing walking toward the orc.

"Release the orc!" he demanded. "Your fight was not with him; it was with my companions and therefore with me."

The six lycaons startled, looked to the same lycaon who was speaking common in the long house the day prior. That lycaon spoke something it their tongue. Bjorn could not understand the language but the body language and unsheathing of their weapons spoke volumes. Bjorn responded in kind.

The large cleric of Matronae blasted the nearest lycaon with a body blow from his shield sending the creature flying into the other lycaon, sending both into the dirt. Another lycaon came on in response to his fellow lycaons being toppled over but was met by the Rose-Mace which crashed through the lycaons meagre leather armour. That lycaon hit the ground hard, gasping for breath due to his now cracked ribs.

Bjorn accepted the blow of a flail to his shield and deflected a stab of a sword by using his mace. Bjorn saw the remaining lycaon, the vocal one from sanctuary, trying to circle him. Bjorn reluctantly had to back away from the pair in an effort to prevent from being surrounded. This was not as Bjorn had planned and hoped his friend would arrive soon. Two more assaults by the pair of lycaon came at him as he reeled backwards. The third lycaon, seeing the meagre retreat instead began a frontal assault with his two lycaon companions. Once Bjorn sensed he was not about to be surrounded he let loose his strength and power of Matronae. He said a silent prayer to give him strength and courage.

With the power of the enchanted Rose-Mace he sent a backhand blow that sent the sword wielding lycaon to the ground, grasping his chest for air. Bjorn then charged forward with his shield leading the way into the flail holding lycaon sending him to the ground. Bjorn accepted the swing of an axe by the talkative lycaon and blocked it with his mace. Bjorn then swung around in a circle with his shield level with the ground to break the jaw of that lycaon. Teeth and a yelp escaped from the creature who staggered and fell to the ground.

The first two lycaons were now back on their feet but ran away as Dru, Leif, Lorez and Damon emerged from the brush. That left four lycaons, three had taken blows by the Rose-Mace and the other lying on the ground relatively unharmed. Each lycaon had a sword pointed at them by now while Bjorn made his way to the orc tied around a tree covered in firewood. It was then to Bjorn's horror that the orc was already dead.

"Why did you take off without us? You could have been killed?" asked Leif but Bjorn did not answer.

"Leif is right, Bjorn. You could have been killed," announced Dru.

"I felt there was no time, I thought they were going to burn him alive," Bjorn said feeling foolish.

Damon Crag, who just put his sword through the neck of his lycaon stated, "You Foehammers are reckless."

"Why did you kill him?" asked an upset Leif.

Lorez did the same to his lycaon as Leif was speaking.

"No, Lorez, I don't want needless bloodshed," shouted Leif. It was then the lycaon under the blade of Dru and Leif sensed their doom. They made a dash for it to get away, only Leif let his depart unscathed. Dru promptly dispatched his lycaon with his sword; however, Leif's lycaon didn't get far as he had to bypass Bjorn who bludgeoned the lycaon with his mighty mace in one stroke. "We didn't need to kill them," stated Leif as Bjorn walked past.

Bjorn ignored him and said to all, "It is my folly, I should have waited. I put you in danger with my rashness. I thought you all heard me. I am sorry. Let us move on from this place and continue our mission."

"Just like that," said Leif. "You just extinguished four lives, needlessly," said Leif.

"No, Lieutenant Foehammer," interrupted Lorez. "They would have never let this orc live and would have killed us given the chance too. Let us be gone from this place before the two escaped can return with more of their clan."

It was then Sker showed up and began picking the pockets of the deceased. No one paid him any mind as the party got used to the little scavenger's presence, especially since Dru continued the conversation.

"Your efforts had merit, Leif," said Dru seeing the frustration still lingering in Leif. "Your father would have been proud of your noble cause, but your arch-goblin friend is probably right, they would have killed us given half a chance. Now, let's get out of here and finish the mission."

The party joined up with Denisia sitting atop Brommel with Grommel was at her side. She refused to partake in the battle, preferring her neutrality in the area. However, even she thought the lycaons were the culprits and although did not want to see anyone killed, she was not sorry with the outcome for the lycaons. Eventually they came to spot to camp. There weren't many trees this high up but was secluded enough in the rocks to build a small fire to remain unseen, keep warm and have a hot meal. Denisia could sense the tension of the botched endeavour.

"Those lycaons should have known better," she said around the camp fire. "Their killing of that orc will likely cause a feud for sure. Hopefully the other two will learn a lesson from this and importance of neutrality up here."

Leif's mind seemed to ease on the subject with those words but felt the blood of those lycaons, much like his soldiers was on his hands.

Bjorn's mind too seemed to relax although he felt foolish for rushing to save an already dead orc.

Lorenz interjected. "Why is neutrality important up here?" he asked.

"My mother says life this far north and this high up is harsh, more harsh than normal. Those that come here do not always make it through their first winter or those do not seek protection of a group or a clan and perish. Neutrality is what is best for all, most of the time."

"And this is why you remained out of sight from the lycaons when we attacked?" asked Lorez.

"Precisely," she responded. "I saw first-hand how they offended you. Unfortunately, from what you say they did to that orc, the peace around here may be shattered, for a time."

"Except when it comes to Rom-Seti," interject Damon Crag who was trying again to stir the pot. "Your mother is keen to help us meet this foe," he said smiling, trying to counter her neutrality theory.

The young girl, undaunted, stared at the man intently. "Perhaps he is more a threat to neutrality than you realise?" she responded.

Erik the wizard giggled under his breath. "Best leave it alone Damon," he said.

"Well played young lady," admitted Damon.

"My bears and I will take first watch tonight," she said staring at Damon still, showing her mistrust. "I will watch for half the night. You all need your rest for you are travelling through the mountain tomorrow and need your wits about you. Who should I wake in the morning?"

"Wake me," said Leif, "I don't need much sleep," he said upset by this evening's events.

* * * * *

The fire was low when Denisia woke Leif. It was well into the morning but still dark. Everyone including the bears were still asleep.

"Tell me elf warrior, you do not plan to parley with this revenant like you tried with the lycaons?" asked the young half dark-elves of Leif.

Leif, chuckled at the direct and clarity with which this young half dark-elves spoke. "No, I do not. It is not the mission. We plan to end this revenant and return home and let peace reign in."

"I hope for your sake you succeed in ending Rom-Seti. However, how long do you think your peace will last?"

"You are very direct in your line of questioning," replied Leif with a surprised smile. "To answer your question, forever; however, I am a realist and know that it will likely not last as long as I dare hope."

"Then why put your own life at risk for a peace that will not last? Abandon this mission and stay here with me and my bears!" she said smiling. "You can help us keep the peace up here."

"That is actually a great idea, my lady," said Leif. "But I owe it to my soldiers that I lost, to the family I miss and the nation I swore to protect."

"You owe them what?" she said curiously.

"Do you always ask these many questions?" he asked Denisia with a warming smile. Before she could answer, he said, "Rest your pretty eye young warrior. It is your turn to sleep and my turn to keep watch. Get some sleep."

Denisia didn't argue as she let a large yawn escape and cuddling up to her warm bear companion was even more incentive to stop quizzing this young elf. She didn't understand it yet, but she admired him for some reason. Maybe even liked him for trying to save that orc. So she did not take her eyes off this warrior, at least not until she fell asleep.

Leif walked around the camp, checking the perimeter and used his *night-vision* to look for heat signatures of those of predators that may be lurking around the camp. When he was certain the camp was secure, Leif contemplated the questions and offer the young half-dark-elves put to him.

What does he owe them? Leif rationalised the answer. He owes his life to his adoptive family; he owes it to his dead fellow soldiers that they had not died in vain and he owed it to Vorclaw that he follows orders for the good of the nation. He then looked at the sleeping young lady, smiled and silently thanked her for reminding him what he stood for.

Chapter 27

Let the Games Begin

The woman possessed not just a presence when she walked into the room but commanded an arrogance about her. She was Lady Sanne Nightingale, whose family bricklaying business helped build and maintain Sedgedunum. Although aunt to now Lord, Handel Nightingale for whom which she abdicated, she was also the silent partner in General Blackpool's plot. Sanne was the same age of Baltus Blackpool and knew him since they were children. They grew up together among the aristocracy of Sedgedunum. Even though her face was hidden by a black mask, Baltus could easily pick her out of the small assembly gathered in the underground ruins.

"Council leader," she began addressing Baltus. It was standard practice to not use names in case someone was to magically scry upon them during their meetings. "I am patient woman, but I have been waiting years for this scheme to come to fruition. Your timetable was originally set for assault to happen by now. What is the delay?" Several people grumbled and commented quietly but all that ceased once the general stood up from the table.

"My friends, all of you have suffered in some form or fashion under the present regime running this country. Which is one of the main reasons why we came together. Whether due to lost property, damaged careers, humiliation or by the untimely death of loved ones, you and your families deserve better from Vorclaw and its leaders." Many Black-Masks held deep resentment to towards many of the elitists of Vorclaw's Council-of-Twelve. Baltus was clever enough to cultivate that hatred for his Black-mask cult. He then used his influence as a military commander to promote those members to gain their allegiance. It took years but he did it. There were some that were the exception, such as Lady Sanne Nightingale, but they have gains to be had.

"And now I say to you," Baltus continued. "Your revenge for what they have done to you or your families is upon us," he said dryly. "As discussed previously, belongings and people you do not wish lost should have been moved by now or at least warded. The hour is late, and the pieces are in motion. Your revenge begins the night of the Festival of the Seas," explained Baltus referring to a local celebration respecting the fisherman, the Navy and the bounty the sea provides. It is an all-day celebration of food, fish, naval displays and fun all along the Sedgedunum docks. It is showcased along the coast of the city, complete with fireworks and magical displays.

"Council leader," Lady Sanne Nightingale again spoke. "When might we expect for the transition of power to happen?"

"Once the city is retaken," replied Baltus. "It is then I make my arrests."

"When should we expect the redistribution of the plunder?" asked another Black-Mask.

"Again, once the city is secure and arrests have been made, I will assign several of you to tally and redistribute the wealth of those arrested. Or at least what the arch-goblins do not take for their own."

"Are the arch-goblins still clueless to our change of plans? I just want to make sure I won't be under siege for longer than a day or two," asked another of General Blackpool.

"The arch-goblins do not know of our plans to rid them of the city after their first full day of looting. They still believe they will be taking over the north half of the city to loot for a full week. However, I would be prepared for several days of siege, aftermath and just in case of...complications," said Baltus.

"The golem moves tomorrow tonight!" finished the general. And the Black-Mask council, hidden beneath the Academy of Arms, erupted in cheer.

* * * * *

"Will you come back and visit Sanctuary one day do you think?" asked Denisia of Leif, again with her warming smile.

Leif returned her smile and bowed. "My lady, I do indeed hope so. You have a wonderful life in this part of the world, and I would love to explore it further."

"Best wishes and safe travels then Master Leif. I look forward to your return," she said. She resisted any further conversation directly with any of them. Her instinct told her that he may be the only trustworthy of this motley crew and did not care for the rest. "Farewell to you all," announced Denisia. "You are an unusual lot and I hope you will return to Sanctuary one day," she said but was looking at Leif. Bjorn and Dru gave her a wave and Leif gave her a wave and a wink farewell. She watched as the they departed the camp and headed for the next leg of their journey. She stared at Leif mostly, hoping to see him again.

It was nearly an entire day of travel to get to the next location on the map, another waterfall but much smaller that gave way into a trickle of a small stream. Behind that waterfall was a crack in the rocks that was the entrance into the mountain. The crew by this time was out of breath, tired and hungry from the day of travel. The saw a large flying creature, maybe a chimera as Denisia mentioned, upon high. Being this high up in the mountains, nothing seemed to thrive. Trees were sparse and the land was mostly eroded rock from the surrounding mountains. It was colder than normal, even for the time of year and some mountains contained snow-capped peaks. Damon was smart enough to ensure the party picked up firewood along the way, for the night would be cold. Damon, who held the map, investigated the small waterfall and indeed found the opening. It appeared to be a carved-out tunnel, one person wide, or at least as far as he could see.

"How about Lorez, Sker and I take a look inside the tunnel to see if we cannot find a better campsite inside?"

"I think it best to remain outside until tomorrow," stated Lorez. "If we're to climb inside the mountain now, it may allow roaming beasts to pick up our scent or prepare for us."

"I agree," stated Damon. "And I did not see any recent tracks in or out so I do not foresee anything coming out of there anytime soon."

Leif felt a little foolish just then, but he was not an experienced leader. Bjorn and Dru felt similar as both in their own mind thought that Leif had a good idea. However, all three young warriors remained quiet and chalked it up as a learning experience.

That night they slept outside if they could call it that, for it was cold and the wind, although slight, made for a colder night.

* * * * *

It was dusk, the sun was set below the horizon and only limited light remained. Chieftain Gutter, the rotund arch-goblin who governed the western arch-goblin city of Ironhold simply relished at his supposed good fortune. His fortress at the base of the Spine-of-Vana Mountains, in the most northern reaches of the Mistful Forest, was called Ironhold for good reason. It boasted many iron ore deposits for mining. He controlled a great source for making weapons and armour for all three arch-goblin tribes. However, it had also become the primary location for Anthon's creation, an iron-golem! Although it took many years to complete and was a drain on his tribes' resources, the time to for pay out had finally come. War was after all what every arch-goblin Chieftain wanted. A victorious battle to lead his army in, spoils of war to be had, it was what the chieftain dreamed of over the last few years.

The rotund arch-goblin admired his legions walking out of his stronghold and into the forest. He did not mind that Chieftain Blist had joined him in this endeavour, it simply meant less blood spilled from his own tribe. He was after all, the architect behind much of the planned assault. His own tribal spies found best routes through the forest and figured which gate of the great wall to crash at Sedgedunum. For Chieftain Gutter, it has been a long but somehow fun few years planning this assault. Most importantly, in his mind, his plans have made Queen Ooktha pleased.

Queen Ooktha was pleased and present as the two columns of arch-goblins, over one thousand strong, marched in silence through the Mistful Forest. She stood between her two Chieftains, Blist and Gutter. The vampire was surprised at how quiet the two columns of soldiers could be. She, however, was not here just to see her hoards move out of the strong hold. She wanted to see if the golem creature would actually work. For if it did not, she would cancel this assault and turn on her human wizard, and his allies.

Anthon was also present along with several other wizard minions of his. However, he was floating upon a magical carpet, large enough for himself and two other wizards with him. One, a young male, was to will the carpet forward while the other wizard, a female, was there for his protection as Anthon willed the golem forward. They steadily built the iron-golem within a great wooden structure, a hanger, complete with iron smelting attached to the side of the large building. A great enchanted mace was also constructed. It was one third the height of the iron-golem and waited outside the large building for the golem to take possession.

Many eyes were upon the scene, Anthon knew. Aside from those in the vicinity, others from The Shadow Company were watching using their own scrying devices. This was Anthon's test and potential elevation into the ranks of his own dark fraternity.

The fire lit by magic within the iron heart of the creation had been burning for two days. Now that the creature was complete with a working heart, it was ready to move. Anthon evoked the final spell to engage the iron-golem's capability. It was time for the creature to fulfil its dark purpose. Anthon closed his eyes and concentrated. His mind called to the beast, connecting his own mind to the creation.

"Come forth, walk forward," he said within himself. The creature obeyed, reluctantly it seemed as a large grinding of metal on metal erupted as the iron-golem emerged; it was the source of the creatures perceived hesitation. All the arch-goblins turned to regard the noisy thing. Anthon anticipated this and had several arch-goblins ready, jamming large mops covered in lubrication oils to lubricate its joints. The noise did ease, and Anthon commanded the creature to stop before the great mace and lift it. The iron-golem performed the action without question. Again, the joints of the thing needed lubrication due to the shrieking metal. Its form was that of an armoured arch-goblin warrior. Although made of iron plates, the arch-goblin craftsman painted the creature in red and black, not unlike their own armour.

"It is over twenty feet tall," Anthon said, now floating towards Queen Ooktha and her Chieftains. "It weighs greater than two elephants. Its body is magically enhanced to withstand assaults and it will smash through the gates and doorways."

"And lead us to plunder!" stated Chieftain Gutter excited at the prospects.

Queen Ooktha boasted a wide smile. She was then handed a goblet of blood from Chieftain Blist. She toasted it to Anthon as he sat upon his magical carpet. When she finished, she said to him with a red-toothed smile, "Delicious, Mage Anthon, I cannot wait to see it in Sedgedunum."

* * * * *

The path was barely wide enough for Bjorn, the largest of the party. But even Erik, the shortest of the party, had to duck in places. It was watery, ankle deep at places. Leif asked Sker to lead the way with a torch so the humans could see in the deep darkness. The first leg appeared to be an old mine. The first large cavern they came to, had a sloped ceiling and several offshoots in various directions. Even an old mining cart, although broken and covered in sediment from dripping waters, it was still discernible. "It is very wet," said Bjorn, stating the obvious.

"It will be less wet as we climb higher," stated Lorez.

"Lizard-goblin," stated Damon, getting Sker's attention, "this way," pointing to a gently sloping passage.

Sker led the way with the torch. This path was wider, enough for two. Damon asked Leif and Lorez to take lead behind Sker's torchlight since the towered over the little lizard-goblin. Lorez had another idea. Since Lorez and Leif could see well enough in the dark, Lorez suggested both Leif and Lorez lead in front of Sker by a several paces so they could see further into the dark with their *night-vision* and let the torched light remain behind them so the humans could see. No one could argue with the logic, and Damon motioned for them to lead. When they were far enough ahead from the light so *night-vision* could be useful, Lorez explained that the light would give them away if anything was present, but their *night-vision* might give them a first look-first shot at any approaching dangers.

Lorez took the left side with his mace in his left hand and scimitar in his right. Leif on their right had his round shield in his left and a *dao* sword in his right hand. Leif preferred this type of arch-goblin sword for it being a one-handed weapon. It was unusually in that it had a thick blade that curve towards the top but narrowed back down to the hilt. It was also an enchanted gift from Queen Ooktha that he graciously accepted from his lover.

"Do you believe we'll encounter anything in these tunnels?" asked Leif quietly of Lorez.

"Always best to assume as much," he said.

"What should we be looking for?" asked Leif.

"Anything that radiates heat," Lorez said. "Then kill it before it tries to eat you. Creatures this far up in the world would like eat most anything and meals are probably scarce."

After about an hour of walking the tunnels, they came upon a large opening. Water was still dripping, and a few small pools dominated the cavern. The water did not appear rising but where the water was draining at was anyone's guess. One of the pools had an island in the middle of it.

It was Lorez who spotted the carved-out stairs off to their right. "Look there," said the arch-goblin pointing to the stairs. "They wrap around the cavern and go up into the back of the falls."

Leif did not pay attention to Lorez. Instead he was transfixed on the small odd rocky island in the centre of one of those small pools. As soon as the remainder approached with their torch light, it was then Leif recognised the island for what it really was. Leif shouted a warning as a larger sticky tongue launched towards Lorez's face.

Leif reacted with his shield to block the assault. The large tongue of a giant bull frog grappled that shield with a powerful driving force. It knocked Lorez from his stance as Leif's forearm knocked into Lorez. Then the tongue retracted, pulling the shield and Leif with it. Leif was able to release his arm from the shield but landed in the water on all fours and submerged before the frog.

The frightened frog, who now had the shield in its mouth but not wishing to engage with such a large force spit out the shield sending it spinning towards Lorez, slamming him in the gut. The arch-goblin dropped backwards onto the hard-wet ground. Then the frog left his muddy puddle and hopped out of the cavern beyond sight.

Leif came up suddenly from the pool gasping for air, his sword swinging out for the large frog that was no longer there. After several moments, Damon Crag started to laugh. As did the rest of the party who just joined them.

Bjorn was the first to comment. "You fools almost got eaten by a large frog!"

As Lorez regained his footing, even he rolled out a belly laugh at the absurdity.

Dru piped in with a joke. "Have a nice swim Leif?"

"Ha, ha, very funny," said Leif emerging from the shallow water. Eventually Leif smiled and laughed at the event. After several moments of rest Leif stated, "Ha! The joke is on all of you now. I believe the map is taking us all behind the falls, correct? I am already wet!"

The map did indeed take them up into the back of the waterfall and they did indeed all get drenched, except Sker who held the torch for the humans; several cloaks were used as improvised umbrellas so the rest of the party could see in the dark. Once clear of the falls, Lorez and Sker scouted ahead to ensure no other creatures lurked. Comfortable of being secure at in this dark tunnel, for the moment, the party poured out the water from their boots and wrung clothing as much as they could.

The air was cool and being wet negatively impacted their body temperature. It was the wizard Erik that started to show signs of fatigue. The wizard was cold and being in a dark cramped cave and facing a mighty revenant soon made him feel uneasy.

"Wizard, have a spell to warm yourself?" asked Lorez who noticed the wizard shivering. Erik shook his head *no* in response. "You priest?" asked Lorez. Bjorn also shook his head *no*.

"Best to keep moving," stated Damon. "It will get your body temperature up again." The party moved onward, albeit soaked. Same positions as before and it did not take long for them to realise they were in a cut tunnel which gave way to stone-blocked walls and floor.

Damon then decided to change tactics. "I want the lizard-goblin to go first with the torch. I want to scan for traps and signs of recent traffic. Dru you are next to me. Elf and arch-goblin, take up the rear."

"We all have names," said Leif as he passed to the rear with Lorez.

Damon didn't respond. In fact, he waited for Leif to pass so he could use his own boot to motion Sker forward. The lizard-goblin let off a little growl that hardly seemed threatening to the assassin. No disturbances or traps were seen by Damon as they came out of the tunnel. They stood high upon another open cavern. A twenty-foot bridge of stone stood before them but about twelve feet of it collapsed for some unknown reason, long ago. Across the missing bridged, there were more cut steps that curved upwards and disappeared behind a natural stone column.

"This might be a good place for us to dry off as we figure out a way across," said Bjorn.

"Well, I agree with the drying off, but I already figured out a way across," replied Damon. He pulled a long rope that was impossibly too long to fit in a small bag around his waist. When the full fifty foot of rope was out, he set it on the stone floor. He then looked at Sker, grabbed the lizard-goblin by the back of his belt and lobbed him over the missing expanse of bridge to land roughly an additional ten feet the other side.

It all happened so quickly that no one could react. Leif, in disbelief, eventually lunged for Damon from behind and made brief contact with his shoulder but the assassin, always aware, half expected Leif to react negatively. The assassin instinctively spun to grab Leif, although smaller and thinner, the assassin's magically enhanced strength surprised everyone, especially Leif as Damon pushed Leif up against the wall. "Don't ever touch me," he said to Leif.

Leif responded, "Sker is not a toy for your amusement!"

"I know," casually responded Damon. "He has been more of a valuable asset that I first thought. The lizard-goblin has held the torch for me so I can scan for traps and is now going to catch my rope so we can get across. No need for you to worry-elf."

By now Dru was trying to get between the two as was Lorez who also crowded the scene with a slight growl on behalf of Leif. It was Bjorn, however, that seemed more convincing. "Warrior," said Bjorn to Damon. "Let him go now!"

Damon complied and backed away, his hands on his sword.

"Know this," said Bjorn now facing Damon, well staring down on the assassin actually. "You harm my brother again, you will be facing me as well?"

Leif wasted no time checking if Sker was all right. "Sker, how are you?"

Sker whimpered a bit at first but responded with, "Iza okay master Leif."

"That won't happen again, I assure you," said Leif looking at Damon holding the rope.

"Tie the rope, little one, around that pillar," announced Damon and threw the rope to Sker. "I will tie it this side and we'll all shimmy across the gap."

Sker looked for Leif for approval and got the nod to do so. Once both ends were secure, Damon offered to Leif, "After you, of course."

Leif shimmied over without incident. Damon went next. It was a tense moment with Sker, Leif and Damon on the other side alone. Leif stared hard but Damon paid him no mind or at least appeared as such. The rest of the party slipped over without incident, leaving the rope in place for the return although Erik, not known for his strength was now visibly fatigued. However, no one noticed Erik, everyone else was worried about the tension mounting in Leif over Damon Crag's treatment of Sker.

The party continued on up the steps, Sker leading the way with the torch. Carvings of snakes, beetles and crocodiles started to adorn the walls up the cut steps. Odd that crocodiles would be carved up in mountain dwellings. Ancient hieroglyphs of a language unknown to them also decorated the walls as they ascended. A creature with the body of a man but containing some unknown head of a bird seemed to be a recurring theme.

As the path continued upward, turned left and then right and came to a landing with a stone door, a stone-tiled floor covered the landing. All around the door was a stone carving of a large cobra, it appeared as if the cobra was about to consume any who were to enter once the door was opened. The cobra's fangs hung like stalactites above the would-be doorway.

"Dru!" called Damon. "Examine for traps. Tell me what you see?" As soon as Dru approached and leaned onto the door, Damon put out his arm and halted him. He pointed down to a slight rise in one tiled stone.

"A pressure plate!" came not from Dru but from Leif.

Damon shot a look at Leif and then an annoyed look at Dru. "It appears Leif Foehammer is better at this than you my young student." Damon knelt down and with a small knife removed the pressure plate to see the mechanism below. It was a small glass and capped bottle filled with a yellow liquid. "If this were to break, it would have erupted in a mist, possibly killing some of us but surely making us all ill. The effects of which would linger here for days," explained Damon. "Well, Foehammer, you just saved us," said Damon but it was more an insult at Dru who did not see it.

The insult was also a way to put a wedge between Leif and Dru which the assassin felt was needed after he was at odds with Leif and Bjorn for the toss of Sker across the chasm. Damon and Dru examined the rest and found another trap behind the fangs of the Cobra's teeth. Small bottles of the same liquid were ready to drop from a fang if the certain stones on the floor or if the door was disturbed. Damon was able to pry the vials loose from behind the fangs. Now that danger was mitigated, he and Dru could inspect the door. Dru did find the loose bricks that would have triggered the drop of the vials. They found the door latch was triggered to drop another vile when moved. They open the door forward slightly, revealing another dark tunnel, climbing steadily upwards.

"Onwards and upwards," mouthed Damon.

"I need to rest and dry off," stated Erik. "I am not feeling well."

"Then let us close the door, dry off and have a meal. Continue on in an hour or so," stated Bjorn. Everyone agreed.

Chapter 28
Festival of the Seas

The Festival of the Seas was a Vorclaw celebration of giving thanks. Mostly celebrated on the coastal cities within the nation, the festivities were a gala for fisherman, the Navy and the bounty of the sea. Worshipers paid homage to appease Lir, the sea god who carried ships from one port to the next.

This was also an opportunity for the Admiralty to open its vessels to families and children to view ship life or inspire them with tales of adventure and song. All in order to gain new recruits of course. Food was sold cheaply all along the Sedgedunum docks, as long as it was sea food causing traders, travellers and residents all flocked to the city seaside to partake in this great event. At the end of the day, at night, mages from the Wizards Tower put on a magical display in the sky to close out the celebration. Everyone wins, the god Lir, venders who peddle seafood or shells and patrons from all over enjoy themselves.

Many of the lords of the Vorclaw were present. Boyd Draconian, Headmaster of Sedgedunum's Wizard's College was on sight to watch his pupils perform their magical display. The wealthy Lord Nightingale, now councilman, was out talking with city merchants. Archbishop Zelana Spool, high priestess of Matronae, Archbishop Storm Evander of Dagda and Archbishop Elman Wisemind, priest of Ogma were also out and about. Lords Igor Frothbeard, the dwarven arms maker of Irons-by-the-Sea was the only councilman not in town for the event; however, he was the furthest city from the capitol and the dwarf hated water travel – the quickest means to get to the capitol.

However, this celebration saw an unusual number of clerics, particularly Matronae, whose celebrations were geared towards autumn harvests. Her followers received communication in dreams and meditations to be present at this event. Some readied with healing spells others postured for defensive or both. Nevertheless, the day seemed enjoyable and most of Matronae's clerics lost focus due to the fray of food, festivities and fun.

The magical display over the harbour commenced when the sun set. Then explosions safely made their presence felt, signalling the commencement of the magic display. Next in the sky came the illusion of watery waves appearing in the night sky. Images of fish, squid and other sea creatures meandered over the harbour. Bards played music in the background, drums beating were the primary music makers.

Next, fishing vessels sailing on the frothy waves appeared. The scene changed suddenly to a bright sun. As the sun shrank in size and intensity, another ship on calm waters now appeared in the illusion. Then the scene changed again to a blue sky that followed a flock of seagulls. That started to circle over a fisherman's haul. A fisherman tossed a fish at a seagull and the scene changed again. Next illusion was in the bowels of a ship. It was a war ship with ballista and Vorclaw navy personnel scurrying about. The scene came up through the wood of the ship and the illusion showed a large Vorclawean Navy vessel. The Illusion widened in view and depicted sailors running about the ship releasing sails. The navy men on the docks watching the large illusion shouted out *hoo-rah!* Lastly a magical display akin to fireworks had begun!

With the illusion at an end, a dozen wizards standing on an anchored barge in the middle of the harbour began their display. They released dozens of magical dancing lights to float into the night sky. They then sent up small fireballs to explode in an array of coloured lights. Specially designed coloured mage's darts raced into the night. Then the mages sent colour sprays up into the air, lighting up the evening in a rainbow of colour.

No one noticed or suspected then that the northern gates to the city were smashed open by an enormous iron-golem wielding a giant mace, followed by a thousand arch-goblins pillaging to the left and right of the northern sections of the city.

* * * * *

General Blackpool arrived at Fort Adamant the day prior by magical means. He arrived at the door of the Tor carrying a small but clearly heavy chest. Major Goldwater and Major Ickingham were expecting him and led him to a private room at the top of the Tor and placed the chest on the table. Then, they closed the door and left.

It was now the day Vorclaw was under attack. The three officers mustered the soldiers, all on horseback. They have been stationing and readying horses at the garrison for weeks in anticipation. Local merchants, mercenaries and others from the small shanty town rising from the building of Fort Adamant also mounted their horses and belongings. It was clear Fort Adamant was being abandoned and they were all about to find out why.

From atop a black steed General Blackpool addressed the formation. "Brothers and sisters in arms!" he shouted. "As general of the Armies of Vorclaw and member of the ruling council, I have decided to empty Fort Adamant for the greater good of our nation! It has come to my attention that our capital city of Sedgedunum is under attack from an arch-goblin hoard that has come forth from the Mistful Forests," he said, letting that statement sink in. "We as a nation," he continued, "have unfortunately been victims of a ruse. The military has been driven to build Fort Adamant so our leaders could profit from mining here in the mountains. While they ignored the real threat that has been in the Mistful Forest all along!" he shouted. "And now, I hear they lay siege to Sedgedunum as I speak."

Murmurs and whispers of uncertainty began to filter among the crowd.

"Soldiers! Friends!" shouted the general. "We are nearly two hundred strong on horseback and another two hundred on foot. We ride throughout the night and day to rescue Sedgedunum to recover our capitol. I sent a few wizards and scouts ahead to light the way with magical fires and torches." The general then raised his sword and shouted, "Follow me, to Sedgedunum. For Vorclaw!"

The soldiers echoed, "For Vorclaw!" Off went the cavalry brandishing torches. Followed by the foot soldiers, double timing their march following behind, some also carrying torches to help guide them.

* * * * *

The north gate of Sedgedunum was smashed to oblivion by both the powerful mace of the iron-golem and its sheer strength. It was night so by the time the city guards even noticed the behemoth the golem knocked down the door. Behind the iron-golem flowed two columns of arch-goblins. Once in through the gate, Chieftain Gutter's Ironhold arch-goblins filtered to the left while Chieftain Blist's Skulls-thorpe arch-goblins filtered right. Once both columns had sent one hundred arch-goblins to either side, the next one hundred went forward behind the advancing iron-golem.

Above and behind, floating invisibly upon a magic carpet, sat Anthon Blackpool guiding the golem, his other two mages, one male who steered the carpet and the other a female, guarded Anthon, expecting an attack by Queen Ooktha that may or may not come; a planned betrayal was leaked by the Chieftain Merka of Blood-helm. Whether it would happen or not, Anthon could not say but he wasn't taking any chances. He wanted his revenge as much as his brother Baltus wanted his. Anthon's revenge stemmed from having been excommunicated from Sedgedunum's Wizard's College due to his association with The Shadow Company. Since that day, Anthon wanted to topple that tower.

There were targets of interest along the path to the spire of Sedgedunum 's Wizard's College such as the residences of council members and mages. A common dining hall and pub used by members of the college, was also along the way; places that frustrated Anthon every time he saw them. Anthon resisted the temptation to level them as the fireworks and magic display along the coats were almost complete. He did not want to make too much noise and arouse premature suspicion. That college was his prize.

* * * * *

Fort Adamant was emptied, even local merchants evacuated. The city walls were locked and fires were left ablaze. However, it mattered little. It was all a ruse. Within the hour, a small army of arch-goblins, some five hundred strong, led by Chieftain Merka scaled the walls of the empty Fort Adamant. The chieftain made is way up the Tor as was previously instructed. He went alone

194

while the rest of his warriors looked for plunder. At the very top of the tower, where General Blackpool left the small chest on the table he was met by another arch-goblin. One with red hair. The large red-haired arch-goblin handed over a key to the arch-goblin chieftain. Merka opened the chest with the key provided.

"I assume we are still in agreement with the arrangement?" asked the red-haired arch-goblin of the chieftain in a very un-arch-goblin-like manner. His language was arch-goblin but the way he spoke was more refined.

Chieftain Merka smiled as he relished in the pieces of gold, silver and cooper. A few gems were also within. A small hoard but a bribe large enough to ensure the arch-goblins of Blood-helm would remain at Fort Adamant and not pursue General Blackpool south. Thereby betraying both his rival, Chieftain Blist and his monarch, Queen Ooktha.

It mattered not to Chieftain Merka if General Blackpool succeeded in routing his fellow arch-goblin forces and killing off his rivals or not. As long as his treasure was hidden and his arch-goblin troops remained alive, that was all that mattered. Merka would simply claim the fort was emptied when he arrived, which was true. When this event was complete, he stood to become one of the more powerful chieftains.

"You now have two forts, Chieftain Merka," stated the red-haired arch-goblin as if reading his mind, perhaps he was. "Now with two forts under your command, it gives you an entire region to plunder with not a single loss to your own warriors."

"Yes, all is to my liking," he said aloud still admiring the treasure with in the chest. "And even the hindrance of the orcs in the north was solved, thanks to Leif Foehammer!" Chieftain Merka then moved to look out a window of the Tor to see his soldiers feasting on the remaining livestock.

"Very well then, I will leave your clan. I will contact you if and when the General Blackpool requires it."

"He will kill her? Yes?" asked Merka.

"For your sake, I would hope so," stated the red-haired arch-goblin. That answer obviously did not sit well with the chieftain and bared his yellow teeth. "If she does manage to kill the wizard Anthon and plunder the city completely, then your best hope of her demise rests with Leif Foehammer, if that one even returns."

"Why do you say that of the elf?" asked Merka.

"Because, once the elf-lover of your queen learns what has transpired here, it is hoped he will seek vengeance upon her. The general will make certain the elf believes it was all her doing."

"She is no queen to me," stated Merka but his angry look turned to a smile and wondered if Lorez, his most trusted arch-goblin and somewhat of a friend to Leif, could help make that happen.

"Forgive me," responded the red-haired arch-goblin.

"How many days of plunder until the garrison from here arrives?" Merka asked. "She is expecting to have weeks of plunder."

"She will get only two days' plunder now that the general escaped your grasp. Sorry to foil her plans but she overreached trying to take Sedgedunum for longer than planned without consent from General Blackpool, not to mention her plan to assassinate the wizard, Anthon," responded the red-haired arch-goblin. "With the general now en route he will become the saviour of Sedgedunum and the vanquisher of the long looming threat in the Mistful Forest. Which of course works out good for you being the only arch-goblin tribe untouched by the war," explained the red-haired arch-goblin.

"You make it sound like I care. I am the one that revealed her betrayal, remember?"

"Of course, but when these events are all said and done, it is expected that you will respect General Blackpool's wishes and reframe from actions that would jeopardise his seizing of Vorclaw, hence the chest and silence in your betrayal," explained the red-haired arch-goblin.

Chieftain Merka nodded his acceptance to the bargain.

"Good, then I will take my leave of you, I wish to see the siege of the city I helped create," stated the red-haired arch-goblin. Merka turned to look at him curiously, wondering how he intended to get there to watch in time.

The red-haired arch-goblin departed the fort taking in a few curious looks from other arch-goblins but some recognised him, other whispered that he was some demon in disguise, having seen him at the battle at the cave. The red-haired began a slow trot south towards General Blackpool's departing army. That trot eventually turned into a run, an elongated run actually as his legs stretched to abnormal lengths growing longer and gaining longer strides. Too long for any arch-goblin. Eventually the red-haired arch-goblin sighted the lights of the distant army. He changed form once again as he closed the gap. His legs shrunk to the length of a man's, in fact he became a man, once again, in the guise of Mr Night.

Mimdrid was overjoyed playing the part of both the red-haired arch-goblin and Mr Night. Liaison to both parties. But only General Baltus Blackpool and his brother Anthon knew the truth of the matter. Why wouldn't they, it was all by their designs. But unfortunately for Mimdrid, the night gave him a false sense of security to transform out in the open.

His elongated trots and transformation from the red-haired arch-goblin into the human Mr Night was seen by a man resting in the darkness from upon a hillock; the newly retired Master Sergeant Dunkin Saltclaw saw the transformation take place.

* * * * *

Chieftain Blist's army went to the right while Chieftain Gutter's moved left. Their soldiers began raiding houses. Most people were not home but a few did not take part in the celebration by the docks but now wish they had.

The sounds of screams and then silence was a melody to Chieftain Blist. The large and ever angry arch-goblin was in a particularly good mood for he knew the northeast of the city held the wealthiest homes, thanks to Anthon parting that knowledge while the rabble and hardworking folk lived in the western parts of the city. It even held a slum in the west. Chieftain Gutter knew nothing of the dynamics of the city populace and for that Chieftain Blist stood to garner much. Wealth such as metal objects, currency, jewels, armour, weapons and even fine cloth were thrown out the doorways of buildings to be collected by the older arch-goblins, ones although capable of fighting but well past their prime and the women arch-goblins. Veen some of the arch-goblin-youth participated in the clean-up of the booty.

For Chieftain Gutter, there was much resistance. Several massage parlours, drunk warriors and poorer families present him pockets of resistance. Still, his arch-goblins too were pillaging where they could. Some families noticed such and throughout their precious items in hope to elude slaughter. Other prizes Chieftain Gutter was after were slaves. He did not care what kind but most were women and children. The chieftain brought lizard-goblins to help funnel and control his captives into pockets and pen them wherever they could. Then the lizard-goblins were immediately chaining them up the residents while the arch-goblins moved onward to pillage and kill any resistance.

* * * * *

From upon high and in the form of a large bat, Queen Ooktha watched the event unfold. It was to her liking. She was dumbfounded how easily her arch-goblins and Anthon's iron-golem could achieve such surprise. She had to admit that when it came following orders and remaining silent to achieve surprise, arch-goblins were very good.

"Not as good as us elves though," she said to herself but then reminded herself she was no longer an elf, at least not accepted as one. Her elven kin could never accept her bloodlust, nor would they try, hence becoming queen to the arch-goblin hoards below. However, longing for elven acceptance was a feeling she thought she would never succumb to again but the appearance of Leif and his tolerance of her condition, no acceptance of her being a vampire was unexpected. Confusing as her feelings for Leif were, she had worked too hard to unify the arch-goblins and this was what she had promised them, a glorious battle with much reward! It was too late to turn back.

She wanted Leif too in her life or undead life but could not have both she knew. Leif, she knew would never accept this; he was too lawful. She would have to turn him but that is not what she wanted, she did not want to turn others into what she had become, she would rather kill them before making them into a vampire. Perhaps she might run away with her elven soldier and leave all this behind and hide this mess she helped create.

She shook Leif from her thoughts and once again concentrated on the battle below. She could not see Anthon. Smartly he was invisible. She intended to kill the wizard once his own revenge was complete, for she intended to allow her arch-goblins to stay much longer than agreed upon with General Blackpool but also needed Anthon to distract the wizards of the city. Additionally, her other arch-goblins, those of the mountain city of Blood-helm should be engaged with the general, bogging him down and preventing him from rescuing his people. Such a fool, or so she thought.

It was too late to turn back, the events she helped put into play here were too delicious to ignore. Down she swooped to land atop a roof that offered her a view of the golem walking its way towards the wizard's tower. She then transformed into her elven self. Adorned in black, several wands hung from her slender hips. She wore knee-high boots, revealing corset armour and black eye make-up that covered part of her face like a mask. She was a beautiful but deadly sight.

Chapter 29
The Wizard's College

The Sedgedunum Wizards tower was a large four-sided fifty-foot square tower that reached nearly two-hundred and fifty feet into the air and sat upon a twenty-foot-high base. The tower base was surrounded by a collection of decorative stone buildings. All the buildings were of the same brownish stone. Statues of past head masters and powerful graduates were placed about these buildings. Carvings of the sun, moon and stars decorated the stone work. Magic symbols too adorned the décor. This surrounding infrastructure hosted additional housing and classrooms for wizards who attended the school. .

The iron-golem, under the direction of Anthon, walked up to the large doorway of the Sedgedunum Wizard's College and smashed at the door with its enchanted mace. Sparks flew as the door's enchantment met the mace's magic. After several attempts by the golem, the large oak and metal door came off its hinges. The golem received a blast of fireballs and lightning by the mages with in the college's ground level.

"It's an iron-golem," shouted a wiry old woman dressed in green robes with unkempt-frizzy hair known as Kayneep. "It is absorbing the heat and burning whatever it touches! Cast lighting or mage's darts or cold spells! Anything but fire!" she shouted.

She did not know Anthon was attuned to the golem and was listening, as well as seeing through the golem. She made herself a target then as Anthon commanded the iron-golem to rush at the wizards who greeted the golem. Kayneep found herself flying through the air, struck by the golems enchanted mace. Her back broken, her lungs filling with smoke, she died a slow and painful death.

Casting spells became problematic for the wizards as heat now radiated from golem due to the fireballs cast upon it. Other wizards were trampled, swatted or escaped the path of the creature as the iron-golem made its way up the steps of the tower base.

Now in the confines of the tower walls, the creature found itself in a large library. Books lay on benches, tables, shelves and racks lined the walls. The iron-golem and Anthon did not care. By Anthon's command, the iron-golem began smashing and wrecking the shelves of books. As it did so, it was done with purpose. It sent this pile of books, shelves tables and chairs back to the large doorway from which it entered, to block it. There was one wizard up along a wooden catwalk of the library that led into an upper level. That wizard, a young male, fired a barrage of mage's darts at the golem. They seemed to cause no ill effect. The iron-golem ignored the young wizard, walked to the most southern wall and began to smash at the stones with that mace. Cracks formed in the walls.

* * * * *

Queen Ooktha could hear the commotion going on inside the tower. The screams and chaos that rang from within echoed even over the fireworks happening over the harbour. However, word had gotten out and wizards were hurrying to the front doors of the college. In addition, a mass exodus of town's folk was running through the streets past her location towards the college. It was those escaping the onslaught of her arch-goblins she realised. There was not much more to see and so she used one of the powers of a vampire and turned herself into a gaseous form to manoeuvre silently in the dark.

She floated through the alleyways back towards her arch-goblins in the northern parts of the city. She noted opposition though, a team on mercenaries and soldiers banded together creating a pocket of resistance. Carts were laid out along a street that ran east to west in Chieftain Gutter's part of the city. That part held several pubs and therefore several mercenaries. Her arch-goblins exchanged arrows and crossbow bolts back and forth. Her arch-goblins outnumbered the resistance nearly five to one but could not make progress into the road. Several arch-goblins of Chieftain Gutter clan lay dead at either end of the road.

She materialised into a dark corner, unseen. With stealth, she made her way up towards the eastern side of the resistance, snapping necks of some of the folk. After her third kill she was noticed by a young warrior, drunk he was but capable with his sword still. Her gaze took control of him quickly, as vampires' capabilities can.

"You can have me, my love," she imparted to him. "If you stab at those men," she said.

The young soldier knew it was wrong and was shaken by the disturbing events of the present situation. Her hold on him was wavering, a sign of the recent events being dramatic, so she beckoned him into the shadows. She killed him quickly. Frustrated, she threw him with one hand from out of the shadows and into the backs of two of those shooting arrows at her arch-goblins. She pulled forth her wand and produced a lightning bolt that jolted the surprised men. There were ten of them shaken and in disarray. Another blast came from her, killing a male soldier and a mercenary female. One female, a wizard, recovered and cast a lightning bolt of her own back into the shadows but only hit the building, no one was there.

It was a tense moment for the remaining eight holding the eastern side of the street. The female launched another blast of lightning hitting only the buildings and lighting the darkness, revealing no one. After an uncomfortable silence, the overturned carts and barrels that made the makeshift barrier of the street exploded and went flying into the air, stunning several. The way was open for the arch-goblins to rush in, but none entered. Nor was there a fire or lightning that might cause the sudden explosion. Instead stood a beautiful black-haired elf, black knee-high boots, black corset armour and war paint of black across her eyes. Then she lunged for the female wizard, baring fangs as only vampires could. The wizard's throat was ripped out, blood sprayed forth over Queen Ooktha.

"Delicious!" she announced. Some of the not-so-stunned folks ran away, others remained either too dazed or frozen with fear. Then the arch-goblins rushed in.

* * * * *

The fireworks ended early and many of the wizards made their way out of the harbour back towards the college. It was then the people noticed the bells ringing from places of worship and guard towers along the perimeter walls. Mass confusion began to erupt as rumours of an invasion began to spread?

When some wizards took flight through magical means, many of the citizens grew more concerned. Then the City Watch began to make their way out of the crowded wharfs toward the city centre. Panic started to set in among the masses as stories of the northern part of the city was overrun with arch-goblins and the wizard's college has been compromised.

Boyd Draconian, Headmaster of Sedgedunum's Wizard's College, along with several other magic-users flew around their college. They saw a large hole in the southern wall of the tower, just above the towers base and it was getting bigger! Something internally was knocking out the wall and the hole started to wrap would the corner to the west of the tower.

"We have to get in there to stop this else it will bring down the whole tower upon the college," shouted the head master to the other wizards.

Down the wizards went, three heading to the opening led by Boyd Draconian and four more headed towards the broken front doors. In the headmaster flew and was met by the enchanted mace of the iron-golem. Although Boyd reinforced his own protections, he was stunned by the power of the mace. The headmaster went flying backwards and landed upon one of the roof tops of the college buildings. Two other wizards made it into the tower though, the third changed his mind at entering the tower and went to check on the headmaster. Bolts of electricity wrecked upon he iron-golem. Attacks from the two wizards that flew in and a third reaching in through the rubble placed at the original entrance way. However, that only seemed to slow the movements of the creature.

In retaliation, on came the golem's powerful mace. It was directed at the two wizards who just flew into the melee. The two wizards, surprised the creature was aware of their presence, dodged the attack by jumping behind and through the rubble of the original entry way. One of the wizards regained enough sense to run through the large hole he just flew in from. The other felt the force of the enchanted mace and became a bloody stain upon the floor.

Chieftain Blist, the giant arch-goblin who ruled the underground city of Skulls-thorpe relished in what was transpiring before him. He walked casually along the streets. Many of the wealthy homes in his captured section were empty, save a few servants or elderly. Wealth of different sorts were pouring into the streets. Metal in all shapes, sizes and kinds were plucked form homes by his invading hordes and deposited in the streets for elderly arch-goblins and lizard-goblins to cart off back from which his warriors came.

"A fine cache of metal works to be made into weapons or sold in the Skagsnest market," he said to his bodyguards as much as to himself. He received reports from lizard-goblins who acted as runners for communication purposes. The lizard-goblin runners told him of the confrontations that Chieftain Gutter was experiencing and a request for support was received. However, Chieftain Blist cared little of the reports and ignored the request, killing the lizard-goblin who brought the news. He was becoming wealthy with each passing moment and wanted to enjoy the scene for the moment. It was then he saw a female house servant, a half-orc tied with rope, with other captured citizens.

"Bring her to me," he said pointing. The Chieftain had cruel intentions with her. An elderly arch-goblin untied her and brought her to his chieftain. The Chieftain grabbed her by the hair and strolled to the nearest residence to have his evil way with her. Fortunately for the half-orc female a black smoke appeared before them both. It took shape into the form of a beautiful female dressed in all black, she had white skin that was almost blue and black war paint across her eyes.

"What news have you for me cousin," stated Queen Ooktha.

Chieftain Blist released the female half orc who went running wild but was chased down by arch-goblins and lizard-goblins. "Thus far, my queen, we have secured four main streets and have been collecting precious metals, slaves and many other spoils with little resistance."

"Chieftain Gutter does not fare as well as you," she responded. "Pockets of resistance and developed among his district and you have found none it seems. Send him some support," she said bluntly.

Chieftain Blist was not pleased at that request, demand. The Chieftain actually almost stammered in defiance and Queen Ooktha caught the agitation in the arch-goblins body language. It was almost comical. Still, Queen Ooktha was a vampire after all and could kill him quickly, or slowly or anyway she liked he realised. Therefore, the chieftain responded, "As you wish, my queen." But the Chieftain's body language showed a clear sign of agitation.

"I know it pains you, my friend," she announced as he began to walk away, "to have to aid Chieftain Gutter after you have claimed so much in spoils. But if his minions are pushed back too quickly, we will all suffer for it."

"I understand, my queen," he responded.

"And Chieftain Blist," she said. "There is a reason why you sit next to me at Skulls-thorpe and not any other chieftain. It is because I can rely upon you to get things done!"

* * * * *

The retired Sergeant Major Magnus Foehammer was mustering every able body with a weapon. His wife Disa was already organising a make-shift recovery centre for the wounded coming from the northern quarters. Like so many other folk, they too were trapped along piers at the Festival of the Seas.

"I am told by the casualty's coming in that the north-east quarter and possibly the northwest quarter of the city is being overrun by arch-goblins," shouted Magnus over the noise of the battle waging in the wizard's college. It was being heard even among the crowds on docks. "Everyone with a weapon and willing to save our loved ones from being pushed into the sea, follow me!" shouted Magnus. "The rest of you use carts and boxes or whatever you can find to put up a defensive wall and perimeter."

Magnus kissed Disa farewell but she halted him and said, "I am going with you this time."

"No, my dear, stay here and take care of the injured, I will send them to you," he replied.

"Magnus, I worry I will not see you again, I am coming!"

"Please, my love, stay here at least until I come back with more news as to what is transpiring," he responded.

With that, Magnus with just his trusted bastardsword, regular clothing, no armour, the brave 'retired' soldier led two dozen men into the northeast section of the city.

The explosions and damage being done to the Sedgedunum's Wizard's College made the apprehensive journey even more frightening. Sudden flashes of light coming from the wizards casting at whoever or whatever enemy they were fighting in the college. Magnus paused as he watched what looked like Headmaster Boyd Draconian being batted out from the college to land somewhere onto one of the roofs of a college building. Wounded and scared people who were fleeing that section were also passing useful information.

"We'll break into two teams," he said. "Half take the road up the right, I will take the other half up the left sight of Sedgedunum's Wizard's College. I want to know what is happening there as well."

Six men who appeared as sailors and all seemed to know one another decided to go with Magnus. They seemed well armed surprisingly! The six all had either a cutlass or sabres. The remaining posy had normal swords.

Magnus now went northward with his elven-person motley crew, keeping to the right of the avenue, so he could glimpse the battle unfold in the college tower on his left. Some of the men with him saw people in the streets, in homes and in shops. They relayed to the citizens to lock their doors and close their windows or head to the docks for safety. With the wizard tower now somewhat behind them, they started to make out the sounds of battle, screaming and of course the grunts and deep growls of arch-goblins.

However, when Magnus cautiously peered around the corner, what he mostly saw was lizard-goblins. About twenty lizard-goblins and only six arch-goblins tying up prisoners. Most were non-combatant women and some young children who were sobbing. Two adult males were lying dead in the street.

"I hate lizard-goblins," said Magnus. Magnus told the rest of the men the numbers. "Wait for me to make some noise first then come charging in."

Not certain of what this large man was planning but he seemed to be the de facto leader and agreed. With that, Magnus silently turned the corner. He creeped up behind an unsuspecting lizard-goblin and swatted the small creature from behind with an upward swipe of his bastard sword. The poor creature went flying apart, covering several arch-goblins and lizard-goblins in blood. Magnus then quickly kicked another into the air with his large boot and cleave another lizard-goblin. Magnus's voice erupted in a large shout as he hacked away at two more lizard-goblins who tried to get out of the way of the large ginger-haired man. As soon as the arch-goblins began to step towards Magnus in defence, the rest of the Magus's motley crew came running into the melee, the six buccaneers leading the way.

Magnus then put an overhead swing of his sword to the nearest arch-goblin who put up his spear with both hands to catch the sword. The spear cracked easily enough, allowing the sward to split the skull of the arch-goblin. The rest of the lizard-goblins were in full retreat as were the rest of the arch-goblins. Some lizard-goblins tried to get through locked doors of buildings only to be cleaved by the crew.

"Well, Mr Magnus, you killed four lizard-goblins before we even got to you," said one of the sailors. "My name is Ruko," said the young black-haired swashbuckler. "How far do you want to press?"

Magnus was at first confused as he did not remember telling this man his name but assumed he heard it when talking to Disa and let it be. "Until we are stalemated or turned back," replied Magnus, examining the dead arch-goblin. "I do not recognise these markings so this clan is not from the mountains," he said aloud referring to the armour and clothing worn by the now dead arch-goblins.

Ruko's men untied the prisoners, some of whom fell over the fallen male family members in tears. After several moments, Ruko said, "Be gone from here, ladies, back to the docks, it is safer there then in the streets." Magnus moved the dead bodies off to the side of the street.

"What else have you seen?" asked Magnus. However, not much more was gained from the rescued prisoners and bade them to make for the harbour as the rest of his motley crew returned from their kills. Ten lizard-goblins and another arch-goblin in total, dead.

"You know, sir, they are probably waiting for us now, down the road," said Ruko to Magnus.

Another explosion rocked the wizard's tower just then. Magnus had an idea then. "I know this city better than any of them. Let us slip down the alley to the west and flank them."

"Are you sure you want to get that close to the havoc that is taking place among the wizard's college?" asked Ruko, seeing the crew's growing concerned looks.

"I am sure everyone is fleeing from that which is why it might be a safer way north," replied Magnus.

On they went then turned west. They came to the centre road that split the city in half. They did not emerge though. Instead they remained in the side alleyway to view the battle waging in the wizard's college before moving northward. From there they could see the college on fire from the battle. Bolts of lightning, mage's darts and other spells were ringing off something inside the tower of the college. A stone block from the tower exploded from the west wall.

"Well, I must say, it looks like a good battle is waging in there," stated Ruko.

"Let me see, please," asked one of the members of the crew, a young man in fine clothing and was very capable with his rapier. "Curious?" he said. "I do not see spells emanating from the tower, only going in?" All gathered a bit closer to the alleyways edge. "Do you know if those wizards flying around the tower are friend or foe?" he asked.

"You bring up an excellent observa—" stated Ruko but was cut short when a flurry of crossbow bolts peppered the party. One of Ruko's men and the young man in fine clothes had several crossbow bolts sticking out of them.

"Back! Hurry!" shouted Magnus. He saw that these arch-goblins were well armoured, they outnumbered them by at least ten and were led by a very large arch-goblin. Magnus carried the young man who would likely be dead soon and Ruko's other men carried their sailor who might not live either. Ruko pulled out a bunch of caltrops from a hidden bag he carried and dropped them as they fled. Small explosions followed by echoes of pain came from back down the alleyway; the caltrops bought them some time to escape.

"It is not as bad as it sounds, the explosions are minor, but it is the sleep potions inside the caltrops that are the real value."

They were back to where they freed the prisoners earlier. They ran into more lizard-goblins, a dozen of them and quickly dispatched them, killing eight. Magnus, covered in blood from the now dead young man, set the man down next to the other fallen men from earlier.

"Do you have any more tricks in that bag of yours to cover our tracks?" asked Magnus.

"I do, but it just puts them to sleep or makes them dreary," Ruko replied.

"Then let us cover our retreat and try and link up with the other party that we broke from earlier. Perhaps they are having better success than us," stated Magnus.

"Um, yes we can do that," stated Ruko reluctantly.

"Captain, perhaps it is time for *our* retreat?" asked one of the sailors of Ruko, pointing to the others of the party now heading back to the docks. Magnus, Ruko and four sailors remained.

"We are done good sir, for now," stated one of the men retuning to the docs. "We are not armoured for this and undermanned. I will, however, try and get more people to join us and let them know where you are headed." Magnus nodded to the man without another word.

"What say you, Magnus?" asked Ruko.

"Return if you must with them," replied Magnus. "However, we might do the city more justice freeing more people or acting as deterrent to the arch-goblins and lizard-goblins until more of the city musters the courage to press forward." Ruko admired this man's determination.

Magnus and his reduced motley crew backtracked to where he split the original party from the docks and made their way northward again. This time further east into the section of the city.

* * * * *

Boyd Draconian, Headmaster of Sedgedunum's Wizard's College was badly bruised and dazed from being batted out of the college by the iron-golem's mace. However, the man was well warded regardless of the day or situation and was able to regain his composure. With his spell of flying exhausted, the man began to run up the roof of the college to grasp the situation.

A huge quarter of the tower was knocked out, bricks scatter over the college roof and put many holes through the tops making the roof he was on, unstable. From the sounds of it, a great magical barrage was taking place inside the tower. If it not for the sounds of explosions, a bystander might thing a magical lightshow was emanating from within the lower part of the tower.

Boyd drew forth a large staff from an *enchanted bag* he kept hidden beneath his orange and black garments. He tapped the large wooden staff on his foot once, activating another spell of flying. The man flew up before the large hole in the wall; the room was on fire!

Spells came in from the inside doorway to damage the back of the iron-golem who took the brunt of them but kept swinging away at the wall, knocking more of the structure loose. It was clear now to Boyd the golem's intent or master's intent was to bring the tower crashing down and levelling the college. Who would want that? The headmaster could only guess for now. Boyd Draconian, Headmaster of Sedgedunum's Wizard's College, now floating outside the gaping hole of the college tower, levelled his staff at the golem, chanted and released a cone of cold. He had hoped the wizards beyond the inner doorway would have enough sense to run form the blast of cold. The headmaster not only needed to stop the iron-golem but also needed to extinguish the fires in the room, it was the library after all. The *wind of frost* did just as he hoped, it extinguished the fires but more importantly it slowed the iron-golem's movements. Its body creaked as it made a now weakened attempt to hit the wall once more with its magical mace. The cold, he hoped would do the trick in slowing down the golem, and it did!

Now the man began his next spell as the slowing iron-golem suddenly stood apparently motionless. In fact, it was completely motionless, and Boyd was surprised by that. He expected the beast to continue its assault.

"No matter," said Boyd to himself as he readied a *mage's gate* to cast the creature away from here, into the ocean he decided, far from here. Boyd would cast the powerful spell so close and behind it that the beast would surely fall into it. It was a spell few could cast, save for truly experienced wizards.

Suddenly, a strange silence fell all about him. His lips moved but no words came forth. A *silence spell* was cast over him! He could not mouth the words to his spells. Then a *dismiss enchantment* was cast upon the man and he then found himself tumbling down onto the roof of the college as his flying spell was expelled.

He hit it so suddenly that he lost hold of his staff. When he looked up into the darkness of night, he saw three robed silhouettes upon a magic carpet high above him. All had wands pointing at him. What followed was a barrage of fire, lighting and acid. The barrage punched the man through the roof and unto the floor beneath him. His magical wards nearly at an end, the room was ablaze now with fire, as was his magic staff now falling down from the roof. Another salvo came through the ceiling though, detonating around the man. The lightning hit that very powerful staff and it exploded, thus Boyd Draconian, Headmaster of Sedgedunum's Wizard's College, was no more.

Two more fireballs entered the tower reigniting some parchments and furniture but also helping the iron-golem by dissolving the frost over it. Anthon then set back down upon the magic carpet to regain control of the golem. The male wizard recast another invisibility spell. The iron-golem then continued its destruction once again.

* * * * *

It didn't take long for Magnus and his motley crew to catch up with the rest of the volunteers they split from initially. They had engaged in battle as well. A dead volunteer was found along the way, as were several dead lizard-goblins and a dead arch-goblin. Clearly, this crew pushed further north, as they were not in eye sight. The sound of battle erupted further on. Magnus quickened his pace and found them engaged in combat with arch-goblins and lizard-goblins. With two more volunteers dead and others bleeding, Magnus charged into the fray, Ruko and his sailors right behind him. It took only moments before Magnus, Ruko and the sailors turned the momentum. Three more arch-goblins dropped and they began a speedy retreat. The lizard-goblins ran away. Magnus and his original motley crew were back together and all came to the same conclusion: the Arch-goblins were pushing south but not at full force. Instead they were looting the northern parts of the city. Unfortunately, that's as far as the conversation got as the arch-goblins were now returning.

"Let's make a stand here," stated Ruko who seemed to be enjoying this.

"Agreed, for now," said Magnus who picked up a shield from a dead arch-goblin. "For the moment, let these ones come to us and then we will chase their arses north," he finished. It did not take long for Ruko to see what Magnus meant by that.

On came a swarm of thirty armoured arch-goblins, against a motley crew of fifteen who were moments ago enjoying the festivities at the Festival of the Seas. Magnus met a charging arch-goblin, allowing the creature to run into him or at least the arch-goblin thought he was running into Magnus. Instead Magnus ducked at the last second, sending the arch-goblin over his own back. As the arch-goblin did so, Magnus stood upright suddenly, launching the creature end-over-end into the air. Magnus did not even turn to finish the creature, instead he was relying on the motley crew behind him to finish the beast off. Magnus moved forward into the charging arch-goblins. He received a cut to his leg, another passing slice to his new-found shield. However, Magnus himself was able to slice two passing arch-goblins and stab a passing third. In the frenzy of battle, he wasn't certain of the ones he cut and stabbed were any of the ones that sliced at him. The whole scene was in a dark cobblestone road, lit by the blaze of the burning tower and the lanterns hanging form buildings.

Ruko and his boys were right behind Magnus at first, cutting, stabbing and killing the ones that Magnus hacked at as the large man pushed forward. But soon everyone in the road was engaged with a one or two arch-goblins.

Magnus suddenly stood still and locked eyes with the large arch-goblin he evaded earlier. The arch-goblin was ugly, taller than Magnus and well armoured. The arch-goblin, who was known to his fellow kin as Chieftain Blist, pulled forth a larger katana. Magnus threw his shield into the back of the head of another arch-goblin who was double teaming a Vorclaw citizen. With both Chieftain Blist and Magnus Foehammer holding their weapons in two hands, they ran at each other, blades ringing off one another three times before they both circled around each other. Again, they attacked, testing one another's metal. Blist threw an overhead chop but Magnus was able to get his trusted bastard sword up to block. Blist was surprised at the strength of Magnus. Both men were well muscled, but the human's sword barely gave way under the weight of the arch-goblin's mighty katana. Both kept their swords raised above their heads. Magnus had the most to concern for caution, he had no armour, no helm. Blist attacked suddenly realising this powerful human's disadvantage was his lack of protection.

Blist led with a series of overhead chops forcing Magnus to back away at first but the old soldier realised he had nowhere to retreat to. So Magnus stepped forward into the assault. Both swords met up high again. Magnus met the large arch-goblin face to face but realised his mistake when Blist started kicking at Magnus with his heavy boot in the shin and knee. Magnus winced and backed down offering Blist a chance to inflict another cut, but it was a ruse. While the pain to Magnus' leg was real, he let on the pain was more severe. Blist made another overhead slice thinking to push Magnus down to one knee however, Magnus side stepped out of the way to his right, spun around with his sword leading in a horizontal swipe, catching the overextended arch-goblin in the shoulder. Blist took the blow but was clearly surprised and hurt but the move.

Magnus would have continued the assault were it not for another arch-goblin coming to his chieftain's aid. Magnus dispatched the new arch-goblin quickly enough and faced Blist once again. Blist was unable to raise his left arm up very high and now kept his katana out vertically in front of him. Magnus grinned a bit, knowing he did some damage.

Magnus took stock of the situation, both human and arch-goblin littered the streets. Ruko was still alive as were his sailors! Magnus took advantage of an arch-goblin engaged with one of those sailors and cut the leg out from under him so one of Rukos's sailors could finish him off. Magnus then motioned for Blist to come at him but the giant arch-goblin merely smiled a toothy grin instead.

Oddly the commotion seemed to wane as several arch-goblins and humans started to look Magnus's way. A cool chill filled Magnus bones as he felt het presence of someone behind him. Magnus felt a sudden weight upon his shoulders, dropping him to his knees. The weight did not cease and the pressure pinched his shoulder with the strength of an ogre at least.

"You cannot kill him," shouted Ruko. "He is Magnus Foehammer!"

Suddenly, Queen Ooktha eased her grip. "You are the father of Leif?" she asked.

Magnus was in great pain from her vice-like grip upon his shoulders that it took him moments to answer yes. Queen Ooktha then grabbed the man again hard by the tunic and threw him back at Ruko. Magnus struck Ruko like a boulder, both went tumbling. The vampiress slowly turned to face the remaining motley crew of Magnus. "Be gone all of you," she said to them.

All began to back away, down the road from which they came while the arch-goblins huddled in triumph around their vampire queen. Then a loud rumble echoed from the city centre. Queen Ooktha smiled, her fangs now evident to all as the wizard's tower began to fall over the western part of the college!

The men of Vorclaw were slowly backing down the street when a new crop of volunteer warriors arrived on the scene. Twenty armed men and women. One woman came to the front of the pack.

"Get out of my city, you bitch!" shouted Disa. She held up her holy symbol of Matronae beaming a bright white light of purity. Queen Ooktha hissed and shielded her eyes. Her arch-goblins too were blinded by the power of Matronae within Disa. They now began a hasty retreat of their own.

Queen Ooktha hissed in defiance but felt her skin beginning to bubble away and turn to ash. So she fled, turning quickly into a bat and vanished into the night sky. So too did her arch-goblins go back down the road. The newcomers did not pursue. They were unsure on how to proceed as dust and dirt began to descend on the town from the fallen tower.

Undaunted, Magnus rose and instructed everyone to build defensive fortifications along the roads and to hold the ground they have gained. "It was hard fight clearly and worth keeping in honour of the lives spent this night," he said to Disa.

He then looked for Ruko to discuss who and what that was and why his name meant anything to the vampire and why she knew Leif's name. But the sailor and his remaining men were gone, presumably back to the docks.

Chapter 30

Necropolis

Through the cobra-mouth door and up another warmer passage which was odd because they were going higher into the mountain. But everyone could feel a slightly warm breeze. It was a welcome relief to Erik who was feeling ill from the cold. The upward hike and nervousness at the prospect of fighting a revenant did not help. But the young wizard assured himself that he was given what he needed by his master to combat the creature.

"This passage contained more carvings of snakes, beetles and crocodiles like the ones from the previously cut steps," stated Leif.

"There is more of that unknown writing as well," stated Erik. "It almost seems otherworldly."

They all stopped at the next landing where a large statue of stone in the form of a slender but muscled man with the head of a dog or a jackal atop it. It was twice the height of Bjorn and stood holding a small shepherd's crook and a sickle shaped sword. Behind the statue was another door made of thick wood. After Damon and Dru checked for traps and Erik did not detect any magic emanations, Dru went to work on picking the lock. It took a long while for Dru. Even Damon was unfamiliar with this type of locking mechanism but together they unlocked the large door. The door creaked slightly, and everyone jumped back a bit as light emanated from the now cracked opened door and heat came through! Once nothing else happened, Damon inched the door open more, another set of stairs came into view. It wrapped around another corridor where more light came through.

"Odd that we're even higher in the mountains from when we started and it's warm," said Damon.

The party went up the stairs, relishing in the warm air. Within moments they emerged upon a small rocky outcrop. What they saw mesmerised and astounded them.

Below them, running east to west, nestled in a large crater like basin was a forest. Rising up through the forest appeared to be an ancient city, a ruin. The east was dominated by a great red stone pyramid. The centre of the city had a fissure running through the length of it that appeared to have no bottom that anyone could see. It wasn't a perfect crater though, high into the mountains. From their perch, a great desert could be seen to the west which stood in contrast to the surrounding snow-capped peaks.

"Was anyone expecting to see this?" asked Leif.

No one answered. All were still mesmerised by the beauty of this place.

"The whole scene is odd. It appears as if a god made a thumbprint into the land and shoved an ancient city into it," said Dru.

"It definitely looks out of place," said Bjorn.

Damon had already found a way down into the forest. "There is plenty of daylight left. Are all your spells prepared?" he asked both Bjorn and Erik. Bjorn and Erik needed another hour to prepare so Dru and Damon decided to try and scout ahead.

"This is all wrong," said Lorez. "No red stone around here to make that giant pyramid."

Leif sat down not really listening. Instead Leif pulled forth the small Jade Tower Queen Ooktha gave him. "So, how do I activate this? This soul sucker. She said you have the activation word."

"Awe yes, I almost forgot," replied Lorez. She said the command word is *Archangel* and will only work on the undead. Must weaken him first but not knowing what Queen Ooktha means by this.

To Leif that sounded oddly familiar. "Was that...a place? Archangel?"

"My mission was to make certain you go in and to pass you the command word for the soul sucker," continued the arch-goblin. "I am not familiar with this item or what the command word refers to. I do not even believe she crafted it. It is said Queen Ooktha has many undead allies and I believe one of them provided it to her."

"Perhaps she has a mutual ally that also wishes the demise of Rom-Seti?" asked Leif studying the small Jade Tower in his hand.

Lorez, who continued to study the red stone pyramid, only shrugged in response, not knowing the answer. Leif stood up then and took notice of the red stone pyramid and the small city before it. "I agree, with your assessment, the whole complex seems out of place. Perhaps the red stones were quarried elsewhere, do you think?" finished Leif.

"Perhaps, but the forest is about right, thick with pines and brush suited for high elevations," said Lorez.

Bjorn interrupted the elf and arch-goblin. "We're ready," said Bjorn referring to himself and Erik.

"Any sign of Dru and his wicked mentor?" asked Bjorn, still upset with Damon threatening Leif.

"I see them," said Leif whose eyes were sharper being an elf. "They are returning through the forest." Dru motioned for the rest to come down the hill. Erik and Bjorn lead the way down.

"Well, my friend this is where we part ways," said Leif to Lorez.

"Sker and I will be waiting for your return, large elf," responded Lorez.

"Iza go with Master Leif," said Sker.

Leif looked at the runty lizard-goblin, squatted and smiled. "You don't have to come with me, you know."

"Iza where my good friend Master Leif goes," replied Sker. "Besides, someone needs to keep watch on the wicked man for you," said Sker referring to Damon.

"You are too good to me, Sker. And I will have an important task for you on this mission my friend," he told the Lizard-goblin and winked.

"Settled then," said Lorez, "I will be waiting inside the cave entrance."

"Farewell, my friend," said Leif.

"Farewell, my friend," said Lorez. Lorez suddenly grabbed Leif by the arm. "Do you *not* know what you are doing, what you are up against?" asked Lorez in all seriousness. "A revenant! Don't do this," he said. "Let us all just leave this behind and find adventure elsewhere. Even bring that arrogant human, Damon. You don't need Queen Ooktha and neither do I. You are great in a fight and we could all have fun wreaking havoc and finding adventure here in the north," he said.

Leif recognised what his arch-goblin friend was driving at but after many moments of consideration he said, "I have to. She could have killed me but let me live and now if I turn my back on this task, then my soldiers would all have died for nothing. I have to do this to set things right in Vorclaw and show how my men did not die in vain against Chieftain Merka."

"But it is a revenant," he whispered so Sker could not fully hear. "You all will not likely survive."

"We all have out magical enchantments. And we have the element of surprise," stated Leif.

Lorez let Leif walk off with Sker in tow, not daring to hope but would wait never the less. The arch-goblin did not have the stomach to tell his elf friend about the webs being spun between Queen Ooktha, Colonel Blackpool and others in Vorclaw. Lorez knew that even if Leif did survive this endeavour, the land he would return to would be very different indeed.

* * * * *

After several moments of surveying the old ruins of the town before the pyramid, Damon gave the signal to come out of the trees. They all hopped over an old stone wall and begin making their way towards the red stone pyramid.

"Everyone," announced Damon quietly. "Draw your weapons, put on your rings and step cautiously."

"Pull forth your lavender-wands," said Bjorn, hang them from their belt loops. "Although they appear to be nothing more than stems and flowers from the lavender plant bound together with white criss-crossed string, they are blessed. These will ward off undead creatures by masking the wearers living scent but also repels minor undead creatures."

The roads were a grey cobblestone but the buildings were made of the same stone as the red stone pyramid.

"The stone is beautiful," said Erik quietly. "But not seen anything like it before."

The sun was still overhead providing ample daylight so they came down a street easily enough, keeping the large pyramid in sight. They were heading directly east down a road that contained what looked like dwellings. Broken doors and windows revealed only empty darkness within each structure.

"If there is anyone living here, they're not home presently," whispered Dru.

They came to the end of the street that opened up into a large open square, possibly used for markets but was void of anything such. Dozens of skeletons lay scattered throughout the square. Most poorly armoured and as if eroded from weather. Some we're clearly not soldiers and notably were children.

"I see human, elf, dwarf, possibly orc and even children!" said Bjorn remarking about the skeletons.

Leif motioned for Sker to climb up on the back of Leif to get a better look from the elf's shoulders. "I see lizard-goblin skeletons, Master Leif. Many dead, maybe hundreds."

"Let's head to that building with all the columns and take a look inside," said Damon. "Looks like a temple of some kind but day light is reaching in from a caved in roof."

"Just keep quiet as we walk across, let us not disturb the dead," said Bjorn.

They made it across the square littered with skeletons without incident. They walked up the temple steps. They turned to get a good look of the ruins behind them. From their new vantage point atop the temple steps, they could see many of the roofs of the buildings had collapsed but the framework of the buildings seemed in tack. After several moments of awe, they turned their attention to the large bronze doors of the temple. They were sundered and the right door was off its top hinge creating a crack that a small child could go through. There was light inside but that came from the open roof. Damon peered inside and around the door for traps but paused. The man had sent in Sker to take a look.

"The lizard-goblin has talent enough to look around for us I take it?" asked Damon who stepped aside with somewhat of annoyed face.

Leif merely rolled his eyes at the man and then focused on Sker. "Just look around my friend, see if there is anything alive or dead. Take my lavender wand, it should provide you some protection. I will give you until a count of two hundred and then I want you back," finished Leif. Sker nodded and accepted his assignment. The small lizard-goblin was back well before the count finished.

"You must see," said Sker. "Come quickly!" he finished and disappeared back through the damaged door way.

Leif went first and crawled through to the other side. Bjorn and Dru began to protest but Leif was already through before they could get to him. Dru walked up to the doorway and could see Leif motioning for the rest of them to come through. One by one they crept through the broken opening of the large bronze doors, all careful not to disturb the large doors as they entered.

They came upon a large hall with stone pillars adorning the right and left, all covered with the strange hieroglyphs. The roof was smashed all over the floor and buried what looked like well-polished red, orange and black marble. Broken statues humanoid bodies but with heads of beasts adorned the place. The opposite end what may have been an altar but was instead a gaping empty space. The whole back of the building had fallen into the rift they all saw before descending.

"So here starts the rift," stated Damon.

"You see, no skeletons," said Sker excited. "No undead."

"Well done, Sker," said Leif. "It looks like the only way out is back the way we came or down into the rift or did you find another way out."

In the distance, they could see the looming pyramid, where they believe Rom-Seti made his lair.

"We are about half a mile away," said Dru. "Best for us to back out the way we came and go around," he said.

"I saw dark holes going under temple but Sker not certain where lead," stated the lizard-goblin. "But no smell of death coming from the holes so I think no undead."

"We need to explore this sight afterwards," said Damon. "There is gold paint on some of the damaged statues and likely other treasures to be found, perhaps in those holes he speaks of."

"Agreed, let's be off then," stated Bjorn. "I am not a fan of pagan religions and this temple looks ancient, foreign and pagan to this land. I do not find appealing."

"Show me the holes, Sker," said Leif winking over at Bjorn who now looked annoyed at Leif for suggesting to stay longer. The lizard-goblin showed Leif and Dru who joined them. Two holes were on the far side of the temple, nearer to rift. The holes had stairs but were covered by rubble.

"They appear to be entrance ways below the temple, hidden by the roof collapsing," stated Dru.

"Again, we'll come back later!" stated an agitated Damon Crag but it was too late, Sker went down the steps. Anyone else would have to crawl through a hole or remove rumble to follow Sker. However, popped back up quickly.

"Large room but empty crypts," stated Sker. "Tops off, no bodies remain," he finished.

Sker was about to say more but halted as Bjorn interrupted. "Leif, let's go!" he half-heartedly whispered but in a stern voice through his teeth.

"We'll talk later, let's get moving," said Leif to Sker. The lizard-goblin tried to say more but Leif had turned to move back to the party and so Sker decided to explain what else he saw, later.

Out they all went, careful not to disturb the bronze doors or make any noise that might bring attention onto them. If there was anyone around to hear them. They made their way down a street to the right of the temple, the south side of the basin, the side of the basin from which they entered the city. Leif looked to see if Lorez was up on the hillside and he was, watching.

The closer they got to the pyramid, the more damage to the buildings became apparent. The rift came to its widest along the road, swallowing whole buildings in fact. Again, skeletons did dot the roads but far fewer than the grounds before the temple. Halfway between the pyramid and the temple the rift was at its widest and they could see clearly into the bottom now. There was water filling the rift or part way as some the buildings that had fallen into the rift were exposed. Water was flowing or falling from somewhere nearer the pyramid. Plant life clung to the sides of the rift where sunlight could still reach and a natural rocky-beach seemed to have formed along the sides at the bottom of the rift. However, no way down seemed possible without ropes or magic.

Many of the building, similar in colours and stone to the red stone pyramid were still intact. Dark windows beckoned Leif's curiosity but Bjorn come up next to his brother raised an eyebrow knowing what Leif was thinking.

They finally came to the end of the city and now stood before the great red pyramid. It was damaged, cracked and a few skeletal remains, still in armour lay along the ramp. They appear to be to have been trying to exit the pyramid. They also found the source of the water. It was coming from the around the north side of the pyramid, through a crack in the rocks to the side. The water meandered to the west side of the ramped entrance of the pyramid and poured down in to the rift.

"It is a good thing we chose to approach from the south of the rift," stated Erik. "Otherwise we would have to cross that water and the slick flat rocks to get there."

"Yeah," said Leif. "Especially since it would have probably been you would have ended up slipping down into the rift, clumsy," finished Leif with a smile.

Dru let out a small laugh as well.

Damon put his hand to his lips to silence everyone. "From here on out, be ready, we do not know what else is in there," he whispered.

"All right," interjected Erik. "Stay close and I will cast the invisibility spell around us as planned using my ring," he said. Everyone took their prescribed positions discussed from the night before.

In the lead were both the shield-bearing warriors, Leif on the left with Sker hanging off his back, Bjorn to the right. In between them but a bit recessed was Damon Crag to try and spot any traps. Behind him was Erik the mage and taking up the rear was Dru and his two enchanted short swords.

Erik pulled forth a ring from his robes and the invisibility spell was cast. They took a moment to acclimate.

Erik then cast a spell to *detect invisibility* so the party to see each other. Although it was ghostly image of themselves, they could, for a time, see each other and anything else that may be lurk invisible.

"We have about one hour before both spells cease," stated Anthon. "But you must remain in close proximity to me to remain invisible. I have to cast one more spell, it will allow us all to see better in the dark. It too will last about an hour."

They walked up the ramp invisible but still capable of seeing each other. They made it to a large triple recessed doorway. The large stone doors to the pyramid's interior were smashed inwards, as if something was trying to get in. There were more remains of the dead around the door but in pieces. The inner chamber was dark and cold. The only light was the natural light from outside. There were three paths, left which went down, right which went down or straight which had stairs that went up.

"I say we go straight," whispered Bjorn. Damon looked the area over for traps with Dru. Quietly, they all agreed and went up the stairs. The passage way was barely wide enough to go two people across. Were it not for Anthon's spell, they would be completely blind, but everyone could see in the room as if a full moon was shining the light everywhere they looked. It took them to a hallway with rooms to both the left and right directly across from each other. The five rooms on each side had doorways but no doors or hinges for doors. The rooms all contained broken tables, ransacked jars, broken pottery and some unfortunate skeletal pieces. The hallway had blackened husk on the ground and soot was along the walls and floors.

At the end of the hallway was a wooden door, intact. Damon looked it over for traps. He even asked Sker if he could smell anything in and around the doorway. There wasn't even a keyhole, just a wooden latch. Damon then put on a small ring with a red gem and felt around the door. Leif looked to Dru for an answer. "Magical detection," explained Dru in a whisper.

Damon lifted the latch slowly and pushed open the door slowly, nothing happened. It was a large rectangular room filled with many rows of scroll tubes and tables covered by parchments known as papyrus.

"It is a library," said Dru. "And there is another door, up there!" he said referring to a balcony at the end of the room. "And it is open."

"Quiet!" demanded Damon.

Into the library they went. Erik reminded them not to spread out too far from his location else they would become visible. "No one touch a thing, else it might alert whatever lurks to our presence," he said. At the end of the long hallway there were stairs off to the right leading up to the balcony. Once up on the balcony they all got a good view of the library. It was lined with decorated pillars of the hieroglyph writing. Side profiles of chariot races, boats ferrying goods down a river and black-haired people playing instruments decorated the walls. The room had gold inlay in the ceiling and walls, painted in the language of the unknown culture that party saw earlier. Again, the images of the large man with the head of a jackal or a dog dominated the hieroglyphs around the room. It seemed a distant cousin to the lycaons.

They moved on through the portal behind the balcony up another passageway that sloped up. At the end was a door. Light was emanating from beneath the door and keyhole, and voices! It was the voice of what sounded like an old woman and an old man arguing!

As previously discussed, Leif signalled Sker to drop and remain behind. The runty lizard-goblin did so nervously, and scurried to the back of the party, the small green tower in hand.

* * * * *

"She insulted me! If you recall!" insisted Rom-Seti, yelling at one of his many mirrors hanging from his own throne room. The revenant used these mirrors to communicate with his allies in the Union of Undead. The only mirror that had an actual recipient presently was Revenant Niss.

Revenant Rom-Seti, who ruled over the Necropolis of Milothia, a city banished from another world to Vana, was a flamboyant, easily aggravated and a demanding dark soul. He sat atop a golden throne seated upon a dais with stairs leading up to the seat. The Revenant himself was adorned in ancient cloth, jewels and golden inlay. Golden sconces with burning torches reflected off the white limestone walls of this room. Beautiful yet old tapestries hung around the room. Every inch of stone had some form of picture or hieroglyph etched into it. Oddly, the only thing plain about the revenant was his shepherd's crook that he used as a staff.

Revenant Ness, however, was a simple, almost recluse yet powerful human female mage. While Rom-Seti allowed all to see into his throne room through their mirrors, Niss only allowed her torso and face to show through the mirror.

Niss was not normally this engaging but the two bickered back and forth over Rom-Seti and his alleged assault upon a fellow member of the Union of Undead – a vampiress known as Queen Ooktha. Niss took a mentoring role to the young Vampire-Queen. Therefore, the confrontation explains her unusual aggression, so Rom-Seti believed. In truth Revenant Niss witnessed the assault herself as she was engaged in conversation with the Vampiress known as Queen Ooktha when Rom-Seti assaulted the undead queen of the arch-goblins.

"It does not justify your assaults," Niss retorted.

"What assault?" stammered Rom-Seti.

"Her word is good enough for the Union and when I inform the rest of the Union, they…"

"They will do nothing? You have no proof," he said flatly. "And whoever attacked her has likely come from her dealings with the war she created with that human general she conspires with," stated Rom-Seti with a dismissive wave of his nearly skinless hand.

He was referring to the war Queen Ooktha conspired to create with General Baltus Blackpool of Vorclaw. "You called her an insulant whelp and referred to her as a pup. Who insulted who?" shouted Niss referring to an argument that happened before the attack on Queen Ooktha.

"Yes, I did when I was merely trying to impart my advice to her and she took an aggressive tone with me," said Rom-Seti, who was now distracted. The revenant sensed something.

Niss pulled his attention back. "You care only for yourself and not the Union. We formed for the betterment of ourselves, not to attack one another. Or did you forget our charter?"

"I forget nothing but it would be my word against hers and she is not a revenant. And what you have said proves nothing," stated Rom-Seti who continued to deny the assault he committed upon the fellow Union member.

"What you don't realise oh-miserable-one," Niss said to Rom-Seti in a sarcastic voice, "is that I was speaking to her when you started your assault." There was silence form Rom-Seti. "Do you not recall me interrupting you shortly after you attacked her?" she said teasingly.

For once Rom-Seti was at a loss for words. He was surprised by the revelation and was actually worried. Not about Revenant Niss nor Queen Ooktha potentially joining forces against him but how the Union of Undead might react to the news of his assault. The angry revenant was so deep in thought he tuned out Revenant Niss and her continued ravings and almost missed the door to his private quarters was now opened!

"Intruders!" he shouted even though there was no one visible in the room.

* * * * *

To Rom-Seti's left appeared Leif Foehammer, the shield bearing elven warrior in black enchanted armour. Behind Leif was Erik, The Shadow Company mage. On Rom-Seti 's right was an even larger shielded man; the warrior-priest with red hair and silvery armour Bjorn Foehammer, wielded a large, enchanted mace. Behind Bjorn was The Shadow Company assassin, Damon Crag with his two short swords that were enchanted. Taking up the rear and between all intruders was the human warrior Dru Blackpool, with his two enchanted short swords drawn. There was plenty of room to spread out around the dais but those without shields stayed behind those with, for now. Lastly, arching towards Rom-Seti, which also dispelled the invisibility of the intruders, was a large *fireball* cast by The Shadow Company mage.

Sparks and fire exploded off Rom-Seti's protective magical shield. The revenant readied a counterattack of his own but his spell failed! It was due to the priestly powers of Bjorn Foehammer, a warrior-priest of Matronae!

"I renounce your power, unholy creature!" shouted Bjorn. The power of Matronae radiated through his body and into his holy weapon.

At the completion of Bjorn's quick chant, a blinding red radiance burst from that mace. That holy weapon doubled as Bjorn's holy symbol. The radiance burned the revenant who lost his concentration and caused his spell to fail.

Another blast came at Rom-Seti but from a lightning wand. This bolt came from over the shoulder of Leif. Erik came equipped with several wands. The revenant accepted the blast as it weakened his magical barrier. The revenant also accepted another divine of burst from the large priest again. The revenant accepted the pain and the loss so he could properly prepare a counter strike that would be quick and hopefully bring a swift end. Within his shepherd's crook dwelled great magic. Much like Eric's wand, the magic within Rom-Seti's shepherd's crook could be released with a mere word.

Rom-Seti shouted a phrase in his native tongue, a language no one in the room understood but Damon Crag guessed at what it meant.

"Prepare your rings!" shouted Daman Crag.

The revenant launched a barrage of four fiery balls, often known as *hail-of-fire*. If Rom-Seti could smile, he would have but his dried lips had worn away long ago. And if he could frown, he would have also done so. For somehow, his magical orbs were all turned away and sent back straight at him, the caster! Two *fireballs* returned from Leif and two *fireballs* returned from Bjorn as the two advanced up the dais towards the revenant. The four orbs exploding against Rom-Seti's *magical barrier*. The room became a light show of red fire and yellow-green sparks. The heat radiating off was colossal as was the noise. It caused the intruders to back away down what few steps they made up the dais. Everyone tried to duck behind the shields Bjorn and Leif. The sconces and artwork around the room became obliterated or ablaze. The intruders would have been too, save for their magical armour and shields.

Both Leif and Bjorn felt as if they both turned the *fireballs* back at Rom-Seti as the power in their rings tingled. "I think I turned that," said the Leif ducking low but the ringing in his ears made hearing difficult.

Bjorn replied, "I think I turned two and you turned two!" he shouted.

Bjorn rose and from behind his shield cast a spiritual weapon, a *divine mace* as it was known. It was a weapon that had no visible welder. It was spectral mace that went straight to attack Rom-Seti!

Eric sent forth another lightning bolt from his wand.

That combined with the spectral mace and having his *hail-of-fire* turned against his own shielding, the revenant fell back into his now damaged throne. Now that the tapestries in the room were destroyed or burning, two opened doorways were revealed behind either side of the dais. Out spilled forth armoured skeleton soldiers.

With his magical shielding now buckling, the revenant used the *mage's gate* saved within his shepherd crook to reappear behind the intruders. Now at the far side of the room from where he once stood and the communication mirrors to his back, Rom-Seti launched another *hail-of-fire*.

Erik instinctively turned around to see the reappearance and shouted a warning. He also saw the incoming swarm of fiery orbs. Erik used his own ring to turn back the incoming attack which again surprised Rom-Seti in fiery explosions all around him, again! Again, the noise and heat were massive but less so as the Revenant was now further away from the party on the other side of the room.

Rom-Seti then saw some of his magical mirrors crack, break and melt from the heat. Only the ones far to the sides, left and right of him were relatively undamaged. Ironically the two remaining were of both Queen Ooktha to his far left and Revenant Niss to his far right. "Are you going to aid me?" he shouted to Revenant Niss.

The human revenant instead put her hand through and cast the spell of *dismiss enchantment* upon Rom-Seti!

"His magical barrier is dispelled, do with him as you please," she shouted in the common tongue to all and closed her mirror portal.

Stunned, Rom-Seti cursed the revenant.

Erik wasted no time launching another lightning bolt from his wand that pinned the revenant against the wall. Both Dru and Damon had to deal with the armoured skeleton warriors entering the room. Bjorn sent his spectral mace at the skeleton to give aid to Damon Crag. Dru, however, was on his own to fend off the skeletons. Leif though was already running towards the revenant. Bjorn eventually followed suit but when he did, his spectral mace was dispelled.

Rom-Seti assumed the wizard was more a threat and ignored the advancing shielded elf. The revenant tapped his shepherd's crook to the ground and five enlarged arms rose up from the ground before around Erik.

Each large arm was tethered to the ground, somehow, and each were completely different. One was black, another was red covered in course red hairs. A yellow arm with three clawed fingers reached for the wizard. A green one came up to the wizards left while a blue one with a pincer came up to his right. All the arms came up to Erik's chest and began to bludgeon or grab the wizard by the clothing and limbs. That gave Rom-Seti the chance to deal with Leif who was upon him with an overhead chop of his *dao* sword. Leif would have sliced the revenant over his head, but the enchanted shepherd's crook came up with the uncanny magically enhanced strength and speed of Rom-Seti and easily defeated the assault.

Leif, stunned and confused by the power of this bony opponent caused the elf to pause. It was all the time the revenant needed and sent a *lightning bolt* into Leif. Most of the blast was absorbed by the enchanted armour and shield but still sent Leif flying backwards to the ground, teeth jittering and muscles twitching.

The revenant then felt a now familiar blast of pain coming again from Bjorn and his damned deity, Matronae. Rom-Seti felt the holy word of Matronae differently from before. It gave him a feeling of exhaustion, as if a layer of strength was ripped from him. It was more intense now due to the loss of his magical barrier.

Bjorn was on the revenant then with his fantastic Rose-Mace coming down for Rom-Seti's face. However, the magically enhanced strength and speed of the revenant caused Bjorn to miss as Rom-Seti side dodged what would have been a crushing blow. With Bjorn off balance, the revenant used this opportunity to use his shepherd's crook to hook over Bjorn's shield and rip it from his hand! Bjorn retaliated with a backhand swing of his mace that was met with an equally strong counterforce from the revenant's crook. The revenant pressed with his staff but was only using one hand to Bjorn's two. The larger Bjorn was forced on his heels and it was then that Rom-Seti reached up with his free hand and grabbed Bjorn by the throat.

The ice-cold of the undead burned Bjorn's skin. Bjorn felt nauseous and his strength began to leave him. His neck burned icy-hot and he started having tunnel vision as his eyesight was failing. Rom-Seti was draining the life from the human priest.

Additionally, what no one knew was Rom-Seti had become a devout follower of the Crom-Cruach, the evil god of the underworld, since arriving on Vana. Through deity's divine guidance, Rom-Seti learned of a poison that was deposited by microscopic parasites beneath his rotting fingernails. The tiny parasites lay dormant until exposed to living flesh. Once on the flesh of a living host, they devour their host and emit poison into the flesh and blood stream of their host. It was difficult to cure being that the parasites were alive and constantly emitting the poisons as waste. The parasite's poison not only kills but the parasites themselves damage the host's body as they consume it. They attacked the body slowly but were devastating if left unresolved. Bjorn may survive the battle with Rom-Seti; however, he will eventually have to deal with the parasites and poisons now entering his body.

Sensing the life-force was draining from this warrior-priest, Rom-Seti grew more confident. He had the wizard engaged with his tentacles and the priest in his clutches. His skeleton warriors were losing but occupied the remaining two warriors. It was then that Rom-Seti realised his error. A magically enhanced blade came down upon the arm holding Bjorn, severing it at the shoulder. The bony grasp released from Bjorn's neck and the undead severed arm fell to the floor. Bjorn too fell to the floor grasping his own neck and breathing intensely.

Leif, wanting to finish the revenant, made an upward backhand swipe of his *dao* sword and hit Rom-Seti in the face, knocking the revenant's cobra-like headgear from his skull. The revenant backed away from both Bjorn and Leif, stumbling towards the centre of the room.

"Now, Sker!" shouted Leif. "Do it now!"

Rom-Seti screamed out more undecipherable words toward his throne or warriors, Leif could not be sure. Not understanding the significance, Leif pressed his attack swinging at the revenant. Rom-Seti leaned heavily upon his crook when he could but also used it in defence from Leif's attacks. Weary of his spells being turned against him again, the revenant cast a less aggressive spell. A cloud emerged from his staff. A *nauseous cloud* began to fill the room. Everyone began to cough at first, then gag. Everyone's eyes watered.

The revenant then started towards the doorway the party used to enter the room. The revenant was clearly in disarray and unaccustomed to intrusions and pain. Rom-Seti found it difficult to concentrate. He leaned upon his crook to help keep him up. He could use a *mage's gate* like before, but he needed to concentrate for that spell and he used up the one saved within his shepherd's crook. The revenant came to a sudden stop when a small lizard-goblin entered the room from the door. The runty creature was holding a small jade object that the revenant could not make out. Rom-Seti first heard the words *Archangel* escape from the mouth of the runty lizard-goblin.

Rom-Seti next felt terror, a sensation he had not felt in a millennium. His own remaining life force began to pull from his body. The revenant instinctively turned away but could not move. The revenant felt disorientated, dizzy. The world around him began to grow large and ominous; no, he was shrinking! There was a wind blowing around the room that much was certain. His invocation of the *nauseous cloud* and attacking appendages upon Erik dissolved. Rom-Seti could see the undead spirits of the skeleton warriors being pulled in with him. Soon his vision took on a green glow until his entire sight was consumed by smooth green walls and floor. All was translucent but not completely see-through. He, no, his remaining lifeforce and that of his ten skeleton warriors were inside that tiny green object held by the lizard-goblin.

End – Book 2

CODEX

Creatures of Vana

Arch-goblin: Arch-goblins who are pale blue with ape-like canines and faces. They live as long as humans. True goblins no longer exist as far as anyone on Vana knows. Arch-goblins are a manipulation of the smaller extinct goblins by human wizards for the purposes of war.

Dark Elves: These outcast elves live within Vana, not on the surface. This breed of elf has ashy-coloured skin, red eyes and golden hair. The sunlight pains them greatly. The reason they're so different from other elfkin was when humans arrived, elves were introduced other gods and ways of thinking. Subsequently those who turned away from the even goddess Airia were punished for their blasphemy. Those banished from the surface often became Crom-Cruach worshipers and atheists. They live about twice as long average humans. However, lore states Airia regrets her punishment.

Dwarves: About half as tall to two-thirds as tall as an average human. These pious Terra worshipers live within mountains and highland forests. Like humans, they come in a variety of skin tones, eye and hair colours. Their height is deceiving as they are stronger physically than any humanoid. They live two to three times longer than average humans.

Elves: Slender humanoid creatures just under the height of an average human. Like humans, they come in a variety of skin tones, eye and hair colours. They have a great grasp of knowledge and fighting prowess but are in retreat due violent interactions with human and arch-goblins. They live two to three times longer than average humans.

Kelpiefolk: A short two-legged aquatic humanoid with webbed hands and feet. Its skin is dark green or brown and smooth, like an amphibian's. These creatures have great orbs for eyes, small fins protruding from their frog-like head. The do not have great intelligence and live more like wild animals.

Lemurian: A two-legged creature with sea green scaly skin and the head of an angry fish. They can breathe in water and on land. They worship to the water god of Mermanta. They live about twice as long average humans.

Lizard-goblin: These are small bipedal lizard-like creatures of various colours. They often act as servants and fodder for larger races. Their scales are often seen as either green, red or orange. They have no relation to arch-goblins who seem to keep them for afore mentioned purposes. They live half as long as an average human.

Lycaon: Tall humanoid creatures with jackal-like heads whose tall pointy ears extended above their heads. Their skin is dark with short dark hair that covered their shoulders up to their tall ears. Their skin and fur are black while elite of the species are golden in fur and skin. They live as long as humans. They are very rare and only seen in the northern mountains.

Mantikhoras: A rare creature found in the mountains. Its body is orange tiger-like but without stripes. It has the head of a man-like creature with a furry face; it has a very long whip-like tail with spikes at the end. The species are rumoured to be a magical creation by human-wizards long ago and is rumoured to have magical capabilities.

Orcs: These creatures have the face of a pig. Their skin varies from dark green to solid black in colour. The have tusks the protrude up from their mouth like a boar. Their hair over their head and body tends to be dark in colour. They live about twice as long as humans.

Shape-changer: These very rare creatures have the ability to take on the shape of those they see. They tend to study first those they intend to imitate. In their basic form they look like an albino human with no hair and blue eyes. These are very rare and believed to be a manipulation of humans by wizardry.

Undead

Note: Depending on their experience, all clergy of all faiths can manipulate the undead by either destroy or control using their own divine power bestowed by the god or goddess.

Ghoul: Horrible undead humanoids who were equally evil in real life; unlike skeletons who were either animated to follow orders, ghouls hunger for flesh and bone of the living.

Mummy: Undead guardians that lay in wait in tombs. Traditionally they are wrapped in bandages to help stem their decay. The creatures animate upon disturbance or on command of a more powerful undead creature like a revenant or vampire.

Revenant: Powerful undead who refuse to truly die; they maintain their consciousness while their body decays. They also must hide away their soul in an item called a soul-sepulchre. The soul-sepulchre allows them to keep their soul from the afterlife so they can toil as undead but retain their consciousness. Once the soul-sepulchre is destroyed, the soul moves into the undead body and then they can then be killed. If a revenant body is destroyed but the soul remains in a soul-sepulchre, the revenant can move its consciousness into another dead form.

Skeleton: Mindless undead used as labour or fighting.

Vampire: Undead creature who have unique powers such as animal control and weather manipulation. However, they require near fresh blood almost daily for sustainment.

Mentioned Lands

Anubia: Rom-Seti homeland from another planet.

Dwarven Mons: Home of the dwarven kings to the West of Vorclaw.

Fort Adamant: Fort built around The Tor to protect the region near Panther-Paw-Pass.

Mistful Forest: Forest area north and west of Sedgedunum.

Sanctuary: A small patch of land in the far north where violence is forbidden and all are allowed to worship whatever gods they see fit.

Skagsnest: A centre for trade under the Spine of Vana Mountain range. It is overseen by Lemurians. It is named for the Lemerian leader, Old Skags.

Spine of Vana: Mountain range all along the north of Vorclaw.

The Land of the Great Glaciers: Lands near the top of Vana.

The Tor: Ancient tower built by elves long ago before the advent of humans to the area.

Human Countries of Vana

Dubravna
Lotus
Karthia
Uden
Vorclaw

Vorclaw's:

Seaside cities and towns
Sedgedunum
Seaforth
Irons-by-the-Sea

Mountain and hilled cities and towns
Cairnloch
Cairnhold

Wooded cities and towns
Exbury
Wrexbury
Nortbury

The arch-goblin cities in the Spine of Vana

Blood-helm
Skulls-thorpe
Iron-hold

The indigenous four elemental gods of Vana and primary worshipers

Terra (Female) Dwarfkin: Depicted as a short muscular woman with white haired woman whose face is light brown in colour. Terra is often depicted in a black armour adorned in silver and trim to match.

Magmum (Female) Orckin: Depicted as a robust orcish woman with black hair and fire-red veins protruding through her black skin.

Airia (Female) Elfkin: Depicted as a winged woman with silver hair and wings whose colour pulsated the colours of a rainbow.

Mermanta (Female) Merfolk: Depicted as a red octopus like creature who has eight arms but two are red-clawed and two are five-fingered arms of sea green.

Non-indigenous Gods of Vana primarily worshipped primarily by humans

Matronae: Is the mother goddesses of birth, harvest, and the seasons. The symbol of Matronae is an X that has four additional symbols within the X. The sun is represented within the top of the X. A circle represents the planet Vana within the bottom of the X. To the left is a wavy line that represents water while a cloud formation on the left represents the wind.

Dagda: The father figure and god of strength, war, weather. The symbol of Dagda are two lightning bolts crossing one another to form an X.

Children of Matronae and Dagda

- **Ogma** (male): God of wisdom, hunting, forestry, good. The symbol of Ogma is an oak tree. He is depicted as a man of the forest with a green beard and hair.

- **Lir** (male): God of endurance, oceans, lakes and river. The symbol of Lir is three wavy lines. He is depicted as a man with blue beard and hair that flows like water.

- **Crom-Cruach** (male): God of the underworld and often prayed to for revenge. The symbol of Crom-Cruach is a cloaked and hunched over figure walking with a scythe. No face can be seen within the hood, only bony hands holding the scythe.

Organisations:

Black-Masks: Underground network of soldiers loyal to Baltus Blackpool.

Dragoons: Vorclaw's cavalry units.

Knights of Uden: A noble elite knights that do the King of Uden's bidding, good or bad. Rumoured to be one hundred strong.

The Council of Twelve: The ruling council of Vorclaw.

The Shadow Company: A greedy network of merchants, wizards, and thieves; believed to be ruled by either a secret council or powerful wizard referred to as The One.

Union of Undead: A confederacy of powerful undead forces whose members are vampires and revenants of different but unknown species.

CPSIA information can be obtained
at www.ICGtesting.com
Printed in the USA
LVHW050918210723
752909LV00048B/10